NAPOLEON ON THE BATTLEFIELD OF BORODINO.

Original Drawing by E. H. Garrett.

WAR AND PEACE

VOL. IV

CONTENTS

PART IX

CONTENTS

CONTENTS

[1] This peculiarity of Prince Bolkonsky is evidently imitated from Napoleon at St. Helena; see Bourrienne's "Memoirs."

CONTENTS

CONTENTS

WAR AND PEACE

PART NINTH

CHAPTER I

TOWARD the end of the year 1811 began a mobilization and concentration of forces in Western Europe; and in 1812, these forces — millions of men, counting those who were concerned in the transport and victualing of the armies — were moved from West to East toward the borders of Russia, where the Russian forces were drawn up just as they had been the year before.

On the twenty-fourth of June, the forces of Western Europe crossed the Russian frontier, and war began: in other words, an event took place opposed to human reason and human nature.

Millions of men committed against one another a countless number of crimes, deceptions, treacheries, robberies, forgeries, issues of false assignats, depredations, incendiary fires, murders, such as the annals of all the courts in all the world could not equal in the aggregate of centuries; and yet which, at that period, the perpetrators did not even regard as crimes.

What brought about this extraordinary event?

What were its causes?

The historians, with naïve credulity, say that the causes of this event are to be found in the affront offered to the Duke of Oldenburg, in the disregard of the "Continental System," in Napoleon's ambition, Alexander's firmness, the mistakes of diplomatists, and what not.

Of course, in that case, to put a stop to the war, it would have merely required Metternich, Rumyantsof, or Talleyrand, between a levee and a rout, to have made a little effort and skilfully composed a state paper; or Napoleon to have written to Alexander: *Monsieur, mon Frère, je consens à rendre le duché au Duc d'Oldenbourg.*

It is easily understood that the matter presented itself in that light to the men of that day. It is easily understood that Napoleon attributed the cause of the war to England's intrigues (indeed he said so on the island of St. Helena); it is easily understood that the members of the British Parliament attributed the cause of the war to Napoleon's ambition; that Prince Oldenburg considered the war to have been caused by the insult which he had received; that the merchants regarded the "Continental System," which was ruining European trade, as responsible for it; that old veterans and generals saw the chief cause for it in the necessity to find them something to do; the legitimists of that day, in the necessity of upholding sound principles; and the diplomatists in the fact that the Russian alliance with Austria, in 1809, had not been cleverly enough kept from Napoleon's knowledge and that memorandum No. 178 was awkwardly expressed.

It is easily understood that these, and an endless number of other reasons — the diversity of which is simply proportioned to the infinite diversity of standpoints — satisfied the men who were living at that time; but for us, Posterity, who are far enough removed to contemplate the magnitude of the event from a wider perspective, and who seek to fathom its simple and terrible meaning, such reasons appear insufficient. To us it is incomprehensible that millions of Christian men killed and tortured each other because Napoleon was ambitious, Alexander firm, English policy astute, and Duke Oldenburg affronted. It is impossible to comprehend what connection these circumstances have with the fact itself of murder and violence: why, in consequence of the affront put on the duke, thousands of men from the other end of Europe should have killed and plundered the people of the governments of Smolensk and Moscow, and have been killed by them.

For us, Posterity, who are not historians, and not carried away by any far-fetched processes of reasoning, and who can, therefore, contemplate the phenomena with unclouded and healthy vision, the causes thereof arise before us in all their innumerable quantity. The deeper we delve into the investigation of causes, the more numerous do they open up before us; and every separately considered cause, or whole series of causes, appears equally efficient in its own nature, and equally fallacious by reason of its utter insignificance in comparison with the prodigiousness of the events; and equally fallacious also by reason of its inability, without the coöperation of all the other causes combined, to produce the events in question.

Such a cause as the refusal of the Napoleon to draw his army back within the Vistula, and to restore the duchy of Oldenburg, has as much weight in this consideration as the willingness or unwillingness of a single French corporal to take part in the second campaign; because, if he had refused, and a second, and a third, and a thousand corporals and soldiers had likewise refused, Napoleon's army would have been so greatly reduced that the war could not have occurred.

If Napoleon had not been offended by the demand to retire his troops beyond the Vistula, and had not issued orders for them to give battle, there would have been no war; but if all the sergeants had refused to go into action, there also would have been no war. And there would also have been no war if there had been no English intrigues, and no Prince Oldenburg; and if Alexander had not felt himself aggrieved; and if there had been no autocratic power in Russia; and if there had been no French Revolution, and no Dictatorship and Empire following it; and nothing of all that led up to the Revolution, and so on. Had any one of these causes been missing, war could not have taken place. Consequently, all of them — milliards of causes — **must** have coöperated to bring about what resulted.

And, as a corollary, there could have been no exclusive final cause for these events ; and the great event was accomplished simply because it had to be accomplished. Millions of men, renouncing all their human feelings, and their reason, had to march from West to East, and kill their fellows ; exactly the same as, several centuries before, swarms of men had swept from East to West, likewise killing their fellows.

The deeds of Napoleon and Alexander, on whose fiat apparently depended this or that occurrence, were just as far from being spontaneous and free as the actions of any soldier taking part in the expedition, either as a conscript or as a recruit. This was inevitably the case, because, in order that Napoleon's or Alexander's will should be executed — they being apparently the men on whom the event depended — the coöperation of countless factors was requisite, one of which failing, the event could not have occurred. It was indispensable that millions of men, in whose hands was really all the power, soldiers who fought, and men who transported munitions of war and cannon, should consent to carry out the will of these two feeble human units ; and they were brought to this by an endless number of complicated and varied causes.

Fatalism in history is unavoidable, if we would explain its preposterous phenomena (that is to say, those events the reason for which is beyond our comprehension). The more we strive by our reason to explain these phenomena in history, the more illogical and incomprehensible to us they become.

Every man lives for himself, and enjoys sufficient freedom for the attainment of his own personal ends, and is conscious in his whole being that he can instantly perform or refuse to perform any action ; but as soon as he has done it, this action, accomplished in a definite period of time, becomes irrevocable and forms an element in history, in which it takes its place with a fully preordained and no longer capricious significance.

Every man has a twofold life : on one side is his personal life, which is free in proportion as its interests are abstract; the other is life as an element, as one bee in the swarm; and here a man has no chance of disregarding the laws imposed on him.

Man consciously lives for himself; but, at the same time, he serves as an unconscious instrument for the accomplishment of historical and social ends. An action once accomplished is fixed; and when a man's activity coincides with others, with the millions of actions of other men, it acquires historical significance. The higher a man stands on the social ladder, the more men he is connected with, the greater the influence he exerts over others, — the more evident is the predestined and unavoidable necessity of his every action.

"The king's heart is in the hand of the Lord."

The king is the slave of history.

History, that is to say, the unconscious, universal life of humanity, in the aggregate, every moment profits by the life of kings for itself, as an instrument for the accomplishment of its own ends.

Napoleon, notwithstanding the fact that never before had it seemed so evident to him as now in this year 1812, that it depended on him whether he should shed or not shed the blood of his people, — *verser le sang de ses peuples*, as Alexander expressed it in his last letter to him, — was in reality never before so subordinated to the inevitable laws that compelled him — even while, as it seemed to him, working in accordance with his own free will — to accomplish for the world in general, for history, what was destined to be accomplished.

The men of the West moved toward the East so as to kill one another. And, by the law of coincidences, thousands of trifling causes made themselves into the guise of final causes, and, coinciding with this event, apparently explained this movement and this war: the dissatisfaction at the non-observance of the "Continental System"; and the Duke of Oldenburg; and the invasion of Prussia, undertaken (as it seemed to Napoleon) simply for the purpose of bringing about an armed peace; and the French emperor's love and habit of war coinciding with the disposition of his people; the attraction of grander preparations, and the outlays for such preparations, and the necessity for indemnities for meeting these outlays; and the intoxicating honors paid at Dresden; and the diplomatic negotiations which, in the opinion of contemporaries, were conducted with a sincere desire to preserve peace, but which merely offended the pride of either side; and millions of millions of other causes, serving as specious reasons for this event which had to take place, and coinciding with it.

When an apple is ripe and falls, what makes it fall? Is it the attraction of gravitation? or is it because its stem withers? or because the sun dries it up? or because it is heavy? or because the wind shakes it? or because the small boy standing underneath is hungry for it?

There is no such proximate cause. The whole thing is the result of all those conditions, in accordance with which every vital, organic, complex event occurs. And the botanist who argues that the apple fell from the effect of decomposing vegetable tissue, or the like, is just as much in the right as the boy who, standing below, declares that the apple fell because he wanted to eat it, and prayed for it.

Equally right and equally wrong would be the one who should say that Napoleon went to Moscow because he wanted to go, and was ruined because Alexander wished him to be ruined; equally right and equally wrong would be the man who should declare that a mountain, weighing millions of tons and undermined, fell in consequence of the last blow of the mattock dealt by the last laborer. In the events of history, so-called great men are merely tags that supply a name to the event, and have quite as little connection with the event itself as the tag.

Every one of their actions, though apparently performed by their own free will, is, in its historical significance, out of the scope of volition, and is correlated with the whole trend of history; and is, consequently, preordained from all eternity.

CHAPTER II

ON the tenth of June, Napoleon started from Dresden, where he had been for three weeks the center of a court composed of princes, dukes, kings, and at least one emperor.

Before his departure, Napoleon showed his favor to the princes, kings, and the emperor, who deserved it; he turned a cold shoulder on the kings and princes who had incurred his displeasure; he gave the empress of Austria pearls and diamonds, which he called his own, though they had been stolen from other kings, and then tenderly embracing the *Empress* Maria Louisa, as the historian terms her, left her heartbroken by his absence, which it seemed to her, now that she considered herself his consort, although he had another consort left behind in Paris, was too hard to be endured.

Although the diplomats stoutly maintained their belief in the possibility of peace, and were working heartily for this end; although Napoleon himself wrote a letter to the Emperor Alexander, calling him *Monsieur mon Frère*, and sincerely assuring him that he had no desire for war, and that he should always love and respect him, — still, he was off for the army, and at every station was issuing new rescripts having in view to expedite the movement of the troops from West to East.

He traveled in a calash drawn by six horses, and accompanied by his pages, aides, and an escort, and took the route through Posen, Thorn, Dantzic, and Königsberg. The army was moving from the West to the East, and relays of fresh horses bore him in the same direction. On the twenty-second of June, he overtook the army, and spent the night in the Wilkowiski forest, on the estate of a Polish count, where quarters had been made ready for him.

On the following day Napoleon, outstripping the army, drove to the Niemen in his calash; and, for the purpose of reconnoitering the spot where the army was

to cross, he put on a Polish uniform, and went down to
the banks of the river.

When he saw on the other side the Cossacks, and the
wide-stretching steppes, in the center of which was
Moscou, la ville sainte, the capital of that empire which
reminded him of the Scythian one, against which Alexander of Macedon had marched, Napoleon, unexpectedly and contrary to all strategical as well as diplomatic
considerations, gave orders for the advance, and on the
next day the troops began to cross the Niemen.

Early on the morning of the twenty-fourth he emerged
from his tent, which had been pitched on the steep left
bank of the river, and looked through his field-glass at
the torrents of his troops pouring forth from the Wilkowiski forest, and streaming across the three bridges
thrown over the Niemen.

The troops were aware of the presence of the emperor;
they searched for him with their eyes, and when they discovered him on the cliff, standing in front of his tent,
and distinguished from his suite by his figure, in an
overcoat and cocked hat, they flung their caps in the
air, and shouted, " *Vive l'empereur !* " and then, rank
after rank, a never-ceasing stream, they poured forth
and still poured forth from the mighty forest that till
now had concealed them, and, dividing into three currents, crossed over the bridges to the other side.

" Something'll be done this time ! Oh, when he takes
a hand, he makes things hot ! .... God .... save us. .... There
he is ! .... Hurrah for the emperor ! "

" So these are the steppes of Asia ? Beastly country
all the same ! "

" Good-by ! Beauché, I 'll save the best palace in
Moscow for you. Good-by ! Luck to you ! " ....

" Have you seen him ? The emperor ? — Hurrah for
the emperor — ror — ror ! "

" If I am made governor of India, Gérard, I 'll appoint
you minister at Cashmir ; that 's a settled thing."

" Hurrah for the emperor ! Hurrah ! hurrah ! hurrah ! "

" Those rascally Cossacks ! how they run ! Hurrah
for the emperor ! "

"There he is! Do you see him? Twice I've seen him as plain as I see you.... the 'Little Corporal?'"

"I saw him give the cross to one of our vets. .... Hurrah for the emperor!"

Such were the remarks and shouts made by men, both young and old, of the most widely differing characters and positions in the world. The faces of all these men bore one universal expression of delight at the beginning of the long-expected campaign, and of enthusiasm and devotion for the man in the gray overcoat, standing on the hill.

On the twenty-fifth of June a small thoroughbred Arab steed was brought to Napoleon, and he mounted and set off at a gallop down to one of the bridges over the Niemen, greeted all the way by enthusiastic acclamations, which he evidently endured for the reason that it was impossible to prevent the men from expressing by these shouts their love for him ; but these acclamations, which accompanied him wherever he went, fatigued him, and distracted his attention from the military task that met him at the moment he reached the army.

He rode across the bridge, which shook under his horse's hoofs, and, on reaching the farther side, turned abruptly to the left, and galloped off in the direction of Kovno, preceded by his mounted guards, who, crazy with delight and enthusiasm, cleared the way for him through the troops pressing on ahead. On reaching the broad river Vistula, he reined in his horse near a regiment of Polish Uhlans, which was halted on the bank.

"Hurrah!" shouted the Polyaks, no less enthusiastically, as they fell out of line, elbowing one another, in their efforts to get a sight of him. Napoleon contemplated the river ; then dismounted and sat down on a log which happened to be lying on the bank. At a mute signal, his telescope was handed him ; he rested it on the shoulder of one of his pages, who came forward beaming with delight, and began to reconnoiter the other shore. Then he remained lost in study of a map spread out over the driftwood. Without lifting his head he said something, and two of his aides galloped off toward the Polish Uhlans.

"What was it? What did he say?" was heard in the ranks of the Uhlans, as one of the aides came hurrying toward them.

The order was that they should find a ford, and cross to the other side.

The Polish colonel who commanded the Uhlans, a handsome old man, flushing, and stumbling in his speech from excitement, asked the aide-de-camp whether he might be permitted to swim the river with his men, instead of trying to find the ford. He was evidently as apprehensive of receiving a refusal as a school-boy who asks permission to ride on horseback; and what he craved was the chance to swim the river under his emperor's eyes.

The aide-de-camp replied that in all probability the emperor would not be displeased with this superfluity of zeal.

As soon as the aide-de-camp had said this, the old mustached officer, with beaming face and gleaming eyes, waved his sword and cried *Vivat!* And, ordering his Uhlans to follow him, he plunged spurs into his horse and dashed down to the river. He angrily struck the horse, which shied under him, and forced him into the water, striking out boldly into the swift current where it was deepest. The water was cold, and the swiftness of the current made the passage difficult. Hundreds of Uhlans galloped after him. The Uhlans clung to one another, in case they were dismounted from their horses. Several of the horses were drowned, and some of the men; the others endeavored to swim, one clinging to his saddle, another to his horse's mane. Their endeavor was to swim to the farther side, and, although there was a ford only half a verst below, they were proud of swimming and drowning in that river under the eye of a man who sat on the log and did not even notice what they were doing!

When the aide-de-camp on his return found a favorable moment, and allowed himself to call the emperor's attention to the devotion of these Polyaks to his person, the little man in the gray surtout got up, and, calling Berthier, began to walk with him back and forth on the river bank, giving him orders, and occasionally casting a dissatisfied glance at the drowning Uhlans, who distracted his attention.

It was nothing new in his experience that his presence in any corner of the world, in the deserts of Africa as well as in the Moscovite steppes, was sufficient to stimulate and drive men into senseless self-sacrifice. He commanded a horse to be brought, and rode back to his bivouac.

Forty Uhlans were drowned in the river, although boats were sent to their aid. The majority gave up the task, and returned to the hither side. The colonel and a few of the men swam across the river, and with great difficulty crept up on the farther shore. But as soon as they were on the land, though their garments were streaming with water, they shouted *Vivat*, gazing with enthusiasm at the spot where Napoleon had been, but from which he had vanished, and counting themselves fortunate.

In the afternoon, after making arrangements for procuring with all possible despatch the counterfeit Russian assignats, which had been prepared for use in Russia; and after issuing an order to shoot a certain Saxon, who, in a letter that had been intercepted, gave information in regard to the disposition of the French army, — Napoleon, in still a third order, caused the Polish colonel who had quite needlessly flung himself into the river, to be enrolled in the *Légion d'Honneur*,[1] of which he himself was the head.

Quos vult perdere — dementat.[2]

---

[1] Instituted by Napoleon, May 19, 1802; carried out, July 14, 1814.
[2] Those whom God wishes to destroy, he first makes mad.

CHAPTER III

The Russian emperor, meantime, had been now for more than a month at Vilna, superintending reviews and manœuvers.

Nothing was ready for the war, though all had foreseen that it was coming, and though the emperor had left Petersburg to prepare for it. The vacillation as to what plan, from among the many that had been prepared, was to be selected, was still more pronounced after the emperor had been for a month at headquarters.

Each of the three divisions of the army had a separate commander; but there was no nachalnik, or responsible chief, over all the forces; and the emperor did not see fit to assume this position.

The longer the emperor stayed at Vilna, the less ready for the war were they who had grown weary of expecting it. The whole purpose of those who surrounded the sovereign seemed directed toward making him pass the time agreeably and forget about the impending conflict.

After a series of balls and festivities, given by Polish magnates, and by the courtiers, and by the emperor himself, one of the Polish general-adjutants proposed in June that the imperial staff should give a banquet and ball, in his majesty's honor.

The suggestion was gladly adopted by all. The sovereign granted his sanction. The imperial aides collected the necessary funds by a subscription. A lady, who it was thought would be most acceptable to the emperor, was invited to do the honors. Count Benigsen, a landed proprietor of the Vilna government, tendered the use of his country-house for the festivity, which was set for the twenty-fifth of June; and it was decided that the ball and banquet, together with a regatta and fireworks, should take place at Zakreto, Count Benigsen's country-place.

On that very day on which orders were given by Napoleon to cross the Niemen, and the vanguard of his army drove back the Cossacks and crossed the Russian frontier, Alexander was spending the evening at Count Benigsen's villa, at a ball given by his staff!

It was a gay, brilliant occasion. Connoisseurs in such matters declared that seldom had so many pretty women been gathered in one place. The Countess Bezukhaya, who, with other Russian ladies, had followed the sovereign from Petersburg to Vilna, was at this ball, by her heavy so-called Russian beauty quite putting into the shade the more refined and delicate Polish ladies. She attracted much attention, and the sovereign condescended to dance with her.

Boris Drubetskoï, having left his wife at Moscow, was also present at this ball *en garçon*, as he expressed it; and, although not a general-adjutant, was a participant in the festivities in virtue of having subscribed a large sum toward the expenses. Boris was now a rich man, who had already arrived at high honors and now no longer required patronage, but stood on an equal footing with those of his own age, no matter how lofty their rank might be.

He met Ellen at Vilna, not having seen her for some time; but he made no reference to the past. But as Ellen was "enjoying the favor" of a very influential individual, and Boris had not been long married, they met as good old friends.

At midnight they were still dancing. Ellen, finding no partner to her taste, had herself proposed to Boris that they should dance the mazurka together. They were in the third set. Boris, with cool indifference glancing at Ellen's dazzling, bare shoulders, set off by a dark gauze dress, shot with gold, was talking about old acquaintances; and, at the same time, neither she nor any one else observed that, not for a single second, did he cease to watch the emperor, who was in the same hall.

The emperor was not dancing; he was standing in the doorway, and addressing, now to one and now to another, those gracious words which he, of all men alone, had the art of speaking.

Just before the beginning of the mazurka, Boris

noticed that the General-Adjutant Balashof, who stood on terms of special intimacy with the sovereign, approached him as he was talking with a Polish lady, and, contrary to court etiquette, stood waiting at a short distance from him. While still talking, the sovereign looked up inquiringly, and, evidently perceiving that only weighty considerations would have caused Balashof to act thus, he gave the lady a slight bow, and turned to Balashof.

At Balashof's very first words, an expression like amazement came over the sovereign's face. He took Balashof's arm, and, together with him, crossed the ball-room, so absorbed that he did not notice how the company parted, making a sort of lane, three sazhens wide, through which he passed.

Boris observed Arakcheyef's agitated face, as the sovereign walked out with Balashof. Arakcheyef, looking askance at the emperor, and snuffing through his red nose, moved out from the throng, evidently expecting that the sovereign would address him. It was clear to Boris that Arakcheyef hated Balashof, and was much dissatisfied that any news of importance should be brought to the sovereign otherwise than through him.

But the sovereign, not heeding Arakcheyef, passed out, together with Balashof, through the open door, into the brilliantly illuminated garden. Arakcheyef, grasping the hilt of his sword, and viciously glancing around, followed them, twenty steps in the rear.

While Boris continued to perform the proper figures of the mazurka, he was continually tortured by the thought of what news Balashof had brought, and how he might get hold of it before the others.

In the figure, when he had to choose a lady, he whispered to Ellen that he wanted to get the Countess Potocka, who, he believed, had gone out on the balcony. Hastily crossing the marquetry floor, he slipped out of the open door into the garden ; and there, perceiving the sovereign walking along the terrace in company with Balashof, he stepped to one side. The sovereign and Balashof were directing their steps toward the door.

Boris, pretending that in spite of all his efforts he had
not time to get out of the way, respectfully crowded up
against the lintel and bowed.

The sovereign, with the agitated face of a man personally offended, uttered these words : —

"To make war against Russia without any declaration! I will never consent to peace so long as a single
armed foe remains in my land!" said he. It seemed to
Boris that the sovereign took a delight in uttering these
words; he was satisfied with the form in which his
thought was couched, but he was annoyed that Boris
had overheard him. "Let not a word of this be known,"
he added, with a frown. Boris understood that this was
a hint to him, and, closing his eyes, he again bowed
slightly. The sovereign returned to the ball-room, and
remained for about half an hour longer.

Boris was the first to learn the news of the French
army having crossed the Niemen ; and, turning his luck
to good use, made several important personages think
that many things concealed from the others were known
to him, and thereby he succeeded in rising still higher
in their estimation.

The news of the French crossing the Niemen, unexpected as it was, was peculiarly unexpected after a long
month of strained expectancy, and by reason of being
announced at a ball! The sovereign, at the first instant
of receiving the news, under the influence of inner revolt and indignation, made use of that bold sentiment
which gave him such satisfaction, and so exactly expressed his feeling, at the time, and afterwards became
famous.

On his return to his residence after the ball, the sovereign sent, at two o'clock in the morning, for his secretary, Shishkof, and dictated a general order to his
troops, and a rescript to Field-Marshal Prince Saltuikof,
strictly charging him to use the words about his refusal
to make peace so long as a single armed Frenchman remained on Russian soil. On the next day, the following
note was written to Napoleon : —

My Brother : — I learned yesterday that, notwithstanding the fidelity with which I have adhered to my engagements toward your majesty, your troops have crossed the Russian frontier ; and I have this moment received from Petersburg a note wherein Count Lauriston, in order to explain this aggression, announces that your majesty considered himself at war with me from the time that Prince Kurakin demanded his passports. The grounds on which the Duke of Bassano refused to grant it would never have allowed me to suppose that this step could serve as a pretext for the aggression. In fact, my ambassador was never authorized to take this step, as he himself explicitly declared ; and, as soon as I was informed of it, I manifested the extent of my disapproval by ordering him to remain at his post. If your majesty is not obstinately bent upon shedding the blood of our peoples through a misunderstanding of this sort, and will consent to withdraw your troops from the Russian territory, I will regard what has passed as non-existent, and we may arrive at some accommodation. In the opposite case, your majesty, I shall be compelled to repulse an attack which I have done nothing to provoke. There is still a chance for your majesty to avoid the calamities of a new war.

I am, etc.,

(Signed) ALEXANDER.[1]

[1] MONSIEUR MON FRÈRE : — J'ai appris hier que malgré la loyauté, avec laquelle j'ai maintenu mes engagements envers votre majesté, ses troupes ont franchi les frontières de la Russie, et je reçois à l'instant de Petersbourg une note par laquelle le Comte Lauriston, pour cause de cette aggression, annonce que votre majesté s'est considérée comme en état de guerre avec moi dès le moment où le prince Kourakine a fait la demande de ses passeports. Les motifs sur lesquelles le duc de Bassano fondait son refus de les lui délivrer, n'auraient jamais pu me faire supposer que cette démarche servirait jamais de prétexte à l'aggression. En effet cet ambassadeur n'y a jamais été autorisé comme il l'a déclaré lui même, et aussitôt que j'en fus informé, je lui ai fait connaître combien je le désapprouvait en lui donnant l'ordre de rester à son poste. Si votre majesté n'est pas intentionnée de verser le sang de nos peuples pour un malentendu de ce genre et qu'elle consente à rétirer ses troupes du territoire russe, je regarderai ce qui s'est passé comme non avenu et un accommodement entre nous sera possible. Dans le cas contraire, votre majesté, je me verrai forcé de repousser une attaque que rien n'a provoquée de ma part. Il depend encore de votre majesté, d'éviter à l'humanité les calamités d'une nouvelle guerre.

Je suis, etc.,

(Signé) ALEXANDRE.

CHAPTER IV

On the twenty-fifth of June, at two o'clock in the morning, the sovereign, having summoned Balashof and read over to him his letter to Napoleon, ordered him to take it and deliver it to the French emperor in person. In despatching Balashof, the sovereign once more repeated what he had said about not making peace so long as a single armed foe remained on Russian soil, and he ordered him to quote these exact words to Napoleon. The sovereign did not incorporate this threat in his letter to Napoleon, because his tact made him feel that they were inappropriate at a moment when the last efforts were making for reconciliation; but he strenuously commanded Balashof to repeat them to Napoleon verbally.

Setting off that very same night, Balashof, accompanied by a bugler and two Cossacks, by daybreak reached the village of Rykonty, on the Russian side of the Niemen, where the French vanguard were stationed. He was brought to a halt by the French videttes. A noncommissioned officer of hussars, in a crimson uniform and shaggy cap, challenged the approaching envoy, and ordered him to halt. Balashof did not come instantly to a pause, but continued to advance at a footpace along the road.

The subaltern, scowling and muttering some abusive epithet, blocked Balashof's way with his horse, and rudely shouted to the Russian general, demanding if he were deaf, that he paid no attention to what was said to him. Balashof gave his name. The subaltern sent a soldier to the officer in command.

Paying no further heed to Balashof, the non-commissioned officer began to talk with his comrades concerning their private affairs, and did not even look at the Russian general.

It was an absolutely new experience for Balashof, after being so accustomed to proximity to the very fountain-head of power and might, after just coming from a three hours' conversation with his sovereign, and having been universally treated with respect, to find, here on Russian soil, this hostile and peculiarly disrespectful display of brutal insolence.

The sun was just beginning to break through the clouds ; the air was cool and fresh with dew. Along the road from the village they were driving the cattle to pasture. Over the fields, one after another, like bubbles in the water, soared the larks with their matin songs.

Balashof looked about him while waiting for the officer to arrive from the village. The Russian Cossacks and the bugler and the French hussars occasionally exchanged glances, but no one spoke.

A French colonel of hussars, evidently just out of bed, came riding up from the village on a handsome, well-fed, gray horse, accompanied by two hussars. The officer, the soldiers, and their horses had an appearance of content and jauntiness.

It was the first period of the campaign, while the army was still in the very best order, almost fit for a review in time of peace, with just a shade of martial smartness in their attire, and with their minds a trifle stirred up to that gayety and cheerfulness and spirit of enterprise which always characterize the beginning of an expedition.

The French colonel with difficulty overcame a fit of yawning, but he was courteous, and evidently appreciated Balashof's high dignity. He conducted him past his soldiers inside the lines, and informed him that his desire to have a personal interview with the emperor would in all probability be immediately granted, since the imperial headquarters, he believed, were not far distant.

They approached the village of Rykonty, riding past pickets, sentinels, and soldiery, who saluted their colonel, and gazed with curiosity at the Russian uniforms, and finally came to the other side of the village. According to the colonel, the chief of division, who would receive Balashof and arrange the interview, would be found two kilometers distant.

The sun had now risen, and was shining gayly over the vivid green of the fields.

They had just passed a pot-house on a hillside, when they saw, coming to meet them up the hill, a little band of horsemen, in front of whom rode a tall man in a red cloak and in a plumed hat, under which long dark locks rolled down over his shoulders. He bestrode a coal-black horse, whose housings glittered in the sun, and his long legs were thrust forward in the fashion affected by French riders. This man came at a gallop toward Balashof, flashing and waving in the bright June sun, with his plumes and precious stones and gold galloons.

Balashof was within the length of two horses from this enthusiastically theatrical-looking individual, who was galloping to meet him in all his bravery of bracelets, plumes, necklaces, and gold, when Iulner, the French colonel, respectfully said, in a deferential whisper, " The king of Naples."

This was indeed Murat, who was still called the king of Naples. Although it was wholly incomprehensible in what respect he was the king of Naples, still he bore that title ; and he himself was convinced of its validity, and consequently he assumed a more majestic and important aspect than ever before. He was so convinced that he was actually king of Naples, that when, on the day before his departure from that city, as he was walking with his wife through the streets of Naples, and a few Italians acclaimed him with *Viva il re,* — Hurrah for the king, — he turned to his consort and said, with a melancholy smile : —

" Oh, poor creatures, they do not know that I am going to leave them to-morrow."

But, though he firmly believed that he was king of Naples, and was grieved for the sorrow that was coming upon his faithful subjects in losing him, still when he was commanded to enter the military service again, and especially since his meeting with Napoleon at Dantzic, when his august brother-in-law had said to him, "I made you king to reign in my way, not in yours," [1] he had

---

[1] *Je vous ai fait roi pour regner à ma manière, mais pas à la vôtre.*

cheerfully taken up the business which he understood so well, and, like a carriage-horse, driven but not over-worked, feeling himself in harness, he was frisky even between the thills, and, decked out in the most gorgeous and costly manner possible, galloped gayly and content-edly along the Polish highway, not knowing whither or wherefore.

As soon as he approached the Russian general, he threw his head back in royal fashion, and solemnly, with his black curls flowing down over his shoulders, looked inquiringly at the French colonel. The colonel respectfully explained to his majesty Balashof's errand, though he could not pronounce his name.

"*De Bal-ma-cheve,*" said the king, his self-confidence helping him to overcome the difficulty that had floored the colonel. "Charmed to make your acquaintance, general," he added, with a royally gracious gesture.

The moment the king began to speak loud and rapidly all the kingly dignity instantly deserted him, and, with-out his suspecting such a thing himself, changed into a tone of good-natured familiarity. He laid his hand on the withers of Balashof's horse.

"Well, general, everything looks like war, it seems," said he, as if he regretted a state of things concerning which he was in no position to judge.

"Sire," replied Balashof, "the emperor, my sovereign, has no desire for war, and, as *your majesty* sees," .... said Balashof, and thus he went on, with unavoidable affecta-tion, repeating the title *votre majesté* at every oppor-tunity during his conversation with this individual, for whom this title was still a novelty.

Murat's face glowed with dull satisfaction while he listened to *Monsieur de Balachoff*. But *royauté oblige;* and he felt that it was indispensable for him, as king and ally, to converse with Alexander's envoy, on matters of state. He dismounted, and, taking Balashof's arm, and drawing him a few paces aside from his suite, waiting respectfully, he began to walk up and down with him, trying to speak with all authority. He in-formed him that the Emperor Napoleon was offended by the demand made upon him to withdraw his forces from Prussia; especially as this demand was made publicly, and, therefore, was an insult to the dignity of France.

Balashof said that there was nothing insulting in this demand, "Because...."

Murat interrupted him. ....

"So then you do not consider the Emperor Alexander as the instigator of the war?" he asked suddenly, with a good-naturedly stupid smile.

Balashof explained why he really supposed that Napoleon was the aggressor.

"Ah, my dear general," again exclaimed Murat, interrupting him, "I desire, with all my heart, that the emperors should come to a mutual understanding, and that the war, begun in spite of me, should be brought to a termination as soon as possible," said he, in the tone of servants who wish to remain good friends, though their masters may quarrel. And he proceeded to make inquiries about the grand duke, and the state of his health, and recalled the jolly good times which they had enjoyed together at Naples. Then, suddenly, as if remembering his kingly dignity, Murat drew himself up haughtily, struck the same attitude in which he had stood during his coronation, and, waving his right hand, said : —

"I will not detain you longer, general; I wish you all success in your mission;" and then, with his embroidered red mantle and plumes waving, and his precious trinkets glittering in the sun, he rejoined his suite, which had been respectfully waiting for him.

Balashof went on his way, expecting, from what Murat said, to be very speedily presented to Napoleon himself. But, instead of any such speedy meeting with Napoleon, the sentinels of Davoust's infantry corps detained him again at the next village — just as he had been halted at the outposts — until an aide of the corps commander, who was sent for, conducted him to Marshal Davoust, in the village.

CHAPTER V

Davoust was the Emperor Napoleon's Arakcheyef — Arakcheyef except in cowardice: just the same, punctilious and cruel, and knowing no other way of manifesting his devotion than by cruelty.

In the mechanism of imperial organism, such men are necessary, just as wolves are necessary in the organism of nature; and they always exist and manifest themselves and maintain themselves, however incompatible their presence and proximity to the chief power may seem. Only by this indispensableness can it be explained how Arakcheyef — a cruel man, who personally pulled the mustaches of grenadiers, and who by reason of weakness of nerves could not endure any danger, and was ill-bred and ungentlemanly — could maintain power and influence with a character so chivalrous, noble, and affectionate as Alexander's.

In the barn attached to a peasant's cottage, Balashof found Marshal Davoust, sitting on a keg, and busily engaged in clerk's business (he was verifying accounts). An aide stood near him. He might have found better accommodations; but Marshal Davoust was one of those men who purposely make the conditions of life as disagreeable as possible for themselves, in order to have an excuse for being themselves disagreeable. Consequently, they are always hurried and obstinate. 'How can I think of the happy side of life when, as you see, I am sitting on a keg, in a dirty barn, and working?' the expression of his face seemed to say. The chief satisfaction and requirement of such men are that they should be brought into contact with men of another stamp, and to make before them an enormous display of disagreeable and obstinate activity. This gratification was granted Davoust when Balashof was ushered into his presence. He buried himself more deeply than ever in his work when the Russian general appeared. He glanced over his spectacles at Balashof's face, which was still glowing under the impression of the beautiful morning and the meeting with Murat, but he did not get up or even stir. He put on a still more portentous frown, and smiled sardonically.

Noticing the impression produced on Balashof by this reception, Davoust raised his head, and chillingly de· manded what he wanted.

Supposing that this insulting reception was given him because Davoust did not know that he was the Emperor Alexander's general-adjutant, and, what was more, his envoy to Napoleon, Balashof hastened to inform him of his name and mission. Contrary to his expectation, Davoust, after listening to Balashof's communication, became still more gruff and rude.

"Where is your packet?" he demanded. "Give it to me; I will send it to the emperor."

Balashof replied that he was ordered to give the package personally to the emperor.

"Your emperor's orders are carried out in *your* army; but here," said Davoust, "you must do as you are told."

And, as if to make the Russian general feel still more keenly how completely he was at the mercy of brute force, Davoust sent an aide for the officer of the day.

Balashof took out the packet containing the sovereign's note, and laid it on the table — a table improvised of a door, with the torn hinges still protruding, and laid on a couple of barrels. Davoust took the packet and read the superscription.

"You have a perfect right to treat me with respect, or not to treat me with respect," said Balashof. "But permit me to remark that I have the honor of being one of his majesty's aides."....

Davoust gazed at him without saying a word; but a trace of annoyance and confusion, betrayed in Balashof's face, evidently afforded him gratification.

"All due respect will be showed you," said he; and, placing the envelop in his pocket, he left the barn.

A moment later, the marshal's aide, Monsieur de Castrier, made his appearance, and conducted Balashof to the lodgings made ready for him; Balashof dined that same day with the marshal, in the barn, the boards

on the barrels serving as the table; early in the morning of the following day, Davoust came, and taking
Balashof to one side, told him confidentially that he was
requested to stay where he was; though if the baggage
train received orders to advance, he was to advance with
it, and not to communicate with any one except with
Monsieur de Castrier.

At the end of four days of solitude, of tedium, of consciousness of his helplessness and insignificance all the
more palpable after the environment of power to which
he had so recently been accustomed, after a number of
transfers with the marshal's baggage and the French
forces which occupied the whole region, Balashof was
brought back to Vilna, now in possession of the French;
he reëntered the town by the same gate by which he
had left it four days before.

On the following day the imperial chamberlain, Monsieur de Turenne, came to Balashof and announced that
the Emperor Napoleon would be pleased to grant him
an audience.

Four days previously sentinels from the Preobrazhen-
sky regiment had been standing in front of the mansion
into which Balashof was conducted; now two French
grenadiers in blue uniforms opened over the chest, and
in shaggy caps, an escort of hussars and Uhlans and a
brilliant suite of aides, pages, and generals, were standing at the steps near his saddle-horse and his Mameluke
Rustan, waiting for him to make his appearance.

Napoleon received Balashof in the same house in Vilna
from which Alexander had despatched him.

CHAPTER VI

THOUGH Balashof was accustomed to court magnifi-
cence, the sumptuousness and display of Napoleon's court
surprised him. Count Turenne conducted him into the
great drawing-room, where a throng of generals, chamberlains, and Polish magnates, many of whom Balashof
had seen at court during the sojourn of the Russian

emperor, were in waiting. Duroc told the Russian general that the Emperor Napoleon would receive him before going out to ride.

At the end of some moments of expectation the chamberlain on duty came into the great drawing-room, and, bowing courteously, invited Balashof to follow him.

Balashof passed into a small reception-room which opened into the cabinet, — into the very same cabinet where the Russian emperor had given him his directions. Balashof stood two minutes waiting. Then quick steps were heard in the other room. The folding doors were hastily flung open. All was silent, and then firm, resolute steps were heard coming from the cabinet : it was Napoleon. He had only just completed his toilet for riding on horseback. He was in a blue uniform coat thrown open over a white waistcoat which covered the rotundity of his abdomen ; he wore white chamois-skin small-clothes that fitted tightly over the stout thighs of his short legs, and Hessian boots. His short hair had evidently only just been brushed, but one lock of hair hung down over the center of his broad brow. His white, puffy neck was in sharp contrast with the dark collar of his uniform coat ; he exhaled a strong odor of eau-de-Cologne. On his plump and youthful-looking face with its prominent chin was an expression of gracious, imperially majestic condescension.

He came in, giving little quick jerks as he walked along, and holding his head rather high. His whole figure, thick-set and short, with his broad, stout shoulders and with the abdomen and breast involuntarily thrust forward, had that portly, stately carriage which men of forty who have lived in comfort are apt to have. Moreover it was evident that on this particular day he was in the serenest frame of mind.

He inclined his head in response to Balashof's low and respectful bow, and, approaching him, began immediately to speak like a man who values every moment of his time, and does not condescend to make set speeches, but is convinced in his own mind that he always speaks well and to the point.

"How are you, general?" said he. "I have received the Emperor Alexander's letter which you brought, and I am very glad to see you."

He scrutinized Balashof's face with his large eyes, and then immediately looked past him. It was evident that Balashof's personality did not interest him in the least. It was evident that only what came into his own mind had any interest for him. Everything outside of him had no consequence, because, as it seemed to him, everything in the world depended on his will alone.

"War I do not desire, and I have not desired it," said he. "But I have been driven to it. Even *now*" — he laid a strong stress on the word — "I am ready to accept any explanation which you can offer."

And he began clearly and explicitly to state the grounds for his dissatisfaction with the Russian government. Judging by the calm, moderate, and even friendly tone in which the French emperor spoke, Balashof was firmly convinced that he was anxious for peace and intended to enter into negotiations.

"*Sire, l'Empereur, mon maître ....*"

Balashof began his long-prepared speech when Napoleon, having finished what he had to say, looked inquiringly at the Russian envoy; but the look in the emperor's eyes, fastened on him, confused him. 'You are confused, — regain your self-possession,' Napoleon seemed to say as he glanced with a hardly perceptible smile at Balashof's uniform and sword. Balashof recovered his self-possession and began to speak. He declared that the Emperor Alexander did not consider Kurakin's demand for his passport a sufficient ground for war, that Kurakin had proceeded on his own responsibility and without the sovereign's sanction, that the Emperor Alexander did not wish for war, and that he had no understanding with England.

"None as yet," suggested Napoleon, and, as if fearing to express his thought, he scowled and slightly inclined his head, giving Balashof to understand that he might go on.

Having said all that he had been empowered to say,

Balashof declared that the Emperor Alexander desired peace, but that he would not enter into negotiations except on condition that — here Balashof stopped short. He recollected the words which the Emperor Alexander had not incorporated in the letter, but which he had strenuously insisted should be inserted in the rescript to Saltuikof, and which he had commanded Balashof to repeat to Napoleon. Balashof remembered these words, "so long as an armed foe remains on Russian soil," but some complicated feeling restrained him. He found it impossible to repeat these words, in spite of his desire to do so. He hesitated, and said, "On condition that the French troops retire beyond the Niemen."

Napoleon remarked Balashof's confusion as he said those last words. His face twitched ; the calf of his left leg began to tremble nervously. Not stirring from the place where he was standing, he began to speak in a higher key, and more rapidly than before. All the time that he was speaking, Balashof, not once shifting his eyes, involuntarily watched the twitching of Napoleon's left calf, which increased in violence in proportion as he raised his voice.

"I desire peace no less than the Emperor Alexander," said he. "Have I not for eighteen months done everything to preserve it? I have been waiting eighteen months for an explanation. But what is demanded of me before negotiations can begin?" he asked, with a frown, and emphasizing his question with an energetic gesture of his little, white, plump hand.

"The withdrawal of the troops beyond the Niemen, sire," replied Balashof.

"Beyond the Niemen," repeated Napoleon. "So that is all that is wanted now, is it, — 'beyond the Niemen,' merely beyond the Niemen," insisted Napoleon, looking straight at Balashof.

Balashof respectfully inclined his head.

"Four months ago the demand was to evacuate Pomerania, but now all that is required is to retire beyond the Niemen."— Napoleon abruptly turned away and began to pace up and down the room. "You say that

it is demanded of me to retire beyond the Niemen before there can be any attempt at negotiations ; but in
exactly the same way two months ago all that was required of me was to retire beyond the Oder and the
Vistula, and yet you can still think of negotiating?"

He walked in silence from one corner of the room to
the other, and then stopped in front of Balashof. Balashof noticed that his left leg trembled even faster than
before, and his face seemed petrified in its sternness of
expression. This trembling of his left calf Napoleon
himself was aware of. He afterwards said, " *La vibra-
tion de mon mollet gauche est un grand signe chez moi.*"

"Any propositions to abandon the Oder or the Vistula may be made to the Prince of Baden, but not to
me," Napoleon almost screamed, the words seeming to
take him by surprise. "If you were to give me Petersburg and Moscow, I would not accept such conditions.
You have said that I began this war. But who went to
his army first? The Emperor Alexander, and not I.
And you propose negotiations when I have spent millions,
when you have made an alliance with England, and when
your position is critical — you propose negotiations with
me! But what is the object of your alliance with England? What has she given you?" he asked hurriedly,
evidently now making no effort to show the advantages
of concluding peace, and deciding on the possibilities of
it, but only to prove his own probity and power, and
Alexander's lack of probity and blundering statecraft.

The beginning of his remarks evidently went to show
what an advantageous position he held, and to prove
that, nevertheless, he would be willing to have negotiations opened again. But he was now fairly launched in
his declaration, and the longer he spoke the less able he
was to control the current of his discourse. The whole
aim of his words now seemed to exalt himself and to
humiliate Alexander, which was precisely what he least
of all wished to do at the beginning of the interview.

"It is said you have concluded peace with the
Turks?"

Balashof bent his head affirmatively. "Peace has

been dec...." he began; but Napoleon gave him no chance to speak. It was plain that he wished to have the floor to himself, and he went on talking with that eloquence and excess of irritability to which men who have been spoiled are so prone.

"Yes, I know that you have concluded peace with the Turks, and without securing Moldavia and Valakhia. But I would have given your sovereign these provinces, just as I gave him Finland! Yes," he went on to say, "I promised the Emperor Alexander the provinces of Moldavia and Valakhia, and I would have given them to him; but now he shall not have those beautiful provinces. He might, however, have united them to his empire, and, in his reign alone, he would have made Russia spread from the Gulf of Bothnia to the mouths of the Danube. Catherine the Great could not have done more," exclaimed Napoleon, growing more and more excited, as he strode up and down the room, and saying to Balashof almost the same words which he had said to Alexander himself at Tilsit. "All that my friendship would have brought to him! Oh, what a glorious reign! what a glorious reign!" he repeated several times. He paused and took out a gold snuff-box, and greedily sniffed at it. "What a glorious reign the Emperor Alexander's *might have been!*"

He gave Balashof a compassionate look, but as soon as the general started to make some remark, Napoleon hastened to interrupt him again.

"What could he have wished or sought for that he would not have secured by being my friend?".... Napoleon asked, shrugging his shoulders in perplexity. "No; he preferred to surround himself with my enemies, and what enemies!" pursued Napoleon. "He has attached to himself Steins, Armfeldts, Benigsens, Winzengerodes! Stein, a traitor banished from his own country; Armfeldt, a scoundrel and intriguer; Winzengerode, a fugitive French subject; Benigsen, a rather better soldier than the others, but still incapable, who had no idea how to act in 1807, and who ought to arouse horrible recollections in the emperor's mind.... We will grant that he might make some use of them, if they had any capacity," pursued Napoleon, scarcely able in his speech to keep up with the arguments that kept rising in his mind in support of his right or might — the two things being one in his view. "But there is nothing of the sort : they are of no use either for war or peace ! Barclay, they say, is better than all the rest of them ; but I should not say so, judging by his first movements. But what are they doing ? What are all these courtiers doing ? Pfuhl proposes ; Armfeldt argues ; Benigsen considers ; and Barclay, when called upon to act, knows not what plan of action to decide on, and time slips away, and nothing is accomplished. Bagration alone is a soldier. He is stupid, but he has experience, a quick eye, and decision. And what sort of a part is your young sovereign playing in this hopeless throng ? They are compromising him, and making him responsible for everything that takes place. A sovereign has no right to be with his army unless he is a general," said he, evidently intending these words to be taken as a direct challenge to the Russian emperor. Napoleon was well aware how desirous the Emperor Alexander was to be a military commander.

"The campaign has not been begun a week, and you could not defend Vilna. You are cut in two, and driven out of the Polish provinces. Your army is already grumbling."

"On the contrary, your majesty," said Balashof, scarcely remembering what had been said to him, and finding it hard to follow this pyrotechnic of words, "the troops are full of zeal...."

"I know all about it," said Napoleon, interrupting him. "I know the whole story ; and I know the contingent of your battalions as well as that of my own. You have not two hundred thousand men ; and I have three times as many. I give you my word of honor," said Napoleon, who forgot that his word of honor might have very little weight, — "I give you my word of honor that I have five hundred and thirty thousand men on this side of the Vistula. The Turks will be no help to you; they are never of any use; and they have proved this by making peace with you. The Swedes — it is their fate to be ruled by madmen. Their king was crazy: they got rid of him, and chose another — Bernadotte, who instantly lost his wits; because it is sure proof of madness if a Swede enters into alliance with Russia."

Napoleon uttered this with a vicious sneer, and again carried the snuff-box to his nose.

To each of Napoleon's propositions, Balashof was ready and willing to give an answer; he kept making the gestures of a man who has somewhat to say; but Napoleon gave him no chance to speak. In refutation of the Swedes' being mad, Balashof was anxious to state that Sweden was isolated if Russia were against her; but Napoleon angrily shouted so as to drown his words. Napoleon had worked himself up into that state of irritation in which a man must talk, and talk, and talk, if for nothing else but to convince himself that he is in the right of a question.

Balashof began to grow uncomfortable: as an envoy he began to fear that he was compromising his dignity, and he felt it incumbent on him to reply; but, as a man, he had a moral shrinking before such an unreasonable passion as Napoleon had evidently worked himself into. He knew that anything Napoleon might say in such circumstances had no significance; that he himself, when he came to think it over, would be ashamed. Balashof stood with eyes cast down, looking at Napoleon's restless stout legs, and tried to avoid meeting his eyes.

"But what do I care for your allies?" demanded Napoleon. "I too have allies — these Poles, eighty thousand of them; they fight like lions, and there will be two hundred thousand of them."

And, probably, still more excited by the fact that in making this statement he was uttering a palpable falsehood, and by Balashof standing there, in silent submission to his fate, he abruptly turned back, came close to Balashof, and, making rapid and energetic gestures with his white hands, he almost screamed: —

"Understand! If you incite Prussia against me, I
assure you, I will wipe her off from the map of Europe,"
said he, his face pale and distorted with rage, and ener-
getically striking one white hand against the other.
"Yes, and I will drive you beyond the Dvina and the
Dnieper; and I will again set up against you that
barrier which Europe was stupid and blind enough to
permit to be overthrown. That is what will become of
you, that is what you will have lost in alienating me,"
said he, and once more paced the room in silence a
number of times, jerking his stout shoulders.

He replaced his snuff-box in his waistcoat pocket, took
it out again, carried it to his nose several times, and
halted directly in front of Balashof. He stood thus
without speaking, and gazed directly into Balashof's
eyes, with a satirical expression; then he said, in a low
tone : —

"*Et cependant quel beau regne aurait pu avoir votre
maître* — what a glorious reign your master *might have
had !*"

Balashof, feeling it absolutely indispensable to make
some answer, declared that affairs did not present themselves to the eyes of the Russians in such a gloomy
aspect. Napoleon said nothing, but continued to look
at him with the same satirical expression, and apparently
had not heard what he said. Balashof declared that in
Russia the highest hopes were entertained of the issue
of the war. Napoleon tossed his head condescendingly,
as much as to say, 'I know it is your duty to say so,
but you do not believe it ; my arguments have convinced
you.'

When Balashof had finished what he had to say,
Napoleon once more raised his snuff-box, took a sniff
from it, and then stamped twice on the floor, as a signal.
The door was flung open ; a chamberlain, respectfully
approaching, handed the emperor his hat and gloves ;
another brought him his handkerchief. Napoleon, not
even looking at them, addressed Balashof : —

"Assure the Emperor Alexander, in my name," said
he, as he took his hat, "that I esteem him as warmly as

before; I know him thoroughly, and I highly appreciate his lofty qualities. *Je ne vous retiens plus, général; vous recevrez ma lettre à l'empereur.*"

And Napoleon swiftly disappeared through the door. All in the reception-room hurried forward and down the stairs.

CHAPTER VII

AFTER all that Napoleon had said to him, after those explosions of wrath, and after those last words spoken so coldly, "*I will not detain you longer, general, you will receive my letter to the emperor,*" Balashof was convinced that Napoleon would not only have no further desire to see him, but would rather avoid seeing him, a humiliated envoy, and, what was more, a witness of his undignified heat. But, to his amazement, he received through Duroc an invitation to dine that day with the emperor.

The guests were Bessières, Caulaincourt, and Berthier.

Napoleon met Balashof with a cheerful face and affably. There was not the slightest sign of awkwardness or self-reproach for his outburst of the morning, but, on the contrary, he tried to put Balashof at his ease. It was plain to see that Napoleon was perfectly persuaded that there was no possibility of his making any mistakes, and that in his understanding of things all that he did was well, not because it was brought into comparison with the standards of right and wrong, but simply because *he* did it.

The emperor was in excellent spirits after his ride through Vilna, where he was received and followed by the acclamations of a throng of people. In all the windows along the streets where he passed were displayed tapestries, flags, and decorations ornamented with his monogram, while Polish ladies saluted him and waved their handkerchiefs.

At dinner he had Balashof seated next himself, and treated him, not only cordially, but even as if he considered him one of his own courtiers, one of those who sympathized in his plans and rejoiced in his successes. Among other topics of conversation he brought up Moscow, and began to ask Balashof about the Russian capital, not merely as an inquisitive traveler asks about a new place which he has in mind to visit, but as if he was convinced that Balashof, as a Russian, must be flattered by his curiosity.

"How many inhabitants are there in Moscow? How many houses? Is it a fact that Moscow is called *Moscou la Sainte?* How many churches are there in Moscow?" he asked.

And when told that there were upwards of two hundred, he asked: —

"What is the good of such a host of churches?"

"The Russians are very religious," replied Balashof.

"Nevertheless, a great number of monasteries and churches is always a sign that a people are backward," said Napoleon, glancing at Caulaincourt for confirmation in this opinion.

Balashof respectfully begged leave to differ from the French emperor's opinion.

"Every country has its own customs," said he.

"But nowhere else in Europe is there anything like it," remarked Napoleon.

"I beg your majesty's pardon," replied Balashof. "In Spain as well as in Russia there are many monasteries and churches."

This reply of Balashof's, which glanced at the recent defeat of the French in Spain, was highly appreciated when Balashof repeated it at the Emperor Alexander's court; but it was very little appreciated at Napoleon's table, and passed unnoticed.

The indifferent and perplexed faces of the marshals plainly betrayed the fact that they did not understand where the point of the remark came in, or realize Balashof's insinuation. 'If that had been witty, then we should have understood it; consequently it could not have been witty,' the marshals' faces seemed to say. So little was this remark appreciated that even Napoleon did not notice it, and naïvely asked Balashof the names of the cities through which the direct road to Moscow led.

Balashof, who throughout the dinner was on the alert, replied, "Just as all roads lead to Rome, so all roads lead to Moscow;" that there were many roads, and that among these different routes was the one that passed through Pultava, which Charles XII. had chosen. Thus replied Balashof, involuntarily flushing with delight at the cleverness of this answer. Balashof had hardly pronounced the word "Pultava" when Caulaincourt began to complain of the difficulties of the route from Petersburg to Moscow and to recall his Petersburg experiences.

After dinner they went into Napoleon's cabinet to drink their coffee; four days before it had been the Emperor Alexander's cabinet; Napoleon sat down, stirring his coffee in a Sèvres cup, and pointed Balashof to a chair near him.

There is a familiar state of mind which comes over a man after a dinner, and, acting with greater force than all the dictates of mere reason, compels him to be satisfied with himself and to consider all men his friends. Napoleon was now in this comfortable mental condition. It seemed to him that he was surrounded by men who adored him. He was persuaded that even Balashof, after having eaten dinner with him, was his friend and worshiper. Napoleon addressed him with a pleasant and slightly satirical smile:—

"This is the very room, I am informed, which the Emperor Alexander used. Strange, is n't it, general?" he asked, evidently not having any idea that such a remark could fail to be agreeable to his guest, as it insinuated that he, Napoleon, was superior to Alexander.

Balashof could have nothing to reply to this, and merely inclined his head.

"Yes, in this room, four days ago, Winzengerode and Stein were holding council," pursued Napoleon, with the same self-confident, satirical smile. "What I cannot understand is that the Emperor Alexander has taken

to himself all my personal enemies. I do not .... understand it. Has it never occurred to him that I might do
the same thing?"

And this question, directed to Balashof, evidently
aroused his recollection of the cause of his morning's
fury, which was still fresh in his mind.

"And have him know that I will do so," said Napoleon, getting up and pushing away his cup. "I will
drive all his kindred out of Germany, — those of Würtemberg, Weimar, Baden .... yes, I will drive them all
out. Let him be getting ready for them an asylum in
Russia!"

Balashof bowed, and signified that he was anxious to
withdraw, and that he listened simply because he could
not help listening to what Napoleon said. But Napoleon paid no heed to this motion; he addressed Balashof
not as his enemy's envoy, but as a man who was for
the time being entirely devoted to him and must needs
rejoice in the humiliation of his former master.

"And why has the Emperor Alexander assumed the
command of his forces? What is the reason of it?
War is my trade, and his is to rule and not to command armies. Why has he taken upon him such
responsibilities?"

Napoleon again took his snuff-box, silently strode
several times from one end of the room to the other,
and then suddenly and unexpectedly went straight up
to Balashof, and with a slight smile he unhesitatingly,
swiftly, simply, ... as if he were doing something not
only important, but even rather agreeable to Balashof,
.... put his hand into the Russian general's face, and,
taking hold of his ear, gave it a little pull, the smile
being on his lips alone.

To have one's ear pulled by the emperor was
considered the greatest honor and favor at the French
court.

"Well, have you nothing to say, admirer and courtier
of the Emperor Alexander?" asked Napoleon, as if it
were an absurdity in his presence to be *courtisan et
admirateur* of any one besides himself. "Are the

horses ready for the general?" he added, slightly bending his head in answer to Balashof's bow. "Give him
mine, he has *far to go*." ....

The letter which was intrusted to Balashof was the
last that Napoleon ever wrote to Alexander. All the
particulars of the interview were communicated to
the Russian emperor, and the war began. ....

CHAPTER VIII

AFTER his interview with Pierre, Prince Andreï went
to Petersburg on business, as he told his relatives, but
in reality to find Prince Anatol Kuragin there, since he
considered it his bounden duty to fight him. But Kuragin, whom he inquired after as soon as he reached
Petersburg, was no longer there. Pierre had sent word
to his brother-in-law that Prince Andreï was in search
of him. Anatol Kuragin had immediately secured an
appointment from the minister of war, and gone to the
Moldavian army.

During this visit to Petersburg Prince Andreï met
Kutuzof, his former general, who was always well disposed to him, and Kutuzof proposed that he should go
with him to the Moldavian army, of which the old general had been appointed commander-in-chief. Prince
Andreï, having thereupon received his appointment as
one of the commander's staff, started for Turkey.

Prince Andreï felt that it would not be becoming to
write Kuragin and challenge him. Having no new pretext for a duel, he felt that a challenge from him would
compromise the Countess Rostova, and therefore he
sought for a personal interview with Kuragin, when he
hoped he should be able to invent some new pretext for
the duel. But in Turkey also he failed of finding Kuragin, who had returned to Russia as soon as he learned of
Prince Andreï's arrival.

In a new country, and under new conditions, life
began to seem easier to Prince Andreï. After the faith-
lessness of his betrothed, which had affected him all the

more seriously from his very endeavor to conceal from all the grief that it had really caused him, the conditions of life in which he had found so much happiness had grown painful to him, and still more painful the very freedom and independence which he had in times gone by prized so highly. He not only ceased to harbor those thoughts which had for the first time occurred to him as he looked at the heavens on the field of Austerlitz, which he so loved to develop with Pierre, and which were the consolations of his solitude at Bogucharovo, and afterwards in Switzerland and Rome; but he even feared to bring up the recollection of these thoughts, which opened up such infinite and bright horizons. He now concerned himself solely with the narrowest and most practical interests, entirely disconnected with the past, and busied himself with these with all the greater avidity because the things that were past were kept from his remembrance. That infinite, ever-retreating vault of the heavens which at that former time had arched above him had, as it were, suddenly changed into one low and finite oppression, where all was clear but there was nothing eternal and mysterious.

Of all the activities that offered themselves to his choice, the military service was the simplest and best known to him. Accepting the duties of general inspector on Kutuzof's staff, he entered into his work so doggedly and perseveringly that Kutuzof was amazed at his zeal and punctuality.

Not finding Kuragin in Turkey, Prince Andreï did not think it worth his while to follow him back to Russia; but still he was well aware that, no matter how long a time should elapse, it would be impossible for him, in spite of all the scorn which he felt for him, in spite of all the arguments which he used in his own mind to prove that he ought not to stoop to any encounter with him, he was aware, I say, that if ever he met him he would be obliged to challenge him, just as a starving man throws himself on food. And this consciousness that the insult had not yet been avenged, that his anger had not been vented, but still lay on his heart, poisoned that artificial serenity which Prince Andreï by his apparently indefatigable and somewhat ambitious and ostentatious activity procured for himself in Turkey.

When, in 1812, the news of the war with Napoleon reached Bukarest, — where for two months Kutuzof had been living, spending his days and nights with his Wallachian mistress, — Prince Andreï asked his permission to be transferred to the western army. Kutuzof, who had already grown weary of the excess of Bolkonsky's activity, which was a constant reproach to his own indolence, willingly granted his request, and gave him a commission to Barclay de Tolly.

Before joining the army, which, during the month of May, was encamped at Drissa, Prince Andreï drove to Luisiya Gorui, which was directly in his route, being only three versts from the Smolensk highway.

During the last three years of Prince Andreï's life, there had been so many changes; he had thought so much, felt so much, seen so much, — for he had traveled through both the East and the West, — that he felt a sense of strangeness, of unexpected amazement, to find at Luisiya Gorui exactly the same manner of life even to the smallest details. As he entered the driveway, and passed the stone gates that guarded his paternal home, it seemed as if it were an enchanted castle, where everything was fast asleep. The same sobriety, the same neatness, the same quietude, reigned in the house; the same furniture, the same walls, the same sounds, the same odor, and the same timid faces, only grown a little older.

The Princess Mariya was the same timid, plain person, only grown into an old maid, and living out the best years of her life in fear and eternal moral sufferings, without profit and without happiness. Bourienne was the same coquettish, self-satisfied person, cheerfully getting profit out of every moment of her life, and consoling herself with the most exuberant hopes; only it seemed to Prince Andreï that she showed an increase of assurance.

The tutor, Dessalles, whom Prince Andreï had brought from Switzerland, wore an overcoat of Russian cut; his unmanageable tongue involved itself in Russian speech with the servants, but otherwise he was the same pious and pedantic tutor of somewhat limited intelligence.

The only physical change in the old prince was a gap left in one corner of his mouth, caused by the loss of a tooth; morally, he was just the same as before, only with an accentuation of his ugly temper and his distrust in the genuineness of everything that was done in the world.

Nikolushka, with his rosy cheeks and dark, curly hair, had been the one person to grow and change; and, when he laughed and was merry, he unconsciously lifted the upper lip of his pretty little mouth, just as the lamented princess, his mother, had done. He, alone, refused to obey the laws of immutability in this enchanted, sleeping castle. But, though externally everything remained as it had always been, the internal relations of all these people had altered since Prince Andreï had seen them.

The members of the household were divided into two alien and hostile camps, which made common cause now simply because he was there, — for his sake changing the ordinary course of their lives. To the one party belonged the old prince, Bourienne, and the architect, to the other, the Princess Mariya, Dessalles, Nikolushka, and all the women of the establishment.

During his brief stay at Luisiya Gorui, all the family dined together; but it was awkward for them all, and Prince Andreï felt that he was a guest for whose sake an exception was made, and that his presence was a constraint on them. At dinner, the first day, Prince Andreï, instinctively feeling this, was taciturn; and the old prince, remarking the unnaturalness of his behavior, also relapsed into a moody silence, and, immediately after dinner, retired to his room. When, later, Prince Andreï joined him there, and, with the desire of entertaining him, began to tell him about the young Count Kamiensky's campaign, the old prince unexpectedly broke out into a tirade against the Princess Mariya, blaming her for her superstition and for her dislike of Mlle. Bourienne, who, according to him, was the only person truly devoted to him.

The old prince laid the cause of his feeble health entirely to the Princess Mariya, insisting that she all the time annoyed and exasperated him; and that, by her injudicious coddling, and foolish talk, she was spoiling the little Prince Nikolaï. The old prince was perfectly well aware that it was he who tormented his daughter, and that her life was rendered exceedingly trying; but he was also aware that he could not help tormenting her, and that she deserved it.

"Why does not Prince Andreï, who sees how things are, say anything to me about his sister?" wondered the old prince. "He thinks, I suppose, that I am a wicked monster, or an old idiot, who has unreasonably estranged himself from his daughter, and taken a Frenchwoman in her place. He does not understand; and so I must explain to him, and he must listen to me," thought the old prince. And he began to expound the reasons that made it impossible to endure his daughter's absurd character.

"Since you ask my opinion," said Prince Andreï, not looking at his father, — for he was condemning him for the first time in his life, — "but I did not wish to talk about it; since you ask me, however, I will tell you frankly my opinion in regard to this matter. If there is any misunderstanding and discord between you and Masha, I could never blame her for it, for I know how she loves and reveres you. And if you ask me further," pursued Prince Andreï, giving way to his irritation, because he had become of late exceedingly prone to fits of irritation, "then I must have one thing to say: if there is any such misunderstanding, the cause of it is that vulgar woman, who is unworthy to be my sister's companion."

The old man at first gazed at his son with staring eyes, and, by his forced smile, uncovered the new gap caused by the loss of the tooth, to which Prince Andreï could not accustom himself.

"What companion, my dear? Ha! Have you already been talking that over? Ha!"

"Batyushka, I do not wish to judge you," said Prince Andreï, in a sharp and choleric voice; "but you have driven me to it; and I have said, and always shall say, that the Princess Mariya is not to blame, but they are to blame — the little Frenchwoman is to blame.".....

"Ha! you condemn me!..... you condemn me!" cried the old man, in a subdued voice, and with what seemed confusion to Prince Andreï; but then suddenly he sprang up, and screamed : —

"Away! away with you! Don't dare to come here again!"

Prince Andreï intended to take his departure immediately; but the Princess Mariya begged him to stay another day. He did not meet his father that day; the old prince kept in his room, and admitted no one except Mlle. Bourienne and Tikhon; but he inquired several times whether his son had yet gone.

On the following day, just before dinner, Prince Andreï went to his little son's apartment. The blooming lad, with his curly hair, just like his mother's, sat on his knee. Prince Andreï began to tell him the story of Bluebeard; but, right in the midst of it, he lost the thread, and fell into a brown study. He did not give a thought to this pretty little lad, his son, while he held him on his knee, but he was thinking about himself. With a sense of horror, he sought, and failed to find, any remorse in the fact that he had exasperated his father; and no regret that he was about to leave him — after the first quarrel that they had ever had in their lives. More serious than all else was his discovery that he did not feel the affection for his son which he hoped to arouse, as of old, by caressing the lad and taking him on his knee.

"Well, go on, papa!" said the boy.

Prince Andreï, without responding, set him down from his knees, and left the room. The moment Prince Andreï suspended his daily occupations, and especially

the moment he encountered the former conditions of
his life, in which he had been engaged in the old, happy
days, the anguish of life took possession of him with
fresh force ; and he made all haste to leave the scene
of these recollections, and to find occupation as soon
as possible.

"Are you really going, André ? " asked his sister.

"Thank God, I can go," replied Prince Andreï.   "I
am very sorry that you cannot also."

"What makes you say so ? " exclaimed his sister.
"Why do you say so, now that you are going to this
terrible war ? and he is so old !   Mlle. Bourienne told
me that he had asked after you."

As soon as she recalled this subject, her lips trembled.
and the tears rained down her cheeks.   Prince Andreï
turned away, and began to pace up and down the room.

"Oh ! my God ! my God ! "[1] he cried.   "And how
do you conceive that any one — that such a contemptible creature can bring unhappiness to others ! " he
exclaimed, with such an outburst of anger that it
frightened the Princess Mariya.   She understood that,
in speaking of "such contemptible creatures," he had
reference not alone to Mlle. Bourienne, who had caused
him misery, but also to that man who had destroyed his
happiness.

"André ! one thing I want to ask you ; I beg of you,"
said she, lightly touching his elbow and gazing at him
with her eyes shining through her tears. — "I understand you." — The Princess Mariya dropped her eyes. —
"Do not think that sorrow is caused by men.   Men are
His instruments."   She gazed somewhat above her
brother's head, with that confident look that people
have who are accustomed to look at the place where
they know a portrait hangs.   "Sorrow is sent by Him,
and comes not from men.   Men are His instruments ;
they are not accountable.   If it seem to you that any
one is culpable toward you, forget it and forgive.   We
have no right to punish.   And you will find happiness
in forgiving."

---

[1] *Akh ! Bozhe moï ! Bozhe moï !*

"If I were a woman I would, Marie! Forgiveness is a woman's virtue. But a man has no right and no power to forgive and forget," said he, and, although he was not at that instant thinking of Kuragin, all his unsatisfied vengeance suddenly surged up in his heart. "If the Princess Mariya at this late day urges me to forgive, it is proof positive that I ought long ago to have punished," he said to himself. And, not stopping to argue with his sister, he began to dream of that joyful moment of revenge when he should meet Kuragin, who (as he knew) had gone to the army.

The Princess Mariya urged her brother to delay his journey yet another day, assuring him how unhappy her father would be if Andreï went off without a reconciliation with him; but Prince Andreï replied that in all probability he should soon return from the army, that he would certainly write to his father, and that now the longer he stayed the more bitter this quarrel would become.

"Adieu, André! remember that sorrows come from God, and that men are never accountable for them;" those were the last words that his sister said as they bade each other farewell.

"Such is our fate!" said Prince Andreï to himself as he turned out of the avenue of the Luisogorsky mansion. "She, poor innocent creature, is left to be devoured by this crazy old man. The old man is conscious that he is doing wrong, but he cannot change his nature. My little lad is growing up and enjoying life, though he will become like all the rest of us, deceivers or deceived. I am going to the army — for what purpose I myself do not know, and I am anxious to meet a man whom I despise, so as to give him a chance to kill me and exult over me."

In days gone by the same conditions of life had existed, but then there was a single purpose ramifying through them and connecting them, but now everything was in confusion. Isolated, illogical thoughts, devoid of connection, arose one after another in Prince Andreï's mind.

CHAPTER IX

P *ince* Andreï reached the army headquarters toward the first of July. The troops of the first division, commanded by the sovereign in person, were intrenched in a fortified camp on the Drissa; the troops of the second division were in retreat, though they were endeavoring to join the first, from which, as the report went, they had been cut off by a strong force of the French. All were dissatisfied with the general conduct of military affairs in the Russian army; but no one ever dreamed of any of the Russian provinces being invaded, and no one had supposed that the war would be carried beyond the western government of Poland.

Prince Andreï found Barclay de Tolly on the bank of the Drissa. As there was no large town or village within easy reach of the camp, all this enormous throng of generals and courtiers who were present with the army were scattered in the best houses of the little villages for a distance of ten versts from the camp, on both sides of the river.

Barclay de Tolly was stationed about four versts from the sovereign.

He gave Bolkonsky a dry and chilling welcome, and, speaking in his strong German accent, told him that he should have to send in his name to the sovereign for any definite employment, but proposed that for the time being he should remain on his staff.

Anatol Kuragin, whom Prince Andreï expected to find at the army, was no longer there; he had gone to Petersburg, and this news was agreeable to Bolonsky. He was absorbed in the interest of being at the very center of a mighty war just beginning, and he was glad to be, for a short time, freed from the provocation which the thought of Kuragin produced in him.

During the first four days, as no special duties were required of him, Prince Andreï made the circuit of the whole fortified camp, and by the aid of his natural intelligence and by making inquiries of men who were well

informed, he managed to acquire a very definite comprehension of the position. But the question whether
this camp were advantageous or not remained undecided
in his mind. He had already come to the conclusion,
founded on his own military experience, that even those
plans laid with the profoundest deliberation are of little
consequence in battle — how plainly he had seen this
on the field of Austerlitz! — that everything depends on
what was done to meet the unexpected and impossible-
to-be-foreseen tactics of the enemy, that all depended
on how and by whom the affair was conducted.

Therefore in order to settle this last question in his
own mind, Prince Andreï, taking advantage of his position and his acquaintances, tried to penetrate the character of the administration of the armies, and of the
persons and parties that took part in it, and he drew up
for his own benefit the following digest of the position
of affairs.

While the sovereign was still at Vilna, the troops had
been divided into three armies: the first was placed
under command of Barclay de Tolly; the second under
the command of Bagration; the third under command
of Tormasof.

The emperor was present with the first division, but
not in his quality of commander-in-chief. In the orders
of the day it was simply announced that the sovereign
would — not take command, but would simply be present with the army. Moreover, the sovereign had no
personal staff, as would have been the case had he been
commander-in-chief, but only a staff appropriate to the
imperial headquarters.

Attached to him were the chief of the imperial staff,
the General-Quartermaster Prince Volkonsky, generals,
flügel-adjutants, diplomatic chinovniks, and a great
throng of foreigners; but these did not form a military
staff. Besides these there were attached to his person,
but without special functions, Arakcheyef, the ex-minister
of war; Count Benigsen, with the rank of senior general; the grand duke, the Tsesarevitch Konstantin Pavlovitch; Count Rumyantsef; the Chancellor Stein, who

had been minister in Prussia; Armfeldt, a Swedish general; Pfuhl, the principal originator of the plan of the campaign; Paulucci, general-adjutant and a Sardinian refugee; Woltzogen, and many others.

Although these individuals were present without any special military function, still by their peculiar position they wielded a powerful influence, and oftentimes the chief of the corps, and even the commander-in-chief, did not know in what capacity Benigsen or the grand duke or Arakcheyef or Prince Volkonsky asked questions or proffered advice, and could not tell whether such and such an order, couched in the form of a piece of advice, emanated from the speaker or the sovereign, and whether it was incumbent on him or not incumbent on him to carry it out. But these were merely a stage accessory; the essential idea why the emperor was present and all these men were present was perfectly palpable to all from the point of view of courtiers, and in the presence of the sovereign all were courtiers.

This idea was as follows: The monarch did not assume the title of commander-in-chief, but he exercised control over all the troops; the men who surrounded him were his aids; Arakcheyef was the faithful guardian of law and order, and the sovereign's body-guard. Benigsen was a landowner in the Vilna government, who, as it were, did the honors of the region, and in reality was an excellent general, useful in council, and ready, in case he were needed, to take Barclay's place. The grand duke was there because it was a pleasure for him to be. Ex-Minister Stein was there because he was needed to give advice, and because the Emperor Alexander had a very high opinion of his personal qualities. Armfeldt was Napoleon's bitter enemy, and a general possessed of great confidence in his own ability, which always had an influence upon Alexander. Paulucci was there because he was bold and resolute in speech. The general-adjutants were there because they were always attendant on the sovereign's movements; and, last and not least, Pfuhl was there because he had conceived a plan for the campaign against Napoleon, and had in-

duced Alexander to place his confidence in the expedi-
ence of this plan, thereby directing the entire action of
the war. Pfuhl was attended by Woltzogen, a keen
self-conceited cabinet-theorist, who scorned all things,
and had the skill to dress Pfuhl's schemes in a more
pleasing form than Pfuhl himself could.

In addition to these individuals already mentioned,
Russians and foreigners, — especially foreigners, who
each day proposed new and unexpected plans with that
boldness characteristic of men engaged in activities in
a land not their own, — there were a throng of subordinates who were present with the army because their
principals were there.

Amid all the plans and voices in this tremendous,
restless, brilliant, and haughty world, Prince Andreï
distinguished the following sharply outlined subdivisions
of tendencies and parties.

The first party consisted of Pfuhl and his followers,
military theorists, who believed that there was such a
thing as a science of war, and that this science had its
immutable laws — the laws for oblique movements, for
outflanking, and so on. Pfuhl and his followers insisted
on retreating into the interior of the country, according
to definite principles prescribed by the so-styled science
of war, and in every departure from this theory they
saw nothing but barbarism, ignorance, or evil intentions.
To this party belonged the German princes, and Woltzogen, Winzengerode, and others, — notably the Germans.

The second party was diametrically opposed to the
first. And, as always happens, they went to quite
opposite extremes. The men of this party were those
who insisted on making Vilna the base of a diversion
into Poland, and demanded to be freed from all pre-
conceived plans. Not only were the leaders of this
party the representatives of the boldest activity, but at
the same time they were also the representatives of
nationalism, in consequence of which they showed all
the more urgency in maintaining their side of the
dispute. Such were the Russians Bagration, Yer-

molof, — who was just beginning to come into prominence, — and many others. It was at this time that Yermolof's famous jest was quoted extensively : it was said that he asked the emperor to grant him the favor of promoting him to be a German! The men of this party recalled Suvorof, and declared that there was no need of making plans or marking the map up with pins, but to fight, to beat the foe, not to let him enter Russia, and not to let the army lose heart.

The third party, in which the sovereign placed the greatest confidence, consisted of those courtiers who tried to find a compromise between the two previous tendencies. These men — for the most part civilians, and Arakcheyef was in their number — thought and talked as men usually talk who have no convictions but do not wish to show their lack of them. They declared that unquestionably the war, especially with such a genius as Bonaparte, — they now called him Bonaparte again, — demanded the profoundest consideration and a thorough knowledge of the science, and in this respect Pfuhl was endowed with genius ; but, at the same time, it was necessary to acknowledge that theorists were often one-sided, and, therefore, it was impossible to have perfect confidence in them ; it was best to heed also what Pfuhl's opposers had to say, and also what was said by men who had had practical experience in military affairs, and then to balance the two. The men of this party insisted the camp along the Drissa should be retained, according to Pfuhl's plan ; the movements of the other divisions should be changed. Although this action answered no purpose whatever, yet it seemed advisable to the men of this party.

The fourth tendency was the one of which the conspicuous representative was the grand duke, the Tsesarevitch [1] Konstantin, heir-apparent to the throne, who could not forget his disappointment at the battle of Austerlitz, when he rode out at the head of his guards, dressed in

---

[1] Any son of the Tsar is properly *tsarevitch*, but the crown prince bears the distinctive title *tsesarevitch* (son of the Cæsar). Count Tolstoï emphasizes his position by using also the term *naslyednik*, successor, heir.

casque and jacket as for a parade, expecting to drive the
French gallantly before him, and, unexpectedly finding
himself at the very front, was, in spite of everything,
involved in the general confusion.   The men of this
party showed in their opinions both sincerity and lack
of sincerity.   They were afraid of Napoleon; they saw
that he was strong while they were weak, and they had
no hesitation in saying so.   They said : —

"Nothing but misfortune, ignominy, and defeat will
come out of all this.   Here we have abandoned Vilna ;
we have abandoned Vitebsk ; we shall abandon the
Drissa in like manner.   The only thing left for us to
do in all reason is to conclude peace, and as speedily as
possible, before we are driven out of Petersburg."

This opinion, widely current in the upper spheres of
the army, found acceptance also in Petersburg, and was
supported by the Chancellor Rumyantsof, who for other
reasons of state was also anxious for peace.

A fifth party was formed by those who were partisans
of Barclay de Tolly not as a man, but simply because he
was minister of war and commander-in-chief.   These said :
"Whatever he is," — and that was the way they always
began, — "he is an honest, capable man, and he has no
superior.   Give him actual power because the war can
never come to any successful issue without some one in
sole control, and then he will show what he can do, just
as he proved it in Finland.   If our army is well organized and powerful, and made the retreat to the Drissa
without suffering any loss, we owe it to this Barclay alone.
If now Barclay is replaced by Benigsen, all will go to
rack and ruin, because Benigsen made an exhibition of
his incapacity in 1807," said the men of this party.

A sixth party — the Benigsenists — claimed the contrary ; that there was no one more capable and experienced than Benigsen, "and, however far they go out
of his way, they 'll have to return to him."   "Let them
make their mistakes now !"   And the men of this
party argued that our whole retreat to the Drissa was a
disgraceful defeat and an uninterrupted series of blunders.

"The more blunders they make now the better, or, at least, the sooner they will discover that things cannot go on in this way," said they. "Such a man as Barclay is not needed, but a man like Benigsen, who showed what he was in 1807. Napoleon himself has done him justice, and he is a man whose authority all would gladly recognize, and only such a man is Benigsen."

The seventh party consisted of men such as are always found especially around young monarchs, — and the Emperor Alexander had a remarkable number of such,— namely, generals and flügel-adjutants who were passionately devoted to their sovereign, not as an emperor, but as a man whom they worshiped heartily and disinterestedly, just as Rostof had worshiped him in 1805, and who saw in him not only all virtues but all human qualities. These men, although they praised their sovereign's modesty in declining to assume the duties of commander-in-chief, still criticized this excess of modesty, and had only one desire which they insisted on, that their adored monarch, overcoming his excessive lack of confidence in himself, should openly announce that he would take his place at the head of his armies, gather around him the appropriate staff of a commander-in-chief, and while consulting in cases of necessity with theorists and practical men of experience, himself lead his troops, who by this mere fact would be roused to the highest pitch of enthusiasm.

The eighth and by all odds the largest group of men, which in comparison with the others all put together would rank as ninety-nine to one, consisted of men who desired neither peace nor war nor offensive operations, nor a defensive camp on the Drissa nor anywhere else, nor Barclay, nor the sovereign, nor Pfuhl, nor Benigsen, but simply wished one and the same essential thing : the utmost possible advantages and enjoyments for themselves. In these troubled waters of intertangled and complicated intrigues which abounded at the sovereign's headquarters, it became possible to succeed in many things which would have been out of the question at any other time. One whose sole desire was not to lose his advantageous position was to-day on Pfuhl's side, to-morrow allied with his opponent, on the day following, for the sake merely of shirking responsibility and pleasing the sovereign, would declare that he had no opinion in regard to some well-known matter.

A second, anxious to curry favor, would attract the sovereign's attention by boisterously advocating at the top of his voice something which the sovereign had merely hinted at the day before, by arguing and yelling at the council meeting, pounding himself in the chest, and challenging to a duel any one who took the other side, and thereby show how ready he was to be a martyr for the public weal.

A third would simply demand between two meetings of the council and while his enemies were out of sight a definitive subvention in return for his faithful service of the state, knowing very well that they would never be able to refuse him. A fourth would as if by accident keep letting the sovereign see how overwhelmed with work he was! A fifth, in order to attain his long-cherished ambition of being invited to dine at the sovereign's table, would stubbornly argue the right or wrong of some newly conceived opinion and bring up for this purpose more or less powerful and well-founded arguments.

All the men of this party were hungry for rubles, honorary crosses, promotions, and in their pursuit of these things they watched the direction of the weathercock of the sovereign's favor, and just as soon as it was seen that the weathercock pointed in any one direction, all this population of military drones would begin to blow in the same direction so that it was sometimes all the harder for the sovereign to change about to the other side. In this uncertainty of position, in presence of a real danger which was threatening and which impressed upon everything a peculiarly disquieting character, amid this vortex of intrigues, selfish ambitions, collisions, diverse opinions and feelings, with all the variety of nationalities represented by all these men, this eighth and by far the largest party of men, occupied with private interests, gave great complication and confusion to affairs in general. Whatever question came up, instantly this swarm of drones, before they had finished their buzzing over the previous theme, would fly off to the new one, and deafen every one and entirely drown out the genuine voices who had something of worth to say.

Just about the time Prince Andreï arrived at the army, still a ninth party was forming out of all these others, and beginning to let its voice be heard. This was the party of veteran statesmen, men of sound wisdom and experience, who, sharing in none of all these contradictory opinions, were able to look impartially upon all that was going on at headquarters and to devise means for escaping from this vagueness, indecision, confusion, and weakness.

The men of this party said and thought that nothing but mischief resulted preëminently from the presence of the sovereign with a military court at the front, introducing into the army that indeterminate, conditional, and fluctuating irregularity of relations which, however useful at court, were ruinous to the troops; that it was the monarch's business to govern, and not to direct the army; that the only cure for all these troubles was for the sovereign and his court to take their departure; that the mere fact of the emperor being with the army paralyzed the movements of fifty thousand men who were required to protect him from personal peril; that the most incompetent general-in-chief, if he were independent, would be better than the best, hampered by the sovereign's presence.

While Prince Andreï was at Drissa, without stated position, Shishkof, the imperial secretary, who was one of the chief members of this faction, wrote the sovereign a letter which Balashof and Arakcheyef agreed to sign. Taking advantage of the permission accorded him by the sovereign to make suggestions concerning the general course of events, he respectfully, and under the pretext that it was necessary for the sovereign to stir the people of the capital to fresh enthusiasm for this war, in this letter proposed that he should leave the army.

The mission of fanning the enthusiasm of the people and of summoning them to defend the fatherland, the very thing that led to the ultimate triumph of Russia, — and his personal presence in Moscow contributed largely to this end, — was therefore offered to the emperor and accepted by him as a pretext for taking his departure from the army.

CHAPTER X

THIS letter had not as yet been placed in the sovereign's hands, when Barclay at dinner informed Bolkonsky that his majesty would be pleased to have a personal interview with him, in order to make some inquiries concerning Turkey, and that he, Prince Andreï, was to present himself at Benigsen's headquarters at six o'clock that evening.

On that day a report had been brought to the sovereign's headquarters concerning a new movement on the part of Napoleon which might prove dangerous for the army — a report which was afterward found to be false, however. And on that same morning, Colonel Michaud, in company with the emperor, had ridden around the fortifications on the Drissa and had proved conclusively to the sovereign that this fortified camp, which had been laid out under Pfuhl's direction and had been up to that time considered a masterpiece of tactical skill destined to be the ruin of Napoleon, — that this camp was a piece of folly and a source of danger for the Russian army.

Prince Andreï proceeded to the headquarters of General Benigsen, who had established himself in a small villa on the very bank of the river. Neither Benigsen nor the sovereign was there; but Chernuishef, one of the emperor's aides, received Bolkonsky and explained that the sovereign had gone with General Benigsen and the Marchese Paulucci for a second time that day on a tour of inspection of the fortified camp of the

Drissa, as to the utility of which serious doubts had begun to be conceived.

Chernuishef was sitting with a French novel at one of the windows of the front room. This room had at one time probably been a ball-room ; there still stood in it an organ on which were piled a number of rugs, and in one corner stood the folding bed belonging to Benigsen's aide. This aide was there. Apparently overcome by some merry-making or perhaps by work, he lay stretched out on the bed and was fast asleep.

Two doors led from this ball-room : one directly into the former drawing-room, the other to the right into the library. Through the first, voices were heard conversing in German and occasionally in French. Yonder, in that former drawing-room, were gathered together at the sovereign's request, not a council of war — for the sovereign was fond of indefiniteness — but a meeting of a number of men whose opinions concerning the existing difficulties he was anxious to learn. It was not a council of war, but a sort of committee of gentlemen convened to explain certain questions for the sovereign's personal gratification. To this semi-council were invited the Swedish general Armfeldt, General-Adjutant Woltzogen, Winzengerode, whom Napoleon had called a fugitive French subject, Michaud, Toll, who was also not at all a military man, Count Stein, and finally Pfuhl himself, who, as Prince Andreï had already heard, was *la cheville ouvrière* — the mainspring — of the whole affair. Prince Andreï had an opportunity of getting a good look at him, as Pfuhl arrived shortly after he did and came into the drawing-room, where he stood for a minute or two talking with Chernuishef.

Pfuhl, dressed like a Russian general, in a badly made uniform which fitted him clumsily, seemed to Prince Andreï at first glance like an old acquaintance, although he had never seen him before. He was of the same type as Weirother and Mack and Schmidt and many other German theorist-generals whom Prince Andreï had seen in 1805; but he was more characteristic of the type than all the rest. Never in his life had Prince Andreï seen a German theorist who so completely united in himself all that was typical of those Germans.

Pfuhl was short and very thin, but big-boned, of coarse, healthy build, with a broad pelvis and prominent shoulder-blades. His face was full of wrinkles, and he had deep-set eyes. His hair had been evidently brushed in some haste forward by the temples, but behind it stuck out in droll little tufts. Looking about sternly and restlessly, he came into the room as if he were afraid of every one. With awkward gestures grasping his sword, he turned to Chernuishef and asked in German where the emperor was. It was evident that he was anxious to make the round of the room as speedily as possible, to put an end to the salutations and greetings, and to seat himself before the map, where he felt quite at home. He abruptly tossed his head in reply to Chernuishef's answer and smiled ironically at the report that the sovereign had gone to inspect the fortifications which Pfuhl himself had constructed in accordance with his theory. In a deep, gruff voice characteristic of all self-conceited Germans, he grumbled to himself : —

"Blockhead! — Ruin the whole business ; pretty state of things will be the result." [1]

Prince Andreï did not listen to him and was about to go, but Chernuishef introduced him to Pfuhl, remarking that he had just come from Turkey, where the war had been brought to a successful termination. Pfuhl gave a fleeting glance, not so much at Prince Andreï as through him, and muttered with a smile : —

"That must have been a fine tactical campaign." [2]

And, scornfully smiling, he went into the room where the voices were heard.

Evidently Pfuhl, who was always disposed to be ironical and irritable, was on this day especially stirred up because they had dared without him to inspect his camp and criticize him.

[1] *Dummkopf! — Zum Grunde die ganze Geschichte — 's wird was gescheites d'raus werden.*
[2] *Da muss ein schöner tactischer Krieg gewesen sein.*

Prince Andreï, simply by this brief interview with Pfuhl, reinforced by his experiences at Austerlitz, had gained a sufficiently clear insight into the character of this man. Pfuhl was one of those hopelessly, unalterably self-confident men who would suffer martyrdom rather than yield his opinion, a genuine German, for the very reason that only Germans are absolutely certain, in their own minds, of the solid foundation of that abstract idea, — Science; that is to say, the assumed knowledge of absolute truth.

The Frenchman is self-confident because he considers himself individually, both as regards mind and body, irresistibly captivating to either men or women. The Englishman is self-confident through his absolute conviction that he is a citizen of the most fortunately constituted kingdom in the world, and because, as an Englishman, he knows always and in all circumstances what it is requisite for him to do, and also knows that all that he does as an Englishman is correct beyond cavil. The Italian is self-confident because he is excitable, and easily forgets himself and others. The Russian is self-confident for the precise reason that he knows nothing, and wishes to know nothing, because he believes that it is impossible to know anything. But the German is self-confident in a worse way than all the rest, above and beyond all the rest, because he imagines that he knows the truth, — the science which he has himself invented, but which for him is absolute truth!

Evidently such a man was Pfuhl. He had his science, — the theory of oblique movements, which he had deduced from the history of the wars of Friedrich the Great, — and everything that he saw in the warfare of more recent date seemed to him nonsense, barbarism, ignorant collisions in which, on both sides, so many errors were committed that these wars had no right to be called wars. They did not come under his theory, and could not be judged as a subject for science.

In 1806 Pfuhl had been one of those who elaborated the plan of the campaign that culminated at Jena and Auerstadt, but the unfortunate issue of that campaign did not open his eyes to see the slightest fault in his theory. On the contrary, the fact that his theory had been, to a certain extent, abandoned, was in his mind the sole cause of the whole failure ; and he said, in the tone of self-satisfied irony characteristic of him, "*Ich sagte ja dass die ganze Geschichte zum Teufel gehen werde*, — I predicted that the whole thing would go to the deuce."

Pfuhl was one of those theorists who are so in love with their theory that they forget the object of the theory, its relation to practice. In his love for his theory he hated everything practical, and could not listen to it. He even delighted in the failure of any enterprise, because this failure, resulting from the abandonment of theory for practice, was proof positive to him of how correct his theory was.

He spoke a few words with Prince Andreï and Chernuishef about the existing war, and his expression was that of a man who knew in advance that all was going to the dogs, and that he, for one, did not much regret the fact. The little tufts of unkempt hair that stuck out on his occiput, and the hastily brushed love-locks around his temples, spoke eloquently of this.

He went into the adjoining room, and instantly they heard the deep and querulous sounds of his voice.

CHAPTER XI

PRINCE ANDREI had no time to let his eyes follow Pfuhl, as Count Benigsen just at that moment came hastily into the room, and, inclining his head to Bolkonsky, but not pausing, went directly into the library, giving his adjutant some order as he went. Benigsen had hurried home in advance of the sovereign in order to make some preparations, and to be there to receive him.

Chernuishef and Prince Andreï went out on the steps. The emperor, looking fatigued, was dismounting from his horse. The Marchese Paulucci was making some remark. The sovereign, with his head bent over to the left, was listening with a discontented air to Paulucci, who was speaking with his usual vehemence. The sovereign started forward, evidently desirous of cutting short this harangue; but the flushed and excited Italian, forgetting the proprieties, followed him, still talking.

" As for the man who advised this camp, the camp of Drissa," Paulucci was saying, just as the sovereign, mounting the steps and perceiving Prince Andreï, glanced into his face, not at first recognizing him. "As to him, sire," pursued Paulucci, in a state of desperation, as if quite unable to control himself, — "as for the man who advised this camp of Drissa, I see no other alternative for him than the insane asylum or the gallows."

The sovereign, not waiting for the Italian to finish what he had to say, and apparently not even hearing his words, came closer to Bolkonsky, and, recognizing him, addressed him graciously : —

"I am very glad to see you. Come in where the meeting is, and wait for me."

The sovereign went into the cabinet. He was followed by Prince Piotr Mikhaïlovitch Volkonsky and Baron Stein, and the doors were shut. Prince Andreï, taking advantage of the sovereign's permission, joined Paulucci, whom he had known in Turkey, and went into the drawing-room where the council was held.

Prince Piotr Mikhaïlovitch Volkonsky held the position of *nachalnik*, or chief, of the sovereign's staff. Volkonsky came out of the cabinet and carried into the drawing-room a quantity of maps and papers, and after he had laid them on the table he communicated the questions in regard to which he was anxious to have the opinions of the gentlemen present. The questions arose from the fact that news, afterwards proved to be false, had been received the night before concerning a movement of the French toward outflanking the camp on the Drissa.

General Armfeldt was the first to begin the debate, and he unexpectedly proposed, as an escape from the impending difficulty, that they should choose an entirely new position at a little distance from the highways leading to Moscow and Petersburg ; and there, as he expressed it, let the army be increased to its full strength, and await the enemy. No one could see any reason for his advocating such a scheme, unless it came from his desire to show that he, as well as the rest, had ideas of his own.

It was evident that Armfeldt had long ago evolved this scheme, and that he proposed it now not so much with the design of responding to the questions laid before the meeting — questions which this scheme of his entirely failed to answer — as it was with the design of using his chance to enunciate it. This was one of the millions of proposals which, not having any reference to the character which the war was likely to assume, had equally as good foundations as others of the same sort for successful accomplishment.

Some of those present attacked his suggestions, others defended them. The young Colonel Toll attacked the opinions of the Swedish general more fiercely than the others, and during the discussion took out of his side pocket a manuscript note-book, which he begged permission to read. In this diffusely elaborated manuscript Toll proposed still another plan of campaign, diametrically the opposite of those suggested by Armfeldt and Pfuhl.

Paulucci, combating Toll, proposed the plan of an advance and attack, which, according to his views, was the only possible way to extricate us from the present suspense, and from the "trap," as he called the camp on the Drissa, in which we now found ourselves.

During the course of these discussions and criticisms Pfuhl and Woltzogen, his interpreter (his "bridge," in court parlance), maintained silence. Pfuhl merely snorted scornfully and turned away, signifying that he would never sink so low as to reply to all this rubbish to which he was now listening. So when Prince Volkonsky, as chairman of the meeting, called on him to express his opinion, he merely said : —

"Why do you ask me ? General Armfeldt has proposed a beautiful position, with the rear exposed, and you have heard about the offensive operations proposed by this Italian gentleman. *Sehr schön!* Or the retreat. *Auch gut!* So why do you ask me?" he replied ; "for, you see, you yourselves know more about all this than I do."

But when Volkonsky frowned, and said that he asked his opinion in the name of the sovereign, then Pfuhl got up, and, growing suddenly excited, began to speak : —

"Everything has been spoiled, everything been thrown into confusion. All pretend to know more than I do, but now they come to me. How can things be remedied? There's no possibility of remedying them. It is necessary to carry out to the letter my design, on the lines which I have laid down," said he, pounding the table with his bony knuckles. "Where is the difficulty? Rubbish! *Kinderspiel!*"

He stepped up to the table and began to talk rapidly, scratching with his finger-nail on the map, and demonstrating that no contingency could alter the effectiveness of the camp on the Drissa ; that everything had been foreseen, and that if the enemy were actually to outflank them, then the enemy would be inevitably annihilated.

Paulucci, who did not understand German, began to question him in French. Woltzogen came to the aid of his leader, who spoke French but badly, and began to translate his words, though he could hardly keep up with Pfuhl, who rapidly demonstrated that everything, everything, not only what had happened, but whatever could possibly happen, had been provided for in his plan ; and that, if there were any complications, the whole blame lay simply in the fact that his plan had not been accurately carried out. He kept smiling ironically as he made his demonstration, and finally he scornfully stopped adducing arguments, just as a mathematician ceases to verify the various steps of a problem which has once been found correctly solved. Woltzogen took his place, proceeding to explain in French his ideas, and occasionally turning to Pfuhl with a "*Nicht wahr, Excellenz?*" for confirmation.

Pfuhl, like a man so excited in a battle that he attacks his own side, cried testily to his own faithful follower, to Woltzogen: —

"Why, of course; it's as plain as daylight!"[1]

Paulucci and Michaud both at once fell on Woltzogen in French, Armfeldt addressed a question to Pfuhl in German, Toll explained the matter in Russian to Prince Volkonsky. Prince Andreï listened without speaking, and watched the proceedings.

Of all these individuals the exasperated, earnest, and absurdly opinionated Pfuhl awoke the most sympathy in Prince Andreï. He alone, of all present, evidently had no taint of self-seeking, nor had he any hatred of any one, but simply desired that his plan, elaborated from his theory which had been deduced from his studies during long years, should be carried into execution. He was ridiculous, his use of sarcasm made him disagreeable; but at the same time he awakened involuntary respect by his boundless devotion to an idea.

Besides, in all the remarks made by those who were present, with the sole exception of Pfuhl's, there was one common feature which had never been manifested in the council of war in the year 1805, and this was the secret but panic fear — dissembled — of Napoleon's genius; it showed itself in every argument. They took it for granted that Napoleon could do anything. They looked for him on every side, and by his terrible name each one of them demolished the proposals of the other. Pfuhl alone, it seemed, regarded even Napoleon as a barbarian, like all the other opponents of his theory.

Pfuhl awakened in Prince Andreï a feeling of pity as well as of respect. By the tone in which the courtiers addressed him, by the way in which Paulucci had permitted himself to speak of him to the emperor, and, chiefly, by a certain despairing expression manifested by Pfuhl himself, it was plain to see that the others

[1] *Nun ja! was soll denn da noch expliziert werden!*

knew, and he himself felt, that his fall was at hand. And, aside from his self-conceit and his grumbling German irony, he was pitiable by reason of his hair brushed forward into little love-locks on his temples, and the little tufts standing out on his occiput. Although he did his best to dissimulate it under the guise of exasperation and scorn, he was in despair because his only chance of showing his theory on a tremendous scale, and proving its value before all the world, was slipping from him.

The discussion lasted a long time, and the longer it lasted the more heated grew the arguments, which were like quarrels by reason of the raised voices and personalities ; and the less possible was it to come to any general conclusion from all that was said. Prince Andreï, listening to this polyglot debate and these propositions, plans and counter-plans, and shouts, was simply astonished at what they all said. The idea which had early and often suggested itself to him during the time of his former military service, — that there was not, and could not be, any such thing as a military science, and consequently could not be any so-called military genius, — now seemed to him a truth beyond a peradventure.

"How can there be any theory and science in a matter the conditions and circumstances of which are unknown and cannot be determined, — in which the force employed by those who make the war is still less capable of measurement ? No one can possibly know what will be the position of our army and that of the enemy's a day from now, and no one can know what is the force of this or that division. Sometimes, when there is no coward in the front to cry, 'We are cut off !' and to start the panic, and there is a jovial, audacious man there to shout, 'Hurrah !' a division of five thousand is worth thirty thousand, as was the case at Schöngraben ; and sometimes fifty thousand will fly before eight, as happened at Austerlitz. What science, then, can there be in such a business, where nothing can be predetermined, as in any practical business, and where everything depends on numberless conditions, the resolving of which is defined at some one moment, but *when* — no one can possibly foretell. Armfeldt says that our army is cut off, and Paulucci declares that we have got the French army between two fires. Michaud says that the uselessness of the camp on the Drissa consists in this, that the river is back of it, while Pfuhl declares that therein consists its strength. Toll proposes one plan, Armfeldt proposes another, and all are good and all are bad, and the advantages of each and every proposition can be proved only at the moment when the event occurs. And why do they all use the term, 'military genius'? Is that man a genius who manages to keep his army well supplied with biscuits, and commands them to go, some to the left and some to the right? Merely because military men are clothed with glory and power, and crowds of sycophants are always ready to flatter Power, ascribing to it the inappropriate attributes of genius. On the other hand, the best generals whom I have ever known were stupid or absent-minded men. The best was Bagration; Napoleon himself called him so. And Bonaparte himself! I remember his self-satisfied and narrow-minded face on the field of Austerlitz. A good leader on the field of battle needs not genius or any of the special qualities so much as he needs the exact opposite, or the lack of the highest human qualities — love, poetry, affection, a philosophical, investigating skepticism. He must be narrow-minded, firmly convinced that what he is doing is absolutely essential (otherwise he will not have patience), and then only will he be a brave leader. God pity him if he is a man who has any love for any one, or any pity, or has any scruples about right or wrong. It is perfectly comprehensible that in old times they invented a theory of geniuses because they held power. Credit for success in battle depends not on them but on that man in the ranks who cries, 'They have fled!' or who shouts 'Hurrah!' And only in these ranks can you serve with any assurance that you are of service."

Thus mused Prince Andreï as he listened to the arguments, and he came out of his brown study only when

Paulucci called him and the meeting was already dissolved.

On the following day, during a review, the sovereign
asked Prince Andreï where he preferred to serve, and
Prince Andreï forever lost caste in the eyes of the
courtiers because he did not ask for a place near the
sovereign's person, but asked permission to enter active
service.

CHAPTER XII

ROSTOF, before the opening of the campaign, received
a letter from his parents, in which, after briefly announcing Natasha's illness and the rupture of the engagement
with Prince Andreï, — this rupture, they explained, was
Natasha's own work, — they again urged him to retire
from the service and come home.

Nikolaï, on receipt of this letter, made no attempt to
secure either a furlough or permission to go upon the
retired list, but wrote his parents that he was very sorry
for Natasha's illness and breach with her lover, and that
he would do all that he possibly could to fulfil their
desires. He wrote a separate letter to Sonya.

"Adored friend of my heart," he wrote, "nothing except
honor could keep me from returning home. But just now, at
the opening of the campaign, I should consider myself dis-
graced not only before all my comrades, but in my own eyes, if
I were to prefer my pleasure to my duty, and my love to my
country. But this is our last separation. Be assured that immediately after the war, if I am alive and you still love me, I
will give up everything and fly to thee to clasp thee forever to
my ardent heart!"

He was telling the truth — it was only the opening
of the campaign that detained Nikolaï and prevented
him from fulfilling his promise by at once returning
home and marrying Sonya. The autumn at Otradnoye,
with its sport, and the winter with the Christmas holidays, and his love for Sonya, had opened up before him

a whole perspective of the pleasures of a country noble-man, and of domestic contentment, which he had never known before and which now beckoned to him with their sweet allurements.

"A glorious wife, children, a good pack of hunting-dogs, a leash of ten or twenty spirited greyhounds, the management of the estate, the neighbors, and service at the elections," he said to himself. But now there was a war in prospect, and he was obliged to remain with his regiment. And, since this was a matter of necessity, Nikolaï Rostof, in accordance with his character, was content with the life which he led in the regiment, and had the skill to arrange it so that it was agreeable.

On his return from his furlough, having met with a cordial reception from his comrades, Nikolaï was sent out to secure fresh horses; and he brought back with him from Little Russia an excellent remount, which gladdened his own heart, and procured for him the praise of his superiors. During his absence he had been pro-moted to the rank of *rotmistr*, or captain of cavalry, and, when the regiment was restored to a war footing, with increased complement, he was put in charge of his former squadron.

The campaign had begun ; the regiment was moved into Poland, double pay was granted ; there were new officers present, new men and horses, and, above all, there was an increase of that excitement and bustle which always accompanies the beginning of a campaign ; and Rostof, recognizing his advantageous position in the regiment, gave himself up, heart and soul, to the pleasures and interests of military service, although he knew well that, sooner or later, he would have to leave it.

The troops evacuated Vilna for various complicated reasons — imperial, political, and tactical. At head-quarters, every step of the retreat was accompanied by a complicated play of interests, arguments, and passions. For the hussars of the Pavlogradsky regiment, all this backward movement, in the best part of the summer, with abundance of provisions, was a most simple and enjoyable affair. At headquarters, men might lose heart, and grow nervous, and indulge in intrigues to their hearts' content; but in the ranks no one thought of asking where or wherefore they were moving. If they indulged in regrets at the retreat, it was simply because they were compelled to leave pleasant quarters and the pretty Polish women. If it occurred to any one that affairs were going badly, then, as became a good soldier, the man who had such a thought would try to be jovial, and not think at all of the general course of events, but only of what nearest concerned himself.

At first, they were agreeably situated near Vilna, having jolly acquaintances among the Polish landed proprietors, and constantly expecting the sovereign, and other commanders highest in station, to review them, and as constantly being disappointed.

Then came the order to retire to Swienciany, and to destroy all provisions that they could not carry away with them. Swienciany was memorable to the hussars simply because it was the "drunken camp," [1] as the entire army called it, from their stay at the place, and because many complaints had been made of the troops having taken unfair advantage of the order to forage for provisions, and had included under this head horses and carriages and rugs stolen from the Polish *pans*, or nobles.

Rostof had a vivid remembrance of Swienciany, because on the first day of their arrival at the place he had dismissed a quartermaster, and had not been able to do anything with the men of his squadron, all of whom were tipsy, having, without his knowledge, brought away five barrels of old beer.

From Swienciany they had retired farther, and then farther still, until they reached the Drissa; and then they had retired from the Drissa, all the time approaching the Russian frontier.

On the 25th of July, the Pavlogradsui, for the first time, took part in a serious engagement.

On the 24th of July, the evening before the engage-

[1] *Pyanui lager.*

ment, there was a severe thunder-storm, with rain and hail. That summer of the year 1812 was throughout remarkable for its thunder-showers.

Two squadrons of the Pavlogradsui had bivouacked in a field of rye, already eared, but completely trampled down by the horses and cattle. It was raining in torrents, and Rostof, with a young officer named Ilyin, who was his *protégé*, was sitting under the shelter of a sort of wigwam, extemporized at short notice. An officer of their regiment, with long mustaches bristling forth and hiding his cheeks, came along, on his way from headquarters, and, being overtaken by the rain, asked shelter of Rostof.

"Count, I have just come from headquarters. Have you heard of Rayevsky's great exploit?"

And the officer proceeded to relate the particulars of the battle of Saltanovo, which he had learned about at headquarters.

Rostof, hunching his shoulders as the water trickled down his neck, lighted his pipe and listened negligently, now and then giving a look at the young officer Ilyin, who was squeezed in close to him. This officer, a lad of only sixteen, had not been very long connected with the regiment, and was now in the same relation to Rostof that Rostof had borne toward Denisof seven years before. Ilyin had taken Rostof as his pattern in every respect, and was in love with him like a woman.

The officer with the long mustaches, Zdrzhinsky by name, declared emphatically that the dike at Saltanovo was the Thermopylæ of the Russians, and that the exploit performed by General Rayevsky was worthy of the deeds of antiquity. Zdrzhinsky described how Rayevsky went out on the dike, with his two sons, under a deadly fire, and, side by side with them, rushed to the attack.

Rostof listened to the story, and not only had nothing to say in response to the narrator's enthusiasm, but, on the contrary, had the air of a man ashamed of what is told him, although he has no intention of rebutting it.

Rostof, after the battle of Austerlitz, and the campaign of 1807, knew, from his own personal experience, that those who talk of military deeds always lie; just as he himself had lied in relating such things. In the second place, his experience had taught him that, in a battle, every event is quite the reverse of what we might imagine and relate it. And, therefore, he took no stock in Zdrzhinsky's story, and was not pleased with Zdrzhinsky himself, who, with his cheeks hidden by those long mustaches, had the habit of leaning over close to the face of the person to whom he was talking, and then, besides, was in the way in the narrow hut.

Rostof looked at him without speaking. "In the first place, there must have been such a crush and confusion on the dike which they were charging that even if Ra-yevsky had led his sons upon it, it could not have had any effect upon any one save perhaps a dozen men who were in his immediate vicinity," thought Rostof. "The rest could not have seen at all how or with whom Ra-yevsky was rushing upon the dike. And then those who did see it could not have been very greatly stimulated, because what would they have cared for Rayevsky's affectionate paternal feeling, when the only thing of interest to them was the caring for their own skin! Then again, the fate of the country in no wise depended on whether they took the dike at Saltanovo or not, as is supposed to have been the case at Thermopylæ. And therefore what was the use of risking such a sacrifice? And, then, why should he have exposed his children in the affair? I should not have exposed my brother Petya to it, no, nor even this Ilyin here, though he is no rela-tion to me, — but a good fellow all the same, — but I should have tried to put them safe out of harm's way somewhere," pursued Rostof, in his thoughts, all the while listening to Zdrzhinsky. But he did not speak his thoughts aloud; in regard to this also he had learned wisdom by experience. He knew that this story re-dounded to the glory of our arms, and therefore it was requisite to make believe that he had no doubt of it. And so he did.

"Well, there's one thing, I can't stand this," ex-

claimed Ilyin, perceiving that Rostof was not pleased
with Zdrzhinsky's chatter; "my stockings and my
shirt are wet through, and it is running under me here.
I am going in search of shelter. It seems to me the
rain is not so heavy."

Ilyin went out and Zdrzhinsky mounted and rode off.

At the end of five minutes Ilyin, slopping through the
mud, came hurrying up to the wigwam.

"Hurrah! Rostof, come on quick! There's a tavern
a couple of hundred paces from here, and a lot of our
men are there already. We can get dry there, and
Marie Heinrichovna is there too."

Marie Heinrichovna was the regimental doctor's wife,
a pretty young German girl whom the doctor had married in Poland. Either because the doctor had no
means, or because he did not wish to be separated from
his bride during the early period of his married life, he
took her wherever he went in his travels with the hussars, and his jealousy became a constant source of
amusement and jest among the officers of the regiment.

Rostof flung his cloak over him, called Lavrushka to
follow with the luggage, and went with Ilyin, plowing
through the mud, plodding straight onward amid the
now rapidly diminishing shower, into the darkness of
the evening, occasionally interrupted by flashes of distant lightning.

"Rostof, where are you?"

"Here I am! what lightning!" was what they said
as they marched along.

CHAPTER XIII

At the tavern, before which stood the doctor's *kibitka*, or traveling carriage, five officers were already
gathered. Marie Heinrichovna, a plump, light-haired
German, in jacket and nightcap, was sitting in the
front room on a wide bench. Her spouse, the doctor,
was asleep behind her. Rostof and Ilyin, welcomed

by acclamations and roars of laughter, walked into the room.

"Ee! you have something very jolly going on," said Rostof, with a laugh.

"And what brings you here so late?"

"You are fine specimens! Look at the way they are streaming! Don't drown out our parlor floor!"

"Be careful how you daub Marie Heinrichovna's dress," cried the voices.

Rostof and Ilyin made haste to find a corner where, without shocking Marie Heinrichovna's modesty, they might change their wet garments. They had gone behind the partition to make the change, but the little room, which was scarcely more than a closet, was entirely filled by three officers, sitting on an empty chest, and playing cards by the light of a single candle; and nothing would induce them to evacuate the place.

Accordingly, Marie Heinrichovna surrendered her petticoat to them, and they hung it up in place of a screen; and behind this, Rostof and Ilyin, with Lavrushka's aid, who had brought their saddle-bags, exchanged their wet clothing for dry.

A fire had been started in a broken-down stove. They procured a board, laid it across a pair of saddles, covered it with a caparison; the samovar was set up, a bottle-case unpacked, and half a bottle of rum got out, and Marie Heinrichovna was requested to do the honors; all gathered around her. One offered her a clean handkerchief to wipe her lovely little hands; another spread his overcoat under her feet, to keep them from the dampness; a third hung his cloak in the window, to keep away the draught; a fourth waved the flies away from her husband's face, so that he would not wake up.

"Never mind him," said Marie Heinrichovna, smiling timidly and happily. "He always sleeps sound and well after he has been up all night."

"Oh, that is all right, Marie Heinrichovna!" exclaimed the officer. "We must take good care of the doctor. All things are possible; and he would have pity on me, if ever he came to saw off an arm or a leg for me."

There were only three glasses; the water was so muddy that it was impossible to tell whether the tea were too strong or too weak; and the samovarchik held only water enough for six glasses; but it was all the more fun to take turns, and to receive, in order of seniority, each his glass from Marie Heinrichovna's plump little hands, though her short nails were not perfectly clean!

All the officers seemed to be, and were, in love that evening with Marie Heinrichovna. Even the three who had been playing cards in the little room made haste to throw up their hands, and came out to the samovar, giving way to the common feeling of worship for Marie Heinrichovna's charms.

Marie Heinrichovna, seeing herself surrounded by these brilliant and courteous young men, fairly beamed with delight, in spite of all her efforts to hide it, and her manifest alarm every time her husband, on the bench back of her, moved in his sleep.

There was only one spoon, while there was a superfluity of sugar; but, as it was slow in melting, it was decided that she should stir each glass of tea in turn. Rostof, having received his glass and seasoned it with rum, asked Marie Heinrichovna to stir it for him.

"But you haven't put the sugar in, have you?" said she, constantly smiling, as if all that she said, and all that the others said, was as funny as it could be, and concealed some deep hidden meaning.

"No, I haven't any sugar yet; all it needs is for you to stir it with your little hand."

Marie Heinrichovna consented, and began to look for the spoon, which some one had meanwhile appropriated.

"Stir it with your dainty little finger, Marie Heinrichovna," said Rostof. "It will make it all the sweeter!"

"It's hot!" exclaimed Marie Heinrichovna, blushing with gratification.

Ilyin took a pail of water, and, throwing a little rum

into it, came to Marie Heinrichovna, begging her to stir it with her finger.

"This is my cup," said he. "Just dip your finger in it, and I will drink it all up."

When the samovar had been entirely emptied, Rostof took a pack of cards, and proposed to play koroli [1] with Marie Heinrichovna. Lots were cast as to who should be first to play with her.

At Rostof's suggestion, the game was so arranged that the one who became "king" should have the privilege of kissing Marie Heinrichovna's little hand; while he who came out *prokhvost*, or provost, as they called the loser, should have to start the samovar afresh for the doctor, when he awoke.

"Well, but supposing Marie Heinrichovna should be king?" asked Ilyin.

"She's our queen anyway. And her word shall be our law!"

The game had hardly begun, before the doctor's disheveled head appeared behind Marie Heinrichovna. He had been awake for some time, and had overheard all that had been said; and it was perfectly evident that he found nothing very jolly, amusing, or diverting in all that had been said and done. His face was glum and sour. He exchanged no greeting with the officers, but scratched his head, and asked them to make way, so that he could get out. As soon as he had left the room, all the officers burst into a roar of laughter, while Marie Heinrichovna blushed till the tears came, and thereby became all the more fascinating in the eyes of all those young men.

On his return from out-of-doors, the doctor told his wife, who had now ceased to smile that happy smile, and was looking at him in timid expectation of a scolding, that the storm had passed, and they must go and camp out in their kibitka, otherwise all their effects would be stolen.

---

[1] *Koroli*, kings, is a South Russian game at cards, somewhat like the French games of *écarté* and *triomphe*. The winner is called *korol*, king, and can make the other pay a forfeit.

"But I will send a soldier to stand on guard — two of them," said Rostof. "What nonsense, doctor!"

"I'll stand guard myself," said Ilyin.

"No, gentlemen; you have had your rest, but I have not had any sleep for two nights," said the doctor, and sat down gloomily next his wife, to wait for the end of the game.

As they saw the doctor's lowering face bent angrily on his wife, the officers became more jovial still, and many of them could not refrain from bursts of merriment, plausible pretexts for which they kept striving to invent. When the doctor went out, taking his wife with him, and ensconced themselves in the snug little kibitka for the night, the officers wrapped themselves up in their damp cloaks and lay down anywhere in the tavern; but it was long before they could go to sleep, because of the talk that still went on; some of them recalling the doctor's jealous fear, and the doktorsha's jollity; while others went out on the steps, and came back to report what was going on in the kibitka.

Several times, Rostof, muffling up his ears, tried to go to sleep; but then some one would make a remark, and arouse his attention; and again the conversation would go on, and again they would break out into nonsensical, merry laughter, as if they were children.

CHAPTER XIV

IT was three o'clock in the morning, and no one had caught a wink of sleep, when the quartermaster made his appearance with the orders to proceed to the little village of Ostrovno.

Still chattering and laughing as before, the officers made haste to get ready; they again set up the samovar, with the same dirty water. But Rostof, not waiting for tea, started off for his squadron.

It was already growing light, the rain had ceased, the clouds were scattering. It was damp and cold, especially in damp clothes. As they came out of the tavern, Rostof and Ilyin looked at the doctor's leathered kibitka, the leather cover of which, wet with the rain, gleamed in the early morning twilight, while the doctor's long legs protruded from under the apron ; and, in the interior, among the cushions, the doktorsha's nightcap could be dimly seen, and her measured breathing heard, as she slept.

" Fact, she 's very pretty ! " said Rostof to Ilyin, who accompanied him.

" Yes, what a charming woman she' is ! " replied the other, with all the seriousness of sixteen.

Within half an hour, the squadron was drawn up on the road. The command was heard : " To saddle." The men crossed themselves, and proceeded to mount. Rostof, taking the lead, gave the command, " Marsch ! " and, filing off four abreast, the hussars, with the sound of hoofs splashing in the pools, the clinking of sabers, and subdued conversation, started along the broad road, lined with birch trees, and following the infantry and artillery, which had gone on ahead.

Scattered purplish blue clouds, growing into crimson in the east, were swiftly fleeting before the wind. It was growing lighter and lighter. More distinguishable became the crisp grass which always grows on country cross-roads; it was still wet with the evening's rain. The pendulous foliage of the birches, also dripping with moisture, shook in the wind, and tossed aside the sparkling drops. Clearer and clearer grew the faces of the soldiers. Rostof rode along with Ilyin, who was his inseparable companion; they kept to one side of the road, which led between a double row of birches.

Rostof, during this campaign, had permitted himself to ride a Cossack horse, instead of his regular horse of the line. Being both a connoisseur and a huntsman, he had recently selected a strong, mettlesome, dun-colored pony, from the Don, which no one could think of matching in a race. It was a perfect delight for Rostof to ride on this steed. His thoughts now ran on horses, the beauty of the morning, the doctor's wife, and not once did he dream of danger being near.

In days gone by, Rostof, on approaching an engage
ment, would have felt a pang of dismay; now he expe·
rienced not the slightest sensation of timidity.   He was
devoid of all fear, not because he was wonted to fire —
it is impossible to become wonted to danger — but
rather because he had learned to control his heart in
the presence of danger.   On going into an engagement,
he had accustomed himself to think about everything
except the one thing which would have been most
absorbing of all — the impending peril.   In spite of all
his efforts, in spite of all his self-reproaches for his
cowardice, during the first term of his service, he had
not been able to reach this point; but in the course of
years it had come of itself.   He rode now with Ilyin,
side by side, between the birch trees, occasionally tearing off a leaf from a down-hanging branch, occasionally
prodding the horse in the groin, occasionally, not even
turning round, handing his exhausted pipe to the hussar
just behind him, with such a calm and unconcerned
appearance that one would have thought he was riding
for pleasure.

He felt a pang of pity to look at Ilyin's excited face,
as he rode along, talking fast and nervously.   He knew
from experience that painful state of mind at the expectation of danger and death which the young cornet was
now experiencing, and he knew that nothing but time
could cure him.

As soon as the sun came into sight, in the clear strip
of sky below the clouds, the wind died down, as if it
dared not mar in the slightest degree the perfect beauty
of the summer morning after the storm; the raindrops
were still falling, but now perpendicularly — and all was
calm and still.

The sun came up, showed himself on the horizon, and
then disappeared behind a long, narrow cloud.   But, in
the course of a few minutes, it burst forth brighter than
ever on the upper edge of the cloud, cutting its edge.

The world was full of light and brilliancy.   And sim·
ultaneously with this burst of light, and as if saluting it,
pealed the reports of cannon toward the front.

Rostof had no time to calculate and decide how far distant these cannon-shots were, when an aide from Count Ostermann-Tolstoï came galloping up from Vitebsk, with the order to advance with all speed.

The squadron outstripped the infantry and artillery, which were also hurrying forward, plunged down a hill, and, dashing through a village deserted by its inhabitants, galloped up a slope at the other side. The horses were all of a lather, the men were flushed.

"Halt! Dress ranks," rang out the command of the division leader, at the front. "Guide left! Shagom marsch!" (that is, forward at a footpace) again rang the command. And the hussars rode along the line of the troops toward the left flank of the position, and drew rein just behind the Russian Uhlans, who were in the front rank. At the right stood the Russian infantry, in a solid mass; they were the reserves; higher up on the slope could be seen in the clear, clear atmosphere our cannon shining in the slanting rays of the bright morning sun, on the very horizon.

Forward, beyond a ravine, were heard our infantry, already involved in the action, and merrily exchanging shots with the enemy.

Rostof's heart beat high with joy, as he heard these sounds which he had not heard for many a long day, and now seemed like the notes of the jolliest music. *Trap-ta-ta-tap*, several shots cracked, sometimes together, suddenly, then rapidly, one after another.

The hussars stood for about an hour in one place. The cannonade had also begun. Count Ostermann and his suite came riding up behind the squadron, and, drawing rein, had a short conversation with the commander of the regiment, and then rode off toward the cannon at the height.

As soon as Ostermann rode away, the Uhlans heard the command: "In column: make ready to charge!"[1]

The infantry in front of them parted their ranks to let the cavalry pass. The Uhlans started away, the pennons on their lances waving gayly, and down the

[1] *V kolonnu, k atakaye stroïsya!*

slope they dashed at a trot, toward the French cavalry, which began to appear at the foot of the slope at the left.

As soon as the Uhlans started down the slope, the hussars were ordered to move forward and protect the battery on the height. While the hussars were stationed in the position before occupied by the Uhlans, bullets flew high over their heads, buzzing and humming through the air.

These sounds, which had not been heard by Rostof for long years, had a more pleasing and stimulating influence than the roar of musketry before. Straightening himself up in the saddle, he scrutinized the battle-field spread full before his eyes from the height where he was stationed, and his whole heart followed the Uhlans into the charge.

They had now flown almost down to the French dragoons; there was a collision in the smoke, and, at the end of five minutes, the Uhlans were being pressed back, not in the same place, indeed, but farther to the left. Mixed in with the orange-uniformed Uhlans, on their chestnut horses, and behind them, in a compact mass, could be seen the blue French dragoons, on their gray horses.

CHAPTER XV

ROSTOF, with his keen huntsman's eye, was one of the first to notice these French dragoons in blue pressing back our Uhlans. Nearer, nearer, in disorderly masses, came the Uhlans, and the French dragoons in pursuit of them.

Now all could see how these men, dwarfed by the distance, were jostling one another, driving one another, and brandishing their arms and their sabers.

Rostof looked down at what was going on, as if he were present at a hunt. His instinct told him that, if the hussars could now add their impetus to that of the Uhlans, the French dragoons could not stand it; but if

the blow was to be struck, it was to be done immediately, on the instant, else it would be too late. He
glanced around; a captain stationed near him had likewise his eyes fixed steadfastly on the cavalry contest
below.

"Andreï Sevastyanuitch!" said Rostof. "See, we
might crush them."....

"'T would be a dashing piece of work," said the
captain, "but still ...."

Rostof, not waiting to hear his answer, gave spurs
to his horse, dashed along in front of his squadron,
and, before he had even given the word for the
advance, the whole squadron to a man, experiencing
exactly what he had, scoured after him.

Rostof himself did not know how and why he did
this thing. The whole action was as instinctive, as
unpremeditated, as if he had been out hunting. He
saw that the dragoons were near at hand, that they
were galloping forward in disorderly ranks. He knew
that they would not withstand a sudden attack; he
knew that it was the matter of a single moment, which
would not return if he let it have the go-by. The bullets whizzed and whistled around him so stimulatingly,
his horse dashed on ahead so hotly, that he could not
but yield. He plunged the spurs still deeper into his
horse's side, shouted his command, and, at that same
instant, hearing behind him the hoof-clatter of his
squadron, breaking into the charge, at full trot, he gave
his horse his head down the hill, at the dragoons. No
sooner had they reached the bottom of the slope than
their gait changed involuntarily from trot to gallop,
growing ever swifter and swifter in proportion as they
approached the Uhlans and the French dragoons who
were driving them back.

The dragoons were close to them. The foremost,
seeing the hussars, started to turn; those in the rear
paused. Feeling as if he were galloping to cut off
an escaping wolf, Rostof, urging his Don pony to his
utmost, dashed on toward the disconcerted French
dragoons. One of the Uhlans reined in his horse; one,

who had been dismounted, threw himself on the ground to escape being crushed; a riderless steed dashed in among the hussars. Almost all the French· dragoons were now in full retreat.

Rostof, selecting one of them, mounted on a gray steed, started in pursuit of him. On the way, he found himself rushing at a bush; his good steed, without hesitating, took it at a leap; and, almost before Rostof had settled himself in his saddle again, he saw that he should within a few seconds have overtaken the man whom he had selected as his objective point. This Frenchman, evidently an officer by his uniform, bending forward, was urging on his gray horse, striking him with his saber. A second later Rostof's horse hit the other's rear with his chest, almost knocking him over; and, at the same instant, Rostof, not knowing why, raised his saber and struck at the Frenchman.

The instant he did so all Rostof's excitement suddenly vanished. The officer fell, not so much from the effect of the saber-stroke, which had only scratched him slightly above the elbow, as it was from the collision of the horses and from panic. Rostof pulled up to look for his enemy, and see whom he had vanquished. The French officer of dragoons was hopping along, with one foot on the ground and the other entangled in the stirrup. With his eyes squinting with fear, as if he expected each instant to be struck down again, he was looking up at Rostof with an expression of horror. His pale face, covered with mud, fair and young, with dimpled chin and bright blue eyes, was not made for the battle-field — not the face of an enemy, but a simple home face.

Even before Rostof had made up his mind what to do with him, the officer cried: "*Je me rends.*" In spite of all his efforts, he could not extricate his foot from the stirrup; and still, with frightened blue eyes, he kept gazing at Rostof. Some of the hussars, who had come galloping up, freed his foot for him, and helped him to mount. The hussars were coming back in all directions with dragoons as prisoners: one was wounded, out, with his face all covered with blood, would not surrender his horse; another was seated on the crupper of a hussar's horse, with his arm around the man's waist; a third, assisted by a hussar, was clambering up on the horse's back.

In front the French infantry were in full retreat, firing as they went.

The hussars swiftly returned to their position with their prisoners. Rostof spurred back with the rest, a prey to a peculiarly disagreeable feeling which oppressed his heart. A certain vague perplexity, which he found it utterly impossible to account for, overcame him at the capture of that young officer and the blow which he had given him.

Count Ostermann-Tolstoï met the hussars on their return, summoned Rostof, and thanked him, saying that he should report to the sovereign his gallant exploit and recommend him for the cross of the George. When the summons to Count Ostermann came, Rostof remembered that the charge had been made without orders; and he was therefore fully persuaded that the commander called for him to punish him for his presumptuous action. Consequently Ostermann's flattering words and his promise of a reward ought to have been all the more agreeable to Rostof; but that same vague, disagreeable feeling still tortured his mind.

"What can it be that troubles me so, I wonder?" he asked himself, as he rode away from the interview. "Ilyin? No, he is safe and sound. Have I anything to be ashamed of? No, nothing of the sort at all." — It was an entirely different feeling, like remorse. — "Yes, yes, that French officer with the dimple. And how distinctly I remember hesitating before I raised my arm."

Rostof saw the prisoners about to be conducted away, and he galloped up to them, in order to have another look at the officer with the dimpled chin. He was sitting, in his foreign uniform, on a hussar's stallion, and was glancing around uneasily. The wound on his arm was scarcely deserving of the name. He gave Rostof a hypocritical smile, and waved his hand at him, as a sort of salute. Rostof had still the same feeling of awkwardness, and something seemed to weigh on his conscience.

All that day, and the day following, Rostof's friends and comrades noticed that he was — not exactly gloomy or surly, but taciturn, thoughtful, and concentrated. He drank, as it were, under protest, tried to be alone, and evidently had something on his mind.

Rostof was, all the time, thinking about his brilliant exploit, which, much to his amazement, had given him the cross of the George, and had even given him the reputation of being a hero; and he found it utterly incomprehensible.

"And so they are still more afraid of us than we are of them!" he said to himself. "Is this all there is of what is called heroism? Did I do that for my country's sake? And wherein was he to blame, with his dimple and his blue eyes? And how frightened he was! He thought I was going to kill him! My hand trembled; but still they have given me the Georgievsky cross. I don't understand it at all, not at all!"

But while Nikolaï was working over these questions in his own mind, and still failed to find any adequate solution of what was so confusing to him, the wheel of fortune, as so often happens in the military service, had been given a turn in his favor. He was promoted after the engagement at Ostrovno, and given command of a battalion of hussars; and when there was any necessity of employing a brave officer, he was given the chance.

CHAPTER XVI

ON learning of Natasha's illness, the countess, still not very well, and weak, went to Moscow, taking Petya and the whole household; and all the Rostofs left Marya Dmitrievna's, and went to their own house, and took up their residence in the city.

Natasha's illness was so serious that, fortunately for

her happiness, and for the happiness of her relatives, the thought of all that had been the cause of her illness, her misconduct, and the breach with her betrothed, were relegated to the background. She was so ill that it was impossible to take up the consideration of how far she had been blameworthy in the matter; for she had no appetite, and she could not sleep, she lost flesh, and had a cough, and her condition was critical, as the doctors gave them to understand.

There was nothing else to be thought of than to give her all the aid they could devise: the doctors came to see her, both singly and in consultation; talked a great deal in French, in German, and in Latin; criticized one another; prescribed the most varied remedies adapted to cure all the diseases known to their science; but it did not occur to one of them, simple as it might seem, that the disease from which Natasha was suffering might be unknown to them, just as every ailment which attacks mortal man is beyond their power of understanding: since each mortal man has his own distinguishing characteristics, and whatever disease he has must, necessarily, be peculiar and new, complicated and unknown to medicine; not a disease of the lungs, of the liver, of the skin, of the heart, of the nerves, and so on, as described in works on medicine, but an ailment produced from any one of endless combinations of these organs in disease.

This simple idea could not occur to the doctors (any more than it could ever occur to a warlock that his incantations were useless), because it is their life-work to practise medicine, because it is their way of earning money, and because they spend the best years of their lives at this business.

But the chief reason why this thought could not occur to the doctors was because they saw that they were unquestionably of service; and, in deed and truth, they were of service to all the Rostof household. They were of service, not because they made the sick girl swallow drugs, for the most part harmful, — though the harmfulness was of little moment, because the noxious drugs were given in small quantities, — but they were of service, they were needful, they were indispensable — and this is the reason that there are, and always will be, alleged "curers," — quacks, homeopaths and allopaths, — because they satisfied the moral demands of the sick girl and those who loved her.   They satisfied that eternal human demand for hope and consolation, that demand for sympathy and activity, which a man experiences at a time of suffering.

They satisfied that eternal human demand — noticeable in a child in its simplest and most primitive form — to have the bruised place rubbed.   A child tumbles, and immediately runs to its mother or its nurse to be kissed, and have the sore place rubbed, and its pains are alleviated as soon as the sore place is rubbed or kissed.   The child cannot help believing that those who are stronger and wiser than he must have the means of giving him aid for his sufferings.   And this hope of alleviation and expression of sympathy at the time when the mother rubs the bump are a comfort.

The doctors in Natasha's case were of service, because they kissed and rubbed the bobo, assuring her that it would go away if the coachman would only hurry down to the Arbatskaya apothecary shop and get a ruble and seventy kopeks' worth of powders and pellets in a neat little box, and if the sick girl would take these powders, dissolved in boiling water, regularly every two hours, neither more nor less.

What would Sonya and the count and the countess have done if they had looked on without taking any part ; if there had been no little pellets every two hours, no warm drinks, no chicken cutlets to prepare, and none of all those little necessary things prescribed by the doctor, the observance of which gave occupation and consolation to the friends ?

How would the count have borne his beloved daughter's illness if he had not known that it was going to cost him some thousands of rubles, and that he would not grudge thousands more to do her any good ; if he had not known that in case she did not recover speedily, he should not grudge still other thousands in taking her

abroad, and then going to the expense of consultations ;
if he had not been able to tell in all its details how
Métivier and Feller had not understood the case, while
Friese had, and Mudrof had still more successfully,
diagnosed the disease ?

What would the countess have done if she could not
have occasionally scolded Natasha because she did not
fully conform to the doctor's orders ?

" You will never get well," she would say, forgetting
her anxiety in her vexation, "if you don't obey the
doctor, and if you don't take your medicine regularly.
You must not treat it lightly, because, if you do, it may
go into pneumonia," the countess would say ; and she
found great consolation in repeating this one word,
which was something incomprehensible for her and
others besides.

What would Sonya have done if she had not had the
joyful consciousness that, during the first part of the
time, she had not undressed for three nights, so that
she might be ready to carry out to the least detail all
the doctor's prescriptions ; and that even now she lay
awake all night, lest she should sleep over the hours
when it was necessary to administer the not very hurt-
ful pellets from the little gilt box ?

Even Natasha herself, who, although she declared
that no medicine could cure her, and that all this was
nonsense, could not help a feeling of gratification that
it was for her they were making so many sacrifices, that
it was she who had to take the medicine at the hours
prescribed. And likewise she felt glad that by her
neglect to carry out the doctor's orders she might show
that she did not believe in medicine, and did not value
her life.

The doctor came every day, felt of her pulse, looked at
her tongue, and, paying no attention to her dejected face,
laughed and joked with her. But afterward, when he had
gone into the next room, and the countess had hastily
followed him, he would pull a serious face and shake
his head dubiously, saying that, though the patient was
in a critical state, still he had good hopes for the efficacy

of the last medicine he had prescribed, and that they must wait and see; that the ailment was more mental, but ....

The countess, who had tried as far as possible to shut her own eyes, and the doctor's, to Natasha's behaviour, thrust the gold piece into his hand, and each time, with a relieved heart, went back to her invalid.

The symptons of Natasha's illness were loss of appetite, sleeplessness, a cough, and a constant state of apathy. The doctors declared that it was impossible for her to dispense with medical treatment, and, consequently, she was kept a prisoner in the sultry air of the city. And, during the summer of 1812, the Rostofs did not go to their country place.

In spite of the immense quantity of pellets, drops, and powders swallowed by Natasha, out of glass jars and gilt boxes, of which Madame Schoss, who was a great lover of such things, had made a large collection; in spite of being deprived of her customary life in the country, — youth at last got the upper hand: Natasha's sorrow began to disappear under the impressions of every-day life; it ceased to lie so painfully on her heart, it began to appear past and distant, and Natasha's physical health showed signs of improvement.

CHAPTER XVII

NATASHA was more calm, but not more cheerful. She not only avoided all the external scenes of gayety, — balls, driving, concerts, the theater; but, even when she laughed, it seemed as if the tears were audible back of her laughter. She could not sing. As soon as she started to laugh, or essayed, when all alone by herself, to sing, the tears choked her: tears of repentance, tears of remembrance, of regret, of the irrevocable happy days; tears of vexation that she had thus idly wasted her young life, which might have been so happy. Laughter and song especially seemed to her like mockery of her sorrow.

She never once thought of coquetry ; it did not even occur to her to refrain from it. She declared, and she felt, that at this time all men were for her no more than the buffoon Nastasya Ivanovna. An inward monitor strenuously interdicted every kind of pleasure. Moreover, she showed no interest, as of old, in that girlish round of existence, so free of care and full of hope. She recalled more frequently, and with keener pain than aught else, those autumn months with the hunting and the "little uncle," and the holidays with Nikolaï at Otradnoye. What would she not have given for the return of even a single day of that vanished time ! But it was past forever ! She had not been mistaken in the presentiment she had felt then that that condition of careless freedom and susceptibility to every pleasant influence would never more return. But to live was a necessity.

It was a consolation for her to think, not that she was better, as she had formerly thought, but that she was worse, vastly worse, than any one else in the world. But this was a little thing. She knew it, and asked herself : "What more is there?" But there was nothing more in store for her. There was no further joy in life ; and yet life went on. Natasha's sole endeavor evidently was that she might not be a burden to any one, and not to interfere with any one, while, for her own personal gratification, she asked for nothing at all. She kept aloof from the other members of the household, and only with her brother Petya did she feel at all at ease. She liked to be with him more than with the others, and sometimes, when they were alone together, she would laugh. She scarcely ever went out of the house ; and, of those who came to call, there was only one man whom she was glad to see, and that was Pierre.

It could not have been possible for any one to have shown more tenderness and discretion, and, at the same time, more seriousness, in his treatment of her, than did Count Bezukhoï. Natasha unconsciously felt the spell of this affectionate tenderness, and, accordingly, she took great delight in his society. But she was not

even thankful to him for his kindness.   Pierre's goodness seemed to her spontaneous.   It seemed to her that
it was so perfectly natural for Pierre to be kind to every
one, that he deserved no credit for his goodness.   Sometimes Natasha noticed his confusion and awkwardness
in her presence, especially when he was desirous of
doing her some favor, or when he was apprehensive lest
something in their talk might suggest disagreeable
recollections.   She noticed this, and ascribed it to his
natural kindness and shyness, which, in her opinion,
as far as she knew, must be shown to all, just as it was
to her.

Since those ambiguous words, "if he were free, he
should, on his knees, sue for her heart and her hand,"
spoken at a moment of such painful excitement on her
part, Pierre had never made any allusion whatever to
his feelings for Natasha ; and, as far as she was concerned, it was evident that those words, so consoling to
her at the time, had had no more meaning to her than
most thoughtless, unconsidered words, spoken for the
consolation of a weeping child.   It never entered her
head that her relations with Pierre might lead to love
on her side — much less on his — or even to that form
of tender, self-acknowledged, poetic friendship between
a man and a woman, of which she had known several
examples ; and this, not because Pierre was a married
man, but because Natasha was conscious that between
him and her, in all its reality, existed that barrier of
moral obstacles, the absence of which she had been
conscious of in Kuragin.

Toward the end of the midsummer's fast[1] of Saint
Peter, Agrafena Ivanovna Bielova, one of the Rostofs'
neighbors at Otradnoye, came to Moscow to worship at
the shrines of the saints there.   She proposed to Natasha
to join in her devotions, and Natasha gladly entertained
the suggestion.   Notwithstanding the doctor's prohibi-
tion of her going out early in the morning, Natasha insisted on preparing for the sacrament, and doing so, not
as it was usually managed at the Rostofs', by listening

[1] Saint Peter's day is June 29 (O.S.), July 11 (N.S.).

to three services in the house, but rather to prepare for it as Agrafena Ivanovna did, that is, taking the whole week, without missing a single vespers, mass, or matins.

The countess was pleased with this zeal of Natasha's. After all the failure of medical treatment, she hoped in her heart that prayer might prove to be a more powerful medicament; and, though she did it with some apprehension, and concealed it from the knowledge of the doctor, she yielded to Natasha's desire, and let her go with Madame Bielova.

Agrafena Ivanovna came at three o'clock in the morning to arouse Natasha; and yet generally she found her already wide awake. Natasha was afraid of sleeping over the hour of matins. Making hasty ablutions, and humbly dressing in her shabbiest gown and an old mantle, shivering with the chill of morning, Natasha would venture out into the empty streets, dimly lighted by the diaphanous light of early dawn.

In accordance with the pious Agrafena Ivanovna's advice, Natasha performed her devotions not in her own parish, but at a church where, according to her, there was a priest of very austere and lofty life. At this church there were always very few people. Natasha would take her usual place with Madame Bielova before the ikon of the Mother of God, enshrined at the back of the choir, at the left; and a new feeling of calmness would come over her before the vast and incomprehensible mystery, when, at that unprecedentedly early hour of the morning, she gazed at the darkened face of the Virgin's picture, lighted by the tapers burning before it, as well as by the morning light that came in through the windows, as she listened to the sounds of the service, which she tried to follow understandingly.

When she understood it, her personal feeling entered into and tinged the meaning of the prayer; but when she could not understand it, it was all the more delicious for her to think that the very desire to comprehend everything was in itself a form of pride, that it is impossible to comprehend everything, and that all that is requisite and necessary is to have faith and trust in God, who at that moment, she was conscious, reigned in her heart. She would cross herself and bow low; and when the service was too deep for her comprehension, then only, horror-stricken at her own baseness, she would beseech God to pardon her for everything, for everything, and have mercy upon her.

The prayers which she followed with the most fervor were those expressing remorse. Returning home in the early hours of the morning, when the only men she met were masons going to their work, and dvorniks sweeping the streets, and every one in all the houses was still asleep, Natasha experienced a new sense of the possibility of being purged of her sins, and the possibility of a new, pure life and happiness.

During all that week, while she was leading this life, this feeling grew stronger every day. And the happy thought of taking the communion — or, as Agrafena, playing on the word, called it, the communication [1] — seemed to her so majestic that it seemed to her she should never live till that blessed Sunday.

But the happy day came, and when Natasha, on this memorable Sunday, returned home in her white muslin dress, from communion, she, for the first time after many months, felt tranquil and not burdened by the thought of living.

When the doctor came that day to see Natasha, he ordered her to continue taking the last prescription of powders which he had prescribed a fortnight before.

"Don't fail to take them morning and evening," said he, evidently feeling honestly satisfied and even elated at the success of his treatment. "Only be more regular, please. .... Rest quite easy, countess," said the doctor, in a jovial tone, skilfully clutching the gold piece in his plump hands. "She will soon be singing and enjoying herself. The last medicine has been very, very efficacious. She has already gained very noticeably."

The countess looked at her finger-nails, and spat [2] as she returned to the drawing-room with a radiant face.

---

[1] *Soobshchitsa,* instead of *priobshchitsa.*   [2] For the omen's sake.

CHAPTER XVIII

DURING the first weeks of July, more and more disquieting rumors about the progress of the war began
to be circulated in Moscow: people talked about the
sovereign's appeal to his people, and about the sovereign's leaving the army and coming to Moscow. And
as the manifesto and summons were not received in
Moscow until the twenty-third of July, exaggerated reports about them and about the position of Russia were
current. It was said that the sovereign was coming
because the army was in a critical position; it was said
that Smolensk had surrendered, that Napoleon had a
million men, and that only a miracle could save Russia.

The manifesto was received on the twenty-third of
July, on a Saturday, but as yet it had not been pub-
lished; and Pierre, who was at the Rostofs', promised to
come to dinner the next day, Sunday, and bring the
manifesto and the proclamation, which he would get of
Count Rostopchin.

On that Sunday the Rostofs, as usual, went to mass
at the private chapel of the Razumovskys. It was a
sultry July day. Even at ten o'clock, when the Rostofs' carriage drew up in front of the church, the heated
atmosphere, the shouts of peddlers, the bright, light-
colored, summer gowns of the ladies, the dust-covered
leaves of the trees along the boulevard, the sounds of
music, and the white trousers of a regiment marching
by on its way to parade, the rattle of carriages over the
pavement, and the dazzling radiance of the hot sun,
gave the impression of that summer languor, that content, as well as discontent, with the present which is
always felt with especial keenness on a bright, sultry
day in the city.

In the chapel of the Razumovskys were gathered all
the *élite* of Moscow, all the acquaintances of the Rostofs — for that year, as if something unusual were about
to happen, very many of the wealthy families who usually
went off to their country estates had remained in town.

Natasha, as she walked in with her mother, preceded by a liveried lackey, who cleared a way through the throng, overheard a young man making a remark about her in an overloud whisper.

" That is the Rostova .... the very one ! "

" How thin she has grown ! but still she is pretty.

She heard or thought she heard the names of Kuragin and Bolkonsky mentioned. However, it often seemed to her so. It always seemed to her that all who looked at her were thinking only of what had happened to her.

With pain and sinking at heart, as always in a throng, Natasha walked on in her lilac silk dress trimmed with black lace, and giving the appearance, as women can do, of being calm and dignified, for the very reason that her heart was full of pain and shame. She knew that she was pretty, and she was not mistaken ; but the knowledge did not now give her the same pleasure as before. On the contrary, it annoyed her above everything of late, and especially on that bright, hot summer day in the city.

" Still another Sunday, still another week gone," she said to herself, as she remembered for what purpose she was there that day. " And forever the same life that is not life, and the same conditions in which it used to be so easy to live in days gone by. I am pretty, I am young, and I know that now I am good whereas before I was naughty ; but now I am good, I know," she said to herself ; "but it 's all for nothing, that the best, best years of my life have gone and are going."

She took her place with her mother, and exchanged greetings with the acquaintances around her. Out of old habit she noticed the toilets of the ladies ; she criticized the *tenue* of one lady who happened to be standing near her, and the indecorous manner in which she held her hand as she crossed herself ; again she thought with vexation that the others were probably criticizing her just as she was criticizing them, and suddenly, as she heard the sounds of the service, she was horror-struck at her depravity, she was horror-struck because her newly acquired purity was again sullied.

A beautiful-looking, clean, little old man officiated with that sweet solemnity which has such a majestic and sanctifying influence upon the hearts of worshipers. The "Holy Gate"[1] was closed, the curtain was slowly drawn, a mysterious, solemn voice on the other side murmured undistinguishable words. Natasha's bosom heaved with tears too deep for comprehension, and she was agitated by a feeling of joy and tormenting pain.

"Teach me what I must do, how to direct my life, how to do right always, always .... " she prayed in her heart.

The deacon came out to the ambon, used his thumb to pull his long hair out from under his surplice, and, pressing his cross to his heart, began to read in a loud and solemn voice the words of the prayer.

"*Let all the people pray unto the Lord!*"

"Let all the people, all united, without distinctions of rank, without enmity, but joined together in brotherly love .... let us all pray," was Natasha's thought.

"*For the world to come and the salvation of our souls!*"

"For the world of the angels and the spirits of all incorporeal existences, which dwell above us," prayed Natasha.

During the prayer for the army, she remembered her brother and Denisof.

During the prayer for those who were traveling on sea or on land, she thought of Prince Andreï, and prayed for him, and prayed that God would pardon the wrong that she had done him.

During the prayer for those who love us, she prayed for those of her household — her father, her mother, Sonya; and now, for the first time, she realized all the wrong that she had done them, and felt how deep and strong was her love toward them.

When the prayer for those who hate us was read, she tried to think of her enemies, and those who hated her, in order to pray for them. Among her enemies she

---

[1] *Tsarskiya dveri.*

reckoned her father's creditors, and all those who had dealings with him, and every time, at the thoughts of her enemies and those who hated her, she remembered Anatol, who had done her such injury, and, although he had not hated her, she prayed gladly for him as for an enemy.

Only during the prayer was she able to think calmly and clearly about Prince Andreï and about Anatol, as about men toward whom her feelings had been entirely swallowed up in her fear and worship of God.

When the prayer was read for the imperial family, and for the Synod, she made a very low bow and crossed herself, with the thought that if she could not understand, she at least could not doubt, and consequently must love, the directing Synod, and pray for it.

Having finished the liturgy,[1] the deacon crossed himself on the front of his stole, and exclaimed : —

"*Let us give ourselves and our bodies to Christ our God.*"

"Let us give ourselves to God," repeated Natasha, in her own heart. "My God, I give myself up to Thy will," said she to herself. "I have no wishes, I have no desires! Teach me what to do, how to fulfil Thy will! Yea, take me, take me!" cried Natasha, in her heart, with touching impatience, forgetting to cross herself, but letting her slender arms drop by her side, and as if expecting that instantly some viewless Power would take her and free her from herself, from her sorrows, desires, shortcomings, hopes, and faults.

The countess many times during the service glanced at her daughter's pathetic face and glistening eyes, and besought God to give her His aid.

Unexpectedly, in the middle of the service, and out of the usual order of things, which Natasha knew so well, a diachok brought out the wooden stool on which the priest kneels when he reads the prayers on Trinity Sunday, and placed it in front of the "Holy Gates."

The priest came forth in his lilac velvet calotte,

---

[1] The *yekteniya*, or liturgical prayer for the imperial family.

smoothed his hair down, and with some effort got down
on his knees.

All followed his example, looking with perplexity at
one another. It was the prayer which had only just
been received from the Synod, the prayer for the salvation of Russia from the invasion of her enemies.

"*Lord God our strength! God our salvation!*" began
the priest, in that clear, undemonstrative, sweet voice,
which the Slavonic clergy only use in their reading, and
which has such an irresistible effect on the Russian heart.

"*Lord God of Hosts! God our salvation! Protect this day in
Thy infinite mercy and bounty Thy humble people, and charitably
hear us and spare us and have mercy upon us. The enemy are
bringing destruction upon Thy land, and would fain make the uni-
verse a wilderness. Rise Thou up against him. This lawless multitude have gathered themselves together to destroy Thine inheritance,
to lay waste Thy holy Jerusalem, Thy beloved Russia; to desecrate
Thy temples, to overturn Thine altars, and to profane our sanctu-
ary. How long, O Lord, how long shall sinners triumph? How
long shall they be permitted to transgress Thy laws?*

"*Sovereign Lord! hear Thou us that cry unto Thee! By Thy
might strengthen Thou our most devout autocrat and ruler, our
great sovereign the Emperor Alexander Pavlovitch! remember his
equity and meekness! Requite him for his virtues, and let them be
the safeguard of us, Thy beloved Israel. Bless his counsels, his
undertakings, and his deeds. Establish by Thine almighty right
hand his realm, and grant him victory over his enemies, as Thou
didst to Moses over Amalek, Gideon over Midian, and David over
Goliath. Protect Thou his armies. Place the brazen bow in the
arms of those who have gone forth to battle in Thy name, and gird
them with strength for the war. Take Thy sword and Thy buckler,
and arise and help us, and put to shame and confusion those that
have plotted evil against us, so that they may fly before the faces of
those that trust in Thee as chaff is driven before the wind, and may
Thy mighty Angel confound them and pursue them. May the net
come upon them without their knowing it, and may the draught of
fish which they meant to take surround them on all sides, and may
they fall under the feet of Thy slaves, and may they be trampled
under the feet of our warriors O Lord! Thou art able to save in
great things and in small. Thou art God and no man can do aught
against Thee.*

"*God of our fathers! Let Thy bounty and Thy mercy guard us
from everlasting to everlasting. Hide not Thy face from us; let
not Thy wrath be kindled against our iniquities; but in the magnitude of Thy mercy and the abundance of Thy grace pardon our law-
lessness and our sin. Create a clean heart within us, and renew a*

right spirit in our inner parts ; strengthen Thou our faith in Thee ; inspire hope ; kindle true love among us ; arm us with a single impulse to the righteous defense of the inheritance which Thou hast given to us and to our fathers, and let not the scepter of the ungodly decide the destiny of those whom Thou hast consecrated.

" O Lord, our God, in Thee do we put our trust, and our hopes are set on Thee. Let us not despair of Thy mercy, and give a sign, in order that those who hate us and our Orthodox Faith may be confounded and destroyed, and that all nations may see that Thy name is the Lord, and we are Thy people. Show us Thy mercy, O Lord, this day, and vouchsafe to us Thy salvation. Rejoice the heart of Thy slaves by Thy grace ; strike our enemies, and crush them under the feet of those that believe in Thee. For Thou art the defense, the succor, and the victory to them that trust in Thee, and to Thee be the glory — to the Father and to the Son and to the Holy Spirit, as it was in the beginning, is now, and ever shall be, world without end. Amen."

In that condition of spiritual excitement to which Natasha had attained, this prayer [1] had a very powerful effect upon her. She listened to every word about "the victory of Moses over Amalek, of Gideon over Midian, and David over Goliath, and the laying waste of Thy Jerusalem," and she prayed to God with that tenderness of spirit and melting of the heart which she now felt. But she did not understand very well what she should pray God for. With all her heart she could join in the petition for a right spirit, for fortifying zeal with faith and hope, and stimulating their love.

But she could not pray that the enemy might be crushed under their feet, because only a few moments before her only regret was that she had no more of them, so that she might pray for them.

But at the same time she could not doubt the rightfulness of the prayer which the kneeling priest had read. She felt in her heart a genuine and anxious terror at the thought of the punishment which must befall men on account of their sins, and especially for her own sins, and she besought God to forgive them all, and her as well, and to give them all and her tranquillity and happiness in life.

And it seemed to her that God heard her prayer.

[1] The effect of this prayer is enhanced in the original by the dignified Slavonic, the Church language, in which it is couched.

CHAPTER XIX

FROM the day when Pierre, as he left the Rostofs' with Natasha's look of gratitude still fresh in his mind, and gazed at the comet stretched across the sky, and felt that he had made a new discovery, the eternally tormenting question as to the vanity and folly of all things earthly had ceased to occupy his thoughts. This terrible question, *Why? Wherefore?* which before had come up before him amid every occupation, had now merged itself for him, not into another problem, and not into any answer to his question, but into *her* image.

Whether he listened or took the lead himself in trivial conversations, whether he read or heard about the baseness and absurdity of men, he no longer felt that sense of horror as before; he did not ask himself what caused men to struggle so, when life was so short and incomprehensible, but he recalled how she looked when he saw her the last time, and all his doubts vanished, not because she had given the answer to his questions, but because her image instantly lifted him into another realm, serene and full of spiritual activity, where there could be no question of right or wrong — the realm of beauty and love which alone makes life worth living. Whatever baseness in life might be brought to his attention, he would say to himself: —

"Well, then, let N. N. plunder the government and the Tsar, and let the government and the Tsar load him with honors; but *she* smiled on me last evening, and asked me to come again, and I love her, and no one shall ever know it!"

And his soul became calm and clear.

Pierre continued as before to go into gay society, and drank heavily, and led the same idle and dissipated life, for the reason that at such times as he was not able to spend at the Rostofs' there were still many hours every day which he had to spend in some manner, and his habits and acquaintances at Moscow invariably allured him to this mode of existence, which had such a firm hold upon him.

But of late, now that the news from the theater of the war became constantly more and more disquieting, and now that Natasha's health had fairly begun to improve, and she ceased to arouse in him that former feeling of anxiety and pity, he began to become the prey of a restlessness which grew more and more incomprehensible. He was conscious that the position in which he found himself could not last very long, that some catastrophe was at hand, which was destined to change his whole life, and he impatiently sought to find in everything the presages of this imminent catastrophe.

One of the brotherhood of Freemasons had called his attention to the following prophecy concerning Napoleon. It was derived from the Revelation of Saint John. In the eighteenth verse of the thirteenth chapter of the Apocalypse it is written: *"Here is wisdom. He that hath understanding, let him count the number of the beast; for it is the number of a man: and his number is six hundred and sixty and six."* And the fifth verse of the same chapter says: *"And there was given unto him a mouth speaking great things and blasphemies. And there was given unto him authority to do his works during forty and two months."*

The letters of the French alphabet when disposed in accordance with the Hebrew enumeration, which gives the first nine letters the value of units, and the rest that of tens, have the following significance: —

a b c d e f g h i k l m n o p q r s t u v w x y z
1 2 3 4 5 6 7 8 9 10 20 30 40 50 60 70 80 90 100 110 120 130 140 150 160

If the words *l'Empereur Napoléon* are written letter for letter with this cipher, the result is that the sum of these letters amounts to six hundred and sixty-six; therefore Napoleon is the beast described in the Apocalypse. Moreover, if you apply to this same alphabetic cipher the words *Quarante deux*, that is the time, forty-two months, during which authority was given to the beast to speak great things and blaspheme, the sum of these letters according to the same scheme will amount to six hundred and sixty-six, whence it results that Napoleon's power was to be allowed to last until the year 1812, when he would have reached the age of forty-two.

Pierre was greatly amazed by this method of divination, and he frequently asked himself what could possibly put an end to the power of the beast, that is to say, Napoleon; and he made use of the same cipher and mode of reckoning, in order to find an answer to the question that he had propounded. Thus he wrote, as an experiment, *l'Empereur Alexandre*, and *La nation russe*, but the sum of the letters came out either greater or less than six hundred and sixty-six.

One time, while occupying himself with this enumeration, he wrote his own name, Comte Pierre Besouhoff; [1] the sum of the figures did not agree. Then changing the spelling, substituting *z* for *s*, he added the "particule" *de*, he added the article *le*, and still he failed to attain the desired result.

Then it occurred to him that if the answer desired for the question was included in his name, it would certainly have also to include his nationality. He wrote *Le Russe Besuhof*, and, reckoning up the figures, he made six hundred and seventy-one. Only five too much! Five corresponds to *e*, the very same *e* which was elided in the article before the word "Empereur." Eliding this *e*, though it was contrary to the rule, Pierre found the wished-for answer, *l'Russe Besuhof*, equal to six hundred and sixty-six.

This discovery excited him. How, by what bond, he was united to this mighty event foreshadowed in the Apocalypse he knew not; but not for an instant did he

---

[1] In the course of "War and Peace," Pierre's family name appears under at least three different forms of spelling: Bezukhoï, — which in this translation is retained throughout, — Bezukhi, and Bezukhof; the Russian character *kh* corresponds to *ch* in German, and is often represented in French by *h*. It may be here remarked, also, *à propos* of the "particule" *de*, that the French and German way of representing titled Russians' names with a *de* or a *von* is incorrect; the Russian nobility is dependent on neither titles nor "particules."

have any doubt of the bond.   His love for Natasha, the Antichrist, Napoleon's invasion, the comet, six hundred and sixty-six, *l'Empereur Napoléon*, and *l'Russe Besuhof*, —all taken together, could not fail to ripen and burst and bring him forth from that enchanted, do-nothing world of Moscovite habits, in which he felt himself a prisoner, and carry him to some mighty exploit and some mighty happiness.

Pierre, on the evening before the Sunday when the prayer was read, had promised the Rostofs to bring them from Count Rostopchin, with whom he was on terms of intimacy, the proclamation to the Russians and the last news from the army.   That morning, on his arrival at Count Rostopchin's, Pierre found a courier, who had just come from the army.   This courier was an acquaintance of Pierre's, a regular attendant of Moscow ball-rooms.

"For God's sake, could n't you help me out ? " asked the courier.   "I have a whole bagful of letters for friends and relatives."

Among these letters was one from Nikolaï Rostof to his father.   Pierre took charge of it.   Besides this, Count Rostopchin gave Pierre a copy of the sovereign's appeal to Moscow, just printed, the last orders to the army, and his own last "placard."   Glancing over the army orders, Pierre found in one of them, which mentioned the names of the killed, wounded, or rewarded, that Nikolaï Rostof had been decorated with a "George" of the fourth class on account of his gallantry in the affair at Ostrovno ; and in the same "general order," the nomination of Prince Andreï Bolkonsky as commander of a regiment of Jägers.   Although he had no wish to remind the Rostofs of Bolkonsky, still he could not restrain the desire to rejoice their hearts by the news of the reward granted their son ; and so, keeping in his own possession the proclamation, the "placard," and the other orders, which he proposed to carry when he went there to dinner, he immediately sent them the printed order and Nikolaï's letter.

His conversation with Count Rostopchin, whose tone of anxiety and nervousness struck him, his meeting with the courier, who had some careless story to tell of things going ill in the army, the rumors of spies found in Moscow, and of a paper circulating in the city which declared that Napoleon by autumn had promised to occupy both of the Russian capitals, the talk about the expected arrival of the sovereign on the morrow, — all this gave new strength to that feeling of excitement and expectation which had not left him since the night when the comet had first appeared, and especially since the outbreak of the war.

The notion of entering the active military service had, for some time, been much in his mind : and he would assuredly have done so if, in the first place, he had not been deterred by the fact that he belonged to that Masonic fraternity, to which he had bound himself by a solemn pledge, and which preached eternal peace and the cessation of war ; and, in the second place, because, as he beheld the great numbers of the inhabitants of Moscow who had donned uniforms and were preaching patriotism, he was somehow ashamed to do so.   But the chief reason that deterred him from carrying out the idea of entering the military service was to be found in that obscure conception that he, *l'Russe Besuhof*, who carried with him the number of the beast, — 666, — was destined to take some great part in putting bounds to the power of the beast that spoke great things and blasphemies ; and that, therefore, he ought not to undertake anything, but to await and see what was meant for him to accomplish.

CHAPTER XX

THE Rostofs, as usual on Sundays, had some of their intimate friends to dine with them.

Pierre went early, so as to find them alone.

Pierre had grown so stout this year that he would

have seemed monstrous had he not been so tall, so broad-shouldered, and so strong that he carried his weight with evident ease.

Panting, and muttering something to himself, he hurried up-stairs. His coachman no longer thought of asking him whether he should wait for him. He knew, by this time, that when the count was at the Rostofs' he would stay till midnight. The Rostofs' lackeys cheerfully hastened forward to take his cloak and receive his hat and cane. Pierre, from club habit, left his cane and hat in the anteroom.

The first person whom he saw was Natasha. Even before he had caught sight of her, and while he was taking off his cloak in the anteroom, he heard her singing solfeggii in the music-room.

He knew that she had not sung a note since her illness, and, therefore, the sounds of her voice surprised and delighted him. He gently opened the door, and saw Natasha in the lilac-colored dress, in which she had been to mass, pacing up and down the room and singing. She was walking up with her back toward him when he opened the door, but, when she turned short about, and recognized his stout, amazed face, she blushed, and came swiftly toward him.

"I want to get into the habit of singing again," said she. "It is quite an undertaking," she added, as if to excuse herself.

"And it is splendid!"

"How glad I am that you have come! I am so happy to-day," she cried, with something of that old vivacity which Pierre had so long missed in her. "You know Nicolas has received the Georgievsky cross. I am so proud of him!"

"Certainly; I sent you the 'order of the day.' Well, I will not interrupt you," he added, "but I will go into the drawing-room."

Natasha called him back.

"Count, tell me, is it wrong in me to be singing?" she asked, with a blush, but looking inquiringly into Pierre's face, without dropping her eyes.

"No! why?.... On the contrary.... but why did you ask me?"

"I am sure I don't know," replied Natasha, quickly; "but I did not wish to do anything that you would not approve. I have such perfect confidence in you! You don't know what you are to me, how much you have done for me!" She spoke rapidly, and noticed not how Pierre reddened at these words. "I saw that *he* — I mean Bolkonsky" — she spoke this name in a hurried whisper — "was mentioned in the same order; so then he is in Russia and serving again. What do you think?" she asked, still speaking rapidly, evidently in haste to finish what she had to say, lest she should not have the strength necessary to do so — "will he ever forgive me? Will he not always bear me ill-will? What do you think about it? What *do* you think about it?"

"I think ...." Pierre began, "I think he has nothing to forgive. .... If I were in his place .... "

By the force of recollection, Pierre was in an instant carried back, in his imagination, to that moment when, in order to comfort her, he had said that if he were the best man in the world, and free, he would, on his knees, ask for her hand; and now the same feeling of pity, tenderness, and love took possession of him, and the same words were on his lips. But she did not give him time to say them.

"Yes, you, *you*," said she, with a peculiar solemnity, repeating and dwelling on the pronoun — "you — that is another thing. I know no man who is kinder, nobler, better; and there could not be. If it had not been for you, then, and now too, I don't know what would have become of me, because .... " the tears suddenly filled her eyes; she turned around, held her music before her face, and began to sing her scales, and started to walk up and down the room once more.

At this moment, Petya came running in from the drawing-room. Petya was now a handsome, ruddy lad of fifteen, with thick, red lips, and looked like Natasha. He was preparing for the university, but lately he and his comrade, Obolyensky, had secretly resolved that they would enter the hussars.

He sprang forward to his namesake, in order to speak with him about this. He had been begging him to find out whether he could be admitted to the hussars. Pierre went into the drawing-room, not heeding the lad.

Petya pulled him by the arm, in order to attract his attention.

"Now tell me, Piotr Kiriluitch, for Heaven's sake, how is my business getting on? Is there any hope for us?" asked Petya.

"Oh, yes, your business. The hussars, is it? I will inquire about it; I will tell you about it, I will tell you the whole story this very day."

"Well now, my dear, have you brought the manifesto?" asked the old count. "The 'little countess' was at mass at the Razumovskys', and heard the new prayer. Very fine, they say!"

"Yes, I have brought it," replied Pierre. "The sovereign will be here to-morrow..... A special meeting of the nobility has been called, and they say there is to be a levy of ten out of every thousand. And I congratulate you!"

"Yes, yes, glory to God. Now tell me what is the news from the army?"

"We are still retreating. At Smolensk by this time, they say," replied Pierre.

"My God! My God!" exclaimed the count. "Where is the manifesto?"

"The proclamation? Oh, yes!"

Pierre began to search his pockets for the papers, but could not find them. While still rummaging through his pockets, he kissed the countess's hand, who, at that moment, came in, and he looked around uneasily, evidently expecting to see Natasha, who had ceased to sing but had not as yet rejoined the others.

"On my word, I don't know what I have done with them!" he exclaimed.

"Well, you're always losing things," exclaimed the countess.

Natasha came in with a softened, agitated expression of countenance, and sat down, looking at Pierre without speaking. As soon as she appeared, Pierre's face, till then darkened with a frown, grew bright, and though he was still searching for the papers, he kept looking at her.

"By Heavens![1] I must have left them at home. I will go after them. Most certainly...."

"But you will be late to dinner."

"Akh! and my coachman has gone too!"

Sonya, however, who had gone into the anteroom to look for the missing papers, found them in Pierre's hat, where he had carefully stuck them under the lining. Pierre wanted to read them immediately.

"No, not till after dinner," said the old count, evidently anticipating the greatest treat in this reading.

At dinner, during which they drank the health of the new knight of St. George in champagne, Shinshin related all the gossip of the town : about the illness of the old Princess of Gruzia, and how Métivier had disappeared from Moscow, and how they had arrested some German and brought him to Rostopchin, claiming that he was a *shampinion*.[2] Count Rostopchin had himself told the story, and how Rostopchin had commanded them to let the shampinion go, assuring the people that he was not a shampinion, but simply an old German toadstool!

"They'll catch it! they'll catch it!" said the count ; "I have been telling the countess that she must n't talk French so much. It is not the time to do it now."

"And have you heard?" proceeded Shinshin. "Prince Golitsuin has taken a Russian tutor — to teach him Russian. It is beginning to be dangerous to speak French in the street."

"Well, Count Piotr Kiriluitch, if they are going to mobilize the landwehr, you'll have to get on horseback, won't you?" asked the old count, addressing Pierre.

[1] *Yeĭ Bogu.*
[2] French *champignon*, a mushroom. — Slang term, meaning a French man.

Pierre was taciturn and thoughtful all dinner-time. As if not comprehending, he gazed at the old count when thus addressed.

"Yes, yes, about the war," said he. "No! what kind of a soldier should I be? But, after all, how strange everything is! how strange! I can't understand it myself. I don't know; my tastes are so far from being military, but as things are now no one can answer for himself."

After dinner the count seated himself comfortably in his chair, and, with a grave face, asked Sonya, who was an accomplished reader, to read.

"*To Moscow, our chief capital: —*

"*The enemy has come with overwhelming force to invade the boundaries of Russia. He is here to destroy our beloved fatherland,*" read Sonya, in her clear voice. The count listened with his eyes shut, sighing heavily at certain passages.

Natasha, with strained attention, sat looking inquiringly now at her father and now at Pierre.

Pierre was conscious of her glance fastened on him, and strove not to look round. The countess shook her head sternly and disapprovingly at each enthusiastic expression contained in the manifesto, for everything made her see that the danger threatening her son would not soon pass by.

Shinshin, with his lips formed to a satiric smile, was evidently making ready to turn into ridicule whatever first gave him a good opportunity: Sonya's reading, or what the count should say, or even the proclamation itself, if that offered him a suitable pretext.

Having read about the perils threatening Russia, the hopes which the sovereign placed in Moscow, and especially in its illustrious nobility, Sonya, with a trembling voice, which was caused principally by the fact that they were following her so closely, read the following words : —

"*We shall not be slow to take our place amidst our people in this capital, and in other cities of our empire, so as to lead in deliberations and to take the direction of all our troops, not only those which are at the present time blocking the way of the foe, but also those that are gathering to cause his defeat wherever he may show himself. And may the destruction in which he thinks to involve us react upon his own head, and may Europe, delivered from servitude, magnify the name of Russia!"*

"That's the talk!" cried the count, opening his moist eyes, and several times catching his breath with a noise as if a bottle of strong smelling-salts had been put to his nose; he went on to say, "Only say the word, sire, and we will sacrifice everything without a regret!"

Shinshin had no time to utter the little joke which he had ready at the expense of the count's patriotism before Natasha sprang up from her place and ran to her father.

"How lovely he is—this papa of mine!" she exclaimed, giving him a kiss; and then she glanced at Pierre again with the same unconscious coquetry which had come back to her together with her animation.

"What a little patriotka[1] she is!" cried Shinshin.

"Not a patriotka at all, but simply ...." began Natasha, offended. "You turn everything into ridicule, but this is no joke."....

"What jokes!" exclaimed the count. "Let him only say the word, and we will all follow.... we are not Germans or ...."

"And did you notice," said Pierre, "that it spoke 'about deliberations'?"

"Well, whatever he is here for ...."

At that moment Petya, to whom no one had been paying any attention, came up to his father, and, all flushed, said, in that voice of his, which was now breaking, and was sometimes bass and sometimes treble, "Now, then, papenka, my mind is perfectly made up—and, mamenka, too, if you please—I tell you both my mind is made up; you must let me go into the military service, because I cannot.... and that's the end of it."....

[1] The feminine of patriot.

The countess raised her eyes to heaven in dismay, clasped her hands, and turned severely to her husband:

"Just think what he has said!"

But the count instantly recovered from his emotion.

"Well, well!" said he. "A fine soldier you are! A truce to such folly! You must study!"

"It is not folly, papenka. Fedya Obolyensky is younger than I am, and he is going; but, even if he were n't, I could never think of studying now when...."

Petya hesitated, and flushed so that the perspiration stood out on his forehead, but still finished, — "When the country is in danger."

"There! there! enough of this nonsense!"....

"But you yourself just said that we would sacrifice everything!"

"Petya! I tell you hold your tongue!" cried the count, glancing at his wife, who had turned white, and was gazing with fixed eyes at her youngest son.

"But I tell you — and here is Piotr Kirillovitch will speak about it...."

"And I tell you it is all rubbish! the milk is n't dry on your lips yet; and here you are wanting to go into the army! Nonsense, I tell you!"

And the count, gathering up the papers, which he evidently intended to read over again in his cabinet before going to bed, started to leave the room.

"Piotr Kirillovitch, come and have a smoke."....

Pierre was in a state of confusion and uncertainty. Natasha's unnaturally brilliant and animated eyes fixed on him steadily rather than affectionately had brought him into this state.

"No, I think I will go home."....

"What? Go home? I thought you were going to spend the evening with us..... And, besides, you don't come as often as you did. And this girl of mine...." said the count, affectionately indicating Natasha, "is merry only when you are here."....

"Yes, but I had forgotten something..... I must certainly go home..... Some business...." said Pierre, hastily.

"Well, then, good-by," [1] said the count, and he left the room.

"Why must you go? Why are you so out of spirits? What is it?" asked Natasha, looking inquiringly into Pierre's eyes.

"Because I love thee!" was what was on his lips to say, but he did not say it; he reddened till the tears came, and dropped his eyes.

"Because it is better for me not to be here so much .... because .... No, simply because I have some business." ....

"What is it? No! Tell me," Natasha began resolutely, but suddenly stopped. The two looked at each other in dismay and confusion. He tried to smile, but it was a vain attempt; his smile expressed his suffering, and he kissed her hand without speaking, and left the house.

Pierre decided that he must not visit at the Rostofs' any more.

CHAPTER XXI

PETYA, after the decided repulse which he had received, went to his room, and there, apart from every one, wept bitterly. All pretended, however, not to remark his red eyes, when he came down to tea, silent and gloomy.

On the following day the sovereign arrived. Several of the Rostofs' household serfs asked permission to go and see the Tsar.

That morning it took Petya a long time to dress, comb his hair, and arrange his collar, so as to make it look as full-grown men wore theirs. He stood scowling before the mirror, making gestures, lifting his shoulders; and, at last, saying nothing to any one, he put on his cap, and left the house by the back door, so as not to be observed.

[1] *Da svidanya,* like *au revoir, auf wiedersehen.*

Petya had made up his mind to go straight to the place where the sovereign was, and to give a perfectly straightforward explanation to one of the chamberlains — he supposed the sovereign was always surrounded by chamberlains — and tell him that he, Count Rostof, in spite of his youth, wished to serve his country, that his youth could not be an obstacle in the way of devotion, and that he was ready. ....

Petya, by the time he was all dressed, was well fortified with fine words which he should say to the chamberlain.

Petya relied for the success of his application to the sovereign on the very fact that he was a mere child — he thought even that they would all be amazed at his youth — and, at the same time, by the arrangement of his nice little collar, and the combing of his hair, and his slow and dignified gait, he was anxious to give the impression of being a full-grown man.

But the farther he went, and the more he was involved in the throngs and throngs of people gathering around the Kreml, the more he forgot to keep up that appearance of dignity and moderation which marks the full-grown man.

As he approached the Kreml, he had a hard struggle to keep from being jostled; and this he did by putting on a decidedly threatening face, and resolutely applying his elbows to opposing ribs. But at Trinity Gate, in spite of all his resolutions, the people, who evidently had no idea what patriotic object brought him to the Kreml, crushed him up against the wall in such a way that he had to make a virtue of the necessity, and pause, while through the gateway rolled the equipages, thundering by under the vaulted arch.

Near Petya stood a peasant woman and a lackey, two merchants, and a discharged soldier. After standing some time at the Gate, Petya determined not to wait until all the carriages had passed, but to push farther on in advance of the others; and he began to work his elbows vigorously; but the peasant woman, who stood next him, and was the first to feel the application of his elbows, screamed at him angrily : —

" Here, my little barchuk,[1] what are you poking me for ? Don't you see every one is standing still ? Where are you trying to get to ? "

" That 's a game more than one can work," said the lackey, and, also vigorously plying his elbows, he sent Petya into the ill-smelling corner of the gateway.

Petya wiped his hot face with his hands, and tried to straighten up his collar, which had collapsed with the perspiration — that collar which, at home, he had so successfully arranged to look like a man's.

He felt that he now was in an unpresentable state, and he was afraid that if he went to the chamberlain in such a plight, he would not be allowed to approach the sovereign. But to put himself to rights, or to get from where he was to another place, was an impossibility, owing to the throng. One of the generals passing by was an acquaintance of the Rostofs. Petya started to ask his help ; but he came to the conclusion that that would not be compatible with manliness.

After all the equipages had passed, the throng burst through, and carried Petya along with it into the square, which was also full of the populace. Not the square alone, but the slopes and the housetops, every available place, was full of people. As soon as Petya got fairly into the square, he clearly heard the sounds of the bells filling all the Kreml, and the joyous shouts of the people.

At one time there was more room on the square, but suddenly every head was bared, and the whole mass of people rushed forward. Petya was so crushed that he could hardly breathe, and still the acclamations rent the air : " Hurrah ! hurrah ! hurrah ! " Petya got upon his tiptoes, pushed and pinched, but still he could see nothing except the people around him.

All faces wore one and the same expression of emotion and enthusiasm. One woman, a merchant's wife, standing near Petya, sobbed, and the tears streamed from her eyes.

---

[1] *Barchenok, barchuk,* is the popular diminutive of *baritch,* that is to say, the son of a *barin,* or nobleman, gentleman.

"Father! angel! batyushka!" she cried, rubbing the tears away with her fingers.

"Hurrah! hurrah!" resounded on every side.

The throng, for a single instant, stood still in one place; then it rushed onward again.

Petya, entirely forgetting himself, set his teeth together like a wild beast, and, with his eyes starting from his head, plunged forward, using his elbows, and shouting "Hurrah!" at the top of his voice, as if he were ready and willing that moment to kill himself and every one else; while on every side of him there were ever the same wild faces uttering the same shouts: "Hurrah! hurrah!"

"So, then, that's the kind of a man the sovereign is!" thought Petya. "No, it would be impossible for me to deliver my petition in person; it would be quite too audacious."

Nevertheless, he still struggled desperately forward, and, just beyond the backs in front of him, he could see an empty space, with a lane covered with red cloth; but at this instant the throng ebbed back; the police in front were driving them away from the path of the procession, which they were incommoding; the sovereign was on his way from the palace to the Uspiensky Cathedral, and Petya unexpectedly received such a blow in the ribs, and was so crushed, that suddenly everything grew confused before his eyes, and he lost consciousness.

When he came to himself, a strange priest, — apparently a diachok, — in a well-worn blue cassock, and with a long mane of gray hair, was supporting him with one arm, and with the other defending him from the pressure of the throng.

"You have crushed a young nobleman!"[1] cried the diachok. "Look out, there! Easy! — You have crushed him! You have crushed him!"

The sovereign entered the Uspiensky Cathedral. The crowd again thinned out a little, and the priest took Petya, pale and hardly able to breathe, to the *Tsar-pushka*, or King of Guns. Several persons expressed their pity

[1] *Barchenok*, nobleman's son.

for Petya, but then suddenly the throng surged up against him again, and he was already involved in the billows of the mob. But those who stood nearest to him gave him a helping hand, while others unbuttoned his coat, and got him up to the top of the cannon, and reviled some of those who had treated him so brutally.

"Would you crush him to death that way!"…. "What do you mean?"…. "Why, it's downright murder!"…. "See the poor fellow, he's as white as a sheet!" said various voices.

Petya quickly recovered himself, the color returned to his cheek, his pain passed off, and, as a compensation for this momentary discomfort, he had his place on the cannon, from which he hoped to see the sovereign pass by on his way back. Petya no longer even thought of preferring his request. If he could only *see* him, then he should consider himself perfectly happy!

During the time of the service in the Uspiensky Cathedral, which consisted of a Te Deum in honor of the sovereign's arrival, and a thanksgiving for the conclusion of peace with Turkey, the throng thinned out, peddlers of kvas, gingerbread, and poppy seeds — which Petya specially affected — made their appearance proclaiming their wares, and the ordinary chatter of a crowd was heard.

A merchant's wife was lamenting her torn shawl and telling how much it had cost her. Another made the remark that at the present time all sorts of silk stuffs were dear. The diachok, Petya's rescuer, was disputing with an official as to who and who were assisting his eminence in the service. The priest several times repeated the word *sobornye*,[1] which Petya did not understand. Two young fellows were jesting with some servant-girls, who were munching nuts.

All these conversations, especially the jokes with the girls, which ordinarily would have been extremely fascinating to Petya at his age, now entirely failed to attract his attention. He sat on his coign of vantage — the

[1] A Slavonic word signifying that all the clergy of the cathedral (*sobor*) assisted.

cannon — just as much excited as ever at the thought of his sovereign and of his love for him. The coincidence of his feeling of pain and terror when they were crushing him, and his feeling of enthusiasm still more strengthened in him the consciousness of the importance of this moment. Suddenly, from the embankment were heard the sounds of cannon-shots, — they were fired in commemoration of the peace with the Turks, — and the throng rushed eagerly toward the embankment to see them fire the cannon.

Petya wanted to go, too, but the priest who had taken the young nobleman under his protection would not permit it. These guns were still firing when from the Uspiensky Cathedral came a number of officers, generals, and chamberlains; then, more deliberately, came still others; again heads were uncovered, and those who had rushed to see the firing came running back. Last of all there emerged from the portal of the cathedral four men in uniforms and ribbons. "Hurrah! hurrah!" shouted the throng.

"Which is he? Which one?" asked Petya, in a tearful voice, of those around him, but no one gave him any answer; all were too much preoccupied; and Petya, selecting one of these four personages, which he had some difficulty in doing, owing to the tears of joy that blinded his eyes, concentrated on him all his enthusiasm — although it happened not to be the monarch! — and shouted "Hurrah!" in a frenzied voice, and made up his mind that, the very next day, cost what it might, he would become a soldier.

The throng rushed after the sovereign, accompanied him to the palace, and then began to disperse. It was already late, and Petya had eaten nothing, and the perspiration was streaming from him; still he had no idea of going home yet, and all through the time that the sovereign was eating his dinner he stood in front of the palace with the diminished but still enormous throng, gazing at the windows of the palace, still expecting something, and envying the dignitaries who came up to the doorway to take part in the dinner, and even the footmen who were serving the tables and passing swiftly in front of the windows.

During the dinner Valuyef, glancing out of the window, remarked to the sovereign:—

"The people are still hoping to have another glimpse of your majesty."

Just before the banquet was finished, the sovereign arose, still eating the last of a biscuit, and went out on the balcony. The throng, Petya in the number, rushed toward the balcony, shouting, "Angel! batyushka! hurrah!"

"Father!".... cried the people, and Petya also, and again the women and some of the men of weaker mold — Petya among the number — wept for joy.

A pretty good-sized piece of the biscuit which the sovereign held in his hand crumbled and dropped on the railing of the balcony, and from the railing to the ground. A coachman in a sleeveless coat, standing nearer than any one else, sprang forward and seized this crumb. Several of the throng flung themselves on the coachman. The sovereign, perceiving this, commanded a plate of biscuits to be handed to him, and began to toss them from the balcony.

Petya's eyes were bloodshot; the danger of being crushed to death again threatened him, but he rushed for the biscuits. He knew not why, but his happiness depended on having one of those biscuits from the Tsar's hand, and he was bound he would not give in. He sprang forward and knocked over an old woman who was just grasping a biscuit. But the old woman had no idea of considering herself vanquished, although she was flat on the ground, for she held the biscuit clutched in her fist, and had not dropped it. Petya knocked it out of her hand with his knee, and seized it, and, as if fearing that he should be too late, he shouted "Hurrah!" with his hoarse voice.

The sovereign retired, and after this the larger part of the crowd began to separate. "I said there'd be something more to see, and so it turned out," said various voices, joyously, amid the throng.

Happy as Petya was, it was, nevertheless, a gloomy prospect for him to go home, and know that all the happiness of the day was done. Instead, therefore, of going home, he left the Kreml, and went to find his comrade, Obolyensky, who was also fifteen years old, and who also was bent upon going into the army.

When, at last, he reached his home, he clearly and definitely declared that, if they would not give him their permission, he would run away. And, on the next day, Count Ilya Andreyitch, though not fully decided to give his assent, went to learn in what way some place might be found for Petya, where he would be least exposed to danger.

CHAPTER XXII

On the morning of the twenty-seventh, three days later, a countless throng of equipages were drawn up in the vicinity of the Slobodsky palace.

The halls were all crowded. In the front room were the nobles in their uniforms; in the second room were the merchants, wearing medals, beards, and blue kaftans.

There was a bustle and movement in the room where the nobles were gathered. Around a great table, over which hung a portrait of the sovereign, sat the most distinguished dignitaries, in high-backed chairs; but the majority of the nobles were walking up and down.

All the nobles — the very men whom Pierre was accustomed to see every day at the club or at their own homes — were in uniforms; some dating from Catherine's time, some from Paul's, some in the newer-fashioned ones that had come in with Alexander, some in the ordinary uniform of the Russian nobility; and those who wore this characteristic uniform, young and old, no matter how much they differed from one another in type or how well-known they were, had something strange and fantastic about them. Especially notice-able were the old men, dull-eyed, toothless, bald, with flesh turning to yellow fat, or wrinkled and thin. These, for the most part, sat in their places and had nothing to say ; and if they walked about and talked, they addressed themselves to men their juniors. Likewise, as in the faces of the throng which Petya had seen on the Kreml square, so here these faces wore a most astounding contrariety of expressions, the general expectation of some solemn event, and the usual evening's routine : the party of Boston, Petrusha the cook, the exchange of greetings with Zinaïda Dmitrievna, and things of the sort.

Pierre, who since early morning had been pinched into an uncomfortable and too tightly fitting court uniform, was present. He was in a high state of excitement ; a meeting extraordinary, not only of the nobility, but also of the merchant class — a legislative assembly, *états généraux* — had awakened in him a whole throng of ideas about the *Contrat social*, and the French Revolution — ideas which he had long ago ceased to entertain, but were, nevertheless, deeply engraven in his mind. The words of the proclamation which said that the sovereign was coming to his capital, for the purpose of *deliberating* with his people, confirmed him in this opinion. And thus supposing that the important reform which he had been long waiting to see introduced would now be tried, he walked about, looked on, listened to the conversations, but nowhere found any one expressing the ideas that occupied him.

The sovereign's manifesto was read, arousing great enthusiasm ; and then the assembly broke up into groups, discussing affairs. Pierre heard men talking, not only about matters of universal interest, but also about such things as where the marshals of the nobility should stand when the sovereign came, when the ball should be given to his majesty, whether the division should be made by districts or taking the whole government, and other questions of the sort. But as soon as the war became a topic of conversation, or the object of calling the meeting of the nobility was mentioned, the discussions became vague and irresolute. All preferred to listen rather than to talk.

One middle-aged man of strikingly gallant bearing,

and wearing the uniform of a retired officer of the navy, was talking in one room, and a group was gathered around him. Pierre joined it and began to listen. Count Ilya Andreyitch, in his Voevode's kaftan of Catherine's time, after making his way through the crowd, with a pleasant greeting for every one, also approached this same group, and began to listen, as he always listened, with his good-natured smile, and nodding his head to signify that his sentiments were in accord with the speaker's.

The retired naval man spoke very boldly — as could be judged by the faces of his listeners, and because certain of Pierre's acquaintances, well known for their submissive and gentle natures, turned away from him, or disagreed with what he said. Pierre forced his way into the center of this group, listened, and came to the conclusion that the speaker was genuinely liberal, but in a very different sense from what Pierre understood by liberality. The naval man spoke in that peculiar, ringing, singsong baritone characteristic of the Russian nobility, with an agreeable slurring of the R's and shortening of consonants — a voice, too, fitted to issue a command.

"Suppose the people of Smolensk have offered to raise militia for the sove'n. Can the Smolenskites lay down the law for us? If the ge'm'en of the Muscovite nobil'ty find it neces'y, they can show their devotion to their sove'n and emp'r in some other way. We haven't forgotten the calling out of the landwehr in '07, have we? Only rasc'ly priests' sons and plund'r's got any good from it."....

Count Ilya Andreyitch, with a shadow of a smile, nodded his head approvingly.

"And I should like to know if our militia have ever done the empire any good? Not the least. They have merely ruined our farming int'rests. A levy is much better — for the militia man comes back to you neither a soldier nor a muzhik, but simply spoiled and good for nothing. The nobles don't grudge their lives; we are perfectly willing to take the field ourselves and bring along recruits with us; the sove'n [1] has only to speak the word and we will all die for him," added the orator, growing excited.

Ilya Andreyitch swallowed down the spittle in his mouth with gratification at hearing such sentiments, and nudged Pierre, but Pierre also had a strong desire to speak. He pushed still farther forward; he felt that he was excited, but he had no idea what should cause him to speak, and as yet he had still less idea of what he was going to say. He had just opened his mouth to speak when a senator, who had absolutely no teeth at all, but who had a stern, intelligent face, suddenly interrupted Pierre. He had been standing near the naval orator. Evidently used to leading in debate, and holding his own in argument, he spoke in a low but audible voice : —

"I suppose, my dear sir," said the senator — the words sounding thick, owing to his toothless mouth — "I suppose that we have been summoned here not for the purpose of deciding whether at the present moment enlistment of soldiers or levies of militia will be most beneficial for the empire, but we have been summoned here to respond to the proclamation which the emperor our sovereign has deigned to address to us. And the decision of the question which is the more advantageous — recruits or militia — we may safely leave to his supreme autho...."

Pierre suddenly found an outlet for his excitement. He was indignant with the senator for taking such a strict and narrow view of the functions of the nobility. Pierre took a step forward and interrupted the senator. He himself knew not what he was going to say, but he began hotly, occasionally breaking out into French expressions, and when he spoke in Russian, "talking like a book."

"Excuse me, your excellency," he began. Pierre was well acquainted with this senator, but now he felt that it was incumbent upon him to address him with perfunctory formality. "Although I cannot agree

---

[1] " He pronounced *Gosudar, gusaï* " : parenthesis in text.

with the gentleman...." Pierre hesitated. He wanted to say *Mon très-honorable préopinant* — "with the gentleman — *que je n'ai pas l'honneur de connaître* — still I suppose that the nobility have been called together now not alone to express their sympathy and enthusiasm, but likewise to decide on the measures by which we may aid the fatherland. I suppose," said he, growing still more animated, "I suppose that the sovereign himself would have been sorry if he saw in us nothing but owners of peasants whom we should give him as meat for — as *chair à canon* — but rather as co— co— counsellors...."

Several moved away from this group as they noticed the senator's scornful smile and the excitement under which Pierre was laboring; only Ilya Andreyitch was content with Pierre's deliverance, just as he had been with the naval man's speech and the senator's, and, as a general rule, with the last one which he ever happened to hear.

"I suppose that before we decide these questions," pursued Pierre, "we ought to ask the sovereign, we ought most respectfully to ask his majesty, to give us a full and definite account of how many troops we have, in what condition they are, and then...."

But Pierre was not allowed to finish his sentence; he was attacked from three sides at once. More violently than by any one else he was assailed by an acquaintance of his of very long standing, always well disposed to him, and frequently his partner at Boston, Stepan Stepanovitch Adraksin. Stepan Stepanovitch was in uniform, and either it was the uniform or some other reason that made Pierre see himself opposed by an entirely different man from what he had ever known. Stepan Stepanovitch, with an expression of senile wrath suddenly flushing his face, screamed out at Pierre: —

"In the first place I would have you understand that we have no right to ask the sovereign any such thing, and in the second place even if the Russian nobility had such a right, even then the sovereign could not answer us. The movements of our troops depend upon those of the enemy.... the troops decrease and increase...."

Another man, of medium height, forty years old, whom Pierre had seen in days gone by at the gipsies', and knew as a wretched card-player, and who now like the rest had a wholly changed aspect in his uniform, interrupted Adraksin: "Yes, and besides it is not the time to criticize," said the voice of this noble, "but we must act; the war is in Russia. The enemy are coming to destroy Russia, to desecrate the tombs of our sires, to lead into captivity our wives and our children." — The nobleman struck his chest a ringing blow. — "Let us all arise, let us all go as one man in defense of our batyushka, the Tsar!" he cried, wildly rolling his bloodshot eyes.

Several approving voices were heard in the throng.

"We Russians will never begrudge our lives for the defense of the faith, the throne, and the fatherland; but we must renounce day-dreams if we are the true sons of the country. Let us show Europe how Russia can defend Russia!" cried a nobleman.

Pierre wanted to make a reply, but he could not say a word. He was conscious that even the sound of his voice — independent of the meaning of what he would say — was less audible than the sound of the excited nobleman's voice.

Ilya Andreyitch stood just behind the circle, looking on approvingly; several applauded the speaker when he finished, and shouted: —

"Hear! Hear!"

Pierre was anxious to say that, while he would be ready to sacrifice himself to any extent, either in money or in his peasants, still he should like to know how affairs were situated before he could help, but he found it impossible to get a word in. Many voices spoke and shouted all at once, so that Ilya Andreyitch had no chance even to nod his head in assent to everything, and the group grew in size, broke asunder, and then formed again swaying and tumultuous, and moved across the room toward the great table.

Not only was Pierre prevented from speaking, but he was rudely interrupted, assailed, and pushed aside, and treated as if he were a common foe. This was not because they were dissatisfied with the sentiments which he expressed, for they had already forgotten what he had said after the multitude of other things spoken since, but what was necessary to excite the throng was some palpable object of love and some palpable object of hatred. Pierre had made himself the latter. Many orators followed the excited nobleman, and all spoke in the same tone. Many spoke eloquently and with originality.

The editor of the *Russky Vyestnik*, Glinka,[1] who was well known, and was greeted with shouts of "The writer! the writer!" declared that hell must contend with hell; that he had seen a child smiling at the flashing of lightning and at the crashing of thunder, but that we should not be like such a child as that.

"No! no! we must not!" was heard approvingly spoken in the most distant circles.

The throng drifted up to the great table where sat the septuagenarian notables, old and gray and bald, in uniforms and ribbons, veterans whom Pierre had seen, almost without exception, at home with jests in their mouths or at the club-house playing Boston. The throng drew near the table, and still the roar of shouting and talk went on. One after the other, and sometimes two at once, pressing up against the high-backed chairs, the orators spoke their thoughts. Those who stood in the rear finished saying what any orator had no time to say to the end, and filled out the omitted passages. Others, in spite of the heat and closeness, racked their brains trying to find some new idea and to give it utterance. Pierre's friends, the aged notables, sat and gazed, now at one, now at the other, and the expression of the majority of their faces merely said that it was very hot.

Pierre, however, felt intensely excited, and a great

---

[1] Sergyeï Nikolayevitch Glinka, born at Smolensk 1776, founded the *Russian Messenger*, 1808, which, in 1812, was the very pillar of nationalism; he also, at his own cost, furnished twenty men for the militia; died 1847, leaving one hundred and fifty volumes of works.

desire came over him to have the meeting understand that he was as ready as the rest to be moved and stirred by that which was expressed more in the sounds of their voices and their looks than in the sense of the words they spoke. He had no intention of renouncing his convictions, but he somehow felt as if he were in the wrong, and he wanted to set himself right.

"I merely said that it would be easier for us to make sacrifices if we could know what was needed," he began to say, trying to outshout the rest.

A little old man who happened to be standing near him looked at him, but was immediately attracted by a shout raised at the other side of the table.

"Yes, Moscow shall be sacrificed! She shall be the deliverer!" some one was shouting.

"He is the enemy of the human race!" cried another.

"Allow me to speak."....

"Gentlemen, you are crushing me!"....

CHAPTER XXIII

AT this moment, Count Rostopchin, in a general's uniform and with a broad ribbon across his shoulder, with his prominent chin and keen eyes, came into the room, and swiftly passed through the throng of nobles, who made way before him.

"Our sovereign, the emperor, will be here immediately," said Rostopchin. "I have just come from there. I think that in the position in which we find ourselves there is very little room for debate. The sovereign has deigned to call us and the merchant class together," said Count Rostopchin. "They in there control millions,"—he pointed to the hall where the merchants were,—"and it is our business to arm the militia, and not to spare ourselves.... That is the least that we can do!"

The notables, sitting by themselves at the table, held a consultation. The whole consultation went more than quietly. It even seemed melancholy when, after all the noise and enthusiasm, these senile voices were heard, one after the other, saying, "I am content," or, for the sake of variety, "That is my opinion," and the like.

The secretary of the meeting was bidden to write that the Moscovites, in a meeting of the nobility, had unanimously resolved to follow the example of Smolensk, and offer a levy of ten men out of every thousand, completely armed and equipped.

The gentlemen who had been sitting arose, as if freed from a heavy task, noisily pushed back their chairs, and stirred about the hall so as to stretch their legs, perchance taking the arm of some acquaintance, and talking matters over.

"The sovereign! the sovereign!" was the cry suddenly shouted through the halls, and the whole throng rushed to the entrance.

Through a broad lane, between a wall of nobles, the sovereign entered the hall. All faces expressed a reverent and awesome curiosity. Pierre was standing at some little distance, and could not fully catch all that the sovereign said in his address.

He comprehended only from what he heard that the sovereign spoke about the peril in which the country stood, and the hopes which he placed upon the Moscovite nobility. Some one spoke in response to the sovereign's address, and merely confirmed the resolution which had just before been engrossed.

"Gentlemen," said the sovereign's trembling voice; a ripple of excitement ran through the throng, and then dead silence reigned again, and this time Pierre distinctly heard the sovereign's extremely agreeable voice, affected with genuine emotion, saying:—

"I have never doubted the devotion of the Russian nobility. But this day it has exceeded my expectations. I thank you in the name of the fatherland. Gentlemen, let us act—time is more precious than anything...."

The sovereign ceased speaking; the throng gathered round him, and on every side were heard enthusiastic exclamations.

"Yes, precious indeed—the Tsar's word!" said Ilya

Andreyitch, with a sob ; he had heard nothing, but put his own interpretation on everything.

The sovereign passed from the hall where the nobles were into that where the merchants were gathered. He remained there about ten minutes. Pierre and several others saw him on his way from their hall with tears of emotion in his eyes. As was learned afterwards, the sovereign had hardly begun his speech to the merchants before the tears had streamed from his eyes, and he had ended it in a voice broken with emotion. When Pierre saw him, he was coming out accompanied by two merchants. One was an acquaintance of Pierre's — a stout leaseholder ; the other was the city provost, a man with a thin yellow face and a peaked beard. Both of them were in tears. The thin man wept, but the stout leaseholder was sobbing like a child, and kept saying : —

"Take our lives and our all, your majesty ! "

Pierre at this moment felt no other desire than to prove how little he treasured anything, and that he was ready to make any sacrifice. He reproached himself for his speech with its constitutional tendency ; he tried to think of some means to efface the impression which it had made. Learning that Count Mamonof had offered a regiment, Bezukhoï immediately announced to Count Rostopchin that he would give a thousand men and their maintenance.

Old Rostof could not refrain from tears when he told his wife what had been done, and he then and there granted Petya's request, and went himself to see that his name was enrolled.

The next day the sovereign took his departure. All the nobles who had assembled took off their uniforms, once more scattered to their homes and their clubs, and, groaning, gave orders to their overseers in regard to the militia, and marveled at what they had done.

PART TENTH

CHAPTER I

NAPOLEON entered upon the war with Russia because he could not help going to Dresden, could not help being befogged with honors, could not help putting on a Polish uniform, could not help feeling the stimulating impression of a June morning, could not help giving way to an outburst of fury in the presence of Kurakin and afterwards of Balashof.

Alexander declined all negotiations, because he felt that he had been personally insulted.

Barclay de Tolly strove to direct the troops in the very best way, so that he might do his duty and win the renown of being a great commander.

Rostof charged the French because he could not resist the temptation to make a dash across an open field.

And thus acted in exactly the same way, in accordance with their own natural characteristics, habits, dispositions, and aims, all the innumerable individuals who took part in this war. They had their fears and their vanities, they had their enjoyments and their fits of indignation, and they all supposed that they knew what they were doing, and that they were doing it for themselves ; but they were in reality the irresponsible tools of history, and they brought about a work which they themselves could not realize, but which is plain for us to see.

Such is the inevitable fate of all who take an active part in life, and the higher they stand in the hierarchy of mankind the less free are they. Now, those who took part in the events of the year 1812 have long ago passed from the scene ; their personal interests have vanished without leaving a trace, and only the historical results of that time are before us.

Let us now once admit that the armies of Europe, under the leadership of Napoleon, *had* to plunge into the depths of Russia, and there to perish, and all the self-contradictory, senseless, atrocious deeds of those who took part in this war become comprehensible for us.

Providence obliged all these men, who were each striving to attain his own ends, to work together for the accomplishment of one tremendous result, of which no man — neither Napoleon nor Alexander any more than the most insignificant participant — had the slightest anticipation.

It is now plain to us what caused the destruction of the French army in the year 1812. No one will attempt to dispute that the cause of the destruction of Napoleon's French troops was, on the one hand, their plunging into the depths of Russia too late in the season, and without sufficient preparation; and, on the other hand, the character given to the war by the burning of the Russian cities, and the consequent awakening in the Russian people of hatred against the foe.

But at that time not only had no one any idea of such a thing, — though now it seems so evident, — that an army of eight hundred thousand men, the best that the world had ever seen, and conducted by the greatest of leaders, could only in this way have met with its destruction in a collision with an army of half its size, inexperienced, and under the lead of inexperienced generals; *not only no one had any idea of such a thing*, but, moreover, all the exertions of *the Russians* were systematically directed toward preventing the only thing that could save Russia, and all the exertions of *the French*, in spite of Napoleon's experience and his so-called military genius, were directed toward reaching Moscow by the end of the summer — in other words, doing the very thing which was bound to prove his ruin.

French authors, in their accounts of the year 1812, are very fond of declaring that Napoleon felt the risk he ran in extending his line, that he sought to give battle, that his marshals advised him to halt at Smolensk.

And they bring forward other arguments of the sort, to prove that even then the peril of the Russian campaign was foreseen.

On the other hand, Russian authors are even more fond of declaring that, at the very beginning of the campaign, the scheme was already conceived of decoying Napoleon into the depths of Russia, — after the manner of the Scythians, — and some ascribe this scheme to Pfuhl, others to some Frenchman, others again to Toll, and still others to the Emperor Alexander himself. For their proof, they cite certain memoirs, suggestions, and letters, in which it really happens that allusions to some such mode of action can be found.

But all these allusions, suggesting that what was done either by the French or the Russians was the result of calculation, are made to look so at the present day simply because what actually took place has justified them.

If the event had not taken place, then these allusions would have been neglected, just as thousands and millions of hints and suggestions of entirely opposite character are now forgotten, though they were all the vogue at that time, but, having been found to be incorrect, are forgotten.

The issue of any event whatever is always involved in so many hypotheses, that no matter how it really turns some one will be found to say, "I told you it would happen so," entirely forgetting that among the numberless hypotheses others were made which proved to be perfectly erroneous.

To suppose that Napoleon foresaw the peril of extending his line and that the Russians thought of alluring the enemy into the depths of their country, evidently belongs to this category, and it is only by very forced reasoning that historians can ascribe such divination to Napoleon and such schemes to the Russian generals.

All the facts are absolutely opposed to such hypotheses.

The Russians throughout the war not only had no thought or desire to decoy the French into the depths of the country, but, on the other hand, everything was done to prevent them from making the first advance beyond their borders ; and Napoleon not only had no fear of extending his line, but he felt a joy amounting to enthusiasm at every onward movement, and he showed no such eagerness as in his earlier campaigns to give battle.

At the very beginning of the campaign our armies are separated, and our single aim, in which we employ all our energies, is to unite them, whereas if it had been our intention to retreat and decoy the enemy into following us, there would not have been the slightest advantage in making a junction of the forces.

The emperor is with the army in order to inspire the troops to defend the Russian land and not to yield an inch of ground. The enormous fortified camp of the Drissa is established according to Pfuhl's design, and there is no thought of retreating. The sovereign reproaches the commander-in-chief for every backward step. The emperor could never have dreamed either of the burning of Moscow or the presence of the enemy at Smolensk, and when the armies are united the sovereign is exasperated because Smolensk is taken and burned, and because a general engagement is not delivered under its walls.

Such are the sovereign's views, but the Russian generals and all the Russian people are still more exasperated at the mere suggestion that our forces are falling back into the interior of the country.

Napoleon, having cut our armies asunder, moves on into the interior of the country, and neglects several opportunities for giving battle. In August he is at Smolensk, and his sole thought is how to advance into Russia, although, as we see now, this forward movement was certain to be destructive to him.

The facts prove that Napoleon did not foresee the risk of an advance on Moscow, and that Alexander and the Russian generals had no idea at that time of decoying Napoleon, but quite the contrary.

The luring of Napoleon into the heart of the country

was not in accordance with any plan, — for no one believed in the possibility of such a plan, — but came about from the complicated play of intrigues, desires, and ambitions of the men who took part in this war and had no conception of what was destined to be, or what would prove, the only salvation of Russia.

Everything proceeds in the most unexpected way. Our armies are divided at the opening of the campaign. We try to unite them, with the evident aim of giving battle and checking the invasion of the enemy ; but in trying to effect this union our troops avoid battle, because the enemy are stronger, and in our involuntary avoidance of them we form an acute angle, and draw the French as far as Smolensk. But it is not enough to say that we give way at an acute angle, because the French are moving between our two armies : the angle grows still more acute and we retreat still farther because Barclay de Tolly,[1] an unpopular German, is odious to Bagration, who has to act under his command, and Bagration, the commander of the other army, endeavors as far as possible to delay the conjunction, in order not to be under Barclay's orders.

Bagration long delays the union of the two armies — though this has been the chief object of all the Russian generals ; and he does so because he imagines that to make this march would endanger his troops, and that it is better for him to draw off farther to the left and south and harass the enemy on the flank and in the rear, and recruit his army in the Ukraïna.

But this is a pretext. He conceives this plan because he is anxious not to put himself under the command of Barclay, the hated German, whose rank is inferior to his own.

The emperor is with the army to inspire it, but his presence, and his tergiversation, and the tremendous throng of his advisers and plans paralyze the energy of the first army, and it beats a retreat.

---

[1] Barclay de Tolly (1759–1818) was not German, but of the old Scotch family of Barclay, a branch of which settled in Russia in the seventeenth century.

The plan then is to make a stand in the camp at Drissa, but suddenly Paulucci, who aims to be commander-in-chief, makes such an impression on Alexander by his energy, that Pfuhl's whole plan is abandoned, and the task is confided to Barclay. But as Barclay is not able to instil confidence, his power is limited.

The armies are separated; there is no unity, no head; Barclay is unpopular; but all this confusion, and division, and the unpopularity of the German commander-in-chief produce irresolution and the evasion of an encounter with the enemy, which would have been inevitable if the union of the armies had been accomplished, and if Barclay had not been designated as commander-in-chief, while on the other hand the same circumstances continually increase the feeling against the Germans, and more and more arouse the spirit of patriotism.

Finally, the sovereign leaves the army under the sole and most reasonable pretext that he is needed at the capital to stir up the people and incite a national war. And the sovereign's journey to Moscow triples the strength of the Russian troops.

The sovereign leaves the army in order that he may not interfere with the power of the commander-in-chief, and hopes that more decisive measures will be taken. But the position of the chief of the army grows more and more confused and helpless. Benigsen, the grand duke, and a whole swarm of general-adjutants remain in the army to watch the actions of the commander-in-chief and to stimulate him to energetic action; and Barclay, feeling himself still less free under the eyes of all these *imperial censors*,[1] grows still more cautious about undertaking any decided operation, and carefully avoids a battle.

Barclay stands on his guard. The tsesarevitch hints at treason and demands a general attack. Liubomirski, Brannitski, Wlotzki, and others of their ilk add so much to all this tumult that Barclay, to rid himself of them, sends the Polish general-adjutants to Petersburg

---

[1] *Glaz gosudarevuikh :* literally, *sovereign eyes.*

with pretended messages for the sovereign, and enters into an open dispute with Benigsen and the grand duke.

At last, against the wishes of Bagration, the union of the two armies is effected at Smolensk.

Bagration drives in his carriage to the house occupied by Barclay. Barclay puts on his scarf, comes out to meet him, and salutes him as his superior in rank. Bagration, in this conflict of magnanimity, places himself under Barclay's command, in spite of his superiority of rank, but though he takes a subordinate position he is still less in agreement with him. Bagration, by the sovereign's express order, makes direct reports. He writes to Arakcheyef:—

My sovereign's will be done, but I can never work with the *minister* [Barclay]. For God's sake send me where you will, give me only a single regiment to command, but I cannot stay here. — Headquarters are full of Germans, so that it is impossible for a Russian to breathe here, and there is no sense in anything. I thought that I was serving the sovereign and my country, but I am really serving Barclay. I confess this does not suit me.

The swarm of Brannitskis, of Winzengerodes, and others like them, still further poisons the relations between the two chiefs, and united action becomes more and more impossible.

They get ready to attack the French at Smolensk. A general is sent to inspect the position. This general, hating Barclay, instead of obeying orders, goes to one of his friends, a corps commander, remains with him all day, and returns at night to Barclay, to criticize at all points a field of battle which he has not even seen.

While quarrels and intrigues concerning the battlefield are in progress, while we are trying to find the French, because we are ignorant of their whereabouts, the French encounter Nevyerovsky's division, and approach the very walls of Smolensk.

It is necessary to accept an unexpected battle at Smolensk in order to save our communications. The battle takes place, thousands of men on both sides are killed.

Contrary to the wishes of the sovereign and the people, Smolensk is abandoned.   But the inhabitants of Smolensk, betrayed by their governor, set fire to the city, and, offering this example to other Russian towns, take refuge in Moscow, thinking only of their losses, and kindling hatred against the enemy.

Napoleon advances ; we retreat, and the result is that the very measure necessary for defeating Napoleon is employed.

CHAPTER II

ON the day following his son's departure, Prince Nikolaï Andreyitch summoned the Princess Mariya.

"There, now, are you satisfied?" he demanded. "You have involved me in a quarrel with my son! Satisfied? That was what you wanted! Satisfied?.... This is painful, painful, to me.   I am old and feeble, and this was what you wished.   Well, take your pleas· ure in it, take your pleasure in it!"....

And after that the Princess Mariya saw no more of her father for a whole week.   He was ill and did not leave his room.

To her amazement, the princess noticed that during this illness the old prince did not permit even Mlle. Bourienne to come near him.   Only Tikhon was admitted.

At the end of the week, the prince came out and began to lead his former life again, occupying himself with special zeal in his buildings and gardens, but discontinuing all his former relations with Mlle. Bourienne.   His looks and his coolness toward the Princess Mariya seemed to say to her : —

'Here, you see, you have lied about me, you have slandered me to Prince Andreï in regard to my relations with this Frenchwoman, and you have made me quarrel with him ; but, you see, I can get along without you or the Frenchwoman either.'

One-half of the day the Princess Mariya spent with Nikolushka, attending to his lessons; she herself taught him Russian and music, and talked with Dessalles; the remainder of the day she spent with her books, her old nurse, and her "God's people," who sometimes came to see her clandestinely by the backstairs.

The Princess Mariya had such thoughts about the war as women generally have regarding war. She trembled for her brother, who was in it; she was horror-struck at the cruelty which led men to slaughter each other, though she had little comprehension of its reality; but she did not appreciate the significance of this particular war, which seemed to her exactly like the wars that had preceded it.

She did not realize it, although Dessalles, with whom she was constantly associated, followed its course with passionate interest, and tried to explain what he felt about it; and although the "God's people" who came to see her brought to her the popular rumors about the invasion of Antichrist; and although Julie, now the Princess Drubetskaya, who had again begun to correspond with her, wrote her patriotic letters from Moscow.

I am going to write to you in Russian, — *pa Russki*, — my dear friend [wrote Julie], because I hate all the French, and their language likewise. I cannot even bear to hear it spoken. Here in Moscow we are all carried away by our enthusiasm for our idolized emperor.

My poor husband is enduring hunger and privations at Jewish taverns; but the tidings which I get from him still further excite me.

You have undoubtedly heard of the heroic action of Rayevsky, who embraced his two sons, saying, "I will perish with them, but we will never yield." And, indeed, though the enemy was twice as strong as we were, we did not yield.

We spend our time as best we can; during war, it must be as during war. The Princesses Alina and Sophie spend whole days with me, and we wretched widows of living husbands, while raveling lint, have good long talks; only you, my dear, are absent.

And so on.

The principal reason why the Princess Mariya did not realize the whole significance of this war was that the old prince never said a word about it, never mentioned it, and, at dinner, often laughed at Dessalles, who would grow eloquent over it.   The prince's tone was so calm and firm that the Princess Mariya believed in him without question.

All through the month of July, the old prince was extraordinarily active and energetic.   He set out another new orchard, and built a new building for the use of his household serfs.   The only thing that disquieted the Princess Mariya was that he slept very little, and, relinquishing his ordinary habit of sleeping in his cabinet, he each day changed his sleeping-room.   One time he gave orders to have his camp bedstead set up in the gallery ; then he would try the sofa, or the Voltaire easy-chair in the drawing-room, and doze without undressing, while the lad Petrusha — and not Mlle. Bourienne — read aloud to him ; then, again, he would spend the night in the dining-room.[1]

Early in August, he received a second letter from Prince Andreï.   In the first, which came soon after his departure for the army, Prince Andreï humbly begged his father's pardon for what he had permitted himself to say to him, and besought him to restore him to favor. The old prince had replied to this in an affectionate letter, and it was shortly after that he gave up his intimacy with·the Frenchwoman.

Prince Andreï's second letter, written from near Vitebsk, after it had been captured by the French, contained a brief account of the campaign, with the plan of it sketched out, and also his ideas as to the ultimate issue of it.   In the same letter Prince Andreï represented to his father the inconvenience of his position so near to the theater of the war, in the very line of march of the armies, and urged him to go to Moscow.

At dinner that day, hearing Dessalles mentioning the rumor that the French had already reached Vitebsk, the old prince remembered his letter from Prince Andreï

[1] This was a characteristic of Napoleon at St. Helena.

"I had a letter from Prince Andreï to-day," said he. "Have n't you read it?"

"No, *mon père*," replied the princess, timidly. She could not possibly have read the letter, as she did not even know that one had been received.

"He writes me about this campaign," said the old prince, with that scornful smile which had become habitual with him, and which always accompanied any mention of the war then in progress.

"It must be very interesting," said Dessalles. "The prince is in a position to know .... "

"Ah, very interesting," interrupted Mlle. Bourienne.

"Go and fetch it to me," said the old prince to Mlle. Bourienne. "It's on the little table, you know, under the paper-weight."

Mlle. Bourienne sprang away with eager haste.

"Oh, no," he cried, scowling; "do you go, Mikhaïl Ivanuitch."

Mikhaïl Ivanuitch got up and went into the cabinet. But, as he did not immediately return with it, the old prince, uneasily glancing around, threw down his napkin and went himself.

"He won't be able to find it; he'll upset everything."

While he was gone, the Princess Mariya, Dessalles, Mlle. Bourienne, and even Nikolushka silently exchanged glances. The old prince came hurrying back, accompanied by Mikhaïl Ivanuitch, and bringing the letter and a plan; but instead of letting them be read during the dinner-time he placed them by his side.

Passing into the drawing-room, he handed the letter to the Princess Mariya, and, spreading out the plan of the new building, he began to study it, but at the same time commanded the Princess Mariya to read the letter aloud. After she had read it, she looked inquiringly at her father. He was studying the plan, apparently immersed in his thoughts.

"What do you think about this, prince?" asked Dessalles, hazarding the question.

"I .... I?" .... exclaimed the prince, as if he were

aroused to some disagreeable reality, but still not taking his eyes from the plan.

"It is quite possible that the theater of the war may be approaching us."....

"Ha! ha! ha! the theater of war!" exclaimed the prince. "I have said, and I still say, that the theater of the war is in Poland, and the enemy will never venture to cross the Niemen."

Dessalles looked in amazement at the prince, who spoke of the Niemen when the enemy was already at the Dnieper; but the Princess Mariya, who had forgotten the geographical position of the Niemen, supposed that what her father said was correct.

"As soon as the snow begins to thaw they will be swallowed up in the swamps of Poland. Only they cannot see it," pursued the old prince, evidently thinking of the campaign of 1807, which, as it seemed to him, had not been so long ago. "Benigsen ought to have marched into Prussia before this; then the affair would have taken another direction."....

"But, prince," timidly suggested Dessalles, "Vitebsk is mentioned in the letter."....

"Ah! in the letter!.... Yes...." involuntarily exclaimed the prince. "Yes.... yes...." His face had suddenly assumed a sour expression. He paused for a moment. "Yes, he writes that the French were beaten.... near some river.... what was it?"

Dessalles dropped his eyes. "The prince wrote nothing about that," said he, in a low tone.

"Did n't he, indeed! Well, I certainly did not imagine it!"

A long silence ensued.

"Yes.... yes.... Well, Mikhaïl Ivanuitch!" he suddenly exclaimed, raising his head and pointing at the plan of the new building. "Tell me how you propose to change this...." Mikhaïl Ivanuitch drew up to the table, and the prince, after discussing the plan of the new edifice, left the room, casting an angry glance on the Princess Mariya and Dessalles.

The princess noticed Dessalles's confused and wondering look fastened on her father, remarked his silence, and was dumfounded at her father having forgotten to take his son's letter from the drawing-room table; but she was afraid to speak or to ask Dessalles the cause of his confusion and silence, and she was afraid even to think what it might be.

In the evening, Mikhaïl Ivanuitch was sent by the prince for his son's letter, which had been forgotten in the drawing-room. The Princess Mariya handed him the letter. And, although it was a trying thing for her to do, she permitted herself to ask him what her father was doing.

"He is always busy," replied Mikhaïl Ivanuitch, with a polite but sarcastic smile which made the Princess Mariya turn pale. "He is very much interested in the new building. He has been reading a little, but just now," continued Mikhaïl Ivanuitch, lowering his voice, "he is at his desk; he must be working over his 'will.'"

Latterly, one of the prince's favorite occupations had been to arrange the papers which were to be left after his death, and which he called his "will."

"And is he sending Alpatuitch to Smolensk?" asked the Princess Mariya.

"He is; he has been waiting for some time."

CHAPTER III

When Mikhaïl Ivanuitch returned to the cabinet, he found the prince sitting at his open bureau, with his spectacles on and his eyes shaded by an *abat-jour*. He was reading by the light of a shaded candle and with a peculiarly solemn expression, holding very far from his eyes the manuscript — his *Remarks*, he called it — which he wished to have presented to the sovereign after his death.

When Mikhaïl Ivanuitch came in, the old prince's eyes were filled with tears, started by the recollection of the time when he had written what he was now reading. He snatched the letter from Mikhaïl Ivanuitch's hand, thrust it into his pocket, replaced the manuscript and summoned the long-waiting Alpatuitch.

He held a sheet of paper on which was jotted down what he wished to be done at Smolensk, and as he paced back and forth through the room past the servant stand-ing at the door, he delivered his instructions.

" First, — do you hear ? — letter-paper like this speci-men, gilt-edged — here's the pattern so as not to make any mistake, — varnish, — sealing-wax," — following Mikhaïl Ivanuitch's memorandum.

He paced up and down the room, and kept glancing at the memorandum of purchases.

" Then be sure to give this letter about the deed to the governor in person."

Then he laid special stress on getting the bolts for his new edifice, which must be of a special pattern in vented by himself. Then a folio was wanted for hold-ing his " will." It took more than two hours to charge Alpatuitch with all the commissions, and still the prince did not let him go. He sat down, tried to think, and, closing his eyes, fell into a doze. Alpatuitch stirred uneasily.

" Well, get you gone ! get you gone ! if I need any-thing more I will send for you."

Alpatuitch left the room. The prince went to the bureau again, glanced into it, touched the papers with his hand, closed it again, and, going to his table, sat down to write his note to the governor.

It was already late when, having sealed the letter, he got up. He wanted to go to bed, but he knew that he should not sleep, and that the most miserable thoughts would haunt him as soon as he lay down. He rang for Tikhon, and went with him through the rooms, so as to select the place where to set the bed for the night. He went about measuring every corner.

There was no place that seemed to please him, but anything was better than his usual divan in his cabinet. This divan was terrible to him, apparently on account of the trying thoughts which passed through his mind as he lay on it. There was no place that satisfied him, but he was best of all pleased with the corner in the divan-room behind the pianoforte; he had never before slept there.

Tikhon and a man-servant brought in the bedstead, and began to make the bed.

"Not that way! Not that way!" cried the prince, and with his own hand he pushed it an inch or two farther away from the corner, and then nearer again.

"Well, at last I have done everything; let me rest," thought the prince, and he commanded Tikhon to un-dress him.

Painfully scowling at the effort required to take off his kaftan and pantaloons, the prince at last got un-dressed, and let himself drop heavily on his bed, and then seemed lost in thought as he gazed scornfully at his yellow, shriveled legs.   Thought, however, was absent; he was merely sluggish about undertaking the labor of lifting those same legs and getting them into bed.

"Okh! what a trial! Okh! why must the end of these labors be so slow in coming! Why can't *you* leave me in peace?" he said to himself. Screwing up his lips, he, for the twenty-thousandth time, made the effort, and then lay down.   But he was scarcely on his back before the whole bed suddenly began, with slow and regular motion, to rock backward and forward, as if it were heavily breathing and tossing. This thing hap-pened to him almost every night. He opened his eyes, which he had just closed.

"No repose! Curse it!" he exclaimed, full of fury against something.   "Yes, yes! there must have been something else of importance, of very great importance, which I kept till I should go to bed.   Was it the bolts? No, I told him about that.   No, it was something that happened in the drawing-room.   The Princess Mariya had some nonsense to repeat.   Dessalles — that idiot! — made some remark.   There was something in my pocket!   I can't remember. .... Tishka! what were we talking about at dinner-time?"

"About Prince Mikharl .... "

"Hold your tongue!"

The prince thumped his hand on the table. "Now, I know .... it was Prince Andreï's letter. The Princess Mariya read it aloud. Dessalles said something about Vitebsk. Now, I will read it."

He bade Tikhon fetch him the letter from his pocket, and place a small table near the bed, with his lemonade and a wax taper, and, putting on his spectacles, he began to read. There only, as he read the letter, in the silence of the night, by the feeble light of the candle under the green shade, he for the first time for a moment took in its full significance.

"The French at Vitebsk! in four marches they can reach Smolensk; maybe they are there now. Tishka!"

Tikhon sprang forward.

"No matter! Nothing! nothing!" he cried.

He slipped the letter under the candlestick, and closed his eyes.

And there arose before him the Danube, — a brilliant noonday, — the rushes, — the Russian camp and himself, a young general with not a single wrinkle on his face: hale and hearty, gay and ruddy, going into Potemkin's bright-colored tent, and the burning feeling of hatred against the "favorite" stirs in him now as violently as it did even then. And he recalls all the words which were spoken at his first interview with Potemkin. And his fancy brings up before him again a stout, short woman, with a fat, sallow face, — *matushka-imperatritsa*, — the little mother empress, — her smile, her words of flattery, when she for the first time gave him audience, and he remembers her face as it appeared on the catafalque, and then the quarrel with Zubof, which took place over her coffin, over the right to approach her hand.

"Akh! would that those old times could return, and that the present would all come to an end .... soon .... soon .... that I might at last find rest!"

CHAPTER IV

LUISIYA GORUI, Prince Nikolaï Andreyitch Bolkonsky's estate, was situated about sixty versts from Smolensk and three versts from the Moscow highway.

That evening, while the prince was giving Alpatuitch
his commissions, Dessalles asked for a few moments'
talk with the Princess Mariya, and told her that as the
prince, her father, was not very well, and refused to
adopt any measures for their safety, while from Prince
Andreï's letter it was evident that to remain at Luisiya
Gorui was attended with danger, he respectfully advised
her to send a letter by Alpatuitch to the nachalnik of
the government at Smolensk, asking him to let her
know the real state of affairs, and the measure of danger
to which Luisiya Gorui was exposed.

Dessalles wrote the letter for her to the governor,
and she signed it, and it was put into Alpatuitch's hands
with strict injunctions to hand it to the governor, and
in case the danger were urgent to return as soon as
possible.

Having received all his instructions, Alpatuitch, in a
white beaver hat, — a gift of the prince's, — with a cud-
gel exactly like that carried by the prince, went, escorted
by all the servants, to get into the leather-covered kibitka, to which a troïka of fat, roan steeds had been
attached.

The duga-bell was tied up, and the little harness bells
were stuffed with paper. The prince would not allow
bells to be used at Luisiya Gorui. But Alpatuitch liked
the sounds of them on a long journey. His fellow-ser-
vants, the *zemsky*, or communal scribe, the house clerk,
the pastry cook, and the scullery maid, two old women,
a young groom, the coachman, and a number of other
household serfs accompanied him.

His daughter stuffed back of the seat and under it
some down cushions covered with chintz. His wife's
sister, an old woman, stealthily thrust in a small bundle.
One of the coachmen helped him to get to his place.

"Well, well! women's fussiness! Oh! women, wo men!" he exclaimed, puffing and speaking in the same short, hurried way as the old prince did; and he took his place in the kibitka. Having given his last orders to the zemsky in regard to the work, Alpatuitch removed his hat from his bald head and crossed himself thrice — and in this respect he certainly did not imitate the prince.

"If anything should.... you.... you will hurry back, Yakof Alpatuitch; for Christ's sake, have pity on us!" screamed his wife, with a covert reference to the rumors of the war and the enemy.

"Oh, women, women! women's fussiness!" growled Alpatuitch to himself, and he rode away, glancing around him at the fields, some of which were covered with yellowing rye, others with thick crops of oats still green, others black where the men were just beginning to do the second plowing. He rode on, admiring the summer wheat, which gave an unusually abundant crop that year; then he gazed with delight at the rye-fields, where the reapers were already beginning to work, and he made mental calculations as to future sowing and gathering of crops, and wondered if he had forgotten any of the prince's commissions.

Having stopped twice on the road to bait his horses, Alpatuitch, on the sixteenth of August, reached the city.

On the way he met and passed wagon-trains and detachments of troops. As he approached Smolensk, he heard the sounds of distant firing, but these reports did not surprise him. He was more surprised than at anything else to see, in the vicinity of the city, tents pitched in the midst of a magnificent field of oats, which some soldiers were mowing apparently for the sake of fodder; this circumstance surprised Alpatuitch, but it quickly slipped his mind, which was absorbed in his own business.

All the interests of Alpatuitch's life had been for more than thirty years confined to fulfilling the prince's wishes, and he had never taken a step outside of this narrow circle. Everything that did not appertain to carrying out the prince's directions did not interest him, and might be said not even to exist for Alpatuitch.

Arriving on the evening of August sixteenth at Smolensk, Alpatuitch put up at an inn, kept by the dvornik Ferapontof, across the Dnieper, in the Gachensky suburb, where he had been in the habit of making his headquarters for the past thirty years. Ferapontof, thirty years before, had, with the connivance[1] of Alpatuitch, bought a piece of woodland of the prince, and begun to trade, and now he had a home of his own, a tavern, and a grain-shop in the province. Feropontof was a stout, dark-complexioned, good-looking muzhik, of middle age, with thick lips, and a thick, knobbed nose, and with knobs over his black, scowling brows, and with a portly belly.

Ferapontof was standing at the street-door of his shop, in his colored chintz shirt and waistcoat. Catching sight of Alpatuitch, he came out to meet him.

"Welcome, Yakof Alpatuitch. The people are leaving town, and here you are coming to town!" exclaimed the landlord.

"What do you mean? Leaving town?" asked Alpatuitch.

"I mean what I say. The people are fools. They're all afraid of a Frenchman!"

"Woman's chatter! woman's chatter!" grumbled Alpatuitch.

"That's my opinion, Yakof Alpatuitch. I tell 'em there's orders not to let *him* in; so, of course, *he* won't get in. And yet those muzhiks ask three rubles for a horse and cart. That isn't Christian of 'em!"

Yakof Alpatuitch paid little attention to what he said. He asked for a samovar, and some hay for his horses, and, after he had sipped his tea, he went to bed.

All night long the troops went tramping by the tavern along the street. The next morning Alpatuitch put on his kamzol, which he always wore only in town, and set

[1] *Legkaya ruka :* literally, 'light hand.'

forth to do his errands. The morning was sunny, and at eight o'clock it was already hot. A fine day for the wheat-harvest, as Alpatuitch considered. Beyond the city the sounds of firing had been audible since early morning. About eight o'clock a heavy cannonading made itself heard in addition to the musketry.

The streets were crowded with people hurrying to and fro; there were many soldiers; but, just as usual, izvoshchiks were driving about, merchants were standing at their shop doors, and the morning service was going on in the churches.

Alpatuitch did his errands at the shops, at the government offices, at the post-office, and at the governor's. At the government offices, at the shops, at the post-office, everywhere, every one was talking of the war and the enemy, who was even now making his descent upon the city. Every one was asking every one else what was to be done, and every one was trying to reassure every one else.

At the governor's house, Alpatuitch found a great throng of people, Cossacks, and a traveling carriage belonging to the governor. On the doorstep Yakof Alpatuitch met two of the local gentry, one of whom he knew. The nobleman whom he knew, a former *ispravnik*, or district captain of police, was talking with some heat.

"But I tell you this is no joke!" he was saying. "It's very well for a man who is alone. One can endure to be single and poor; but to have thirteen in your family, and your whole property at stake!.... What do the authorities amount to if they let such things come on us? Ekh! they ought to hang such cutthroats...."

"There, there! they'll hear you!" said the other.

"What difference does it make to me; let them hear! Why, we are not dogs!" said the ex-ispravnik, and, looking round, he caught sight of Alpatuitch: —

"Ah! Yakof Alpatuitch, what brings you here?"

"On an errand from his illustriousness to the governor," replied Alpatuitch, proudly lifting his head, and placing his hand in the breast of his coat — which he always did when he remembered the prince. "He sent me to ascertain the position of affairs," said he.

"Well, then, ascertain it," cried the proprietor. "Not a cart to be had — nothing !.... There, do you hear that ?" he exclaimed, calling their attention to the direction in which the firing could be heard. "That's the pass they've brought us to! ruining us all .... the cutthroats!" he muttered again, and turned down the steps.

Alpatuitch shook his head, and went up-stairs. In the reception-room were merchants, women, chinovniks, silently exchanging glances. The door into the governor's cabinet was opened, and all stood up and crowded forward. Out of the room hurried a chinovnik, exchanged some words with a merchant, beckoned to a stout chinovnik, with a cross around his neck, to follow him, and again disappeared behind the door, evidently avoiding all the glances and questions that followed him.

Alpatuitch pressed forward, and, when the chinovnik came out again, placing his hand under the breast of his overcoat, he addressed the official, and handed him the two letters.

"For the Baron Asch, from General-in-Chief Prince Bolkonsky," he said, so solemnly and significantly that the chinovnik turned round to him and took the letters. At the end of a few moments the governor summoned Alpatuitch, and said to him hurriedly : —

"Inform the prince and the princess that I knew nothing about it at all. I have been acting in accordance with superior instructions. — Here !" ....

He gave a paper to Alpatuitch.

"However, as the prince is ill, my advice to him is to go to Moscow. I am going there myself .... immediately. Tell him .... "

But the governor did not finish his sentence ; an officer, breathless and covered with sweat, came rushing in, and hurriedly said something in French. An expression of horror crossed the governor's face.

"Go," said he, nodding to Alpatuitch ; and then he began to ply the officer with questions. Pitiful, fright-

ened, helpless glances followed Alpatuitch as he came
out of the governor's cabinet. Involuntarily listening
now to the cannonading, constantly growing nearer and
more violent, Alpatuitch hastened back to the inn.

The paper which the governor had given him was as
follows : —

I assure you that the city of Smolensk is not in the slightest
danger, and it is entirely unlikely that it will be threatened.
I, on the one hand, and Prince Bagration, on the other, shall
effect a junction before Smolensk ; and this will take place on
the 2d instant, and the two armies, with united forces, will defend their fellow-countrymen of the government committed to
your charge, until their efforts shall have driven away the foes
of the fatherland, or until the last warrior shall have perished
from their gallant ranks. You will see from this that you have
a perfect right to calm the inhabitants of Smolensk, since any
one defended by two such brave armies may well be confident
that victory will be theirs.[1]

The inhabitants were roaming restlessly about the
streets.

Teams, loaded to repletion with domestic utensils,
chairs, clothes-presses, and furniture of every description, were coming out of the courtyard gates of the
houses and proceeding along the streets. At the house
next Ferapontof's stood a number of teams, and the
women were bidding one another good-by, and exchanging parting gossip. The house-dog was barking and
frisking around the heads of the horses.

Alpatuitch, with a brisker gait than he usually took,
went into the courtyard and proceeded directly to the
barn where his team and horses were. The coachman
was asleep ; he aroused him, told him to hitch up, and
went into the house. In the landlord's room were
heard the wailing of a child, the broken sobs of a
woman, and Ferapontof's furious, harsh tones. The
cook, fluttering about the bar-room like a frightened hen,
cried as soon as she saw Alpatuitch : —

"He's been beating her to death.... been beating

[1] Order of the day, from Barclay de Tolly to Baron Asch, the civil governor of Smolensk, 1812.

the missis!.... He just beat her, and dragged her round!"....

"What made him do it?" asked Alpatuitch.

"She begged him to go! Just like a woman! 'Take us away,' says she, 'don't let 'em kill me and the little ones; everybody,' says she, ''s going, and why,' says she, 'should n't we go too?' And so he began to beat her. He just thrashed her and dragged her round!"

Alpatuitch nodded his head as if he approved, and, not caring to hear any more about it, went to the room where his purchases had been left. It was opposite the landlord's family room.

"You villain, you wretch!" at this moment cried a thin, pale woman, with a baby in her arms, and with a torn kerchief on her head, who came rushing out of that room, and flew down-stairs into the court.

Ferapontof came out behind her, and when he saw Alpatuitch, he pulled down his waistcoat, smoothed his hair, and followed Alpatuitch into the room.

"And so you are going so soon?" he asked.

Not paying any attention to this question, and not looking at the landlord, Alpatuitch, after making a bundle of his purchases, asked how much he should pay for the accommodation.

"We will settle that by and by. How was it at the governor's?" asked Ferapontof. "What was the talk there?"

Alpatuitch replied that the governor had not said anything very decisive to him.

"How can we possibly get away with our things?" Why, they ask seven rubles to go to Dorogobuzh! And I tell you there's mighty little Christianity about them!" said he. "Selivanof made a good thing Thursday, sold some flour to the army at nine rubles a sack. Say, will you drink some tea?" he added.

While the horses were being put to, Alpatuitch and Ferapontof sipped their tea and talked about the price of wheat, about the crops, and the splendid weather for harvest.

"Well, it seems to be calming down a little," said Ferapontof, getting up after his three cups of tea. "Ours must have had the best of it. They told us they would not let 'em in. Of course we're strong enough. They say Matvyeï Ivanuitch Platof drove eighteen thousand of 'em into the Marina t'other day and drowned 'em all."

Alpatuitch picked up his purchases and gave them to the coachman, who came in; then he settled his account with the landlord. The sound of carriage-wheels was heard outside the door, the trampling of the horses, and the jingling of bells, as the kibitka drove up.

By this time it was far into the afternoon. One side of the street was in shadow; the other was brightly lighted by the sun. Alpatuitch glanced out of the window, and went to the door. Suddenly he heard the strange sound of a distant whizzing, and a dull thud, immediately followed by the long reverberating roar of a cannon, which made the windows rattle.

Alpatuitch went out into the street; a couple of men were running down toward the bridge. In various directions could be heard the whistling and crashing of round shot, and the bursting of bombshells falling into the city. But these sounds attracted little attention among the citizens compared with the roar of the cannonading heard beyond the city. This was the bombardment which Napoleon commanded to be opened at five o'clock, from one hundred and thirty cannon. The people at first did not realize the significance of this bombardment. The crash of falling shells and cannon-balls at first wakened only curiosity. Ferapontof's wife, who had been steadily wailing and weeping in the barn, dried her tears, and came out to the gates with her baby in her arms, and gazed silently at the people and listened to the noise.

The cook and the shop-tender came down to the gates. All looked with eager curiosity at the projectiles flying over their heads. Around the corner came several men, talking with great animation.

"What force there was!" one was saying. "Smashed the roof and the ceiling all into kindling-wood."

"And it plowed up the ground just like a hog!" said another.

"It was a good shot! Lively work!" said he, with a laugh.

"You had to look out mighty sharp and jump, else 't would have smeared you!"

The people gathered round these men. They stopped and told how shots had been falling into a house near them. Meantime, other projectiles, now round shot, with a pleasant whistling, now shells, with a swift, melancholy hissing, kept flying over the heads of the people. But not a single projectile fell near them; all flew over and beyond. Alpatuitch took his seat in his kibitka. The landlord was standing at his gates.

"You are showing too much!" he cried to the cook, who, with sleeves rolled up above her bare elbows, and holding up her red petticoat, had gone down to the corner to hear the news.

"But it was miraculous," she was just saying, but when she heard the sound of the landlord's voice she turned round and let her petticoat drop.

Once more, but very near this time, came something with a whistling sound, like a bird flying toward the ground; there was a flash of fire in the middle of the street, a loud, stunning crash, and the street was filled with smoke.

"You rascal, what did you do that for?" cried the landlord, rushing down to the cook.

At the same instant, the pitiful screaming of women was heard on various sides; a child wailed in terror, and the people gathered in silence with pale faces round the cook. Above all other sounds were heard the groans and exclamations of the cook.

"Oï-o-okh! my darlings! my poor darlings! Don't let them kill me! My poor darlings!"

Five minutes later, not a soul was left in the street. The cook, whose thigh had been broken by a fragment of the bomb, was carried into the kitchen. Alpatuitch, his coachman, and Ferapontof's wife and children and the hostler, were cowering in the cellar, with ears alert. The roar of cannon, the whistle of projectiles, and the pitiful groans of the cook, which overmastered all else, ceased not for a single instant. The landlord's wife rocked and crooned her infant at one moment, and at the next she would ask in a terrified whisper of all who came down into the cellar where her husband, who had remained in the street, was.

The shop-tender came down into the cellar, and reported that her husband had gone with the crowd to the cathedral to get the wonder-working ikon of Smolensk.

Toward twilight, the cannonade began to grow less violent. Alpatuitch went out of the cellar and stood in the doorway. The evening sky, which before had been cloudless, was now shrouded in smoke. And through this smoke strangely shone the sickle of the young moon high in the west. After the cessation of the terrible roar of the cannon, silence fell upon the city, broken only by what seemed to be a constantly increasing rumble of hurrying steps, groans, distant shouts, and the crackling of flames. The cook's groaning had ceased. In two different directions, volumes of black smoke arose from the conflagrations and spread over the city. Soldiers in various uniforms, mixed all in together, no longer in orderly ranks, but like ants from a demolished ant-hill, came running and walking from various directions down the street. It seemed to Alpatuitch that some of them were making for Ferapontof's tavern. Alpatuitch went down to the gates. A regiment marching in serried ranks and hurrying along blocked the street from side to side.

"The city is surrendered! Off with you! off with you!" cried an officer who noticed him, and then he turned to his soldiers: "Loot the yards if you want," he cried.

Alpatuitch went back to the tavern, and, summoning the coachman, bade him start away. Alpatuitch and the coachmen were followed by all Ferapontof's household. When they saw the smoke and the even flames of the burning buildings which now began to blaze up in the gathering gloom, the women, till now perfectly silent, suddenly unloosed their tongues as they looked at the conflagrations; as it were echoing them, rose similar lamentations at the other end of the street. Alpatuitch and the coachman, with trembling hands, straightened the tangled reins and traces under the shed.

As Alpatuitch drove out of the gates, he saw half a score of soldiers in Ferapontof's open shop, with loud discussion, engaged in filling bags and knapsacks with wheaten flour and sunflower seeds. Just at that time Ferapontof himself happened to come into his shop from the street. When he saw the soldiers, he started to give them some abuse; but suddenly paused, and, clutching his hair, he broke out into laughter that was like a lamentation.

"Take it all, boys. Don't leave any for those devils," he cried, grasping the bags himself, and helping to fling them out into the street. Some of the soldiers, frightened, ran away; others still continued to fill their sacks. Seeing Alpatuitch, Ferapontof called to him: —

"It 's all up with Roosha,"[1] he shouted. "Alpatuitch, it 's all up with us! I myself helped set the fires. .... All ruined!"

Ferapontof started into the courtyard.

The passing regiments so completely blocked the street that Alpatuitch could not make his way along, and he had to wait. Ferapontof's wife and family also were seated in a telyega, waiting for a chance to get away.

Night had now fully come. The sky was studded with stars, and occasionally the young moon gleamed out from behind the billows of smoke. On the slope down towards the Dnieper, the teams of Alpatuitch and the landlord, which had at last been slowly advancing amid the ranks of soldiery and other equipages, were obliged to halt. A short distance from the cross-roads where the teams had halted, a house and some shops were

---

[1] He calls it *Rasseya* instead of *Rossiya*.

burning on the side street.   The fire was burning itself
out.   The flame would die down and lose itself in black
smoke, then suddenly flash forth brilliantly again, bringing out with strange distinctness the faces of the specta-
tors standing on the cross-roads.   In front of the fire,
the dark forms of men were darting to and fro, and
above the still audible crackling of the fire were heard
shouts and cries.   Alpatuitch, dismounting from his
kibitka, as he saw that he should not be able to proceed
for some time yet, walked down the cross-street to look
at the conflagration.   Soldiers were constantly busying
themselves with the fire, passing back and forth, and
Alpatuitch saw two soldiers, in company with another
man in a frieze coat, dragging from the fire some burning
lumber across the street into the next dvor ; others were
adding fagots of straw.

Alpatuitch joined the great throng of people who
were standing in front of a tall warehouse that was one
mass of roaring flames.   The walls were all on fire, the
rear had fallen in, the timbered roof was giving way,
the girders were blazing.   The throng were evidently
waiting for the roof to cave in.   At all events, that was
what Alpatuitch was waiting for.

"Alpatuitch !"

A well-known voice suddenly called the old man by
name.

"Batyushka! your illustriousness!" replied Alpatuitch, instantly recognizing the voice of his young
prince.

Prince Andreï, in a riding-cloak, and mounted on a
black horse, was stationed beyond the crowd and looking
straight at Alpatuitch.

"How are you here?" he asked.

"Your.... your illustriousness," stammered Alpatuitch, and he sobbed.   "Your — your.... I — I.... is ....
are we lost?   Your father...."

"How are you here?" demanded Prince Andreï a
second time.

The flame blazed out again at that moment and
revealed to Alpatuitch his young barin's pale, weary face.

Alpatuitch told how he had been sent and what difficulty he had met with in getting out of town.

"But tell me, your illustriousness, are we really lost?" he asked once more.

Prince Andreï, without replying, drew out a note-book, and, spreading it on his knee, hastily penciled a few lines on a torn leaf. He wrote his sister: —

Smolensk is abandoned; Luisiya Gorui will be occupied by the enemy inside of a week. Go immediately to Moscow. Send me word as soon as you start, by an express to Usviazh.

Having written this note and handed it to Alpatuitch, he was giving him some verbal instructions about the arrangements for the journey of the prince and princess and his son and the tutor, and how and where to communicate with him immediately. He had not had time to finish these instructions when a mounted staff nachalnik accompanied by a suite came galloping up to him.

"You, a colonel?" cried the staff nachalnik in a German accent and a voice that Prince Andreï instantly recognized. "In your very presence they are setting houses on fire, and you allow it? What is the meaning of this? You shall answer for it!"

This was Berg, who now had the position of deputy chief of staff to the deputy chief of staff of the nachalnik of the infantry corps of the left flank of the first division of the army [1] — a place which was very agreeable and "in sight," as Berg expressed it.

Prince Andreï glanced at him, and, without replying, went on with his instructions to Alpatuitch: —

"Tell them that I shall expect an answer by the twenty-second, and that if by the twenty-second I do not get word that they have all gone, I myself shall be obliged to throw up everything and go to Luisiya Gorui."

"I — prince, I only spoke as I did," exclaimed Berg, as soon as he recognized Prince Andreï, "because, because it is my duty to carry out my orders, and I am

[1] *Pomyeshchik nachalnika shtaba pomyeshchika nachalnika shtaba na-chalnika Dlyevava flanka pyekhotnuikh voïsk pyervoï armii.*

always very scrupulous in carrying them out. .... I beg
you to excuse me," said Berg, trying to apologize.

There was a crash in the burning building.   The fire
for an instant died down ; volumes of black smoke rolled
up from the roof.   Again there was a strange crashing
sound in the fire and something enormous fell in.

"Urroorooroo!" yelled the throng, with a roar rival-
ing that of the fallen grain-house, from which now
came an odor like hot cakes, caused by the burning
flour.   The flames darted up and sent a bright reflection
over the throng standing around the fire with gleefully
excited or exhausted faces.

The man in the frieze coat waved his arm and cried : —

"Well done! she draws well now! Well done,
boys!".....

"That's the owner himself," various voices were
heard saying.

"So then," said Prince Andreï, addressing Alpatuitch,
"give the message just as I have told you," and, not
vouchsafing a single word to Berg, who silently stood
near, he set spurs to his horse and rode down the side
street.

CHAPTER V

THE armies continued to retreat from Smolensk.
The enemy followed.   On the twenty-second of August
the regiment which Prince Andreï commanded was
moving along the highroad past the "prospekt" which
led to Luisiya Gorui.

For more than three weeks there had been a hot
spell and drought.   Each day cirrus clouds moved
across the sky and occasionally veiled the sun ; but by
evening the heavens were clear again, and the sun set
in brownish purple haze.   The only refreshing that the
earth got was from the heavy dew at night.   The standing crops of wheat were parched, and wasted their seed.
The marshes dried up.   The cattle bellowed from
hunger, finding no pasturage along the ponds, which

had shrunk to nothing in the sun. Only at night and in the depths of the forest, before the dew evaporated, was there any freshness.

But on the roads, on the highroad where the troops were marching, even at night, even in the shelter of the forests, this coolness was not to be found. The dew was imperceptible on the sandy dust, which was more than a quarter of an arshin deep.

At the first ray of dawn the troops were set in motion. The baggage train and the field-pieces plowed along noiselessly, sinking almost up to the hubs of the wheels, and the infantry struggled through the soft, stifling, heated dust which settled not even at night. One part of this sandy dust impeded feet and wheels; the other arose in the air and hovered like a cloud over the troops, filling eyes, hair, ears, and nostrils, and above all the lungs, of men and beasts alike as they moved slowly along this highway. The higher the sun rose, the higher rose this cloud of dust; and, though the sky was cloudless, the naked eye could endure to look at the sun through this curtain of fine hot dust.

The sun looked like a great purple ball. There was not a breath of air stirring, and the men suffocated in the motionless atmosphere. They tramped along, covering their noses and mouths with handkerchiefs. If they reached a village, they rushed pell-mell for the wells. They fought for water, and drank it every drop till nothing but mud was left.

Prince Andreï was the commander of the regiment, and deeply concerned in its organization and the well-being of his men, and the carrying out of the urgent orders which had to be given and received. The burning of Smolensk and its abandonment marked an epoch in his life. The new feeling of hatred against the enemy made him forget his own personal sorrow. He devoted himself exclusively to the affairs of his command; he was indefatigable in the service of his men and his subordinate officers, and was courteous to them. In the regiment they all called him "*our prince*"; they were proud of him and loved him.

But his kindness and affability were only for his own men — Timokhin and the like, men who were perfect strangers to him and his life, men who could not know him or recall his past; the moment he fell in with any of his former acquaintances, his fellow staff-officers, he immediately became all bristles; he grew fierce, sarcastic, and scornful. Everything that served as a connection with the past revolted him, and consequently in his relations with this former society he simply tried not to be unjust and to do his duty.

It is true, everything appeared to Prince Andreï gloomy and even desperate, especially after the eighteenth of August and the abandonment of Smolensk, — which in his opinion might and should have been defended — and after his sick father had been forced to fly to Moscow, and consign to spoliation his too-well-beloved Luisiya Gorui, which he had taken such pains to cultivate and settle; but, in spite of this, thanks to Prince Andreï's occupation with his regiment, he could let his mind be engrossed with other thoughts, entirely disconnected with the general course of events; namely, his regiment.

On the twenty-second of August the column of which his regiment formed a part was opposite Luisiya Gorui. Prince Andreï, two days before, had received word that his father, his little son, and his sister had gone to Moscow. Although there was nothing to call him to Luisiya Gorui, he determined that it was his duty to go there, feeling a peculiar morbid desire to enjoy the bitterness of his grief.

He ordered his horse to be saddled, and started off to ride to the estate where he had been born and had spent his childhood.

As he rode by the pond, where generally there were a dozen chattering women beating and rinsing their linens, Prince Andreï noticed that it was deserted, and the little float had drifted out into the middle of the pond, and was tipped over and half full of water. Prince Andreï rode up to the gatekeeper's lodge; but there was no one near the stone gateway, and the door was unlocked. The garden paths were already overgrown, and calves and horses were wandering about the " English park." Prince Andreï went to the orangery ; the panes of glass were broken ; some of the tubs were overturned; some of the trees were dried up.

He shouted to Taras, the gardener. No one replied. Passing around the orangery, he saw that the carved deal fence was broken down, and the plum trees were stripped of their fruit. An old muzhik — Prince Andreï had seen him in his childhood at the gates — was plaiting bast shoes as he sat on the green-painted bench.

He was deaf, and did not hear Prince Andreï approach. He was sitting on the bench which had been the old prince's favorite seat, and near him, on the branches of a broken and dried-up magnolia, hung his strips of bast.

Prince Andreï went to the house. Some of the linden trees in the old park had been felled ; a piebald mare, with her colt, was browsing in front of the house itself, among the rose bushes. The window-shutters were closed. One window only, on the ground floor, was open. A little peasant lad, catching sight of Prince Andreï, ran into the house.

Alpatuitch, having got the household away, was the only one left at Luisiya Gorui. He was sitting in the house, and reading "The Lives of the Saints." When he heard that Prince Andreï had come, he came out, with his spectacles on his nose, buttoning up his clothes, and hurried up to the prince, and, before he said a word, burst into tears, kissing Prince Andreï's knee.

Then he turned away, angry at his own weakness, and began to give him an account of the state of affairs. Everything of any value and worth had been despatched to Bogucharovo. One hundred chetverts [1] of wheat had also been sent; the crops of hay and corn, which, according to Alpatuitch, had been wonderful that year, had been taken standing and carried off by the troops. The peasantry were all ruined ; some had gone to Bogucharovo, a very few were left.

Prince Andreï, without heeding what he said, asked

[1] A chetvert is 5.77 bushels.

when his father and sister had left, meaning when had they gone to Moscow. Alpatuitch, supposing he knew that they had gone to Bogucharovo, replied that they had started on the nineteenth, and then again began to enlarge on the condition of the estate, and ask what arrangements he should make.

"Do you order to let them have the oats in return for a receipt? We have still six hundred chetverts left," said Alpatuitch.

"What answer shall I give him?" queried Prince Andreï, looking down at the bald head gleaming in the sun, and reading in the expression of his face a consciousness that the old man himself realized the incongruity of such questions, but asked them simply for the sake of drowning his own sorrow.

"Yes, do so," said he.

"If you will deign to notice the disorder in the garden," pursued Alpatuitch; "but it was impossible to prevent it: three regiments came and camped here for the night. The dragoons especially — I took down the rank and the name of the commander, so as to lodge a complaint."

"Well, but what are you going to do? Shall you remain if the enemy come?" asked Prince Andreï.

Alpatuitch, turning his face full on Prince Andreï, looked at him. And then suddenly, with a solemn gesture, he raised his hands to heaven. "He is my protector; His will be done!" he exclaimed.

A throng of muzhiks and household serfs came trooping across the meadow, and approached Prince Andreï with uncovered heads.

"Well, prashchaï — farewell," said Prince Andreï, bending down to Alpatuitch. "Escape yourself, take what you can, and tell the people to go to the Riazan property, or our pod-Moskovnaya."

Alpatuitch pressed up against his leg, and sobbed. Prince Andreï gently pushed him away, and, giving spurs to his horse, rode at a gallop down the driveway.

To all appearance as impassive as a fly on the face of a dear dead friend, still sat the old man, and thumped

on his shoe-last.   Two young girls, with their skirts
full of plums, which they had gathered from the trees,
were coming away from the orangery, and met Prince
Andreï.   When they saw their young barin, the older
of the two girls, with an expression of terror on her face,
seized her little companion by the hand, and the two hid
behind a birch tree, without having time to gather up
the green plums that had fallen from their skirts.

Prince Andreï, with a feeling of compunction, hastened to look the other way, so that they might think
he had not seen them.   He felt sorry to have frightened
the pretty little girl.   He was afraid to look at them,
but, at the same time, he had an overwhelming desire
to do so.   A new, joyful, and tranquilizing sense took
possession of him at the sight of these little girls ; he
recognized that there existed other human interests
entirely apart from his, and yet just as lawful as those
with which he was occupied.   These two young girls
had evidently only one passionate desire — to carry off
and eat those green plums, and not be found out ; and
Prince Andreï sympathized with them, and hoped for
the success of their enterprise.   He could not refrain
from looking back at them once more.

Supposing that their peril was happily past, they had
sprung out from their hiding-place, and, shouting something in shrill voices, they were running gayly across
the meadow as fast as their bare, sun-burned little legs
would take them.

Prince Andreï felt somewhat refreshed by his digres-
sion from the dusty highroad, where the troops had
been marching.   But not very far from Luisiya Gorui
he again struck the main thoroughfare, and found his
own regiment halting on the embankment of a small
pond.

It was about two o'clock in the afternoon.   The sun,
shining through the dust like a red ball, was unendurably
hot, and burned his back under his black coat.   The
dust still hung like a cloud over the companies while
they halted amid a hum of voices.   There was no wind.
As Prince Andreï rode along the embankment, he caught

the faint scent of the mud and fresh coolness of the pond.
He felt an inclination to take a plunge into the water,
muddy as it was.   He gazed at the pond, from which
rose the sounds of shouts and laughter.   The little sheet,
muddy, and green with slime, had evidently risen an
inch or two, and was now washing up against the embankment, simply because it was full of human bodies,
— the bare bodies of soldiers floundering about in it,
their white skins making vivid contrast to their brick-
red arms, faces, and necks.   All this mass of bare human
flesh was wriggling about, with shouts and laughter, in
that filthy water, like carps flopping in a scoop.   This
wriggling carried the name of enjoyment, and for that
very reason it was particularly melancholy.

One light-complexioned young soldier — Prince Andreï
had already noticed him — of the third company, with a
leather string around his calf, crossed himself, stepped
back a little so as to get a good start, and dived into the
water ; another man, a dark-complexioned non-commissioned officer, with rumpled hair, was up to his middle
in the water, ducking his muscular form, and, snorting
joyfully, was pouring the water over his head from hands
black even to the wrists.   There was a sound of splashing and yelling and grunting.

On the shores, on the embankment, in the pond itself,
everywhere, was the spectacle of white, healthy, muscular human flesh.   The officer, Timokhin, with his short,
red nose, was rubbing himself down with a towel on the
embankment, and was rather ashamed at seeing the
prince ; however, he addressed him : —

"Pretty good, your illustriousness ; you ought to try
it," said he.

"Dirty," said Prince Andreï, making up a face.

"We will have it cleared out for you, in a moment."
And Timokhin, still undressed, ran down to the water,
shouting, "The prince wants a bath."

"What prince ?   Ours ?" shouted various voices, and
all were so zealous that Prince Andreï had some difficulty in appeasing them.   He felt that he would much
rather take a bath in a barn.

"Flesh, body! cannon-meat!" said he to himself, as he looked down at his bare body, and he trembled, not so much from chill as from his aversion and horror, incomprehensible even to himself, at the sight of that monstrous mass of bodies rinsing themselves in that filthy pond.

On the nineteenth of August, Prince Bagration, at his encampment of Mikhaïlovko on the Smolensk highway, had written the following letter to Arakcheyef; but he knew that it would be read by the sovereign, and, consequently, he weighed every word to the very best of his ability : —

My dear Count Alekseï Andrevevitch : — I suppose the minister has already reported to you concerning the surrender of Smolensk to the enemy. It is saddening and painful, and the whole army are in despair that such an important place should have been abandoned to no purpose. I, for my part, personally besought him most earnestly, and at last even wrote him. I swear on my honor that never before was Napoleon "in such a box," and he might have lost half of his army, but he could not have taken Smolensk. Our troops have been and still are fighting as never before. I held out with fifteen thousand men for more than thirty-five hours, and beat them, but *he* was not willing to wait even fourteen hours. It is a shame and a blot on our army, and methinks he ought not to live in this world. If he reports that our losses are heavy, it is false — possibly four thousand, not more than that ; even if it had been ten thousand, what would it have been? This is war. But, to offset it, the enemy lost a host.

What was to prevent him holding out two days longer? Without question they would have been forced to give it up; they had no water for men and horses. He gave me his word that he would not give way, but suddenly he sent me word that he was going to desert the city by night. We cannot make war in such a way, and we shall soon be having the enemy at Moscow. ....

There is a rumor prevalent that you are contemplating peace. Peace? God forbid ! After all our sacrifices, and after such an idiotic retreat, the idea of making peace ! You will have all Russia against you, and we shall all be ashamed of wearing the

Russian uniform. Since things have gone as far as they have, we must fight as long as Russia can, and so long as we have a man alive. ....

It is essential that one man and not two should have supreme command. Your minister is perhaps excellent in the ministry, but as a general it is not enough to say that he is bad ! he is abominable ! and yet in his hands is intrusted the fate of our whole country. ....

I assure you I am beside myself with vexation ; forgive me for writing so frankly. It is plain to my mind that any one who advises peace, and approves of confiding the command of the troops to the minister, is no true friend to the sovereign, and wishes to involve us all in a common destruction. And so I write you the truth. Arm the militia ! Here the minister, in the most masterly fashion, is conducting his guests to the capital.

Mr. Woltzogen, the flügel-adjutant, is giving the army great cause for suspicion. They say he is even less favorable to us than Napoleon himself, and that he inspires all that the minister does.

I am not merely polite to him, I am as obedient as a corporal, although I am older than he is. It is painful, but, as I love my sovereign and benefactor, I submit. Only I am sorry that the sovereign should intrust him with such a glorious army. Imagine ! In our retreat we have lost more than fifteen thousand through fatigue and in hospitals ; now, if we had attacked the enemy, this would not have happened. For God's sake, tell me what will our Russia — our mother — say? She will ask why we are such cowards, and why we have handed over such a good and glorious country to villains, and why we stir up hatred and humiliation in the heart of every subject. What should make us cowards? Whom do we fear? It is not my fault that the minister is irresolute, cowardly, dull of apprehension, dilatory, and has all the worst qualities. The whole army is entirely discouraged, and load him with execrations.

CHAPTER VI

AMONG the numberless subdivisions into which the phenomena of life may be disposed, you may place them all in a category where substance predominates, or into another where form predominates. A contrast of this kind may be observed between life in the country, in the village, in the governmental town — nay, even in Moscow, and that which can be seen at Petersburg, and especially in the Petersburg salons. This sort of life goes on always the same.

Since 1805 we had been quarreling and making up with Bonaparte; we had been making constitutions and unmaking them, but Anna Pavlovna's salon and Ellen's salon were exactly the same as they had been seven years before and five years before. Just exactly as before, at Anna Pavlovna's, they were amazed and perplexed at Bonaparte's successes, and detected, not only in his successes, but also in the subservience of the sovereigns of Europe, a wicked conspiracy, the sole object of which was to disgust and alarm the courtly circle that regarded Anna Pavlovna as its representative.

And just exactly the same way at Ellen's (where Rumyantsof himself was gracious enough to be a frequent visitor, considering her a remarkably intelligent woman), in 1812 as in 1808, they talked with enthusiasm of the "great nation" and the "great man," and regretted the rupture with the French, which in the opinion of the *habitués* of Ellen's salon ought to end with peace.

Latterly, since the sovereign's departure from the army, these rival *clique-salons* were the scenes of some excitement; and demonstrations of mutual hostility were made, but the general characteristics of the two cliques remained the same.

Anna Pavlovna's clique received no Frenchmen, except a few inveterate legitimists. It was here originated the patriotic idea of people being in duty bound to stay away from the French theater, and the criticism was made that it cost as much to maintain the troupe as to maintain a whole army corps. Here the course of military affairs was eagerly followed, and the most advantageous reports of our armies found ready credence.

In Ellen's clique, where Rumyantsof and the French were in favor, the reports as to the barbarities of the enemy and of the war were contradicted, and all Napoleon's overtures for reconciliation were discussed. In this clique they reproached those who showed what they considered too great haste in making preparations to remove to Kazan, the "Imperial Institute for the education of young ladies of the nobility," the patroness of which was the empress-dowager. As a rule those who frequented Ellen's salon regarded the war merely as an empty demonstration, which would be very quickly followed by peace, and here they made great use of a witticism of Bilibin's, — who was now a frequent visitor at Ellen's, as indeed it behooved every clever man to be, — to the effect that the affair should be settled not by gunpowder, but by the man who invented it.[1]

This clique in an ironical, witty, though always guarded, manner made sport of the enthusiasm at Moscow, news of which had arrived at Petersburg simultaneously with the return of the sovereign.

Anna Pavlovna's clique, on the contrary, were enraptured with this enthusiasm, and spoke of the acts of the Moscovites as Plutarch speaks of the glorious deeds of antiquity.

Prince Vasili, who, just the same as of yore, held important functions, formed a bond of union between the two cliques.

He was equally at home with *ma bonne amie*, Anna Pavlovna, and in the *salon diplomatique de ma fille;* and frequently, owing to his constant visits from one camp to the other, he got confused, and said at Ellen's what he should have said at Anna Pavlovna's, and *vice versa*.

Shortly after the sovereign's arrival, Prince Vasili was at Anna Pavlovna's, conversing about the war, sharply criticizing Barclay de Tolly, and frankly confessing his doubt as to the fit person to call to the head of the armies.

One of the visitors, who was known as the man of great merit, mentioning the fact that he had that day seen Kutuzof, the newly appointed chief of the Peters-burg militia, at the Court of Exchequer, enrolling vol-

---

[1] *Il n'a pas inventé la poudre:* He will never set the Thames on fire The Russian idiom is similar.

unteers, allowed himself cautiously to suggest that Kutuzof would be the man to satisfy all demands.

Anna Pavlovna smiled sadly, and remarked that Kutuzof caused the sovereign nothing but unpleasantness.

"I have said, and I have said in the chamber of nobles," interrupted Prince Vasili, "but they would not heed me, — I have said that his election as commandant of the militia would not please the sovereign. They would not listen to me. It is this everlasting mania for petty intrigue," pursued Prince Vasili. "And for what purpose? Simply because we want to ape that stupid Moscow enthusiasm," said Prince Vasili, becoming confused for a moment, and forgetting that it was at Ellen's where it was considered correct to make sport of Moscow enthusiasm, but the fashion to praise it at Anna Pavlovna's. But he instantly corrected himself.

"Now, then, is it fit for Count Kutuzof, Russia's oldest general, to be holding such sessions at the court? and that's as far as he will get. Is it possible to make a man commander-in-chief who cannot sit a horse, who dozes during council meetings, — a man of the worst possible manners? He won a fine reputation for himself at Bukarest! And I have nothing to say about his qualities as a general; but is it possible, under present circumstances, to nominate to such a place a man who is decrepit and blind, simply blind? A blind general would be a fine thing! He can't see anything at all! He might play blind-man's-buff — but, really, he can't see anything!"

No one raised any objection to this.

On the fifteenth of August this was perfectly correct. But, five days later, Kutuzof was made a prince. This advance in dignities might also signify that they wanted to shelve him, and, therefore, Prince Vasili's criticism would continue to be well received, although he was not so eager to deliver himself of it. But, on the twentieth of August, a committee was summoned, composed of Field-Marshal Saltuikof, Arakcheyef, Viazmitinof, Lopukhin, and Kotchubey, to consider the con duct of the war. The committee decided that the failures were attributable to the division of command; and, although the individuals composing the committee well knew the sovereign's dislike of Kutuzof, they determined, after a brief deliberation, to place him at the head of the armies.

And, on that same day, Kutuzof was made plenipotentiary commander-in-chief of the armies, and of the whole district occupied by the troops.

On the twenty-first, Prince Vasili and "the man of great merit" met again at Anna Pavlovna's. "The man of great merit" was dancing attendance on Anna Pavlovna, with the hope of securing the appointment of trustee to a woman's educational institute.

Prince Vasili entered the drawing-room with the air of a rejoicing conqueror who had reached the goal of all his ambitions.

"Well, you know the great news: Prince Kutuzof is appointed field-marshal. All discords are at an end! I am so happy, so glad!" exclaimed Prince Vasili. "There's a man for you!" he added, with significant emphasis, surveying all in the room with a stern glance.

"The man of great merit," in spite of his anxiety to obtain a place, could not refrain from reminding Prince Vasili of his former criticism. This was an act of discourtesy both toward Prince Vasili, in Anna Pavlovna's drawing-room, and toward Anna Pavlovna herself, who had also been greatly delighted with the news; but he could not refrain.

"But it is said that he is blind, prince," he suggested, quoting Prince Vasili's own words.

"Oh, pshaw! he sees well enough," replied Prince Vasili, in quick, deep tones, and clearing his throat — with the same voice and the same clearing of the throat which he always used in getting himself out of an awkward situation. "Certainly he sees well enough," he repeated. "And what makes me glad," he went on to say, "is that the sovereign has given him full powers over all the forces, and over the whole district — such

powers as never commander-in-chief enjoyed before.
This makes him the second autocrat," he said, in con
clusion, with a triumphant smile.

"God grant it, God grant it," said Anna Pavlovna.

"The man of great merit," who was still somewhat
of a novice in courtly circles, wishing to flatter Anna
Pavlovna by taking the ground which she had formerly
taken in regard to the same subject, said: —

"They say it went against the sovereign's heart to
allow these powers to Kutuzof. They say that Kutuzof
blushed like a school-girl hearing 'Joconde,' when the
emperor said: 'The sovereign and your country confer
this honor on you.'"

"Possibly his heart had nothing to do with it," said
Anna Pavlovna.

"Oh, no, certainly not," hotly cried Prince Vasili, coming to his defense. He could not now allow any one to
surpass him in his zeal for Kutuzof. According to his
idea at the present time, not only was Kutuzof himself
the best of men, but every one worshiped him. — "No,
that is impossible, because his majesty long ago appreciated his worth," said he.

"Only, God grant," — ejaculated Anna Pavlovna, —
"God grant that Prince Kutuzof may have actual power,
and will not allow *any one* whatever to put a spoke in
his wheels — *des batons dans les roues.*"

Prince Vasili instantly understood whom she meant
by *any one.* He said in a whisper : —

"I know for a certainty that Kutuzof demanded as
an indispensable condition that the tsesarevitch should
not have anything to do with the army. You know
what he said to the emperor ?" — and Prince Vasili repeated the words which it was supposed Kutuzuf spoke
to the sovereign, — 'I cannnot punish him if he does
wrong, or reward him if he does well.' Oh! he is a
shrewd man, that Prince Kutuzof — I have known him
for a long time."

"But they do say," insisted "the man of great
merit," not as yet having the tact required at court,--
"they do say that his serene highness made it a *sine*

qua non that the sovereign himself should keep away from the army."

The moment he had spoken those words, Prince Vasili and Anna Pavlovna simultaneously turned their backs on him, and, with a sigh of pity for his simplicity, exchanged a melancholy look.

CHAPTER VII

WHILE this was going on at Petersburg, the French had already left Smolensk behind, and were constantly drawing nearer and nearer to Moscow.

Thiers, the historian of Napoleon, like other historians of Napoleon, in trying to justify his hero, says that he was drawn on to the walls of Moscow against his will. He and all similar historians are correct in the assumption that the explanation of all historical events is to be found in the will of a single man. He is right, just as the Russian historians are right, who assert that Napoleon was lured on to Moscow by the skill of the Russian generals. Here, unless one goes according to the laws of retrospection, by which, from the vantage-ground of distance, all that is gone before is seen to be the preparation for a given event, everything will seem confused and complicated.

A good chess-player, on losing a game, becomes convinced that the cause of it was to be found in his own blunder, and he seeks to find what false move he made at the beginning of his game; but he forgets that at each step throughout the game there were similar blunders, so that not a single move of his was correct. The blunder to which he directs his attention he notices because his opponent took advantage of it. But how much more complicated is this game of war, which proceeds under the temporal conditions where it is impossible that a single will should animate the lifeless machine, but where everything results from the numberless collisions of various volitions !

After quitting Smolensk, Napoleon tried to force a

battle near Dorogobuzh, at Viazma, then at Tsarevo-Zaïmishche[1]; but it happened through these same "innumerable collisions of circumstances" that the Russians were unable to meet the French in battle until they reached Borodino, one hundred and twelve versts from Moscow. At Viazma, Napoleon issued his orders to march straight against Moscow: "Moscow, the Asiatic capital of this great empire, the sacred city of Alexander's populations, Moscow with its countless churches like Chinese pagodas."

This *Moscou* allowed Napoleon's imagination no rest. On the march from Viazma to Tsarevo-Zaïmishche, Napoleon rode his English-groomed bay ambler, accompanied by his Guards, his body-guard, his pages, and his aides. His chief of staff, Berthier, had remained behind to interrogate a Russian who had been taken prisoner by the cavalry. And now, accompanied by his interpreter, Lelorme d'Ideville, he overtook Napoleon at a gallop, and with a beaming face reined in his horse.

"*Eh, bien?*" asked Napoleon.

"One of Platof's Cossacks says Platof's corps is just joining the main army, that Kutuzof has been appointed commander-in-chief. Very intelligent and talkative."

Napoleon smiled, ordered this Cossack to be furnished with a horse and brought to him. He wished to have a talk with him. Several aides galloped off, and within an hour Denisof's serf, who had been turned by him over to Rostof, Lavrushka, in a denshchik's roundabout, came riding up to Napoleon on a French cavalryman's saddle, with his rascally, drunken face shining with jollity. Napoleon ordered him to ride along by his side, and proceeded to question him.

"You are a Cossack, are you?"

"I am, your nobility."

"The Cossack," says Thiers, in relating this episode, "not knowing his companion, for there was nothing in Napoleon's appearance that could suggest the presence of a sovereign to an Oriental imagination, conversed with the utmost familiarity concerning the occurrences of the war."

---

[1] *Zaïmishche* means "a field frequently overflowed."

In reality, Lavrushka, who had been drunk the evening before and had failed to provide his barin with any
dinner, had been thrashed and sent off to some village
after fowls, and there he was tempted by his opportunity for marauding, and was taken prisoner by the
French.

Lavrushka was one of those coarse, insolent lackeys
who have seen every kind of life, who consider it to
their advantage to do everything by treachery and trick-
ery, who are ready to subserve their masters in anything, and are shrewd in divining their evil thoughts,
especially those that are vain and petty.

Being brought now into the company of Napoleon,
whom he was sharp enough to recognize, Lavrushka did
not in the slightest degree lose his presence of mind, and
merely set to work with all his soul to get into the good
graces of his new masters.

He knew perfectly well that it was Napoleon himself,
and there was no more reason for him to be abashed in
Napoleon's presence than in Rostof's or the sergeant's
with his knout, for the simple reason that there was
nothing of which either the sergeant or Napoleon could
deprive him.

He glibly rattled off all the gossip that was current
among the denshchiks.   Much of this was true.   But
when Napoleon asked him whether the Russians anticipated winning a victory over Napoleon or not, Lavrushka frowned and deliberated.

Here he saw some subtile craft, just as men like Lavrushka always see craft in everything, and he contracted
his brows and was silent for a little.

"This is about the way of it : if there's a battle
pretty soon," said he, cautiously, "then yours will beat.
That's a fact.   But if three days pass, and after that
the same number, then if there's a battle it'll be a long
one."

This was interpreted to Napoleon as follows : " *Si la
bataille est donnée avant trois jours, les Français la
gagneraient, mais que si elle serait donnée plus tard,
Dieu sait ce qui en arriverait* — If the battle takes

place within three days, the French would win, but if it were postponed longer, Heaven knows what would come of it.''

Thus it was delivered by Lelorme d'Ideville with a smile. Napoleon, though he was evidently in a genial frame of mind, did not smile, and ordered these words to be repeated.

Lavrushka noticed this, and, in order to amuse him, pretended that he did not know who he was.

"We know that you have Bonaparte on your side: he's whipped everybody on earth, but then he'll find us of a different mettle, ..." said he, himself not knowing how or why such boastful patriotism leaped to his tongue. The interpreter translated these words without curtailing them, and Napoleon smiled. "*La jeune Cosaque fit sourire son puissant interlocuteur*—The young Cossack's remark made his powerful companion smile," says Thiers.

After riding a few steps farther in silence, Napoleon spoke to Berthier and said that he would like to try the effect that would be produced on this son of the Don on learning that the man with whom he, this *enfant du Don*, had been conversing was the emperor himself, the very emperor who had written his immortally victorious name on the Pyramids.

The information was communicated.

Lavrushka, — comprehending that this had been done so as to embarrass him, and that Napoleon would expect him to show signs of fear, — and wishing to please his new masters, immediately pretended to be overwhelmed with astonishment and struck dumb; he dropped his eyes and made up a face as he usually did when he was led off for a thrashing.

Says Thiers : — "Hardly had Napoleon's interpreter revealed his name, ere the Cossack was overwhelmed with confusion ; he did not utter another word and rode on with his eyes steadily fixed on that conqueror whose name had reached even his ears across the steppes of the East. All his loquacity was suddenly checked and gave place to unaffected, silent admiration. Napoleon,

having rewarded him, set him at liberty, as a bird is
restored to its native fields." [1]

Napoleon went on his way, dreaming of that *Moscou*
which so enthralled his imagination, but "the bird restored to its native fields" galloped off to the picket
lines, thinking up beforehand what sort of a romance
he should tell his acquaintances. The thing that had
actually happened to him he had no intention of telling,
for the simple reason that it seemed to him unworthy
of narration. He rode up to the Cossacks and made
inquiries as to where he should find his regiment, which
now formed a part of Platof's division, and toward evening he reported to his barin, Nikolaï Rostof, who was
bivouacking at Yankovo and had just mounted in order
to make with Ilyin a reconnoissance of the neighboring
villages. He gave Lavrushka a fresh horse and took
him with him.

CHAPTER VIII

THE Princess Mariya was not at Moscow and out of
harm's way, as her brother supposed.

When Alpatuitch returned from Smolensk, the old
prince seemed suddenly to wake, as it were, from a
dream. He ordered the peasantry from his villages to
be enrolled in the militia and armed, and wrote a letter
to the commander-in-chief, informing him of his resolution to remain at Luisiya Gorui and defend himself till
the last extremity, leaving it to his consideration
whether to take measures or not for the defense of the
place where one of the oldest of Russian generals proposed to be taken prisoner or to die. At the same time
he announced to his household that he should remain at
Luisiya Gorui.

---

[1] *À peine l'interprète de Napoléon avait-il parlé, que le Cosaque, saisi
d'une sorte d'abaissement, ne proféra plus une parole, et marcha les yeux
constamment attachés sur ce conquérant, dont le nom avait pénétré jusqu'à
lui, à travers les steppes de l'orient. Toute sa loquacité s'était subitement
arrêtée, pour faire place à un sentiment d'admiration naïve et silencieuse.
Napoléon, après l'avoir récompensé, lui fit donner la liberté comme à un
oiseau qu'on rend aux champs qui l'ont vu naître.*

But, while he was determined to remain at Luisiya
Gorui, he insisted that the princess with Dessalles and
the young prince should go to Bogucharovo, and from
there to Moscow.   The princess, alarmed by her father's
feverish, sleepless activity so suddenly taking the place
of his former lethargy, could not bring herself to leave
him alone, and for the first time in her life permitted herself to disobey him.   She refused to leave, and this drew
upon her a terrific storm of fury from the prince.   He
brought up against her everything which he could find
that was most unjust toward her.   In his endeavors to
incriminate her, he declared that she was a torment to
him, that she had made him quarrel with his son, that
she had harbored shameful suspicions of him, that
she made it the task of her life to poison his life, and
finally he drove her out of his cabinet, saying that if he
never set eyes on her again, it would be all the same to
him.

He declared that he would never have her name mentioned, and henceforth she might do what she pleased,
but let her never dare to come into his sight again.   The
fact that, in spite of the Princess Mariya's apprehen-
sions, he did not order her to be carried away by main
force, but simply forbade her to come into his sight, was
a comfort to her.   She knew this proved that in the
secret depths of his heart he was glad of her determina-
tion to stay at home and not go.

On the morning of the day after Nikolushka's departure, the old prince put on his full uniform and prepared
to visit the commander-in-chief.   The carriage was already at the door.   The Princess Mariya saw him as he
left the house in his uniform and all his orders and
went down into the park to review his peasantry and
household serfs under arms.   The Princess Mariya sat
at the window and listened to the tones of his voice
echoing through the park.   Suddenly a number of men
came running from the avenue with frightened faces.

The Princess Mariya hastened down the steps, along
the flower-bordered walk, and into the avenue.   Here
she was met by a great throng of the militia and the

household serfs, and in the center of this throng several men were carrying the poor little veteran in his uniform and orders.

The Princess Mariya ran up to him, and, in the shift-ing play of the sunbeams falling in little circles through the linden boughs, and flecking the ground, she could not clearly make out what change had taken place in her father's face. The one thing that she noticed was that the former stern and resolute expression of his face had changed into an expression of timidity and submission. When he caught sight of his daughter, he moved his lips, but his words were unintelligible, and the only sound that came forth was a hoarse rattling. It was impossible to understand what he wished to say. They lifted him in their arms, carried him into his cabinet, and laid him on that divan which he had of late so dreaded.

The doctor who was summoned that same night took blood from him, and announced that paralysis had affected his right side.

As it grew more and more dangerous to remain at Luisiya Gorui, the day after the stroke the prince was removed to Bogucharovo. The doctor went with him.

When they reached Bogucharovo, Dessalles and the little prince had already started for Moscow.

For three weeks the old prince, helpless with paraly-sis, lay in the same condition, neither better nor worse, in the new house which his son had built at Bogucha rovo. He was unconscious. He lay like a mutilated corpse. He kept muttering something with twitching brows and lips, but it was impossible to make out whether or not he realized what was going on around him.

The only thing that was certain was that he struggled and felt the necessity of saying something; but no one could divine whether it was the whim of a sick and semi-delirious man, or whether it referred to the general course of affairs, or whether it was in regard to the circumstances of the family.

The doctor insisted that there was no significance to be found in this restlessness, that it proceeded wholly from physical causes; but the Princess Mariya felt certain that he wished to say something to her, and the fact that her presence always increased his agitation confirmed her in this supposition.

He apparently suffered both physically and morally. There was no hope of his recovery. It was impossible to remove him. And what would have been done had he died on the road?

" Would not the end, would not death, be far better ? " the Princess Mariya sometimes asked herself. She sat by him night and day, almost denying herself sleep ; and, terrible to say, she often watched him closely, not with the hope of discovering symptoms of improvement, but rather with the *wish* that she might discover the approaching end.

Strange as it was for the princess to confess to this feeling, still it was there. And what was still more horrible for her was that since the illness of her father — even if it were not earlier, the time, say, when with some vague expectation she had elected to stay by him — all her long-forgotten hopes and desires seemed to wake and take possession of her once more. What she had long years ago ceased to think of — the thought of a life free from the terror of her father's tyranny, even the dream of love, and the possibility of family happiness — constantly arose in her imagination like the suggestions of the evil one.

No matter how strenuously she tried to put them all away, the thought would constantly arise in her mind how she would henceforth, after *this* was over, arrange her life. This was a temptation from the devil, and the Princess Mariya knew it. She knew that the only weapon against *this* was prayer, and she tried to pray. She put herself into the attitude of prayer, she looked at the holy pictures, she read the words of the breviary, but she could not pray. She felt that now she was going to be brought into contact with the world of life, of hard and yet free activity, so different, so wholly opposed to that moral world by which she had been hitherto surrounded, in which her best consolation had been prayer. She could not pray, could not weep, and the concerns of daily life occupied her.

It was becoming dangerous to remain at Bogucharovo. From every direction came rumors of the approach of the French, and in a village only fifteen versts from Bogucharovo a farm-house had been pillaged by French marauders.

The doctor insisted that it was necessary to get his patient farther away. The *predvodityel*, or marshal of the nobility, sent an officer to the Princess Mariya, urging her to get away as speedily as possible. The district-ispravnik, coming in person to Bogucharovo, insisted on the same thing, declaring that the French were only forty versts off, that the French proclamations were circulating among the villages, and that, if the princess did not get her father away by the twenty-seventh, he would not answer for the consequences.

The princess resolved to start on the twenty-seventh. The labors in preparation, the manifold orders which she had to give, as every one came to her for directions, kept her busy all day long. The night of the twenty-sixth she spent as usual, without undressing, in the room next to that occupied by the prince. Several times, arousing from her doze, she heard his hoarse breathing and muttering, the creaking of his bed, and the steps of Tikhon and the doctor as they turned him over. Several times she listened at the door, and it seemed to her that he muttered more distinctly than hitherto, and turned over more frequently. She could not sleep, and many times she went to the door and listened, wishing to go in, and yet not having the courage to do so. Although he could not tell her so, still she had seen and she knew how much he was annoyed by every expression of solicitude on his account. She had observed how he impatiently avoided her eyes, which she sometimes fixed on him, in spite of herself, full of anxiety. She knew that her intrusion at night, at such an unusual time, would annoy him.

But never before had she felt so sad, so terribly sad, at the thought of losing him. She recalled all her life

with him, and discovered the expression of his love for
her in his every word and every deed. Occasionally
these recollections would be interrupted by those prompt-
ings of the devil, the thoughts of what would happen
after he was gone, and how she would arrange her new
life of freedom. But she dismissed such thoughts with
loathing. Toward morning he became quieter, and she
fell into a sound sleep.

She awoke late. The clear-sightedness which is a
concomitant of our waking hours made her realize that
her father's illness was the one predominant occupation
of her life. As she woke up she listened for what was
going on in the next room, and, hearing his hoarse
breathing, she said to herself with a sigh that there
was no change.

"But what should it be? What is it that I wish? I
am looking forward to his death," she told herself, revolted at the very thought.

She changed her gown, made her toilet, said her
prayers, and went out on the steps. In front of the
door the carriages were standing without horses; a
number of things had been already packed.

The morning was warm and hazy. The Princess
Mariya was standing on the steps, her mind still full of
horror at the thought of her moral depravity, and striving to bring some order into her mental state before
going to him.

The doctor came down-stairs and approached her.

"He is better to-day," said he. "I was looking for
you. You may be able to catch something of what he
says. His mind is clearer. Come. He is calling for
you." ....

The Princess Mariya's heart beat so violently at this
news that she turned pale and leaned up against the
door lest she should fall. To see him, to speak with
him, to come under the power of his eyes now when her
soul had just been full of these terrible, criminal, sinful
temptations was too painful a union of joy and horror.

"Come," said the doctor.

The princess went to her father's room and approached his bed. He was lying propped high up, with his small, bony hands covered with knotted purple veins resting on the counterpane, with his left eye straight as it always had been, and with his right eye drawn down, though now his brows and lips were motionless. He was the same little lean, weazened, pitiful old man. His face seemed all dried up or shriveled, his features without character. The Princess Mariya approached him and kissed his hand. His left hand gave her hand a returning pressure which made it evident he had been for some time expecting her. He held her hand, and his brows and lips moved impatiently.

She looked at him in terror, striving to divine what he wanted of her. When she changed her position and moved so that he could see her face with his left eye, he seemed satisfied and for several seconds did not let her out of his sight. Then his brows and lips quivered; he uttered sounds and began to speak, looking at her timidly and supplicatingly, evidently apprehensive that she would not understand him.

The Princess Mariya, concentrating all her powers of attention, looked at him. The comic difficulty he had in managing his tongue caused her to drop her eyes and made it hard for her to choke down the sobs that rose in her throat. He said something, several times repeating his words. The Princess Mariya could not understand them, but in her attempts to guess at what he said she uttered several sentences questioningly.

"*Gaga .... boï .... boï ....*" he repeated several times. It was impossible to make any sense out of those sounds. The doctor thought that he had found the clue, and, trying to come the nearest to those sounds, asked: "Do you mean, Is the princess [1] afraid?"

He shook his head and again repeated the same sounds.

"His mind, his mind troubles him!" [2] suggested the princess. He uttered a sort of roar by way of affirmation, seized her hand and pressed it here and there on

---

[1] *Knyazhnya boïtsa.*
[2] *Dusha, dusha bolit.*

his chest, as if trying to find a place suitable for it to rest.

"Think .... all .... the time .... about .... thee," he then said far more distinctly than before, — now that he was persuaded that they understood him. The Princess Mariya bowed her head down to his hand to hide her sobs and tears.

He smoothed her hair.

"I was .... calling thee .... all night," he went on saying.

"If I had only known," said she, through her tears. "I was afraid to come in."

He pressed her hand.

"Were you not asleep?"

"No, I was not asleep," replied the princess, shaking her head. Involuntarily falling under the influence of her father's condition, she now, in spite of herself, had to speak, as he did, more by signs, and almost found it difficult to manage her tongue.

"Darling," [1] — or did he say little daughter? — she could not tell, — but she was assured by his look that he had called her some affectionate, caressing name, which he had never before done, — "why did you not come in?"

"And I was wishing him dead, wishing him dead," thought the Princess Mariya.

He lay silent.

"Thank thee .... daughter, dearest .... for all .... for everything. .... Forgive. .... Thank thee .... forgive .... thank thee!"

And the tears trickled from his eyes.

"Call Andryusha," said he, suddenly, and, making this request, a childishly puzzled and distrustful expression came into his face. It seemed as if he himself knew that this request had no sense. So at least it seemed to the Princess Mariya.

"I have had a letter from him," replied the Princess Mariya. He gazed at her in puzzled amazement.

"Where is he?"

"He is with the army, *mon père*, at Smolensk."

---

[1] *Dushenka* (little soul), or *Druzhok*, diminutive of friend or love.

He closed his eyes and remained long silent. Then he opened his eyes and nodded his head affirmatively as if in answer to his own doubts, as much as to say that now he understood and remembered everything.

"Yes," said he, in a low but distinct voice. "Russia is ruined, lost! They have ruined her!"

And again he sobbed and the tears rolled down his cheeks. The Princess Mariya could no longer contain herself, and she also wept as she looked into his face.

He again closed his eyes. His sobs ceased. He made a gesture toward his eyes with his hand, and Tikhon, understanding what he meant, wiped away the tears.

Then he opened his eyes and made some remark which no one for some time understood; at last Tikhon made out what he had said, and said it over after him. The Princess Mariya had been trying to connect the sense of his words with what he had just before been speaking about. She thought he might be speaking of Russia, or of Prince Andreï, or of herself, or of his grandson, or of his own death. And consequently she could not make it out.

"Put on your white dress; I like it," was what he had said.

On hearing this, the Princess Mariya sobbed still more violently; and the doctor, taking her by the arm, led her from the room, out upon the terrace, telling her to calm herself and then finish the preparations for the departure. After his daughter had left him he again spoke about his son, about the war, about the sovereign, and scowled angrily, and tried to raise his hoarse voice, and then came the second and finishing stroke.

The Princess Mariya had remained on the terrace. The weather was now clear; it was sunny and hot. She found it impossible to realize anything, or to think of anything, or to feel anything, except her passionate love for her father, a love which, it seemed to her, she had never felt until that moment. She ran into the park, and, still sobbing, hastened down to the pond, along the avenues of lindens which her brother had recently planted.

"Yes.... I.... I.... I wished for his death. Yes, I wished it to end quickly !.... I wanted to rest..... But what will become of me ? What peace shall I ever find when he is gone?" muttered the princess, aloud, as she walked through the park with swift steps and beat her breast, which was heaving with convulsive sobs.

After having made the round of the park, which brought her back to the house again, she saw Mlle. Bourienne — who had remained at Bogucharovo, and had refused to go away — coming toward her, in company with a man whom she did not recognize. This was the district-predvodityel, who had come in person to impress upon the princess the imperative need of their immediate departure.

The Princess Mariya heard what he said, but his words had no meaning for her ; she conducted him into the house, asked him to remain to breakfast, and sat down with him. Then, excusing herself, she went to the old prince's door. The doctor, with a frightened face, came to her, and said she could not go in. "Go away, princess ; go away, go away !"

The princess went into the park again, and down the slope to the pond, and threw herself on the turf, where no one could see her. She knew not how long she remained there. Women's steps running along the avenue roused her from her reverie. She got up and saw her maid Dunyasha, who was evidently in search of her, suddenly stop with a terrified face at sight of her mistress.

"Please, princess.... the prince.... " stammered Dunyasha, in a broken voice.

"Instantly, I am coming, I am coming," cried the princess, not giving Dunyasha time to finish telling what she had to say, and ran to the house, trying not to look at the maid.

"Princess, God's will is done; you must be prepared for the worst," said the predvodityel, who met her at the doorway.

"Leave me ! It is false !" she cried angrily.

The doctor tried to hold her back. She pushed him

away, and ran into the room. "Why do these people look so frightened? Why do they try to keep me away? I do not need them. What are they doing here?"

She opened the door, and the bright sunlight in the room which a short time ago had been kept so dark filled her with terror. The old nyanya and other women were busy in the room. They all moved away from the bed, and made room for her to approach. He still lay on the same bed; but the stern aspect of his face, calm in death, rooted the Princess Mariya to the threshold.

"No! he is not dead! It cannot be!" said the Princess Mariya to herself; she went to him, and, overcoming the horror which seized her, she pressed her lips to his cheek. But instantly she recoiled from the bed. Suddenly all the affection for him which she had just felt so powerfully, vanished, and instead came a feeling of horror for what was before her.

"No! he is no more! He is gone! And in his place here, where he was, is this strange and unfriendly thing; this frightful, blood-curdling, repulsive mystery!"

And, covering her face with her hands, the Princess Mariya fell into the arms of the doctor, who sustained her.

Under the superintendence of Tikhon and the doctor, the women laved that which had been the prince; they tied a handkerchief around his head, so that his jaw might not stiffen with the mouth open, and they bound together his legs with another handkerchief. Then they dressed him in his uniform, with his orders, and laid out his little weazened body on a table. God knows under whose direction and at what time all this was accomplished, but everything seemed to be done of itself.

By night the candles were burning around the coffin, the pall was laid over it; juniper was strewn on the floor; a printed prayer was placed under the wrinkled head of the dead, and in the room sat the diachok reading the psalter.

Just as horses shy and crowd together and neigh

at the sight of a dead horse, so in the drawing-room, around the coffin of the dead prince, gathered a throng of strangers and the members of the household, — the pre-dvodityel, and the starosta, and peasant women, — and all, with staring eyes and panic-stricken, crossed themselves and bowed low, and kissed the aged prince's cold, stiff hand.

CHAPTER IX

UNTIL Prince Andreï went to reside at Bogucharovo, the place had always been an "absentee" estate, and the peasantry bore an entirely different character from those of Luisiya Gorui. They differed in speech and in dress and in customs. They called themselves "children of the steppe." The old prince praised them for their endurance in work when they came over to Luisiya Gorui to help get in the crops or dig ponds and ditches; but he did not like them, because of their boorishness.

Their manners had not been softened since Prince Andreï's last residence there, in spite of his dispensaries and schools, and the lightening of the *obrok* or quit-rent; on the contrary, those traits of character which the old prince called *boorishness* seemed to have been intensified. Strange, obscure rumors were always finding credence among them; at one time they got the notion that they were all to be enrolled as Cossacks; another time, it was a new religion which they were to be forced to accept; then, again, there was talk about certain imperial dispensations; then, at the time they took the oath of allegiance to Paul Petrovitch, in 1797, they got the notion that their freedom had been granted them, but that their masters had deprived them of it; and, again, it was the return of Peter Feodorovitch[1] to the throne, who would be Tsar in seven years, and give them absolute freedom, so that everything would be simple and easy, and they would have no laws at all.

The rumors of the war and of Napoleon and his inva-

[1] Peter III.

sion were connected in their minds with obscure notions
of Antichrist, the end of the world, and perfect freedom.

In the vicinity of Bogucharovo were a number of large
villages, belonging to the crown or to non-resident proprietors. It was very rarely that these proprietors came
to reside on their estates; there were also very few
domestic serfs, or peasants, who knew how to read and
write; and the lives of the peasantry of this region were
more noticeably and powerfully affected than elsewhere
by those mysterious currents characteristic of the common people in Russia, the significance and causes of
which are so inexplicable to contemporaries.

A phenomenon which illustrates this had taken place
a score of years before, when an exodus of the peasantry
was made toward certain "hot rivers." Hundreds of
peasants, including some from Bogucharovo, suddenly
sold their cattle and set off with their families "somewhere" toward the southeast. Just as birds fly "somewhere" across the sea, so these men, with their wives
and children, made every endeavor to reach that unknown Southeast, where none of them had ever been
before. They marched in caravans; here and there
one bought his freedom; others ran away, and set
forth in wagons or on foot for the "hot rivers"! Many
were caught and punished; many were sent to Siberia;
many perished of cold and starvation on the road; many
returned of their own accord; and, at last, this migration
died out of itself, just as it had begun — without any
visible reason. But these underground currents ceased
not to flow among this people, and they were gathering
impetus for some new outbreak, likely to prove just as
perplexing, as unexpected, and, at the same time, as
simple, natural, and violent.

At the present time, in 1812, any man whose life
brought him in contact with the people might have
observed that these hidden currents were working
with extraordinary energy, and were all ready for an
eruption.

Alpatuitch, who had arrived at Bogucharovo some
little time before the old prince's decease, had observed

that there was considerable excitement among the peasantry; while in the region of Luisiya Gorui — only
sixteen versts distant — all the peasants had deserted
their homes, leaving their villages to be marauded by
the Cossacks; here, on the contrary, in the "Steppe"
belt, in the region of Bogucharovo, the peasantry, so
the report ran, had dealings with the French, were in
receipt of certain papers which were circulating among
them, and had no thought of leaving their homes.

He knew, through certain of the household serfs who
were faithful to him, that a muzhik named Karp, who
had great influence over the *mir*, or peasant commune,
had lately returned from driving a crown wagon-train,
and was spreading the report that the Cossacks were
ravaging the villages which had been deserted by their
inhabitants, while the French were not touching them.

He was informed on good authority that another
muzhik, the evening before, had brought from the village
of Visloukhovo, where the French were, a proclamation from a French general, representing to the inhabitants that no harm would be done to them, and that
cash should be paid for whatever was taken, provided
they remained in their homes.   As proof positive of
this, the muzhik brought with him from Visloukhovo a
hundred rubles in assignats — he did not know that they
were counterfeit — which had been paid to him for his
hay.

Finally, and more important than all, Alpatuitch found
that on that very day when he had commanded the
starosta to procure wagons for the conveyance of the
princess's effects from Bogucharovo, the peasants had
held a morning meeting in the village, at which it had
been voted that they should not stir from the place, but
wait.   And meantime there was no time to lose.

The predvodityel, on the very day on which the prince
had died, — the twenty-seventh, — had come to urge the
princess to depart without further delay, as the risk was
growing constantly more imminent.   He had declared
that after the twenty-eighth he would not be responsible for the consequences.   That same evening, after

the prince's demise, he had gone away, promising to be
present at the funeral on the next day.   But on the
next day it was impossible for him to be present, since
news had been brought to him of an unexpected approach of the French, and he had barely time to remove
his own family and valuables from his estate.

For thirty years, Dron, whom the old prince always
called by the affectionate diminutive, Dronushka, had
exercised the functions of *starosta*, or bailiff, at Bogucharovo.

Dron was one of those muzhiks — powerful, physically and morally — who, as soon as they come to years
of discretion, grow a beard, and live on without change
till they are sixty or seventy years old, without a gray
hair or the loss of a tooth, just as erect and powerful at
sixty as they were at thirty.

Dron, shortly after his returning from his expedition
to the "hot rivers," in which he had taken part, had
been made *starosta-burmistr*, or bailiff headman, of the
village of Bogucharovo; and, since that time, he had
performed without reproach all the functions of that
office.   The muzhiks feared him more than they feared
their barin.   His masters — both the old prince and the
young prince — respected him, and, in jest, called him
"minister."   During all the time of his service, Dron
had never once been drunk or sick.   Never, even after
sleepless nights or after the most exhausting labors, was
he known to show the slightest slothfulness, and, though
he did not know his letters, he never made the slightest
mistakes in his money accounts, or as to the number of
poods of flour which he carried in monstrous loads and
sold, or as to the amount of a single rick of corn harvested in the fields of Bogucharovo.

Alpatuitch, on his arrival from the devastated Luisiya
Gorui, summoned this Dron on the very day of the
funeral, and ordered him to have ready a dozen horses
for the princess's conveyance, and eighteen teams
for the luggage which she was to take with her
from Bogucharovo.   Although the peasantry paid an
obrok, or quit-rent, Alpatuitch never dreamed that there

would be any difficulty in having this order carried out, since the villages contained two hundred and thirty taxable households, and the muzhiks were well-to-do.

But the starosta, Dron, on receiving this order, dropped his eyes and made no answer. Alpatuitch named certain peasants whom he knew, and ordered him to make the requisitions on them.

Dron replied that these men's horses were off on carrier duty. Alpatuitch named still other muzhiks. And these men, also, according to Dron, had no horses: some were off with the government trains; others were out of condition; still others had lost theirs through lack of forage. According to Dron's report, it was impossible to secure horses for the carriages, to say nothing of those for the baggage wagons.

Alpatuitch looked sharply at the starosta and scowled. In the same way as Dron was a model of what a peasant starosta should be, in the same way Alpatuitch had not managed the prince's estates for nothing all those twenty years, and he also was a model overseer. He was in the highest degree qualified to understand, as by a sort of scent, the wants and instincts of the people with whom he had to do, and this made him a surpassingly excellent overseer.

He knew by a single glance at Dron, that Dron's answers were not the expression of Dron's individual opinions, but merely the expression of the general disposition of the Bogucharovo commune, in which the starosta was evidently involved. But, at the same time, he knew that Dron, who had grown rich and was hated by the commune, must necessarily waver between the two camps, the peasants' and the master's. This wavering he could detect in his eyes, and, therefore, Alpatuitch, with a frown, drew near to Dron.

"Listen, you, Dronushka!" said he. "You need not tell me idle tales. His illustriousness Prince Andreï Nikolaitch himself gave me orders that all the peasantry should leave, and not remain behind with the enemy; and those are the Tsar's orders also. So any one who stays is a traitor to the Tsar. Do you hear?"

"I hear," replied Dron, not raising his eyes.

Alpatuitch was not satisfied with this answer.

"Ah, Dron! ill will come of it!" exclaimed Alpa-tuitch, shaking his head.

"You have the power," returned Dron, mournfully.

"Ah, Dron! give it up!" exclaimed Alpatuitch, taking his hand out from the breast of his coat, and with a solemn gesture pointing under Dron's feet. "Not only do I see through and through you, but I can see three arshins under you; everything there is," said he, looking down at Dron's feet.

Dron grew confused; he gave Alpatuitch a fleeting look, and then dropped his eyes again.

"Stop all this nonsense, and tell the people to get ready to leave for Moscow, and have the teams ready to-morrow morning for the princess, and mind you don't attend any more of their meetings! Do you hear?"

Dron suddenly threw himself at his feet.

"Yakof Alpatuitch! discharge me! Take the keys from me! Discharge me, for Christ's sake!"

"Stop!" said Alpatuitch, sternly. "I can see three arshins deep under you!" he repeated, knowing that his skill in going after bees, his knowledge of the times and seasons for sowing, and the fact that for a score of years he had succeeded in satisfying the old prince had long ago given him the reputation of being a *koldun*, or wizard, and that to kolduns was attributed the power of seeing three arshins under a man.

Dron got to his feet, and tried to say something, but Alpatuitch interrupted him.

"Come now! What is your idea in all this? Ha? What are you dreaming of? Ha?"

"What shall I do with the people?" asked Dron. "They are all stirred up! And, besides, I have told them...."

"Told them?" repeated Alpatuitch. "Are they drunk?" he demanded laconically.

"All stirred up, Yakof Alpatuitch! They have just brought another cask!"

"Now, then, listen! I will go to the ispravnik, and

you hasten back to the people, and bid them quit all this sort of thing, and get ready the teams."

"I obey," replied Dron.

Yakof Alpatuitch insisted on nothing more. He had been in control of the people too long not to know that the principal way of bringing the people to subordination was not to show the slightest doubt that they would become subordinate. Having wrung from Dron the submissive " *Slushayu-s* — I obey," Yakhof Alpatuitch contented himself with that, although he not merely suspected, but was even certain in his own mind, that, without the assistance of a squad of militia, nothing would be done.

And, in point of fact, there were no teams forthcoming, as he supposed. Another meeting of the peasantry was held at the village tavern; and this meeting voted to drive the horses out into the woods and not to furnish the teams. Saying nothing of all this to the princess, Alpatuitch gave orders to have the carts that had brought his own effects from Luisiya Gorui unloaded, and to have his horses put to the Princess Mariya's carriage; and he himself went to consult with the authorities.

CHAPTER X

THE Princess Mariya, after her father's funeral, shut herself up in her room, and admitted no one. Her maid came to the door to say that Alpatuitch was there to learn her wishes in regard to the departure. (This was before his interview with Dron.) The princess sat up on the divan where she had been lying, and spoke through the closed door, declaring that she would never go away anywhere, and asked her to leave her in peace.

All the windows of the room which the Princess Mariya occupied faced the south. She lay on the divan with her face turned toward the wall, and picking with her fingers at the buttons on the leathern cushion, which was the only thing that she could see, while her vague thoughts were concentrated on one thing: she was thinking about the unavoidableness of death and of her own moral baseness, which she had never before realized and which came to light during her father's illness. She wanted, but she dared not, to pray; she dared not, in that state of mind in which she found herself, to turn to God in prayer.   Long she lay in that position.

The sun had gone round to the other side of the house, and its slanting afternoon beams fell through the opened windows and lighted up the room and the part of the morocco cushion at which she was looking. The train of somber thoughts suddenly ceased. She instinctively sat up, smoothed her hair, got to her feet, and went to the window, where, without thinking, she breathed in the coolness of the bright but windy afternoon.

"Yes, now you can enjoy your fill of the evening! He is gone, and no one is here to interfere with you," said she to herself, and, dropping into a chair, leaned her head on the window-seat.

Some one, in a soft, affectionate voice, called her name from the park side of the window, and kissed her on the head.   She looked up.

It was Mlle. Bourienne, in a black dress trimmed with white.   She had softly approached the Princess Mariya, kissed her with a sigh, and immediately burst into tears. The princess looked at her.   All her previous collisions with her, her jealousy of her, came back to her remembrance; she also remembered how *he* of late had changed toward Mlle. Bourienne, could not even bear to see her, and consequently how unjust had been the reproaches which the Princess Mariya had in her heart made against her.

"Yes, and can I, I who have wished for his death, can I judge any one else?" she asked herself.

The Princess Mariya had a keen sense of Mlle. Bourienne's trying situation, held by her at a distance as she had recently been, and yet at the same time dependent on her, and dwelling under a stranger's roof. And she began to feel a pity for her.   She looked at her with a sweet, questioning look, and stretched out her hand. Mlle. Bourienne immediately had a fresh paroxysm of tears, began to kiss the princess's hand, and to speak of the affliction that had come upon her, and claimed to be a sympathizer in that affliction. She declared that her only consolation in this sorrow was that the princess allowed her to share it with her. She said that all their previous misunderstandings ought to be forgotten in presence of this terrible loss, that she felt that her conscience was clear before all men, and that *he* from above would bear witness to her love and gratitude.

The princess listened to her without comprehending what she was saying, but she looked at her from time to time, and heard the sounds of her voice.

"Your position is doubly terrible, dear princess," said Mlle. Bourienne, after a short silence. "I understand how it is that you could not have thought .... that you cannot think about yourself; but, from the love which I bear you, I am compelled to do so for you. .... Has Alpatuitch been to see you? Has he said anything to you about going away?" she asked.

The Princess Mariya made no reply. She could not realize who was going away or where they were going.

"How could they undertake anything just now? Why think of anything? What difference does it make?"

She made no answer.

"Do you know, *chère Marie,*" asked Mlle. Bourienne, — "do you know that we are in peril, that we are surrounded by the French? It is dangerous to go now. If we were to start, we should almost certainly be taken prisoner, and God knows ...."

The Princess Mariya looked at her friend without comprehending what she was saying.

"Akh! if you could only know how little, how little I care now," said she. "Of course, I should never wish such a thing as to go away and leave *him.* .... Alpatuitch said something to me about going away. .... Talk it over with him; I cannot and I will not hear ...."

"I have spoken with him. He hopes that we shall be able to get away to-morrow; but it is my opinion that we had better remain here now," said Mlle. Bourienne. "Because — you must agree with me, *chère Marie* — to fall into the hands of the soldiers or insurgent peasants would be horrible."

Mlle. Bourienne drew forth from her reticule a proclamation — printed on paper different from that used generally in Russia — from the French general Rameau, in which the inhabitants were advised not to abandon their homes, since full protection would be vouchsafed them by the French authorities; this she handed to the princess.

"I think it would be better to apply to this general," said Mlle. Bourienne. "And I am convinced that we should be treated with due consideration."

The Princess Mariya read the paper, and her face contracted with a sort of tearless sob.

"From whom did you get this?" she demanded.

"They probably knew that I am French from my name," said Mlle. Bourienne, with a blush.

The princess, with the paper in her hand, got up from the window, and with a pale face left the room, and went into Prince Andreï's cabinet, which adjoined.

"Dunyasha, summon Alpatuitch, Dronushka, any one," exclaimed the Princess Mariya; "and tell Amalie Karlovna not to come near me," she added, hearing Mlle. Bourienne's voice. "Go quick! quick!" exclaimed the Princess Mariya, panic-stricken at the thought that she might be left in the power of the French.

"What if Prince Andreï knew that she were under the protection of the French! That she, the daughter of Prince Nikolaï Andreyitch Bolkonsky, had asked General Rameau to grant her his protection, and put herself under obligations for benefits received from him!"

The mere suggestion of such a thing filled her with horror, made her shudder, turn red, and feel still more violently than ever before those impulses of anger and outraged pride.

She now vividly realized all the difficulties, and, above all, the humiliations of her position.

"They — the French — will take possession of this house; *M. le général* Rameau will make use of Prince Andreï's cabinet; for their amusement they will ransack and read his letters and papers. *Mademoiselle Bourienne lui fera les honneurs de Bogucharovo!* They will out of special favor grant me a sleeping-room; the soldiers will tear open my father's newly made grave in order to rob him of his crosses and stars; they will boast before me of their victories over the Russians, they will pretend to sympathize in my grief," thought the Princess Mariya, not in her own thoughts, but feeling herself compelled to think as her father and brother would have thought.

For her personally it was a matter of utter indifference where she stayed or what happened to her; but at the same time she felt that she was the representative of her late father and of Prince Andreï. She could not help thinking these thoughts and feeling these feelings. Whatever they would have said, whatever they would have done, now this she felt that it was indispensable for her to do. She went into Prince Andreï's cabinet, and, in her endeavors to follow out what would be his ideas, she reviewed her position.

The demands of life, which she had felt had been annihilated at the moment of her father's death, suddenly, with new, never-before-experienced violence, rushed up before her, and took possession of her.

Flushed with excitement, she walked up and down the room, summoning first Alpatuitch, then Mikhaïl Ivanovitch, then Tikhon, then Dron. Dunyasha, the old nurse, and all the maids were equally unable to say how far Mlle. Bourienne was correct in what she had declared. Alpatuitch was not at home; he had gone to consult with the authorities. Mikhaïl Ivanuitch, the architect, on being summoned, came into the Princess Mariya's presence with sleepy eyes, and could tell her nothing. He replied to her questions with precisely the same non-committal smile with which for fifteen years he had been in the habit of dealing with the old prince, and she could get nothing definite from his replies.

Then the old valet Tikhon was called, and, with a downcast and impassive face, bearing all the symptoms of incurable woe, he replied to all her questions with his "*Slushayu-s* — I obey," and could scarcely refrain from sobbing as he looked at her.

At last the starosta Dron came into the room, and, making her a low obeisance, stood respectfully at the threshold.

The Princess Mariya glided through the room and paused in front of him.

"Dronushka!" said she, seeing in him an undoubted friend, the same Dronushka who had always brought home pieces of gingerbread with him from his trips to the *yarmarka*, or annual bazaar, at Viazma, and presented to her with a smile. — "Dronushka! now, since our sad loss...."

She began and then paused, unable to proceed.

"All our goings are under God," said he, with a sigh. Neither spoke.

"Dronushka! Alpatuitch has gone; I have no one to turn to; is it true, what I am told, that we cannot get away?"

"Not get away? Certainly you can get away, princess," said Dron.

"They tell me there is danger from the enemy. My friend,[1] I am helpless, I don't understand anything about it, I am entirely alone. I decidedly wish to start to-night or to-morrow morning early."

Dron stood silent. He looked from under his brows at the princess.

"No horses," said he at last, "and I have told Yakof Alpatuitch so."

"How is that?" asked the princess.

"It is God's punishment," said Dron; "what horses we had have been taken by the troops, and the rest have perished. That's the way it is this year. 'T would n't

[1] *Galubchik.*

so much matter about feeding the horses, if we ourselves were n't perishing of starvation. Often for three days at a time we go without a bite. We have nothing at all; we are utterly ruined."

The Princess Mariya listened attentively to what he said.

"The peasantry are ruined? You say they have no corn?" she asked.

"They are perishing of famine," said Dron. "And as for teams...."

"But why have n't you told me of this before, Dronushka? Can't they be helped? I will do all in my power...."

It was strange for the Princess Mariya to think that now, at this moment when her heart was filled with such sorrow, there could be poor men and rich, and that the rich did not help the poor. She had a general notion that, when the masters had a reserve of corn, it was distributed among the serfs. She knew also that neither her father nor her brother would refuse to help the peasantry in case of need; all that she feared was that she might make some blunder in speaking about this distribution of corn which she was anxious to make. She was glad of some pretext for active work, something that would allow her without pangs of conscience to forget her own sorrow. She proceeded to question Dronushka in regard to the necessities of the muzhiks and the store of reserve corn belonging to the estate at Bogucharovo.

"We have corn belonging to the estate, have we not, brother?" she demanded.

"The master's corn is untouched," said Dron, with pride. "Our prince had not ordered it to be sold."

"Give that to the peasantry; give them all they need. I grant it in my brother's name," said the Princess Mariya.

Dron made no reply, and drew a long sigh.

"You give them this corn, if there is enough for them. Give it all to them. I order it in my brother's name, and tell them: 'What is ours is always theirs. We shall not grudge it for them.' Tell them so."

Dron looked steadily at the princess while she was saying this.

"Discharge me, matushka, for God's sake; order the keys to be taken from me," said he. "I have been in service for twenty-three years! I have never done anything dishonest; discharge me, for God's sake!"

The Princess Mariya could not understand what he wanted of her, or why he wished to be relieved of his office. She replied that she had never conceived a doubt of his devotion, and that she was always ready to do anything for him or for any of the muzhiks.

CHAPTER XI

AN hour later Dunyasha came to the princess with the news that Dron was there, and that all the muzhiks had collected in accordance with the princess's orders at the granary, and wished to have speech with their mistress.

"But I never called them," said the Princess Mariya; "I merely told Dronushka to give them corn."

"Then, for God's sake, princess-matushka, order them to disperse and don't go to them. They are deceiving you," exclaimed Dunyasha. "But Yakof Alpatuitch will soon be back, and then we will go .... and don't you allow .... "

"How are they deceiving me?" asked the princess in amazement.

"But I am certain of it! Only heed my words, for God's sake. Just ask nurse here. They declare they will not go away at your orders."

"You have got it entirely wrong. .... Besides, I have never ordered them to go away," said the Princess Mariya. "Fetch Dronushka." ....

Dron came in and confirmed what Dunyasha said: the muzhiks had assembled at the princess's orders.

"But I never summoned them," said the princess. "You did not give my message correctly. I only told you to give them corn."

Dron made no reply, but sighed.

"If you order it they will disperse," said he.

"No, no, I will go to them," said the princess.

In spite of the persuasion of Dunyasha and the old nurse, the Princess Mariya went down the steps.   Dronushka, Dunyasha, the old nurse, and Mikhaïl Ivanuitch followed her.

"They apparently think that I give them the corn so that they should stay at home, while I myself am going away, abandoning them to the mercy of the French," thought the Princess Mariya.   "But I will promise them rations and quarters at our pod-Moskovnaya ; I am sure André would do even more in my place," she said to herself as she went toward the throng that had gathered in the twilight on the green near the granary.

The throng showed some signs of confusion, and moved and swayed a little, and hats were quickly removed as she approached.   The Princess Mariya, with downcast eyes, and getting her feet entangled in her dress, went toward them.   So many different eyes from faces young and old were fixed on her, and so many different people were collected, that the princess did not distinguish any particular person ; and, as she felt the necessity of addressing them all at once, she did not know how to set about it.   But once more the consciousness that she was the representative of her father and brother gave her courage, and she boldly began to speak.

"I am very glad that you came," she began, not raising her eyes, and conscious of her heart beating fast and strong.   "Dronushka told me that you were ruined by the war.   That is our common misfortune, and I shall spare no endeavor to help you.   I myself am going away because it is dangerous here .... and the enemy are near .... because .... I will give you everything, friends, and I beg of you to take all, all our corn, so that you may not suffer from want.   And if you have been told that I distribute the corn among you so as to keep you here, that is a falsehood.   On the contrary, I beg of you to go with all your possessions to our pod-Moskovnaya, and I will engage and promise that you shall not suffer. You shall be given homes and provisions."

The princess paused. In the throng sighs were heard, and that was all.

"I do not give this of myself," continued the princess ; "but I do it in the name of my late father, who was a good barin to you, and in behalf of my brother and his son."

She again paused. No one broke in on her silence. "Our misfortune is universal, and we will share everything together. All that is mine is yours," said she, gazing at the faces ranged in front of her.

All eyes were fixed on her with one expression, the significance of which she could not interpret. Whether it were curiosity, devotion, gratitude, or fear, or distrust, that expression, whatever it was, was the same in all.

"Very grateful for your kindness, but we don't want to take the master's corn," said a voice in the rear of the throng.

"Yes, but why not?" asked the princess.

No one replied, and the Princess Mariya, glancing around the throng, observed that now all eyes which met hers immediately turned away.

"Why are you unwilling?" she asked again.

No one replied.

The Princess Mariya felt awkward at this silence. She tried to catch some one's eye.

"Why don't you speak?" demanded the princess, addressing an aged man, who, leaning on his cane, was standing in front of her. "Tell me if you think that anything else is needed. I will do everything for you," said she, as she caught his eye. But he, as if annoyed by this, hung his head and muttered : —

"Why should we? We don't want your corn."

"What! us abandon everything? We don't agree to it."...."We don't agree to it."...."Not with our consent."...."We are sorry, but it shan't be done with our consent."...."Go off by yourself alone!" rang out from the mob on different sides.

And again all the faces of the throng had one and

the same expression; but this time it was assuredly not curiosity or gratitude, but one of angry, obstinate resolution.

"Oh, but you have not understood me," exclaimed the Princess Mariya, with a melancholy smile. "Why are you unwilling to go? I promise to give you new homes and feed you. But if you stay here the enemy will ruin you."

But her voice was drowned by the voices of the mob.

"Not with our consent. Let him destroy us. We won't touch your corn. Not with our consent."

The Princess Mariya tried again to catch the eyes of some other person in the crowd; but not one was directed toward her; their eyes evidently avoided her. She felt strange, and ill at ease.

"There now! she's a shrewd one. Follow her to prison. They want to get our houses, and make serfs of us again — the idea! We won't touch your corn," rang the various voices.

The Princess Mariya, hanging her head, left the crowd, and went back to the house. Reiterating her orders to Dron to have the horses ready against their daparture the next day, she went to her room and remained alone with her thoughts.

CHAPTER XII

The Princess Mariya sat long that night beside her open window in her room, listening to the hubbub of voices which came up to her from the peasant village; and yet she was not thinking of them. She felt that the more she thought about them, the less she should understand them. Her mind was concentrated on one thing: her affliction, which now, after the interruption caused by her labors in connection with the present situation, seemed already far in the past. She could now think calmly, could weep, and could pray.

With the sunset the breeze had died down. The night was calm and cool. By twelve o'clock the voices began to grow still; a cock crowed; the full moon began to rise up from behind the lindens; a cool, white dew-mist arose, and peace reigned over the village and over the house.

One after the other passed before her mind the pictures of the recent past: the illness and the last moments of her father. And, with a melancholy joy, she now dwelt on these pictures, repelling with horror only one: the vision of his death, a thing which she felt wholly unable to contemplate, even in imagination, at that calm, mysterious hour of night. And these pictures came before her with such vividness, and with such fullness of detail, that they seemed to her now like the reality, and then, again, like something past, or, again, like something that was to come.

Now she vividly recalled the moment when he received the stroke, and was borne in the arms of his men into the house at Luisiya Gorui, muttering unintelligible words with his disobedient tongue, knitting his grizzled brows, and looking anxiously and timidly at her.

"Even then, he wanted to tell me what he said on the very day of his death," she said to herself. "What he said to me then was all the time in his mind."

And then she imagined, with all its details, that night at Luisiya Gorui, on the evening before he received the stroke, when, with a presentiment of evil, she remained with him against his will. She could not sleep, and she went down late at night on her tiptoes, and, going to the door of the greenhouse, where her father had tried to sleep that night, had listened to him. He was talking to Tikhon in a peevish, weary voice. He was telling him something about the Crimea, about the genial nights, about the empress. He was evidently in a talkative mood.

"And why did he not call me? Why did he not allow me then to take Tikhon's place?"

She asked herself that question then, and again she asked it now.

"He was never one to confide in any one what he kept locked up in the chambers of his heart. And now never again for him and for me will return that moment when he might say all he wished to say, and then I, and not Tikhon, might have listened and understood him. Why did I not go in where he was?" wondered the Princess Mariya. "Maybe even then he would have told me what he said on the day of his death. While he was talking with Tikhon he twice asked about me. He wished to see me, and there I was standing at the door. He found it tiresome and stupid to talk with Tikhon, for he could not understand him. I remember how he spoke with him about Liza, as if she were still alive, — he had forgotten that she was dead, — and Tikhon reminded him that she had passed away, and he cried, 'Durak — idiot!' It was hard for him. As I stood outside I heard him groan, and lie down on the bed and cry aloud, 'My God!' Why did n't I go in then and there? What would he have done to me? What trouble might I not have made? Perhaps even then he would have been comforted; perhaps he would have called me — what he did." And the Princess repeated aloud the caressing word which he had spoken to her on the day of his death: "Dushenka," — Dear heart, — "Du-shen-ka," repeated the princess, and she burst into tears which lightened the sorrow of her soul.

Now she saw his face plainly before her: and not that face which she had known ever since her earliest remembrance, and which she had always seen afar off, as it were, but that weak, submissive face which she, for the first time in her memory, as she bent down close to it to catch the last words that fell from his mouth, saw near at hand with all its wrinkles and details.

"Dushenka!" she repeated.

"What thoughts were in his mind when he said that word? What is he thinking now?"

That question suddenly occurred to her, and for answer to it she seemed to see him before her with that same expression of face which he had worn in his coffin with the white handkerchief binding up his face. And that horror which had seized her then, when she had touched him, and then felt so assured that this thing not only was not he, but something mysterious and repulsive, came over her again. She tried to think of something else, she tried to pray, and she could do neither. With wide, staring eyes she gazed at the moonlight and at the shadows, every instant expecting to see his dead face, and she felt that the silence that hung over the house and in the house was turning her to stone.

"Dunyasha!" she whispered. "Dunyasha!" she cried, in a wild voice; and, tearing herself away from the silence, she ran into the domestics' room, meeting the old nurse and the women, who came to meet her at her cry.

CHAPTER XIII

ON the twenty-ninth of August Rostof and Ilyin, accompanied only by Lavrushka, just back from his brief captivity, and an orderly sergeant of hussars, set forth from their bivouac at Yankovo, fifteen versts from Bogucharovo, to make trial of a new horse which Ilyin had recently purchased, and to find whether there was any fodder in the villages round about.

Bogucharovo, during the last three days, had been midway between two hostile armies, so that it was just as likely to be occupied by the Russian rear-guard as by the French vanguard; and consequently Rostof, like the thoughtful squadron commander that he was, conceived the notion of taking possession of the provisions at Bogucharovo in anticipation of the French.

Rostof and Ilyin were in the most jovial mood. On the way to Bogucharovo, to the princely estate and farm where they hoped to find a great throng of domestics and pretty young girls, they now questioned Lavrushka about Napoleon, and made merry over his tale, and then they ran races to test Ilyin's horse.

Rostof had not the slightest notion that this village where he was bound was the estate of that very same Bolkonsky who had been betrothed to his sister.

He and Ilyin made a final spurt in trial of their horses down the slope in front of Bogucharovo, and Rostof, outriding Ilyin, was the first to enter the street of the village.

"You got in first!" cried Ilyin, growing red in the face.

"Yes, always ahead, not only on the level, but here also," replied Rostof, smoothing the flank of his foam-flecked Donets.

"And I on my Franzuska, your illustriousness," exclaimed Lavrushka, coming up behind them on his cart-jade, which he called "Franzuska," or "Frenchy," in honor of his adventure. "I'd ha' come in first only I didn't want to mortify you."

They rode at a footpace up to the granary, near which a great crowd of muzhiks were gathered.

Some of them took off their caps; some, not taking off their caps, gazed at the newcomers. Two old lean muzhiks, with wrinkled faces and thin beards, came out from the public-house, reeling, and trolling some incoherent snatch of a song, and approached the officers.

"Say, my hearties," sang out Rostof, with a laugh, "have you any hay?"

"Like as two peas," exclaimed Ilyin.

"We're jo-ol-ly g-oo-d f-fel-el-lo-ows," sang one of the men, with a grin of happiness.

A muzhik came out of the throng and approached Rostof.

"Which side are you from?" he asked.

"The French," replied Rostof, jokingly, with a smile "And that's Napoleon himself," he added, pointing to Lavrushka.

"Of course, you're Russians, ain't you?" asked the muzhik.

"Is there a large party of you?" asked another, a little man, who also joined them.

"Ever so many," replied Rostof. "And what brings you all together here?" he added. "A holiday festival?"

"The elders have collected for communal business," replied the muzhik who first came out.

At this time two women and a man in a white hat made their appearance on the road from the mansion, coming toward the officers.   "The one in pink is mine! Don't dare cheat me of her!" exclaimed Ilyin, catching sight of Dunyasha, coming resolutely toward him.

"She shall be yours," replied Lavrushka, with a wink.

"What do you want, my beauty?" asked Ilyin, with a smile.

"The princess has sent to ask what is your regiment and your name."

"I am Count Rostof, squadron commander, and I am your humble servant."

"De-e-ev-lish jol-ol-ly g-ga-gals," sang one of the drunken muzhiks, with a jovial grin, and giving Ilyin a meaning look, as he stood talking with the maid. Dunyasha was followed by Alpatuitch, who, at some distance, took off his hat in Rostof's presence.

"I make bold to trouble your nobility," said he, politely, but manifesting a certain scorn of the officer's youthful appearance, and placing his hand in the breast of his coat.   " My mistress, the daughter of General*ongshef* the late Prince Nikolaï Andreyevitch Bolkonsky, who died on the twenty-seventh instant, finds herself in difficulty on account of the insubordination and boorishness of these individuals here " — he pointed to the muzhiks. " And she begs you to confer with her — if it would not be asking too much," said Alpatuitch, with a timid smile, — "if you would come a few steps farther .... and besides it is not so pleasant in presence of .... "

He indicated the two drunken muzhiks, who were circling round them and in their rear like gadflies round a horse.

"Hey!   Alpatuitch — Hey!   Yakof Alpatuitch " .... "Ser'ous shing!   'Scuse us!   Ser'ous shing!" .... "'Scuse us, for Christ's sake!   Hey!" said the muzhiks, leering at him.   Rostof looked at the drunken muzhiks, and smiled.

"Or perhaps this amuses your illustriousness?" suggested Alpatuitch, with a sedate look, and indicating the old men with his other hand — the one not in the breast of his coat.

"No, there's no amusement in that," said Rostof, and started off. "What is the trouble?" he asked.

"I make bold to explain to your illustriousness that these coarse peasants here are not willing that their mistress should leave her estate, and they threaten to take her horses out; and though everything has been packed up since morning, her illustriousness can't get away."

"Incredible!" cried Rostof.

"I have the honor of reporting to you the essential truth," maintained Alpatuitch.

Rostof dismounted, and, throwing the reins to his orderly, went with Alpatuitch to the house, questioning him on the state of affairs. In point of fact, the offer of corn which the princess had made to the muzhiks the evening before, her explanations to Dron and to the meeting, had made affairs so much worse that Dron had definitively laid down his keys, and taken sides with the peasantry, and had refused to obey Alpatuitch's summons; and that morning, when the princess had ordered to have the horses put in so as to take her departure, the muzhiks had gone in a regular mob to the granary, and sent a messenger declaring that they would not allow the princess to leave the village, that orders had come not to leave and they should unharness the horses. Alpatuitch had gone to them, and reasoned with them, but they had replied — Karp being their spokesman for the most part — Dron did not show himself at all — that it was impossible to let the princess take her departure, that there was a law against it; "only let her stay at home, and they would serve her as they always had done, and obey her in everything."

At the moment that Rostof and Ilyin had come spurring up the avenue, the Princess Mariya, in spite of the dissuasion of Alpatuitch, the old nurse, and her women, had given orders to have the horses put in, and had made up her mind to start; but when the coachmen saw the cavalrymen galloping up, they took them for the

French, and ran away; and wailing and lamentations of
women were heard in the house.

"Batyushka!".... "Blessed father!".... "God has sent
you," were the words of welcome that met him, as Rostof
passed through the anteroom.

The Princess Mariya, entirely bewildered and weak
with fright, was sitting in the drawing-room when Rostof
was brought in to her. She had no idea who he was
and why he was there and what was going to become
of her. When she saw his Russian face, and recognized
by his manner and the first words he spoke that he was
a man of her own walk in life, she looked at him with
her deep, radiant eyes, and began to speak in broken
tones, her voice trembling with emotion.

Rostof immediately found something very romantic
in this adventure. "An unprotected maiden, overwhelmed with grief, left alone to the mercy of rough,
insurgent muzhiks! And what a strange fate has
brought me here!" thought Rostof, as he listened to
her and looked at her. "And what sweetness and
gratitude in her features and her words!" he said to
himself, as he listened to her faltering tale.

When she related all that had taken place on the day
after her father's obsequies, her voice trembled. She
turned aside, and then, as if she were afraid Rostof
would take her words to be an excuse for rousing his
pity, she glanced at him with a timidly questioning look.

The tears stood in Rostof's eyes. The Princess
Mariya observed it, and she looked gratefully at him
with those brilliant eyes of hers, which made one forget
the plainness of her face.

"I cannot tell you, princess, how happy I am at the
chance that brought me here and puts me in a position
to show you how ready I am to serve you," said Rostof,
rising. "You can start immediately, and I pledge you
my word of honor that no one shall dare to cause you
the slightest unpleasantness, if you will only permit me
to serve as your escort;" and, making her a courtly bow
such as are made to ladies of the imperial blood, he went
to the door. By the courtliness of his tone, Rostof

seemed to show that, in spite of the fact that he should consider it an honor to be acquainted with her, he would not think of taking advantage of her hour of misfortune to inflict his acquaintance upon her.

The Princess Mariya understood and appreciated this delicacy.

"I am very, very grateful to you," said she, in French. "But I hope that this was merely a misunderstanding, and that no one is to blame for it...." She suddenly broke down. "Forgive me," said she.

Rostof once more made a low bow, and left the room with an angry scowl.

CHAPTER XIV

"WELL, now, pretty? ah, brother, my pink one's a beauty, and her name is Dunyasha...."

But as he glanced into Rostof's face Ilyin held his tongue. He saw that his hero and commander had come back in an entirely different frame of mind.

Rostof gave Ilyin a wrathful glance, and, without deigning to give him any answer, he strode swiftly down to the village.

"I will teach them! I will give it to those cutthroats," he muttered to himself.

Alpatuitch, with a sort of swimming gait that was just short of running, found it hard to overtake him.

"What decision have you been pleased to come to?" he asked, at last catching up with him. Rostof halted and, doubling his fists, made a threatening movement toward Alpatuitch suddenly.

"Decision? What decision? You old dotard!" cried he. "What are you staring at? Ha?—The muzhiks are in revolt and you can't bring them to terms? You yourself are a traitor! I know you. I'll take the hide off you, the whole of you." And, as if afraid of wasting the reserve fund of his righteous wrath, he left Alpatuitch and hastened forward.

Alpatuitch, evidently crushing down his sense of in-

jured innocence, hastened after Rostof with that swimming gait of his, and continued to give him his opinions
in regard to the matter. He declared that the muzhiks
had got themselves into such a state of recalcitrancy,
that at the present moment it would be imprudent *to
contrarize* them, unless one had a squad of soldiers,
so that it would be better to send after the soldiers
first.

"I'll give them a squad of soldiers.... I'll show how to
contrarize them," replied Rostof, not knowing what he
was saying, and breathing hard from his unreasoning,
keen indignation and the necessity which he felt of expressing this indignation. With no definite plan of
action he rushed with strong, resolute steps straight at
the mob.

And the nearer he approached it, the more firmly
convinced grew Alpatuitch that this imprudent action
of his might lead to excellent results. The muzhiks in
the throng felt the same thing as they saw his swift,
unswerving movements and his resolute, scowling face.

After the hussars had entered the village and Rostof
had gone to see the princess, a certain perplexity and
division of counsels had prevailed among the peasantry.
It began to be bruited among them that these visitors
were Russians, and some of the muzhiks declared that
they would be angry because their young mistress was
detained. Dron was of this opinion, but as soon as he
had so expressed himself, Karp and the other muzhiks
attacked their former starosta.

"How many years have you been getting your belly
full of this commune?" cried Karp. "It's all the
same to you. You'll dig up your pot of money and be
off! What do you care whether they burn up our
houses or not?"

"The order was to keep good order: no one to go
from their homes and not carry off the value of a speck
o' dust — and there she goes with all she's got," cried
another.

"'T was your son's turn, but you were too soft on
your young noodle," suddenly exclaimed a little old

man, pitching into Dron. "But they shaved [1] my
Vanka. Ekh! we shall die!"

"Certainly we shall die!"

"I'm not quit of the commune yet," said Dron.

"Of course you're not. You've filled your belly!"....

Then two long, lank muzhiks said their say. As
soon as Rostof, accompanied by Ilyin, Lavrushka, and
Alpatuitch, drew near the mob, Karp, thrusting his
fingers in his belt, and slightly smiling, came forward.
Dron, on the contrary, got into the rear ranks, and the
throng crowded closer together.

"Hey! Which of you is the starosta here?" cried
Rostof, coming up to the mob with swift strides.

"The starosta? What do you want of him?" asked
Karp.

But before he had a chance to utter another word
his cap flew off, and he was sent reeling with a powerful
blow.

"Hats off, you traitors!" cried Rostof, in a stentorian
voice. "Where is the starosta?" he thundered, in a
voice of fury.

"The starosta, he wants the starosta.... Dron Zaka-
ruitch.... you!" was spoken by various officiously submissive voices, and every hat was doffed.

"We should never think of rebelling; we are keeping
order," insisted Karp, and several voices in the rear
ranks at the same instant suddenly shouted:—

"It was what the council of elders decided; we have
to obey."....

"Do you dare answer back?.... Mob!.... cutthroats!
.... traitors!" sang out Rostof, beside himself with
rage and in an unnatural voice, seizing Karp by the
collar. "Bind him! Bind him!" he cried, though
there was no one to execute his orders except Lavrushka
and Alpatuitch.

Lavrushka, however, sprang forward and seized Karp
by the arms from behind.

"Do you wish us to summon *ours* from below?"
he cried.

[1] *Zabrit lob*, "to shave the brow," that is to enlist a soldier, to conscript.

Alpatuitch turned to the muzhiks, calling two by name, to bind Karp's arms. These muzhiks submissively stepped forth from the throng and began to unfasten their belts.

"Where is the starosta?" cried Rostof.

Dron, pale and scowling, stood forth.

"Are you the starosta? — Bind him, Lavrushka," cried Rostof, as if it was impossible for this command to meet with resistance. And, in point of fact, two other muzhiks began to bind Dron, who, in order to facilitate the operation, took off his girdle and handed it to them.

"And see here .... do you all obey me!" — Rostof had turned to the muzhiks. — "Disperse to your homes instantly, and don't let me hear a word from one of you!"

"Come, now! we've done no harm!" .... "We've only been acting silly." .... "Made fools of ourselves, that's all." .... "I said there wasn't no such orders," said various voices, reproaching one another.

"That's what I told you," said Alpatuitch, reassuming his rights. "'T'wasn't right of you, boys."

"Our foolishness, Yakof Alpatuitch," replied the voices, and the crowd immediately began to break up and scatter to their homes.

The two muzhiks, with their arms bound, were taken to the master's house.[1] The two drunken men followed.

"Ekh! now I get a good look at you!" said one of them, addressing Karp.

"How could you speak to your betters in that way? What were you thinking of? Durak! idiot!" exclaimed the other. "Truly you were an idiot!"

Inside of two hours the teams were ready in the dvor of the Bogucharovo mansion. The men were zealously lugging out and packing up the master's belongings, and Dron, at the princess's intercession let out of the shed where he had been locked up, directed the muzhiks at their work, standing in the court.

"Don't pack that away so clumsily," said one of the muzhiks, a tall man, with a round, smiling face, taking

[1] *Barsky dvor.*

a casket from the hands of a chambermaid. "You see, that's worth something. Don't sling it in that way, or poke it under a pile of rope — why, it'll get spoiled! I don't like it that way. Let everything be done neat, according to law! There, that's the way — under this mat, and tuck hay round it. That's the way to do it!"

"Oh, these books! these books!" exclaimed another muzhik, bending under the weight of the bookcases from Prince Andreï's library. "Don't you touch them! Heavy, I tell you, boys! healthy lot of books!"

"Yes, that man kept his pen busy, and did n't gad much," said the tall, moon-faced muzhik, winking significantly, and pointing to some lexicons lying on top.

Rostof, not wishing to impose his acquaintance on the princess, did not return to her, but remained in the village, waiting for her to pass on her way. Having waited until the Princess Mariya's carriages had left the house, Rostof mounted and accompanied her on horseback along the highway occupied by our troops for a dozen versts.

At Yankovo, where his bivouac was, he politely took leave of her, and for the first time permitted himself the liberty of kissing her hand.

"Ought you not to be ashamed of yourself!" replied Rostof, reddening, as the Princess Mariya expressed her gratitude for his having saved her — for so she spoke of what he had done. "Any policeman [1] would have done as much. If we had only peasants to fight with, we should not have let the enemy advance so far," said he, feeling a twinge of shame, and anxious to change the topic. "I am only delighted that this has given me a chance of making your acquaintance. Farewell, — prashchaïte, princess. I wish you all happiness and consolation, and I hope that we shall meet under more favorable circumstances. If you wish to spare my blushes, please do not thank me."

But the princess, if she did not thank him further in word, could not help expressing her gratitude in every

[1] *Stanovoï.*

feature of her face, which fairly beamed with acknowl-
edgement and gentleness.   She could not believe him
when he said that she had nothing for which to thank
him.   On the contrary, it was beyond question that if
it had not been for him, she would have been utterly
lost either at the hands of the insurgent peasants, or
the French ; that *he*, in order to rescue her, had exposed
himself to the most palpable and terrible peril ; and still
less was it a matter of doubt that he was a man of high,
noble spirit, capable of realizing her position and misfortune.   His kindly, honest eyes, which had filled with
sympathetic tears when she herself was weeping, and
seemed to speak with her about her loss, she could not
keep out of her thoughts.

When she bade him farewell, and was left alone, the
Princess Mariya suddenly felt her eyes fill with tears,
and then, it seemed not for the first time, the strange
question came into her mind, " Did she love him ? "

During the rest of the journey to Moscow, though her
position was far from agreeable, the princess, as Dunyasha, who rode with her in the carriage, more than
once observed, looked out of the window and smiled
a sweet and melancholy smile.

" Well, supposing I did fall in love with him," mused
the Princess Mariya.

Mortifying as it was for her to acknowledge to herself
that she fell in love at first sight with a man who, perhaps, might never reciprocate her love, still she comforted herself with the thought that no one would ever
know it, and that she would not be to blame if, even to
the end of her life, she, without ever telling any one, loved
this man whom she loved for the first time and the last.

Sometimes she recalled his looks, his sympathetic
interest, his words, and happiness seemed to her not
impossible.   And it was at such times that Dunyasha
observed that she smiled as she gazed out of the carriage window.

" And it was fate that he should come to Bogucharovo,
and at such a time ! " said the Princess Mariya.   " And
it was fate that his sister should jilt Prince Andréї ! "

And in all this the Princess Mariya saw the workings of Providence.

The impression made on Rostof by the Princess Mariya was very agreeable. When his thoughts recurred to her, happiness filled his heart; and when his comrades, learning of his adventure at Bogucharovo, joked him because, in going after hay, he had fallen in with one of the richest heiresses of Russia, Rostof lost his temper. He lost his temper for the very reason that the idea of marrying the princess, who had impressed him so pleasantly, and who had such an enormous property, had more than once, against his will, occurred to him. As far as he personally was concerned, he could not wish a better wife than the Princess Mariya. To marry her would give great delight to the countess, his mother, and would help him to extricate his father's affairs from their wreck; and then, again, — Nikolaï felt this, — it would be for the Princess Mariya's happiness.

But Sonya? And his plighted troth? And that was the reason Rostof grew angry when they joked him about the Princess Bolkonskaya.

CHAPTER XV

HAVING accepted the command of the armies, Kutuzof remembered Prince Andreï, and sent word to him to join him at headquarters.

Prince Andreï reached Tsarevo-Zaïmishche on the very day and at the very time when Kutuzof was making his first review of the troops. He stopped in the village, at the house of a priest, in front of which the chief commander's carriage was standing, and took his seat on the bench in front of the door, waiting for his "serene highness," [1] as every one now called Kutuzof. From the field back of the village came the sound of martial music, then the roar of a tremendous throng of men shouting, "Hurrah! Hurrah!" in honor of the commander-in-chief.

[1] *Svietleïshiï.*

A dozen steps or so from Prince Andreï stood two of Kutuzof's servants, — the courier and his house-steward, — profiting by the prince's absence and the beautiful weather to come out to the gates.

A dark-complexioned little lieutenant-colonel of hussars, with a portentous growth of mustache and side-whiskers, came riding up to the gates, and, seeing Prince Andreï, asked if his serene highness lodged there, and if he would soon return.

Prince Andreï replied that he did not belong to his serene highness's staff, and had, likewise, only just arrived.

The lieutenant-colonel turned to the spruce-looking denshchik with the same question; and the chief commander's denshchik answered him with that contemptuous indifference with which the servants of commanders-in-chief are apt to treat under-officers.

"What? His serene highness? Likely to be here before long. What do you want?"

The lieutenant-colonel laughed in his mustaches at the denshchik's tone, dismounted from his horse, gave the bridle to his orderly, and joined Bolkonsky, making him a stiff little bow. Bolkonsky made room for him on the bench. The lieutenant-colonel of hussars sat down next him.

"So you're waiting for the commander-in-chief, too, are you?" asked the lieutenant-colonel. "He's weported to be vewy accessible! Thank God for that! That was the twouble with those sausage-stuffers. There was some weason in Yermolof asking to be weckoned as a German. Now pe'w'aps we 'Ussians may have something to say about things now. The devil knows what they've been doing! Always wetweating — always wetweating! Have you been making the campaign?" he asked.

"I have had that pleasure," replied Prince Andreï. "Not only have I taken part in the retreat, but I have lost thereby all that I hold dear, to say nothing of my property and the home of my ancestors.... my father, who died of grief. I am from Smolensk."

"Ah? Are you Pwince Bolkonsky? Wight glad to make your acquaintance : — Lieutenant-Colonel Denisof, better known as Vaska," said Denisof, shaking hands with Prince Andreï, and looking with a peculiarly gentle expression into his face. "Yes, I heard about it," said he, sympathetically ; and, after a short pause, he continued : "And so this is Scythian warfare. It 's all vewy good except for those whose wibs are bwoken. And you are Pwince Andweï Bolkonsky?" He shook his head. "Vewy, vewy glad, pwince, vewy glad to make your acquaintance," he repeated for the second time, squeezing his hand.

Prince Andreï had known from Natasha that Denisof was her first suitor. This recollection, at once sweet and bitter, brought back to him those painful sensations which of late he had not allowed himself to harbor, but which were always in his heart. Recently so many other and more serious impressions — like the evacuation of Smolensk, his visit to Luisiya Gorui, the news of his father's death — and so many new sensations had been experienced by him, that it was some time since he had even thought of his disappointment, and now, when he was reminded of it, it seemed so long ago that it did not affect him with its former force.

For Denisof, also, the series of recollections conjured up in his mind by Bolkonsky's name belonged to a distant, poetic past, to that time when he, after the supper, and after Natasha had sung for him, himself not realizing what he was doing, offered himself to a maiden of fifteen ! He smiled at his recollection of that time and of his love for Natasha, and immediately proceeded to the topic which at the present passionately occupied him to the exclusion of everything else.

This was a plan of campaign which he had developed during the retreat, while on duty at the outposts. He had proposed this plan to Barclay de Tolly, and was now bent on proposing it to Kutuzof. The plan was based on the fact that the French line of operations was too widely spread out, and his idea was that, instead of attacking them in front, or, possibly, in connec-

tion with offensive attacks at the front, so as to block
their road, it was necessary to act against their communications. He began to outline this plan to Prince
Andreï.

"They can't sustain such a long line. It is impossible! I'll pwomise to bweak thwough them; give me
five hundwed men and I'll cut my way thwough, twuly.
A sort of system of guwillas."

Denisof had got up in his excitement, and as he laid
his plan before Bolkonsky he gesticulated eagerly. In
the midst of his exposition, the acclamations of the
military, more than ever incoherent, more than ever
diffused and mingled with music and songs, were heard
in the direction of the review-grounds. The trampling
of horses and shouts were heard in the village.

"Here he comes," shouted the Cossack guard. Bolkonsky and Denisof went down to the gates, where
were gathered a little knot of soldiers, composing the
guard of honor, and saw Kutuzof coming down the
street, mounted on his little bay cob. An enormous
suite of generals accompanied him; Barclay de Tolly
was riding almost abreast of him. A throng of officers
followed them and closed in around them on all sides,
shouting "Hurrah!"

His aides galloped on ahead of him into the yard.
Kutuzof, impatiently spurring his steed, which cantered
along heavily under his weight, kept nodding his head
and raising his hand to his white cavalier-guard cap,
which was decorated with a red band and was without a
vizor. As he came up to his guard of honor, composed
of gallant grenadiers, — for the most part cavalrymen,
— who presented arms, he for an instant gazed silently
and shrewdly at them with the stubborn look of one
used to command, and turned back to the throng of generals and other officers standing around him. Over his
face suddenly passed an artful expression; he shrugged
his shoulders with a gesture of perplexity.

"The idea of retreating, and retreating with such
gallant fellows!" said he. "Well, good-by,[1] general,'

[1] *Da svidanya.*

he added, and turned his horse into the gates, past Prince Andreï and Denisof.

"Hurrah! hurrah! hurrah!" The acclamations rent the air behind him.

Kutuzof, since Prince Andreï had last seen him, had grown stouter than ever; his face was wrinkled and he fairly weltered in fat. But the whitened eye, and the scar, and that expression of lassitude in face and figure, which he knew so well, were the same. He was dressed in a military long coat, a whip hung by a slender ribbon over his shoulder, and he wore his white cavalier-guard cap. Heavily sprawled out and swaying, he sat his little horse. His *fiu — fiu — fiu* could be heard almost distinctly as he rode into the courtyard.

His face had that expression of relief which a man shows when he makes up his mind to have a rest after a public exhibition. He extricated his left leg from the stirrup, leaned back with his whole body, and, scowling with the exertion of getting his leg up over the saddle, rested with his knee a moment, and then with a quack like a duck he let himself down into the arms of the Cossacks and aides who were waiting to assist him.

He straightened himself up, looked around with blinking eyes, and, glancing at Prince Andreï, but evidently failing to recognize him, he set out with his clumsy, plunging gait for the steps. *Fiu — fiu — fiu —* he puffed, and again he glanced at Prince Andreï. The impression made by Prince Andreï's face, though it was reached only after several seconds, — as is often the case with old men, — at last connected itself with the recollection of who he was.

"Ah! how are you, prince, how are you, my good fellow?[1] come with me," he said wearily, glancing round, and beginning heavily to mount the steps, which groaned under his weight. Then he unbuttoned his uniform and sat down on the bench at the top of the steps.

"Well, how is your father?"

"Yesterday I received news of his death," said Prince Andreï, abruptly.

---

[1] *Galubchik.*

Kutuzof looked at Prince Andreï with startled, wide-opened eyes; then he took off his cap and crossed himself.

"The kingdom of heaven be his. God's will be done to us all."

He drew a deep, heavy sigh and was long silent. "I loved him dearly and I realized his worth, and I sympathize with you with all my heart."

He embraced Prince Andreï, pressed him to his fat chest, and held him there long. When at last he released him, Prince Andreï saw that his blubbery lips trembled, and that his eyes were full of tears. He sighed and took hold of the bench with both hands so as to rise.

"Come, come to my room, and let us talk!" said he; but just at that instant Denisof, who was as little apt to quail before his superiors as before his enemies, strode with jingling spurs to the steps, in spite of the aides, who with indignant whispers tried to stop him. Kutuzof, still clinging to the bench, gave him a displeased look.

Denisof, introducing himself, explained that he had something of the greatest importance for the good of the country to communicate to his serene highness. Kutuzof, with his weary look, continued to stare at Denisof, and, with a gesture of annoyance, released his hands and folded them on his belly, repeating: "For the good of the country? — Well, what is it? Speak!"

Denisof reddened like a girl, — it was so strange to see the blush on the veteran's mustached, bibulous face, — and he began boldly to evolve his plan for breaking through the enemy's effective line between Smolensk and Viazma. Denisof's home was in this region, and he was well acquainted with every locality. His plan seemed unquestionably excellent, especially owing to the force of conviction which he put into his words. Kutuzof regarded his own legs, and occasionally looked over into the *dvor*, or yard, of the adjoining cottage, as if he were expecting something unpleasant to appear from there. And in reality, from the cottage at which he was looking, during Denisof's speech, emerged a general with a portfolio under his arm.

"What?" exclaimed Kutuzof, interrupting Denisof in the midst of his exposition. "Ready so soon?"

"Yes, your serene highness," replied the general. Kutuzof shook his head as much as to say, 'How can one man have time for all this?' and went on listening to Denisof.

"I give my twuest word of honor as a 'Ussian officer," insisted Denisof, "that I will cut off Napoleon's communications."

"What! is Kirill Andreyevitch Denisof, Ober-intendant, any relation of yours?" asked Kutuzof, interrupting him.

"My own uncle, your sewene highness."

"Oh, we were good friends," exclaimed Kutuzof, jovially. "Very good, very good, my dear.[1] Stay here at headquarters; we will talk it over to-morrow."

Nodding to Denisof, he turned away, and stretched out his hand for the papers which Konovnitsuin had brought him.

"Would not your serene highness find it more comfortable to come into the house?" suggested the officer of the day, in a dissatisfied tone. "It's absolutely necessary to look over some plans, and to sign a number of documents."

An aide, appearing at the door, announced that his rooms were all ready. But Kutuzof evidently wanted not to go indoors until he was free. He scowled.

"No, have a table brought out, my dear; I'll look at them here," said he. — "Don't you go," he added, addressing Prince Andreï. Prince Andreï remained on the steps, and listened to the officer of the day.

During the rendering of the report, Prince Andreï heard in the passageway the whispering of a woman's voice and the rustling of a woman's silken gown. Several times, as he glanced in that direction, he caught sight of a round, ruddy-faced, pretty woman, in a pink dress, and with a lilac silk handkerchief over her head

[1] *Galubchik.*

holding a dish in her hands, and evidently waiting for the return of the commander-in-chief. One of Kutuzof's aides explained to Prince Andreï in a whisper that this was the mistress of the house, the pope's wife, who was all ready to offer his serene highness the *khleb-sol*.[1] Her husband had already met his highness with the cross at the church, and here she was at home with the bread and salt.

"Very pretty," added the aide, with a smile. Kutuzof looked up on hearing that. He had been listening to the general's report, — the principal feature of which was a critique on the position at Tsarevo-Zaïmishche, — just exactly as he had listened to Denisof, just exactly as he had listened to the discussions at the council on the night before the battle of Austerlitz, seven years previously. It was evident that he listened merely because he had ears, which could not help hearing, although one of them was stuffed full of tarred hemp; but it was plain that nothing that the general on duty could say could either arouse him or interest him, and that he knew in advance what would be said, and listened only because he had to listen, as he might have to listen to the singing of a Te Deum.

All that Denisof said was practical and sensible. What the general on duty said was still more practical and sensible, but it was evident that Kutuzof scorned both knowledge and sense, and took for granted that something else was needed to decide the matter; something else, and quite independent of sense and knowledge.

Prince Andreï attentively watched the expression of the chief commander's face, and the only expression which he could distinguish in it was one of tedium, or of curiosity as to the meaning of a woman's whispering inside the door, and the desire to save appearances.

It was evident that Kutuzof scorned sense and knowledge, and even the patriotic feeling shown by Denisof, but that he did not scorn them by his own superior sense and knowledge and feeling — for he did **not try**

[1] Bread and salt, typical of Russian hospitality.

to manifest these qualities, but he scorned them for some other reason. He scorned them because of his advanced age, because of his experience of life.

The one single disposition which Kutuzof felt called on to make in connection with this report related to the marauding of the Russian soldiers. The general on duty, on finishing his report, presented to his serene highness, to sign, a paper granting a favorable answer to a proprietor who had petitioned for the military authorities to reimburse him for the loss of his standing oats, which had been taken on requisition.

Kutuzof smacked his lips and shook his head when he heard about this.

"Into the stove with it.... burn it! I tell you, once and for all, my dear," said he, "throw all such things into the fire. Let 'em reap the grain and burn the wood as they need. I don't order it, and I don't allow it; but if it is done, I can't pay for it. It can't be helped. 'If wood is cut, the chips fly.'[1]" He glanced once more at the paper. "Oh, German punctilio!" he exclaimed, shaking his head.

CHAPTER XVI

"WELL, that is all, is it?" asked Kutuzof, affixing his name to the last of the documents; and, rising laboriously and settling the folds of his white, puffy neck, he went to the door with a cheerful face.

The pope's wife, with flushed face, grasped for the plate, which, though she had prepared it so long in advance, she nevertheless failed to present in time. And, with a low obeisance, she offered the bread and salt to Kutuzof. Kutuzof's eyes twinkled; he smiled, chucked her under the chin, and said:—

"What a pretty woman you are! Thanks, sweetheart!"[2]

He drew out of his trousers pocket a few gold pieces,

---

[1] *Drova rubyat, shchepki letyat*, Russian proverb.
[2] *Galubushka.*

and laid them in the plate. "Well, then, how are we situated?" said he, going toward the room reserved for his private use.

The pope's wife, with every dimple in her rosy face smiling, followed him into the chamber.

An aide came to Prince Andreï, as he stood on the steps, and invited him to breakfast. In half an hour he was again summoned to Kutuzof. Kutuzof was sprawled out in an easy-chair, with his uniform coat unbuttoned. He held a French book in his hand, and, when Prince Andreï came in, he laid it down, marking the place with a knife. This book, as Prince Andreï could see by the cover, was "Les Chevaliers du Cygne," a work by Madame de Genlis.

"Well, now, sit down, sit down here," said Kutuzof. "It's sad, very sad. But, remember, my boy, that I am a father to you — a second father." ....

Prince Andreï told Kutuzof all that he knew about his father's death, and what he had seen at Luisiya Gorui as he passed through.

"To what — to what have they brought us!" suddenly exclaimed Kutuzof, in an agitated voice, evidently getting from Prince Andreï's story a clear notion of the state in which Russia found herself.

"Wait a bit! wait a bit!" he added, with a wrathful expression; and then, evidently not wishing to dwell on this agitating topic, he went on to say:—

"I have summoned you to keep you with me."

"I thank your serene highness," replied Prince Andreï. "But I fear that I am not good for staff service," he explained, with a smile which Kutuzof remarked. "And chiefly," added Prince Andreï, "I am used to my regiment. I have grown very fond of the officers, and the men, so far as I can judge, are fond of me. I should be sorry to leave my regiment. If I decline the honor of being on your staff, believe me, it is...."

A keen, good-natured, and at the same time shrewdly sarcastic expression flashed over Kutuzof's puffy face. He interrupted Bolkonsky.

"I am sorry. You might have been useful to me;

but you are right, you are right. We don't need *men* here!
There are everywhere plenty of advisers, but not of men.
Our regiments would be very different if all the advice-
givers would serve in them as you do. I remember you
at Austerlitz — I remember you, I remember you with
the standard," said Kutuzof; and a flush of pleasure
spread over Prince Andreï's face at this recollection.
Kutuzof drew him close, and stroked his cheek, and
again Prince Andreï observed tears in his eyes. Though
Prince Andreï knew that tears were Kutuzof's weak
point, and that he was especially flattering to him, and
was anxious to express his sympathy for his loss, still
Prince Andreï felt particularly happy and gratified at
this allusion to Austerlitz.

"Go, and God bless you! I know, your road .... is
the road of honor."

He paused.

"I missed you sadly at Bukarest. I needed a messenger to send."

And, changing the conversation, Kutuzof began to
talk about the Turkish war and the peace which had
been concluded.

"Yes, they abused me not a little," said he, "both for
the war and for the peace; but all came about in time.
All things come to those who wait. There I had just
as many advisers as I have here".... he went on to
say, turning to the counselors, who evidently were an
annoyance to him. "Okh! these counselors, these
counselors!" he exclaimed. "If their advice had
been taken, we should still be in Turkey, and peace
would not have been signed, and the war would not be
over yet. Everything in haste, but 'fast never gets
far.'   If Kamiensky had not died, he would have been
ruined. He stormed a fortress with thirty thousand
men. It is not hard to take a fortress; it's hard
to gain a campaign. And to do that, not to storm and
attack, but patience and time are what is required.
Kamiensky sent his soldiers against Rushchuk; and
while I employed nothing but time and patience, I took
more fortresses than Kamiensky ever did, and I made

the Turks feed on horse-flesh." He shook his head. "And the French will do the same. Take my word for it," he exclaimed, growing more animated, and pounding his chest, "if I have anything to do with it, they will be eating horse-flesh too!"

And again his eyes overflowed with tears.

"Still, it will be necessary to accept a battle, won't it?" asked Prince Andreï.

"Certainly, if all demand it, there's no help for it. But trust me, my boy.[1] There are no more powerful fighters than these two, — Time and Patience; they do everything. But our advisers — they won't see it in that light, that's the trouble. Some are in favor, and some are opposed. What's to be done?" he asked, and waited for an answer. "Yes, what is it you advise doing?" he repeated, and his eyes gleamed with an expression of deep cunning. "I will tell you what is to be done," he went on to say, when Prince Andreï still refrained from expressing any opinion. "I will tell you what is to be done, and I shall do it. *Dans le doute, mon cher,*" — he hesitated, — "*abstiens-toi.* When in doubt, *don't,*" he repeated, after an interval. "Well, good-by, prashchaï, my dear boy. Remember that I sympathize with all my heart in your loss, and that to you I am not his serene highness nor prince nor commander-in-chief, but a father to you. If you want anything, apply directly to me. Good-by, my dear."[2]

He again embraced and kissed him. And before Prince Andreï had actually reached the door, Kutuzof drew a long sigh of relief, and had resumed his unfinished novel by Madame de Genlis, "Les Chevaliers du Cygne."

Prince Andreï could not account to himself for the why or wherefore of it, but it was a fact that, after this interview with Kutuzof, he returned to his regiment much relieved as to the general course of affairs, and as to the wisdom of intrusting them to this man whom he had just seen. The more he realized the utter absence of all self-seeking in this old man, who seemed to have

---

[1] *Galubchik.*
[2] *Prashchaï, galubchik.*

outlived ordinary passions, and whose intellect — that is, the power of coördinating events and drawing conclusions — had resolved itself into the one faculty of calmly holding in check the course of events, the more assured Prince Andreï felt that everything would turn out as it should.

"There is nothing personal about him. He won't give way to his imaginations; he won't do anything rash," said Prince Andreï to himself, "but he will listen to all suggestions; he will remember everything; he will have everything in its place; he will hinder nothing that is useful, and permit nothing that is harmful; he will remember that there is something more powerful and more tremendous than his will, — the inevitable course of events, — and he will have the brains to see them; he will have the ability to realize their significance, and, in view of this significance, he will be sensible enough to see what a small part he himself, and his own will, have to play in them. But chief of all," thought Prince Andreï, "what makes me have confidence in him is that he is Russian, in spite of his French romance of Madame de Genlis and his French phrases; because his voice trembled when he exclaimed, 'What have they brought us to!' and because he sobbed when he declared that he would make them eat horse-flesh."

It was due to this feeling, which all felt more or less vaguely, that Kutuzof's selection as commander-in-chief, in spite of court cabals, met with such unanimous and general recognition among the people.

CHAPTER XVII

AFTER the sovereign's departure from Moscow, the life in the capital flowed on in its ordinary channels, and the current of this life was so commonplace that it was hard to recall those days of patriotic enthusiasms and impulses, and hard to believe that Russia was actually in peril, and that the members of the English Club were at the same time "Sons of the Fatherland," and had declared themselves prepared for any sacrifice.

The only thing that recalled the general spasm of patriotic enthusiasm that had taken place during the sovereign's recent visit to Moscow was the demand for men and money, which, coming now in legal, official form, had to be met, the sacrifice having once been offered.

Though the enemy were approaching Moscow, the Moscovites were not inclined to regard their situation with any greater degree of seriousness; on the contrary, the matter was treated with peculiar lightness, as is always the case with people who see a great catastrophe approaching.

At such a time, two voices are always heard speaking loudly in the heart of man : the one, with perfect reasonableness, always preaches the reality of the peril, and counsels him to seek for means of avoiding it; the other, with a still greater show of reason, declares that it is too painful and difficult to think about danger, since it is not in the power of man to foresee everything or to escape the inevitable course of events; and, therefore, it is better to shut the eyes to the disagreeable, until it actually comes, and to think only of what is pleasant.

When a man is alone, he generally gives himself up to the first voice, but in society, on the contrary, to the second. This was the case at the present time with the inhabitants of Moscow.

Moscow had not been so gay for a long time as it was that year. Rostopchin's placards, called *affiches*, or *afishki*, were read and criticized just as were the couplets of Vasili Lvovitch Pushkin.[1] On the top of them

---

[1] Vasili Lvovitch Pushkin, the uncle of the poet Aleksandr Sergyeyevitch Pushkin, was born at Moscow in April, 1770; served in the bodyguard in the Izmaïlovsky regiment till 1797; began to contribute to the Petersburg *Mercury*, 1793; wrote an immense number of epistles, elegies, fables, epigrams, madrigals, etc. The war of 1812 sent him to Nizhni-Novgorod, where he remained till 1815. He died September 1, 1830, about seven years before his more famous namesake was killed. His best known work, "*Opasnui Sosyed* — A Dangerous Neighbor," has been thrice republished: Munich, 1815; Leipsic, 1855; Berlin, 1859.

were represented the picture of a drinking-house and the tapster and Moscovite meshchanin, Karpushka Chigirin, *who, having been an old soldier, on hearing that Bonaparte was marching upon Moscow, fortified himself with a brimming nog of liquor in the shop, flew into a passion, heaped every sort of vile epithets on all the French, stepped forth from the drinking-house, and harangued the crowd collected under the eagle.*

At the club, in the corner room, men collected to read these bulletins, and some were pleased when Karpushka make sport of the French, and said : —

" They would swell up with cabbage, burst their bellies with kasha gruel, choke themselves with shchi, that they were all dwarfs, and that a peasant woman would toss three of them at once with a pitchfork."

Some, however, criticized this tone, and declared that it was rude and stupid. It was reported that Rostopchin had sent the French, and, indeed, all other foreigners, out of Moscow; that Napoleon had spies and agents among them; but this story was told merely for the sake of repeating certain sardonic words which Rostopchin was credited with saying about their destination. These foreigners were embarked on the Volga at Nizhni, and Rostopchin said to them : —

"Creep into yourselves," — that is, keep out of sight — "creep on board the boat, and try not to let it become a Charon's bark for you."

It was also reported that the courts of justice had been removed from the city, and here there was a chance given for repeating one of Shinshin's jests, to the effect that for this, at least, Moscow ought to be grateful to Napoleon.

It was said that Mamonof's regiment would cost him eight hundred thousand, that Bezukhoï was spending still more on his warriors; but the best joke of all was that the count himself was going to buckle on his uniform and ride in front of his regiment, and those who would be in the front would not sell their chances to see this great sight for any money.

"You have no mercy on any one," said Julie Drubetskaya, picking up and squeezing a bunch of picked lint between her slender fingers covered with rings.

Julie had determined to leave Moscow the next day, and she was giving her last reception. "Bezukhoï is absurd, but he is so good, so kind! What is the pleasure *to be* so *caustique?*"

"Fined!" exclaimed a young man, in a militia uniform, whom Julie called "*Mon chevalier*," and who was going to accompany her to Nizhni.

In Julie's set, as in many other sets of Moscow society, it had been agreed to speak only in Russian, and those who forgot themselves and made use of French words in conversation, had to pay a fine, which was turned over to the committee of public defense.

"That's a double fine, for a Gallicism," said a Russian author who was in the drawing-room. "'*Pleasure to be'* is not good Russian."

"You show no mercy upon any one," pursued Julie, paying heed to the author's criticism.

"For using the word *caustique*, I admit my guilt, and will pay my fine for it, and for the *pleasure to tell* you the truth, I am ready to pay another fine; but for Gallicisms I am not to be held answerable," she said, turning to the author. "I have neither the money nor the time to hire a teacher and take Russian lessons, as Prince Galitsuin is doing."

"Ah, there he is," exclaimed Julie. "*Quand on —* No, no," said she to the militiaman, "do not count that one, I'll say it in Russian: 'When we speak of the sun we see his rays,'" said the hostess, giving Pierre a fascinating smile — "we were just talking about you. We were saying that your regiment would be really much better than Mamonof's," said she, with one of those white lies so characteristic of society women.

"Akh! don't speak to me about my regiment," replied Pierre, kissing the hostess's hand, and taking a chair near her. "I am tired to death of it."

"But surely you are going to take the command of it yourself?" asked Julie, shooting a glance of cunning and ridicule at the militiaman.

The militiaman in Pierre's presence was no longer so *caustique*, and his face expressed some perplexity at the meaning expressed in Julie's smile. In spite of his absent-mindedness and good humor, Pierre's personality immediately cut short all attempts to make a butt of him in his own presence.

"No," replied Pierre, with a glance down at his big, portly frame, "I should be too good a mark for the French, and I am afraid that I could not get on a horse."

Among those who came up as a subject for gossip in the course of the shifting conversation were the Rostofs.

"They say their affairs are in a very bad condition," remarked Julie. "And the count himself is so utterly lacking in common sense! The Razumovskys wanted to buy his house and his pod-Moskovnaya, and it is still in abeyance. He asks too much."

"No, I believe the sale was effected a few days ago," said some one. "Though now it is nonsense for any one to buy property in Moscow."

"Why?" asked Julie. "Do you imagine there is any real danger for Moscow?"

"What makes you go away?"

"I? That is an odd question. I am going because .... because .... well, I am going because everybody's going, and because I am not a Jeanne d'Arc and not an Amazon."

"There, now, give me some more rags."

"If he can only economize, he may be able to settle all his debts," pursued the militiaman, still speaking of Count Rostof.

"A good old man, but a very *pauvre sire*. And why have they been living here so long? They intended long ago to start for the country. Natalie, I believe, is perfectly restored to health? — Is n't she?" asked Julie of Pierre, with a mischievous smile.

"They are waiting for their youngest son," replied Pierre. "He was enrolled among Obolyensky's Cossacks and was sent to Byelaya Tserkov.[1] The regiment

[1] White Church.

was mobilizing there. But now he has been transferred
to my regiment and is expected every day. The count
wanted to start long ago, but the countess utterly refused to leave Moscow until her son came."

"I saw them three days ago at the Arkharofs'. Natalie has grown very pretty again and was very gay. She
sang a romanza. How easy it is for some people to
forget everything."

"Forget what?" asked Pierre, impulsively.

Julie smiled.

"You know, count, that knights like you are to be
found only in the romances of Madame de Souza."

"What sort of knights? Why, what do you mean?"
asked Pierre, reddening.

"Oh, fie now! dear count, *c'est la fable de tout Moscou. Je vous admire, ma parole d'honneur!*"

"Fined! Fined!" exclaimed the militiaman.

"Very well, then! It's impossible to talk; how
annoying!"

"What is the talk of all Moscow?" asked Pierre,
angrily rising to his feet.

"Oh! fie! count. You know!"

"I don't know at all what you mean," said Pierre.

"I know that you and Natalie were good friends, and
consequently.... No, I always liked Viera better. *Cette
chère Véra!*"

"*Non, Madame*," pursued Pierre, in a tone of annoyance. "I have never in the slightest degree taken upon
myself to play the *rôle* of knight to the Countess Rostova, and I have not been at their house for almost a
month. But I do not understand the cruelty...."

"*Qui s'excuse s'accuse*," said Julie, smiling, and waving
the lint ; and, in order to have the last word herself, she
abruptly changed the conversation. "What do you
suppose I heard last night? Poor Marie Bolkonskaya
arrived in Moscow yesterday. Have you heard? She
has lost her father!"

"Really? Where is she? I should like very much
to see her," said Pierre.

"I spent last evening with her. She is going to-day

or to-morrow morning with her little nephew to their pod-Moskovnaya."

"But what about her? How is she?" insisted Pierre.

"Well, but sad. But do you know who rescued her? It 's a perfect romance! Nicolas Rostof! Her people surrounded her; they would have killed her. She was already wounded. ..... He rushed in and saved her." ....

"Lots of romances!" exclaimed the militiaman. "Really, this general stampede seems to have been made for providing husbands for all the old maids. Catiche is one, the Princess Bolkonskaya two ...."

"Do you know, really I think that she is *un petit peu amoureuse du jeune homme?*"

"Fined! Fined! Fined!"

"But really, how do you say that in Russian?"[1]

CHAPTER XVIII

WHEN Pierre reached home he was handed two of Rostopchin's bulletins, which had been distributed that day.

In the first the count denied having forbidden any one to leave Moscow, and declared that, on the contrary, he was delighted to have ladies of rank and merchants' wives leave town. "Less panic, less gossip!" said the bulletin. "But I 'll answer for it with my life that the villain will never be in Moscow."

By these words Pierre was for the first time fairly convinced that the French would get to Moscow.

The second placard proclaimed that our headquarters were at Viazma, that Count Wittgenstein had beaten the French, but that, as very many of the inhabitants had expressed a desire to arm themselves, there were plenty of weapons for them at the arsenal: sabers, pistols, muskets, — all of which the inhabitants might buy at the lowest prices.

The tone of this placard was not nearly so full of grim

---

[1] The author answers that question by printing the Russian in a footnote: *Nemnozhetchko vliublena f etova molodova chelovyeka.*

humor as those which had been before attributed to the tapster Chigirin. Pierre pondered over these placards. Evidently that threatening storm-cloud which he looked forward to with all the powers of his soul, and which at the same time aroused in him involuntary horror— evidently this storm-cloud was drawing near.

" Shall I enter the military service and join the army, or shall I wait ? " This question arose in his mind for the hundredth time. He took a pack of cards which was lying on the table near him, and began to lay out a game of patience.

" If this game comes out," said he to himself, as he shuffled the cards, held them in his hand and looked up — " if it comes out right, then it means .... What shall it mean ? "

Before he had time to decide on what it should mean, he heard at the door of his cabinet the voice of the oldest princess, asking if she might come in.

"Well, it shall mean that I must join the army," said Pierre to himself. — " Come in, come in," he added, replying to the princess.

Only the oldest of the three princesses — the one with the long waist — continued to make her home at Pierre's; the two younger ones were married.

" Forgive me, *mon cousin*, for disturbing you," said she, in an agitated voice. " But you see it is high time to reach some decision. What is going to be the outcome of this ? Every one is leaving Moscow, and the people are riotous. Why do we stay ? "

"On the contrary, everything looks very propitious, *ma cousine*," said Pierre, in that tone of persiflage which, in order to hide his confusion at having to play the part of benefactor before the princess, he always adopted in his dealings with her.

"Yes, everything is propitious ! .... Certainly a fine state of affairs ! This very day Varvara Ivanovna was telling me how our armies had distinguished themselves. It brings them the greatest possible honor. But still the servants are exceedingly refractory ; they won't obey at all ; my maid — why, she was positively insolent! And before we know it they will be massacring us. It is impossible to go into the streets. But worst of all the French are liable to be here to-day or to-morrow! Why should we wait for them? I ask for only one favor, *mon cousin*," pleaded the princess. "Give orders to have me taken to Petersburg. Whatever I am, I cannot endure to live under the sway of Bonaparte!"

"There, there, *ma cousine!* Where have you got your information? On the contrary...."

"I will not submit to your Napoleon! Others may. .... If you do not wish to do this for me...."

"Yes, I will do it. I will give orders immediately."

The princess was evidently annoyed that she had no one to quarrel with. She sat on the edge of her chair, muttering to herself.

"Nevertheless, this has been reported to you all wrong," said Pierre. "All is quiet in the city, and there is not the slightest danger. Here, I was just this moment reading...." Pierre showed the princess Rostopchin's placards. "The count writes that he will answer for it on his life that the enemy shall never enter Moscow."

"Akh! this count of yours," exclaimed the princess, angrily. "He's a hypocrite, a rascal! who has himself been exciting the people to sedition. Wasn't he the one who wrote in these idiotic *affiches* that, if there was any one found, to take him by the topknot and drag him to the police office — how stupid! And whoever should take one should have glory and honor. That is a fine way of doing! Varvara Ivanovna told me that the mob almost killed her because she spoke French."

"Well, there's something in that. But you take everything too much to heart," said Pierre, and he began to lay out his patience.

His game of patience came out correctly, and yet Pierre did not join the army; but he remained in deserted Moscow, in the same fever of anxiety and indecision and fear, and, at the same time, joy, though he was expecting something horrible.

Toward evening of the following day the princess

took her departure, and Pierre's head overseer came to him with the report that the money required by him for the equipment of his regiment could not possibly be raised except by selling one of his estates. The head overseer explained to him that such expensive caprices as fitting out regiments would be his ruin. Pierre, with difficulty repressing a smile, listened to the man's despair.

"Well, sell it, then," he replied. "There's no help for it now. I cannot go back on my promise now."

The worse the situation of affairs in general, and his own in particular, the more agreeable it was to Pierre; the more evident it seemed to him that the long-expected catastrophe was drawing near. Already there was almost none of his acquaintances left in town. Julie had gone; the Princess Mariya had gone. Of near acquaintances only the Rostofs were left; but Pierre stayed away from their house.

That day, in order to get a little recreation, Pierre drove out to the village of Vorontsovo to see a great air-balloon, which Leppich had built for the destruction of the enemy, and a trial balloon, which was to be let off on the next day. This balloon was not yet ready; but, as Pierre knew, it had been constructed at the sovereign's desire. The emperor had written to Count Rostopchin as follows, in regard to this balloon: —

As soon as Leppich is ready, furnish him with a crew for his basket, composed of tried and intelligent men, and send a courier to General Kutuzof to inform him. I have already instructed him concerning the affair.

I beg of you to enjoin upon Leppich to be exceedingly careful where he descends for the first time, that he may not make any mistake and fall into the hands of the enemy. It is essential that he should coöperate with the commander-in-chief.

On his way home from Vorontsovo, as he was crossing the Bolotnaya Ploshchad, Pierre saw a great crowd collected around the Lobnoye Myesto, or place of executions; he stopped and got out of his drozhsky. They were watching the punishment of a French cook, charged with being a spy. The flogging had only just come to an end, and the executioner was untying from "the mare," or whipping-post, a stout man, with reddish side-whiskers, dressed in blue stockings and a green kamzol. He was piteously groaning. Another prisoner, lean and pallid, was also standing there. Both, to judge by their faces, were French. Pierre, with a face as scared and pale as that of the lean Frenchman, elbowed his way through the throng.

"What does this mean? Who is it? What have they done?" he demanded.

But the attention of the throng — chinovniks, bur-ghers, merchants, peasants, and women in cloaks and furs — was so eagerly concentrated on what was taking place on the Lobnoye Myesto that no one replied to him.

The stout man straightened himself up, shrugged his shoulders with a scowl, and, evidently wishing to make a show of stoicism, and not looking around him, tried to put on his kamzol; but suddenly his lips trembled, and he burst into tears, as if he was angry at himself, just as full-grown men of sanguine temperament are apt to weep. The crowd gave vent to loud remarks — as it seemed to Pierre, for the sake of drowning their own sense of compassion.

"Some prince's cook...."

"Well, Moosioo, evidently Russian sauce goes well with a Frenchman..... Set your teeth on edge? Hey'?" cried a wrinkled law clerk, standing near Pierre, as the Frenchman burst into tears. The law clerk glanced around, expecting applause for his sarcasm. A few laughed, a few continued to gaze with frightened curi-osity at the executioner, who was stripping the second.

Pierre gave a snort, scowled deeply, and, swiftly re-turning to his drozhsky, kept muttering to himself even after he was once more seated. During the transit he several times shuddered, and cried out so loud that the driver asked him : —

"What do you order?"

"Where on earth are you going?" shouted Pierre, as the coachman turned down the Lubyanka.

"You bade me drive to the governor-general's," replied the coachman.

"Idiot! ass!" screamed Pierre, berating his coachman as he scarcely ever had been known to do. "I ordered you to drive home, and make haste, you blockhead!.... I have got to get off this very day," muttered Pierre to himself.

Pierre, at the sight of the flogged Frenchman and the throng surrounding the Lobnoye Myesto, had come to so definite a decision not to stay another day in Moscow, but to join the army immediately, that it seemed to him he had already spoken to his coachman about it, or at least that the coachman was in duty bound to have known it.

On reaching home Pierre gave his coachman, Yevstafyevitch, who knew everything, and could do everything, and was one of the notabilities of Moscow, orders to have his saddle-horses sent to Mozhaïsk, where he was going that very day to join the army.

It was impossible to do everything on that one day, however, and accordingly Pierre, on Yevstafyevitch's representation, postponed his departure to the following day, so that relays of horses might be sent on ahead.

On the fifth of September foul weather was followed by fair, and that day after dinner Pierre left Moscow. In the evening, while stopping to change horses at Perkhushkovo, Pierre learned that a great battle had been fought that afternoon. He was told that there at Perkhushkovo the cannon had shaken the ground; but when Pierre inquired who had been victorious, no one could give him any information.

This was the battle of Shevardino, which was fought on the fifth of September.

By daybreak Pierre was at Mozhaïsk. All the houses at Mozhaïsk were filled with troops; and at the tavern, in the yard of which Pierre was met by his grooms and coachman, there were no rooms to be had. All the places were preëmpted by officers.

In the town and behind the town, everywhere, regiments were stationed or on the move. Cossacks,
infantry, cavalry, baggage wagons, caissons, cannons,
were to be seen on all sides.

Pierre made all haste to reach the front, and, the
farther he went from Moscow, and the deeper he pene-
trated into this sea of troops, the more he was overmastered by anxiety, disquietude, and a feeling of joy,
such as he had never before experienced. It was somewhat akin to that which he had experienced at the Slobodsky palace, at the time of the sovereign's visit, — a
feeling that it was indispensable to do something and
make some sacrifice.

He now felt the pleasant consciousness that all that
constitutes the happiness of men — the comforts of life,
· wealth, even life itself — was rubbish, which it was a
delight to renounce in favor of something else.

Still Pierre could not account to himself, and indeed
he made no attempt to decide, for whom or for what the
sacrifice of everything, which gave him such a sense of
charm, was made. He did not trouble himself with the
inquiry for what he wished to sacrifice himself; the
mere act of sacrifice constituted for him a new and
joyful feeling.

CHAPTER XIX

On the fifth of September was fought the battle at
the redoubt of Shevardino; on the sixth not a single
shot was fired on either side; on the seventh came the
battle of Borodino.

For what purpose and how was it that these battles
at Shevardino and Borodino were fought? Why was
the battle of Borodino fought? Neither for the French
nor for the Russians had it the slightest sense. The
most immediate result was, and necessarily was, for the
Russians an onward step toward the destruction of
Moscow — a thing that we dreaded more than anything
else in the world; and for the French an onward step
toward the destruction of their entire army — a thing

that they also dreaded more than anything else in the world. This result was even then, perfectly obvious, and yet Napoleon offered battle and Kutuzof accepted it.

If the commanders had been governed by motives of reason, it would seem as if it ought to have been clear to Napoleon that, at a distance of two thousand versts in an enemy's country, to accept a battle under the evident risk of losing a quarter of his army was to march to certain destruction; and it should have been equally as clear to Kutuzof that, in accepting an engagement, and in likewise risking the loss of half of his army, he was actually losing Moscow. For Kutuzof this was mathematically demonstrable, just as in a game of checkers, if I have one draught less than my adversary, by exchanging I lose, and, therefore, I ought not to risk the exchange.

If my adversary has sixteen checkers, and I have fourteen, then I am only one-eighth weaker than he is; but when he and I have each lost thirteen draughts, then he becomes thrice as strong as I am.

Up to the battle of Borodino our forces were to the French in the approximate proportion of five to six, but after the battle, of one to two. That is, before the battle, 100,000 : 120,000 ; but after the battle 50 : 100. And yet the wise and experienced Kutuzof accepted battle.

Napoleon, also, the leader of genius, as he was called, offered battle, losing a fourth of his army, and still farther extending his line. If it be said that he expected, by the occupation of Moscow, to end the campaign, as he did in the case of Vienna, this theory can be rebutted by many proofs. The historians of Napoleon themselves admit that he was anxious to call a halt at Smolensk; that he knew the risk he ran in his extended position, and knew that the capture of Moscow would not be the end of the campaign, because he had seen, by the example of Smolensk, in what a state the Russian cities would be left to him, and he did not receive a single response to his reiterated offers for negotiations.

In offering and accepting the battle of Borodino, Kutuzof and Napoleon both acted contrary to their intentions and their good sense. But the historians have affected to fit to these accomplished facts an ingeniously woven tissue of proofs of the foresight and genius of these commanders, who, of all the involuntary instruments for the execution of cosmic events, were the most totally subject and involuntary.

The ancients left us examples of heroic poems in which the heroes themselves constitute all the interest of the story ; and we cannot as yet accustom ourselves to the fact that history of this kind, applied to our own day, is wholly lacking in sense.

As to the second question : How came the battle of Borodino and the battle of Shevardino, which preceded it, to be fought ? there exists an explanation just as positive and universally known, but absolutely fallacious. All the historians describe the affair as follows : —

The Russian army, in its retreat from Smolensk, sought the most favorable position for a general engage= ment, and found such a position at Borodino.

The Russians beforehand fortified this position at the left of the Moscow-Smolensk road, almost in a right angle from Borodino to Utitsa, the very point where the battle was fought.

In front of this position, to keep watch of the enemy, a fortified redoubt was established upon the hill of Shevardino. On the fifth of September, Napoleon attacked the redoubt, and took it by storm ; September 7, he attacked the entire Russian army, which was then in position on the field of Borodino.

Thus it is described in the histories ; and yet the whole thing is perfectly wrong, as any one may be easily convinced who will care to investigate the facts.

The Russians did not seek the most favorable position ; but, on the contrary, in their retreat they passed by many positions which were more favorable than the one at Borodino. They did not halt at any one of these positions, because Kutuzof would not occupy any position he had not himself selected, and because the popular demand for an engagement was not yet expressed with sufficient force ; and because Miloradovitch had not come up with the militia ; and for many other reasons besides, too numerous to mention.

It is a fact that the former positions were superior in strength, and that the position at Borodino — the one where the battle was fought — was not only not strong, but was in no respect superior to any other position in the whole Russian empire, such as one might at haphazard point out on the map with a pin.

The Russians not only did not fortify their position on the field of Borodino, at the left, at a right angle to the road, — in other words, at the place where the battle took place, — but, moreover, up to the sixth of September, they never even dreamed of the possibility of a battle taking place there.

This is proved, in the first place, by the fact that until the sixth of September there were no fortifications on the ground ; but, moreover, the defenses begun on the sixth were not even completed on the seventh.

In the second place, this is proved by the position of the Shevardino redoubt : a redoubt at Shevardino, in front of the position where the battle was accepted, had no sense. Why was this redoubt fortified more strongly than all the other points ? And why were the troops weakened, and six thousand men sacrificed, in vain attempts to hold this position until late on the night of the fifth ? For all observations of the enemy, a Cossack patrol would have been sufficient.

In the third place, that the position where the battle was fought was not a matter of foresight, and that the Shevardino redoubt was not the advanced work of this position, is proved by the fact that Barclay de Tolly and Bagration, up to the sixth instant, were convinced that the Shevardino redoubt was the *left* flank of the position ; and even Kutuzof himself, in his report, written in hot haste after the battle, calls the Shevardino redoubt the *left* flank of the position.

It was only some time subsequently, when the report of the battle of Borodino was written, with abundant time for reflection, that, probably for the sake of smoothing over the blunder of the commander-in-chief, who had to be held infallible, the false and strange ideas were promulgated that the Shevardino redoubt made the advanced post — when, in reality, it was only an intrench-ment on the left flank ; and that the battle of Borodino was accepted by us in a position well fortified, and selected in advance — when, in reality, it was fought in a position perfectly unpremeditated, and almost unfortified.

The affair, evidently, happened this way : a position was selected on the river Kalotcha, where it crosses the highroad, not at right, but at acute angles, so that the left flank was at Shevardino, the right not far from the vil-lage of Novoye, and the center at Borodino, near the con-fluence of the rivers Kalotcha and Voïna. That this was the position, covered by the river Kalotcha, for an army having for its end to check an enemy moving along the Smolensk highway, against Moscow, must be evident to any one who studies the battle-field of Borodino, and forgets how the battle really took place.

Napoleon, who reached Valuyevo on the fifth of Sep-tember, failed — so the histories tell us — to discover the position of the Russians, stretching from Utitsa to Borodino, — he could not have discovered this position because there was no such position, — and did not dis-cover the advanced post of the Russian army, but, in pursuing the Russian rear-guard, he drove them in on the left flank of the position of the Russians at the Shevardino redoubt, and, unexpectedly to the Russians, crossed the Kalotcha with his troops. And the Rus-sians, not having succeeded in bringing on a general engagement, withdrew their left wing from a position which they had intended to hold, and took up another position, which was not anticipated and not fortified.

Napoleon, having crossed over to the left bank of the Kalotcha at the left of the highway, transferred the en-suing battle from the right to the left (relative to the Russians) and brought it into the field between Utitsa, Semenovskoye, and Borodino, — into a field which had no earthly advantage over any other field that might have been chosen at random anywhere in Russia, — and on this field was fought the whole battle of the seventh.

Roughly sketched, the plan of the imaginary battle and of the actual battle is here appended: —

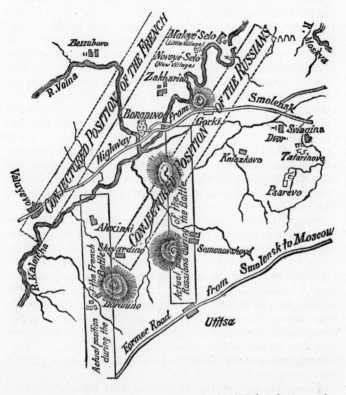

If Napoleon had not reached the Kalotcha on the afternoon of the fifth and had not given orders immediately to storm the redoubt, but had postponed the attack until the next morning, no one could seriously doubt that the Shevardino redoubt would have been the left flank of our position, and the battle would have been fought as we expected. In such a contingency, we should have defended still more stubbornly the Shevardino redoubt as being our left flank; we should have attacked Napoleon at his center or right, and on the fifth of September there would have been a general engagement in that position which had been previously selected and defended.

But as the attack on our left flank was made in the afternoon, after the retreat of our rear-guard, that is to say, immediately after the skirmish at Gridneva, and as the Russian leaders would not or could not begin a general engagement in the afternoon of the fifth, therefore the principal action of the battle of Borodino was already practically lost on the fifth, and undoubtedly led to the loss of the battle that was fought on the seventh.

After the loss of the Shevardino redoubt on the morning of the sixth, we were left without any position on our left flank, and were reduced to the necessity of straightening our left wing and of making all haste to fortify it as best we could.

But, in spite of the fact that the Russian troops on the seventh of September were protected by feeble, unfinished intrenchments, the disadvantage of this situation was still further enhanced by the Russian leaders' refusing to recognize a condition of things settled beyond a peradventure, namely, the loss of their defenses on the left flank and the transfer of the whole ensuing engagement from right to left, and remaining in their altogether too extended position from Novoye to Utitsa; and the consequence was they were obliged, during the engagement, to transfer their troops from right to left.

Thus, throughout the engagement, the Russians had the entire force of the French army directed against their left wing, which was not half as strong.

Poniatowski's demonstration against Utitsa and Uvarovo on the right flank of the French was independent of the general course of the battle.

Thus the battle of Borodino was fought in a way entirely different from the descriptions of it which were written for the purpose of glossing over the mistakes of our leaders and consequently dimming the glory of

the Russian army and people.   The battle of Borodino
did not take place on a selected and fortified position,
or with forces only slightly disproportioned; but the
battle, in consequence of the loss of the Shevardino
redoubt, was accepted by the Russians at an exposed
and almost unfortified position, with forces doubly strong
opposed to them, — in other words, under conditions
whereby it was not only unfeasible to fight ten hours
and then leave the contest doubtful, but unfeasible to
keep the army even three hours from absolute confusion
and flight.

CHAPTER XX

PIERRE left Mozhaïsk on the morning of the seventh.
On the monstrously steep and precipitous hillside
down which winds the road from the city, just beyond
the cathedral which crowns the hill on the right, where
service was going on and the bells were pealing, Pierre
dismounted from his carriage and proceeded on foot.

Behind him came, laboriously letting themselves down,
a regiment of cavalry led by its singers.

A train of telyegas, full of men wounded in the last
evening's engagement, met him on its way up the hill.
The peasant drivers, shouting at their horses and lash-
ing them with their knouts, ran from one side to the
other.   The telyegas, on which lay or sat three and
four wounded soldiers, bumped over the rough stones
which were scattered about and did duty as a causeway
on the steep road.   The soldiers, bandaged with rags,
pale, and with compressed lips and knit brows, clung to
the sides as they were bounced and jolted in the carts.
Nearly all of them looked with naïve, childlike curiosity
at Pierre's white hat and green coat.

Pierre's coachman shouted angrily to the ambulance
train to keep to one side.   The cavalry regiment with
their singers, as they came down the hill, overtook Pierre's
drozhsky and blocked up the whole road.   Pierre halted,
squeezing himself to the very edge of the road, which
was hollowed out of the hillside.   The hillside shelved

over, and as the sun did not succeed in penetrating into
this ravine, it was cool and damp there. Over Pierre
was the bright August morning sky, and the merry
pealing of the chimes rang through the air.

One team with its load of wounded drew up at the
edge of the road near where Pierre had halted. The
teamster, in his bast shoes, and puffing with the exer-
cise, came running up with some stones, and hastily
blocked the hind wheels, which were untired, and proceeded to arrange the breeching of his little, patient
horse.

An old soldier who had been wounded and had one arm
in a sling, and was following the telyega on foot, took
hold of it with his sound hand and looked at Pierre.

"Say, friend,[1] will they leave us here, or is it to
Moscow?"

Pierre was so absorbed in his thoughts that he did not
hear what the man said. He stared now at the cavalry
regiment, which had met face to face with the ambulance train, and now at the telyega, which had halted
near him with two wounded men sitting up and one
lying down, and it seemed to him that here was the
definite solution of the question that perplexed him so.

One of the two soldiers sitting in the cart had been
evidently wounded in the cheek. His whole head was
bound up in rags, and one cheek was swollen up as big
as the head of a child. His mouth and nose were all
on one side. This soldier looked at the cathedral, and
crossed himself.

The other, a young lad, a raw recruit, light complex-
ioned, and as pale as if his delicate face was completely
bloodless, gazed at Pierre with a fixed, good-natured
smile.

The third was lying down, and his face was hidden.

The cavalry singers had now come abreast of the
telyega : —

> "Akh! zapropala — da yezhova golova. ....
> Da! na chuzhoï storone zhivutchi." ....

[1] *Zemliatchek*, affectionate diminutive of *zemliak*, countryman, fellow-
countryman.

" Yes, living in a foreign land," rang out the voices, trolling a soldier's dancing-song. As if echoing the merry song, but in a different strain, far up from the heights above pealed the metallic sounds of the cathedral chimes. And, in still another strain of gayety, the bright sunbeams flooded the summit of the acclivity over opposite. But under the hillside where Pierre stood, near the telyega with the wounded men and the little panting horse, it was damp, and in shadow and in gloom.

The soldier with the swollen cheek looked angrily at the cavalry singers.

" Okh ! the dandies ! " he muttered scornfully.

" I have seen something besides soldiers to-day : muzhiks is what I have seen ! Muzhiks, and whipped into battle, too ! " said the soldier standing behind the telyega, and turning to Pierre with a melancholy smile. " Not much picking and choosing nowadays. They are trying to sweep in the whole nation — in one word, Moscow. They want to do it at one fell swoop."

In spite of the incoherence of the soldier's words, Pierre understood all that he meant, and he nodded his head affirmatively.

The road was at last cleared, and Pierre walked to the foot of the hill, and then proceeded on his way. He drove along, glancing at both sides of the road, trying to distinguish some familiar face, and everywhere encountering only strangers belonging to the various divisions of the troops, who, without exception, looked with amazement at his white hat and green coat.

After proceeding about four versts he met his first acquaintance, and joyfully accosted him. This acquaintance was one of the army physicians. Pierre met him as he came driving along in his britchka, accompanied by a young doctor, and when he recognized Pierre he ordered the Cossack who was seated on the box in place of his coachman to stop.

" Count ! your illustriousness ! How come you here?" asked the doctor.

" Why, I wanted to see what was going on." ....

"Well, you 'll have enough to see." ....

Pierre got out again, and paused to talk with the doctor, to whom he confided his intention of taking part in the battle.

The doctor advised Bezukhoï to apply directly to his serene highness. "God knows what would become of you during a battle if you are not with friends," said he, exchanging glances with his young colleague; "but his serene highness, of course, knows you, and will receive you graciously. I 'd do that if I were you, batyushka," said the doctor.

The doctor looked tired and sleepy.

"You think so, do you? .... But I was going to ask you .... where is our position?" said Pierre.

"Our position?" repeated the doctor. "That is something that is not in my line. Go to Tatarinovo. Lot of them digging something or other there. There you 'll find a mound, and from the top of it you can get a good view," said the doctor.

"A good view?" .... repeated Pierre. "If you would only ...."

But the doctor interrupted him, and turned to his britchka.

"I would show you the way; yes, I would, by God .... but" — and the doctor indicated his throat — "I am called to a corps commander. You see how it is with us! .... You know, count, there 's to be a battle to-morrow: out of a hundred thousand, we must count on at least twenty thousand wounded. And we have no stretchers or hammocks or assistant surgeons or medicines enough for even six thousand! We have ten thousand telyegas, but something else is necessary, certainly. We must do the best we can." ....

The strange thought that out of all these thousands of living, healthy men, young and old, who looked at his white hat with such jovial curiosity, probably twenty thousand were doomed to suffer wounds and death (very possibly the very men whom he that moment saw), struck Pierre.

"They, very possibly, will be dead men to-morrow;

why, then, can they be thinking of anything besides death?"

And, suddenly, by some mysterious association of ideas, he had a vivid recollection of the steep descent from Mozhaïsk — the telyegas with the wounded, the chiming bells, the slanting rays of the sun, and the songs of the cavalrymen.

"The cavalry are going into action, and they meet the wounded, and not for a single instant do they think of what is awaiting them, but they gallop by and greet the wounded; and out of all these men, twenty thousand are doomed to die, and yet they are interested in my hat! Strange!" thought Pierre, as he proceeded on his way to Tatarinovo.

At the mansion of a landed proprietor, on the left-hand side of the road, stood equipages, baggage wagons, a throng of denshchiks and sentinels. Here his serene highness was quartered, but when Pierre arrived he was out, and almost all of his staff. All were at a Te Deum service.

Pierre drove on farther, to Gorki. Mounting the hill, and passing beyond the narrow street of the village, Pierre saw for the first time the peasant militia, with crosses on their caps, and in white shirts, working with a will, with boisterous talk and laughter, at something, on a high, grass-grown mound to the right of the road.

Some of them had shovels, and were digging at the hill; others were transporting dirt in wheelbarrows, along planks; still others were standing about, doing nothing. Two officers were stationed on the mound, directing operations.

Pierre, seeing these muzhiks evidently enjoying the novelty of military service, again recalled the wounded soldiers at Mozhaïsk, and he saw still deeper meaning in what the soldier had tried to express when he said *they are trying to sweep in the whole nation.* The sight of these bearded muzhiks working in the battle-field, in their clumsy boots, with their sweaty necks, and some with shirt-collars rolled back, exposing to sight their sunburned collar-bones, made a deeper impression on

Pierre than all else that he had seen or heard hitherto concerning the solemnity and significance of the actual crisis.

CHAPTER XXI

PIERRE left his equipage, and, passing by the laboring militia, he directed his steps to the mound, from which, as the doctor had told him, the whole battle-field was visible.

It was eleven o'clock in the morning. The sun stood a trifle to Pierre's left and rear, and sent its beams down through the pure, rarefied atmosphere, brilliantly lighting up the immense panorama of hill and vale that spread before him, as in an amphitheater.

Above, and to the left, cutting across this amphitheater, he could see the Smolensk highway, passing through a village with a white church situated five hundred paces distant from the mound and below it. This was Borodino. Near this village the road crossed the river by a bridge, and, winding and bending, mounted higher and higher, till it reached Valuyevo, visible six versts away. (Here Napoleon now was.) Beyond Valuyevo the road was lost to sight in a forest, which showed yellow against the horizon. In this forest of birches and firs, to the left from the highway, could be seen glistening in the sun the distant cross and belfry of the Kolotsky monastery. Over all this blue distance, to the left and to the right of the forest and the road, in various positions, could be seen the smoke of camp-fires, and indeterminate masses of the French and Russian troops.

At the right, looking down the rivers Kalotcha and Moskva, the country was full of ravines and hills. Among these hills, far away, could be seen the villages of Bezzubovo and Zakharino. At the left the country was more level; there were corn-fields, and the ruins of a village which had been set on fire, Semenovskoye, were still smoking.

All that Pierre saw on his right hand and his left was

so confused that he found nothing that in any degree
answered to his expectations. Nowhere could he find
any such field of battle as he had counted on seeing,
but only fields, clearings, troops, woodland, bivouac
fires, villages, hills, brooks ; and in spite of all his efforts
he could not make out any definite position in this
varied landscape, nor could he even distinguish our
troops from the enemy's.

"I must ask of some one who knows," he said to himself, and he addressed himself to one of the officers, who
was looking inquisitively at his huge, unmilitary figure.

"May I ask," said Pierre, turning to this officer,
"what that village is yonder?"

"Burdino, is n't it?" replied the officer, referring to
his comrade.

"Borodino," said the other, correcting him.

The officer, evidently pleased to have a chance to
talk, approached Pierre.

"Are those ours yonder?" asked Pierre.

"Yes, and still farther are the French," said the
officer. "There they are, there. Can you see?"

"Where? where?" asked Pierre.

"You can see them with the naked eye. See there."

The officer pointed at the columns of smoke rising at
the left, on the farther side of the river, and his face
assumed that stern and grave expression which Pierre
had noticed on many faces which he had lately seen.

"Ah! is that the French? But who are yonder?"....

Pierre indicated a mound at the left, where troops
were also visible.

"Those are ours."

"Oh, ours! But there?"....

Pierre pointed to another hill in the distance, where
there was a tall tree near a village showing up in a
valley, and with smoking bivouac fires and something
black.

"That is *he* again," explained the officer (this was the
Shevardino redoubt). "Yesterday it was ours, but now
it 's *his*."

"What is our position?"

"Our position," repeated the officer, with a smile of satisfaction: "I can explain it to you clearly, because I arranged almost all our defenses. There, do you see? our center is at Borodino, over yonder." He pointed to the village with the white church, directly in front. "There is where you cross the Kalotcha. Then here, do you see, down in that bottom-land, where the wind-rows of hay are lying? — there is a bridge there. That is our center. Our right flank is about yonder," — he indicated a place far distant, between the hills at the extreme right, — "the river Moskva is there, and there we have thrown up three very strong earthworks. Our left flank...." here the officer hesitated. "You see, that is somewhat hard to explain to you. Yesterday our left flank was yonder at Shevardino; there, do you see, where that oak tree is? but now we have withdrawn the left wing, and now, — now do you see, yonder, that village and the smoke, that is Semenovskoye, — it is about there." He pointed to the hill of Rayevsky. "But it's hard to tell if the action will come off there. *He* has brought his forces in that direction, but that's a *ruse*. *He* will probably try to outflank us from the side of the Moskva. Well, at all events, a good many of us will be counted out to-morrow," said the officer.

An old non-commissioned officer, who had approached the speaker while he was talking, waited until his superior should finish, but at this juncture, evidently dissatisfied with what the officer was saying, interrupted him. "We must send for gabions," said he, gravely.

The officer seemed to be abashed, as if realizing that, while it was permissible to think how many would be missing on the morrow, it was not proper to speak about it.

"All right, send Company Three again," said the officer, hurriedly. "And who are you? One of the doctors, are you?"

"No, I was merely looking."

And Pierre again descended the hill, past the militia-men.

"Akh! curse 'em!" exclaimed the officer, following him and holding his nose as he ran by the laborers.

"There they are!".... "They've got here, they're coming!".... "There they are!".... "They'll be here in a minute!"—such were the exclamations suddenly heard, and officers, soldiers, and the militiamen rushed down the road.

Up the long slope of the hill came a church procession from Borodino. At the forefront, along the dusty road, in fine order, came a company of infantry with their shakoes off, and trailing arms. Back of the infantry was heard a church chant.

Soldiers and militiamen, outstripping Pierre, ran ahead with their hats off to meet the coming procession.

"They are bringing our Matuskha!.... The Intercessor. The Iverskaya Virgin!"

"The Smolensk Matushka," said another, correcting the former speaker.

The militiamen, both those who belonged to the village and those who had been working at the battery, threw down their shovels and ran to meet the procession.

Behind the battalion which came marching along the dusty road walked the priests in their chasubles,—one little old man in a cowl, accompanied by the clergy and chanters. Behind them, soldiers and officers bore a huge ikon, with tarnished face, in its frame. This was the ikon which had been brought away from Smolensk, and had ever since followed the army. Behind it and around it and in front of it came hurrying throngs of soldiers, baring their heads and making obeisances to the very ground.

When the ikon reached the top of the hill it stopped. The men who had been lugging the holy image on carved staves were relieved, the diachoks again kindled their censers, and the Te Deum began. The sun poured his hot rays straight down from the zenith; a faint, fresh breeze played with the hair on the uncovered heads, and fluttered the ribbons with which the ikon was adorned; the chant sounded subdued under the vault of heaven.

An enormous throng of officers, soldiers, and militiamen, all with uncovered heads, surrounded the ikon. Back of the priest and diachok, on a space cleared and reserved, stood the officers of higher rank. One bald-headed general, with the *George* around his neck, stood directly back of the priest and did not cross himself, — he was evidently a German, — but waited patiently for the end of the Te Deum, which he considered it necessary to listen to, as being calculated to arouse the patriotism of the Russian nation.

Another general stood in a military position, and kept moving his hand in front of his chest and glancing around.

Pierre, who had taken his position amid a throng of muzhiks, recognized a number of acquaintances in this circle of officers ; but he did not look at them ; his whole attention was absorbed by the serious expression on the faces of the throng of soldiers and militia, with one consent gazing with rapt devotion at the wonder-working ikon.

When the weary sacristans — who had been performing the Te Deum for the twentieth time — began to sing "Save from their sorrows thy servants, Holy Mother of God!" and the priest and diachok, in antiphonal service, took up the strain, "Verily we all take refuge in Thee, as in a steadfast bulwark and defense," Pierre noticed that all faces wore that expression of consciousness of the solemnity of the moment, which he had marked at the foot of the hill near Mozhaïsk, and by fits and snatches on many faces that had met him that morning. Heads were bent even more frequently, hair tossed up, and sighs and the sounds of crosses striking chests were heard.

The throng surrounding the ikon suddenly opened its ranks and jostled against Pierre.

Some one, evidently a very important personage, to judge by the eagerness with which they made way for him, approached the ikon.

It was Kutuzof, who had been out reconnoitering the position. On his way to Tatarinovo, he came to hear the Te Deum service. Pierre instantly recognized him by the peculiarity of his figure, which distinguished him from all the throng.

In a long overcoat, covering the huge bulk of his body, with a stoop in his back, with his white head bared, and with his hollow, white eye and puffy cheeks, Kutuzof advanced with his plunging, staggering gait, passed through the circle, and stood behind the priest. He crossed himself with a reverent gesture, touched his hand to the ground, and with a deep sigh bent his gray head. Behind Kutuzof were Benigsen and his suite. Notwithstanding the presence of the commander-in-chief, who attracted the attention of all those of higher rank, the militiamen and the soldiers, without looking at him, continued to offer their prayers.

When the service was concluded, Kutuzof went to the ikon, knelt down heavily, bowed to the ground; then he tried for some time to rise ; his weight and feebleness made his efforts vain. His gray head shook from side to side in his exertion.

At last he got to his feet again, and, with a childishly naïve thrusting-out of his lips, kissed the ikon, and again bent over and touched the ground with his hand. The generals present followed his example ; then the officers, and then, crowding, pushing, jostling, and stepping on each other, with excited faces came the soldiers and militia.

CHAPTER XXII

EXTRICATING himself from the crowd that pressed about him, Pierre looked around.

"Count, Piotr Kiriluitch! How come you here?" cried some one's voice. Pierre looked round. Boris Drubetskoï, brushing the dust from his knee, — he had apparently, like the rest, been making his genuflections before the ikon, — came up to Pierre, smiling. Boris was elegantly attired, with just a shade of the wear and tear from having been on service. He wore a long frock coat and a whip over his shoulder in imitation of Kutuzof.

Kutuzof, meantime, had returned to the village, and sat down in the shadow cast by the adjoining house, on a bench brought out in all haste by a Cossack, while another had covered it with a rug. A large and brilliant suite gathered about him.

The ikon had gone farther on its way, accompanied by a throng. Pierre, engaged in talking with Boris, remained standing about thirty paces from Kutuzof. He was explaining his intention of being present at the battle, and of reconnoitering the position.

"You do this way," said Boris. "I will do you the honors of the camp. The best thing is for you to see the whole affair from where Count Benigsen will be. You see, I am with him. I will propose it to him. And if you would like to ride round the position we will do it together; we are just going over to the left flank. And when we return I will beg you to do me the favor of spending the night with me, and we will get up a party. I think you are acquainted with Dmitri Serge-yevitch. He lodges over yonder."

He indicated the third house in Gorki.

"But I should like to see the right flank; they say it is very strong," protested Pierre. "I should like to ride over the whole position, from the Moskva River."

"Well, you can do that afterwards; but the main thing is the left flank."

"Yes, yes. But where is Prince Bolkonsky's regiment? Can't you show me?" demanded Pierre.

"Andreï Nikolayevitch's? We shall ride directly past it; I will take you to him."

"What were you going to say about the left flank?" asked Pierre.

"To tell you the truth, *entre nous*, God knows in what a condition our left flank is placed," said Boris, lowering his voice to a confidential tone. "Count Benigsen proposed something entirely different. He proposed to fortify that hill yonder; not at all this way.... but " — Boris shrugged his shoulders — "his serene highness would not hear to it, or he was overpersuaded. You see...."

But Boris did not finish what he was going to say, because just at that instant Kaïsarof, one of Kutuzof's aides, approached Pierre.

"Ah! Païsi Sergeyitch," exclaimed Boris, with a free and easy smile, addressing Kaïsarof. "Here I was just trying to explain our position to the count. It is a marvel to me how his serene highness could have succeeded so well in penetrating the designs of the French!"

"Were you speaking of the left flank?" asked Kaïsarof.

"Yes, yes, just that. Our left flank is now very, very strong."

Although Kutuzof had dismissed all superfluous members from his staff, Boris, after the changes that had been made, had managed in keeping his place at headquarters. He had procured a place with Count Benigsen. Count Benigsen, like all the other men under whom Boris had served, considered the young Prince Drubetskoï an invaluable man.

In the headquarters of the army were two sharply defined parties : that of Kutuzof and that of Benigsen, chief of staff. Boris belonged to the latter party; and no one was more skilful than he, even while expressing servile deference to Kutuzof, to insinuate that the old man was incapable, and that really everything was due to Benigsen.

They were now on the eve of a decisive engagement, which would be likely either to prove Kutuzof's ruin, and put the power in Benigsen's hands, or, even supposing Kutuzof were to win the battle, to make it seem probable that all the credit was due to Benigsen. In any case, great rewards would be distributed in the next few days, and new men would be brought to the fore. And, in consequence of this, Boris had been all that day in a state of feverish excitement.

Pierre was joined by other acquaintances, who came up after Kaïsarof, and he had no time to answer all the inquiries about Moscow with which they inundated him; and he had no time to listen to the stories which they told him. Excitement and anxiety were written in all faces. But it seemed to Pierre that the cause of these emotions, in some cases at least, was to be attributed rather to the possibility of personal success; and he found it impossible to help comparing them with that other expression of emotion which he had seen on other faces, and which was eloquent of something besides merely personal matters, but of the eternal questions of life and of death.

Kutuzof caught sight of Pierre's figure, and the group that had gathered round him.

"Bring him to me," said Kutuzof. An aide communicated his serene highness's message, and Pierre started to the place where he was sitting. But, before he got there, a private of militia approached Kutuzof.

It was Dolokhof.

"How comes this man here?" asked Pierre.

"He's such a beast! He's sneaking in everywhere!" was the answer. "He has been cashiered. Now he must climb up again. He has all sorts of schemes, and one night he crept up as far as the enemy's picket lines .... he's brave."

Pierre, taking off his hat, bowed respectfully to Kutuzof.

"I had an idea that if I made this report to your serene highness, you might order me off, or tell me that what I had to say was already known to you, and then all would be up with me ...." Dolokhof was saying.

"Very true, very true!"

"But if I am correct, then I am doing a service for my country, for which I am ready to die."

"Very true .... very true!"....

"And if your serene highness needs a man who would not care if he came out with a whole skin or not, then please remember me .... maybe I might be of use to your serene highness."

"Very true .... very true!".... said Kutuzof, for the third time, looking at Pierre with his one eye squinted up, and smiling.

At this instant, Boris, with his usual adroitness, came

up in line with Pierre close to the chief, and, in the most natural manner in the world, said to Pierre, in his ordinary tone of voice, as if he were pursuing what he had already begun to say : —

"The militia have put on clean white shirts, so as to be ready for death. What heroism, count!"

Boris said this to Pierre evidently for the sake of being overheard by his serene highness. He knew that Kutuzof would be attracted by these words, and, in fact, his serene highness turned to him.

"What did you say about the militia?" he asked of Boris.

"I said, your serene highness, that they had put on white shirts for to-morrow, as a preparation for death."

"Ah!.... They are a marvelous, incomparable people!" exclaimed Kutuzof, and, closing his eyes, he shook his head. "An incomparable people," he repeated, with a sigh. "So you wish to smell gunpowder?" he asked, addressing Pierre. "Well, it's a pleasant odor. I have the honor of being one of your wife's adorers; is she well? My quarters are at your service."

And, as often happens with old men, Kutuzof glanced about absent-mindedly, apparently forgetting all that he ought to say or to do. Then, apparently coming to a recollection of what his memory was searching for, he beckoned up Andreï Sergeyevitch Kaïsarof, the brother of his aide : —

"How .... how .... how do those verses .... those .... those verses of Marin's .... how, how do they go? Something he wrote on Gerakof : '*Thou shalt be a teacher, in the corpus.*' Repeat 'em, repeat 'em!" exclaimed Kutuzof, evidently in a mood to have a laugh.

Kaïsarof repeated the poem. Kutuzof, smiling, nodded his head to the rhythm of the verses.

When Pierre left Kutuzof, Dolokhof approached and took him by the arm.

"Very glad to meet you here, count," said he, in a loud tone and with peculiar resolution and solemnity, not abashed by the presence of strangers. "On the eve of a day when God knows which of us may quit this life, I am glad of the opportunity to tell you that I am sorry for the misunderstandings which have existed between us, and that I hope you bear me no grudge. I beg you to pardon me."

Pierre, smiling, gazed at Dolokhof, not knowing what answer to make. Dolokhof, with tears in his eyes, threw his arms around Pierre and kissed him.

Boris made some remark to his general, and Count Benigsen turned to Pierre and invited him to join him in a ride along the lines.

"It will be interesting to you," said he.

"Yes, very interesting," replied Pierre.

Half an hour later Kutuzof had gone back to Tatarinovo, and Benigsen with his suite, including Pierre, set off on their tour of inspection along the lines.

CHAPTER XXIII

Benigsen set forth from Gorki along the highway to the bridge to which Pierre's attention had been called by the officer on the hilltop as being the center of the position, and where, along the intervale, the windrows of hay lay filling the air with perfume. They crossed the bridge into the village of Borodino, whence they turned to the left, and, passing a great quantity of troops and field-pieces, made their way to a high mound where the militia were constructing earthworks. This was the redoubt which as yet was not named, but was afterwards known as Rayevsky's redoubt, or the Kurgannaya[1] battery. Pierre did not pay any special attention to this redoubt. He did not know that this spot would come to be for him the most memorable of all the positions on the field of Borodino.

Then they rode down through the ravine to Semenovskoye, where the soldiers were dragging off the last remaining beams from the cottages and corn-kilns. Then

[1] From *kurgan,* a mound or hill.

down a hill and up a hill they rode, forward across a field of rye crushed down and beaten as if by a hail-storm, and over a road newly formed by the artillery through a plowed field until they reached the fleches [1] which had just been started.

Benigsen drew up at the fleches and proceeded to scrutinize the Shevardino redoubt, — which had been ours the evening before, — where a number of horsemen could be distinguished.

The officers said that Napoleon or Murat was among them, and all gazed eagerly at the little knot of horse-men. Pierre also looked in the same direction, trying to make out which of these scarcely distinguishable men was Napoleon. At last the horsemen descended from the hill and disappeared.

Benigsen addressed a general who had approached him, and proceeded to explain the whole position of our troops. Pierre listened to Benigsen's words, exerting all the powers of his mind to comprehend the nature of the approaching engagement, but he was mortified to discover that his intellectual powers were not capable of it. He got no idea whatever. Benigsen ceased speaking, and, noticing that Pierre was listening attentively, he said, suddenly addressing him : —

" I am afraid this does not interest you ? "

" Oh, on the contrary, it is very interesting," replied Pierre, not with absolute veracity.

From the fleches they took the road still farther to-ward the left ; it wound through a dense but not lofty forest of birch trees. In the midst of these woods a cin-namon-colored hare with white legs bounded up before them, and, startled by the trampling of so many horses' feet, was so bewildered that for some time it ran along the road in front of them, exciting general attention and amusement, and only when several of the men shouted at it did it dart to one side and disappear in the thicket.

Having ridden two versts through the wood, they came to the clearing where the troops of Tutchkof's

---

[1] A kind of fortification. — AUTHOR'S NOTE.

corps were stationed, whose duty it was to defend the left flank.

Here, at the very extremity of the left flank, Benigsen had a wordy and heated conversation, and made what seemed to Pierre a very important disposition. In front of Tutchkof's division there was a slight rise of ground. This rise had not been occupied by our troops.

Benigsen vigorously criticized this blunder, declaring that it was a piece of idiocy to leave unoccupied a height commanding a locality, and to draw up the troops at the foot of it. Several of the generals expressed the same opinion. One in particular, with genuine military fervor, declared that the men were left there to certain destruction. Benigsen, on his own responsibility, commanded the troops to occupy this height.

This disposition on the left flank still further compelled Pierre to doubt his capacity to understand military manœuvers. As he listened to Benigsen and the generals who were criticizing the position of the troops at the foot of the knoll, he perfectly understood them and agreed in their strictures; but for this very reason he found himself utterly unable to comprehend how the one who had placed the men there at the foot of the knoll could have made such a palpable and stupid blunder.

Pierre did not know that these troops had been stationed there, not to guard the position, as Benigsen supposed, but were set in ambuscade; in other words, in order to be hidden and to fall unexpectedly on the enemy as they approached. Benigsen did not know this, and he moved these troops forward by his own understanding of the case, and without first informing the commander-in-chief.

CHAPTER XXIV

PRINCE ANDREÏ, that bright September afternoon of the sixth, was stretched out with his head leaning on his hand, in a dilapidated cow-shed, at the village of Kniazkovo, at the end of the position occupied by his regiment. Through a hole in the broken wall he was gazing at a row of thirty-year-old birches which ran along the edge of the inclosure, with their lower limbs trimmed off, and at a plowed field over which were scattered sheaves of oats, and at the coppice where the smoke of bivouac fires was rising, where the soldiers were cooking their suppers.

Narrow and useless and trying as Prince Andreï's life now seemed to him, he felt excited and irritable on the eve of the battle, just as he had seven years before at Austerlitz.

The orders for the morrow's battle were given and received by him. There was nothing further left for him to do. But his thoughts, the simplest, clearest, and therefore most terrible thoughts, refused to leave him to repose. He was aware that the morrow's engagement would be the most formidable of all in which he had ever taken part, and the possibility of death, for the first time in his life without reference to any worldly aspect, without consideration as to the effect it might produce upon others, but in its relation to himself, to his own soul, confronted him with vividness, almost with certainty, in all its grim reality.

And from the height of this consideration, all that which hitherto tormented and preoccupied him was suddenly thrown into a cold white light, without shadow, without perspective, without distinction of features.

All his life appeared to him as in a magic lantern, into which he had long been looking through a glass and by means of an artificial light.

Now he could suddenly see without a glass, by the clear light of day, these wretchedly painted pictures.

"Yes, yes, here are those false images which have

excited and enraptured and deceived me," said he to himself, as he passed in review, in his imagination, the principal pictures of his magic-lantern life, now looking at them in this cold white light of day — the vivid thought of death.

"Here they are, these coarsely painted figures which pretended to represent something beautiful and mysterious. Glory, social advantages, woman's love, the country itself — how great seemed to me these pictures, what deep significance they seemed to possess. And all that seems now so simple, so cheap and tawdry, in the cold white light of that morning which, I am convinced, will dawn for me to-morrow."

The three chief sorrows of his life especially arrested his attention — his love for a woman, the death of his father, and the French invasion which was ingulfing half of Russia.

"Love!.... That young girl seemed to me endowed with mysterious powers. How was it? I loved her, I dreamed poetic dreams of love and happiness with her. .... Oh, precious boy!" he cried aloud savagely. "How was it? I had faith in an ideal love which should keep her faithful to me during the whole year of my absence. Like the tender dove of the fable, she should have pined away while separated from me. But the reality was vastly more simple. .... It was all horribly simple, disgusting!

"My father was building at Luisiya Gorui and supposing that it was his place, his land, his air, his peasants; but Napoleon came, and, not even knowing of his existence, swept him aside like a chip from the road, and his Luisiya Gorui was swallowed up and his life with it. But the Princess Mariya says that this is a. discipline sent from above. For whom is it a discipline, since he is no more and will never be again? He will never be seen again. He is no more. Then to whom is it a discipline?

"The fatherland, the destruction of Moscow! But to-morrow I shall be killed — perhaps not even by the French, but by one of our own men, just as I might have been yesterday when the soldier discharged his musket near my head — and the French will come, will take me by the legs and shoulders and fling me into a pit, so that I may not become a stench in their nostrils, and new conditions of existence will spring up, to which other men will grow just as accustomed, and I shall not know about them, for I shall be no more!"

He gazed at the row of birches shining in the sun, with their motionless yellow, green, and white boles.

"I must die; suppose I am killed to-morrow, suppose it is the end of me,.... the end of all, and I no longer existent!"

He vividly pictured the world, and himself not in it. The birches, with the lights and shades, and the curling clouds, and the smoke of the bivouac fires, — all suddenly underwent a change, and assumed for him something terrible and threatening. A cold chill ran down his back. Quickly leaping to his feet, he left the shed, and began to walk up and down.

Voices were heard behind the shed.

"Who is there?" asked Prince Andreï.

The red-nosed Captain Timokhin, who had formerly been Dolokhof's company commander, and now, owing to the lack of officers, had been promoted to battalion commander, came shyly to the shed. Behind him came an aide and the paymaster of the regiment.

Prince Andreï got up, listened to what the officers had to report to him, gave them a few extra directions, and was just about to dismiss them when he heard from behind the shed a familiar lisping voice.

"*Que diable!*" exclaimed the voice of this man, who tripped up over something.

Prince Andreï, peering out of the shed, saw advancing toward him his friend Pierre, who had just succeeded in stumbling and almost falling flat over a pole which was lying on the ground. As a general thing, it was disagreeable for Prince Andreï to see men from his own rank in life, and especially to see Pierre, who brought back to his remembrance all the trying moments which he had experienced during his last visit at Moscow.

"Ah! how is this?" he exclaimed. "What chance brings you here? I was not expecting you."

While he was saying these words his eyes and his whole face expressed something more than mere coolness — it was rather an unfriendliness, which Pierre instantly remarked. He had approached the shed in the most animated frame of mind, but when he saw Prince Andreï's face he felt suddenly embarrassed and awkward.

"I came.... well.... you know.... I came.... it was interesting to me," stammered Pierre, who had already used that word "interesting" no one knows how many times during the course of that day. "I wanted to see a battle."

"So, so, but what do your brotherhood of Masons say about war? How can it be prevented?" asked Prince Andreï, ironically. "Well, how is Moscow? How are my family? Have they got to Moscow at last?" he asked gravely.

"Yes, they got there. Julie Drubetskaya told me. I went to call upon them, and failed to find them. They had gone to your pod-Moskovnaya."

CHAPTER XXV

THE officers were going to take their leave, but Prince Andreï, as apparently not wishing to be left alone with his friend, invited them to sit down and take tea. Stools and tea were brought. The officers, not without amazement, gazed at Pierre's enormously stout figure, and listened to his stories of Moscow, and the position of our troops which he had chanced to visit.

Prince Andreï said nothing, and the expression of his face was so disagreeable that Pierre addressed himself more to the good-natured battalion commander, Timokhin, than to Bolkonsky.

"So you understood all the arrangement of our forces, did you?" suddenly interrupted Prince Andreï.

"Yes — that is, to a certain extent," said Pierre ; "so far as a civilian can. I don't mean absolutely, but still I understood the general arrangements."

"Then you are ahead of any one else!" said Prince Andreï.[1]

"Ha?" exclaimed Pierre, looking in perplexity over his glasses at Prince Andreï. "Well, what do you think about the appointment of Kutuzof?" he asked.

"I was very much pleased with it; that is all I can say about it," replied Prince Andreï.

"Now, then, please tell me your opinion in regard to Barclay de Tolly. They are saying all sorts of things about him in Moscow. What is your judgment about him?"

"Ask these gentlemen," suggested Prince Andreï, indicating the officers.

Pierre looked at Timokhin with that condescendingly questioning smile with which all treated him in spite of themselves.

"It brought light[2] to us, your illustriousness, as soon as his serene highness took charge," said Timokhin, who kept glancing timidly at his regimental commander.

"How so?" asked Pierre.

"Well, now, take, for instance, firewood or fodder: I will explain it to you. We retreated from Swienciany, and did not dare to touch a dry branch or a bit o' hay or anything. You see, we marched off and left it for *him*. Wasn't that so, your illustriousness?" he asked, addressing "his prince." "It was, 'Don't you dare.' In our regiment, two officers were court-martialed for doing such things. Well, then, when his serene highness came in, it became perfectly simple as far as such things were concerned. We saw light." ....

"Then, why did he forbid it?"

Timokhin glanced around in some confusion, not knowing what to say in reply to this question. Pierre turned to Prince Andreï, and asked the same thing.

"In order not to spoil the country which we were

---

[1] *Eh bien, vous êtes plus avancé que qui cela soit.*
[2] *Svyet,* light; a play on the first syllable of *svyetleïshii* (most serene).

leaving to the enemy," replied Prince Andreï, with savage sarcasm. "It is very judicious never to allow the country to be pillaged and soldiers taught to be marauders. Well, then, at Smolensk, he also very correctly surmised that the French might outflank us since they outnumbered us. But one thing he could not understand," shouted Prince Andreï, in a high key, as if he had lost control of his voice. "He could not understand that we were for the first time fighting in defense of Russian soil, that the troops were animated by a spirit such as I, for one, had never seen before; that we had beaten the French two days running, and that this victory had multiplied our strength tenfold. He gave the orders to retreat, and all our efforts and losses were rendered useless. He never dreamed of playing the traitor; he tried to do everything in the best possible manner; his foresight was all-embracing, — but for that very reason he is good for nothing. He is good for nothing now, for the very reason that he lays out all his plans beforehand very judiciously and punctiliously, as it is natural for every German to do. How can I make it clear? .... See here! Your father has a German lackey, and he is an excellent lackey, and he serves him in all respects better than you could do, and so you let him do his work; but if your father is sick unto death, you send the lackey off, and with your own unaccustomed, unskilful hands, you look after your father, and you are more of a comfort to him than the skilful hand of a foreigner would be. And that is the case with Barclay. As long as Russia was well, a stranger could serve her and was an excellent servant; but as soon as she was in danger, she needs a man of her own blood. Well, you have accused him at the club of being a traitor. The only effect of traducing him as a traitor will be that afterwards, becoming ashamed of such a false accusation, the same men will suddenly make a hero or a genius of him, and that will be still more unjust. He is an honorable and very punctilious German." ....

"At all events, they say he is a skilful commander," interposed Pierre.

"I don't know what is meant by a skilful commander," said Prince Andreï, with a sneer.

"A skilful commander," explained Pierre, "well, is one who foresees all contingencies.... reads his enemy's intentions."

"Well, that is impossible," said Prince Andreï, as if the matter had been long ago settled.

Pierre looked at him in amazement.

"Certainly," said he, "it has been said that war is like a game of chess."

"Yes," replied Prince Andreï; "only with this slight difference : that in chess you can think over each move as long as you wish, that you are in that case freed from conditions of time ; and with this difference also, that the knight is always stronger than the pawn, and two pawns are always stronger than one, while in war a single battalion is sometimes stronger than a division, and sometimes weaker than a company. The relative strength of opposing armies can never be predicted. Believe me," said he, "if it depended on the dispositions made by the staff-officers, then I should have remained on the staff and made my dispositions ; while as it is, instead, I have the honor of serving here in the regiment with these gentlemen, and I take it that, in reality, the affair of to-morrow will depend on us, and not on them. .... Success never has depended, and never will depend, either on position or on armament or on numbers, and least of all on position."

"What does it depend on, then ? "

"On the feeling that is in me and in him," — he indicated Timokhin, — "and in every soldier."

Prince Andreï glanced at Timokhin, who was staring at his commander, startled and perplexed. Contrary to his ordinary silent self-restraint, Prince Andreï seemed now excited. Evidently he could not refrain from expressing the thoughts which had unexpectedly occurred to him.

"The battle will be gained by the one who is resolutely bent on gaining it. Why did we lose the battle of Austerlitz ? Our loss was not much greater than that of the French, but we said to ourselves very early in the engagement that we should lose it, and we did lose it. And we said this because there was no reason for being in a battle there, and we were anxious to get away from the battle-field as soon as possible. ' We have lost, so let us run,' and we did run. If we had not said this till evening, God knows what would have happened. But to-morrow we shall not say that. You say our position, the left flank, is weak, the right flank too much extended," he pursued, " but that is all nonsense. It is not so at all. For what is before us to-morrow? A hundred millions of the most various possibilities, which will be decided instantaneously by the fact that either they, or our men, will start to run; this one or that one will be killed. All that is being done now, though, is mere child's play. The fact is, those with whom you rode round inspecting the position, instead of promoting the general course of events, rather hinder it. They are occupied only with their own petty interests."

" At such a moment?" asked Pierre, reproachfully.

" Yes, even *at such a moment*," repeated Prince Andreï. " For them this is only a propitious time to oust a rival or win an extra cross or ribbon. I will tell you what I think to-morrow means. A hundred thousand Russian and a hundred thousand French soldiers meet in battle to-morrow, and the result will be that when these two hundred thousand soldiers have fought, the side will win that fights most desperately and is least sparing of itself. And, if you like, I will tell you this : Whatever happens, whatever disagreements there may be in the upper circles, *we* shall win the battle to-morrow. To-morrow, whatever happens, we shall win."

" You are right there, your illustriousness, perfectly right," echoed Timokhin. " Why should we spare ourselves now? The men in my battalion — would you believe it? — would not drink their vodka. ' It is not the time for it,' said they."

All were silent. The officers got up. Prince Andreï

went with them behind the shed, giving his final directions to his aide.

When the officers had gone, Pierre joined Prince
Andreï, and was just about to renew his conversation
with him, when along the road that ran not far from the
shed they heard the trampling hoofs of three horses,
and, looking in that direction, Prince Andreï recognized
Woltzogen and Klauzewitz, accompanied by a Cossack.
They rode rapidly by, talking as they went, and Pierre
and Andreï could not help hearing the following snatches
of their conversation : —

"The war must spread into the country. I cannot
sufficiently advocate this plan," said one.

"Oh, yes," replied the other, "our only object is to
weaken the enemy, so of course we cannot consider the
loss of private individuals."[1]

"*O ja !*" cchoed the first again.

"Yes, 'spread into the country,'" repeated Prince
Andreï, with an angry snort, after they had ridden past.
"'The country !' And there my father and son and
my sister have had to bear the brunt of it at Luisiya
Gorui. To him it is all the same. Now, that illustrates
the very thing I was telling you. These German gentlemen will not win the battle to-morrow, but will only
muddle matters as far as they can, for in their German
heads there are only arguments which are n't worth a
row of pins, while in their hearts they have nothing of
what is alone useful at such a time — not one atom of
what is in Timokhin. They have abandoned all Europe
to *him*, and now they come here to teach us. Splendid
teachers !" and again his voice became high and sharp.

"So you think that we shall win a victory to-morrow ?"
asked Pierre.

"Certainly I do," replied Prince Andreï, absently.
"One thing I should have done if I could," he began,
after a short pause ; "I would have allowed no prisoners

---

[1] "*Der Krieg muss im Raum verlegt werden. Der Ansicht kann ich
genug Preis geben.*" — "*O ja, der Zwech ist nur den Feind zu schwächen,
so kann mann gewiss nicht den Verlust der privat-Personen in Achtung
nehmen.*"

to be taken. What is the taking of prisoners? It is chivalry. The French have destroyed my home, and they are coming to destroy Moscow; they have insulted me, and they go on insulting me every second. They are my enemies, they are in my opinion criminals. And that expresses the feeling of Timokhin and the whole army. They must be punished. If they are my enemies, they cannot be my friends, whatever may have been said at Tilsit."

"Yes, you are right," assented Pierre, with gleaming eyes glancing at Prince Andreï. "I entirely agree with you."

The question which had been troubling Pierre ever since his delay on the hillside of Mozhaïsk, and all that long day, now became to him perfectly clear and settled beyond a peradventure. He now comprehended all the meaning and significance of this war and of the impending battle. All that he had seen that day, all the stern faces full of thoughtfulness, of which he had caught a cursory glimpse, now were illuminated with a new light for him. He comprehended that latent heat of patriotism — to use a term of physics — which was hidden in all the men he had seen, and this explained to him why it was all these men were so calm, and, as it were, heedless in their readiness for death.

"Let no quarter be given," pursued Prince Andreï. "That alone would change all war, and would really make it less cruel. But, as it is, we play at making war. That's the wretchedness of it; we are magnanimous and all that sort of thing. This magnanimity and sensibility — it is like the magnanimity and sensibility of a high-born lady, who is offended if by chance she sees a calf killed; she is so good that she cannot see the blood, but she eats the same calf with good appetite when it is served with gravy. They prate to us about the laws of warfare, chivalry, flags of truce, humanity to the wounded, and the like. It's all nonsense. I saw what chivalry, what our 'parliamentarianism' was in 1805; they duped us, we duped them. They pillage our homes, they issue counterfeit assignats, and worse than all, they kill our children and our fathers, and then talk about the laws of warfare and generosity to our enemies. Give no quarter, but kill and be killed! Whoever has reached this conclusion, as I have, by suffering ...."

Prince Andreï, who had believed that it was a matter of indifference to him whether Moscow were taken or not taken, — just as Smolensk had been, — suddenly stopped short in the middle of his argument, owing to an unexpected cramp that took him in the throat. He walked up and down a few times in silence; but his eyes gleamed fiercely, and his lip trembled, when he again resumed the thread of his discourse.

" If there were none of this magnanimity in warfare, then we should only undertake it when, as now, it was a matter for which it was worth while to meet one's death. Then there would not be war because Pavel Ivanuitch had insulted Mikhaïl Ivanuitch. But if there must be war like the present one, let it be war. Then the zeal and intensity of the troop would always be like what it is now. Then all these Westphalians and Hessians, whom Napoleon has brought with him, would not have come against us to Russia, and we should never have gone to fight in Austria and Prussia without knowing why. War is not amiability, but it is the most hateful thing in the world, and it is necessary to understand it so and not to play at war. It is necessary to take this frightful necessity sternly and seriously. This is the pith of the matter; avoid falsehood, let war be war, and not sport. For otherwise war becomes a favorite pastime for idle and frivolous men. The military are the most honored of any class.

"But what is war, and what is necessary for its success, and what are the laws of military society? The end and aim of war is murder; the weapons of war are espionage, and treachery and the encouragement of treachery, the ruin of the inhabitants, and pillage and robbery of their possessions for the maintenance of the troops, deception and lies which pass under the name of finesse; the privileges of the military class are the lack of freedom, that is discipline, enforced inactivity, ignorance, rudeness, debauchery, drunkenness. And yet this is the highest caste in society, respected by all. All rulers, except the emperor of China, wear military uniforms, and the one who has killed the greatest number of men gets the greatest reward.

"Tens of thousands of men meet, just as they will to-morrow, to murder one another, they will massacre and maim ; and afterwards thanksgiving Te Deums will be celebrated, because many men have been killed, — the number is always exaggerated, — and victory will be proclaimed on the supposition that the more men killed, the greater the credit. Think of God looking down and listening to them !" exclaimed Prince Andreï, in his sharp, piping voice. "Ah! my dear fellow,[1] of late life has been a hard burden. I see I have obtained too deep an insight into things. It is not for a man to taste of the knowledge of good and of evil — well, it is not for long, now," he added. "However, it is your bedtime ; and it is time for me to turn in too. — Go back to Gorki !" suddenly exclaimed Prince Andreï.

"Oh, no," cried Pierre, looking at Prince Andreï with frightened, sympathetic eyes.

"Go, go ; before an engagement one must get some sleep," insisted Prince Andreï. He came swiftly up to Pierre, threw his arms around him, and kissed him. "Farewell, — prashchaï ; go now," he cried. "We may not meet again — no" — and, hurriedly turning his back on his friend, he went into the shed.

It was already dark, and Pierre could not make out the expression of Prince Andreï's face, whether it was angry or tender.

Pierre stood for some time in silence, deliberating whether to follow him or to go to his lodgings.

"No, he does not want me," Pierre decided, "and I know that this is our last meeting."

He drew a deep sigh, and went back to Gorki.

Prince Andreï, retiring into his shed, threw himself down on a rug, but he could not sleep.

---

[1] *Akh, dusha moya.*

He closed his eyes. One picture after another rose before him. One in particular held him long in rapt, joyous attention. He had a vivid remembrance of an evening at Petersburg. Natasha, with her eager, vivacious face, was telling him how, the summer before, while she was out after mushrooms, she had lost her way in the great forest. She gave him a disconnected description of the darkness of the woods, and her sensations, and her conversation with a bee-hunter whom she had met; and every little while she had interrupted her story and said: "No, I can't tell you, you won't understand," although Prince Andreï had tried to calm her by assuring her that he understood; and in reality he had understood all that she wanted to say.

Natasha had been dissatisfied with her own words; she felt that she could not express the passionately poetical sensation which she had felt that day, and which she desired to express in words.

"The old man was so charming, and it was so dark in the forest .... and he had such good .... but, O dear, I can't tell you," she had said, blushing and becoming agitated.

Prince Andreï smiled even now the same joyous smile which he had smiled then as he looked into her eyes.

"I understood her," said he to himself; "not only did I understand her, but I loved that moral power of hers, that frankness, that perfect honesty of soul, — yes, her soul itself, which seemed to dominate her body, — her soul itself I loved — so powerfully, so happily I loved .... "

And suddenly he recalled what it was that had put an end to his love.

"*He* needed nothing of the sort. *He* saw nothing, understood nothing, of all this. All he saw was a very pretty and *fresh* young girl, with whom he did not even think it worth his while to join his fate. But I ? .... and he is still alive and enjoying life!"

Prince Andreï, as if something had scalded him, sprang up and once more began to pace up and down in front of the shed.

CHAPTER XXVI

On the sixth of September, the day before the battle of Borodino, M. de Beausset, grand chamberlain to the emperor of the French, and Colonel Fabvier arrived, the first from Paris, the other from Madrid, with despatches to the Emperor Napoleon at his camp at Valuyevo.

After M. de Beausset had put on his court uniform, he ordered a packet which he had brought to the emperor to be taken in, and he entered the outer division of Napoleon's tent, where, while talking with Napoleon's aides-de-camp who crowded round him, he busied himself with undoing the wrapper of the case.

Fabvier, not entering the tent, paused at the entrance, and entered into conversation with generals of his acquaintance.

The Emperor Napoleon had not yet left his bedroom, where he was engaged in making his toilet. Sniffing and grunting, he was turning first his stout back, then his fat chest, to the valet who was plying the brush. A second valet, holding his fingers over the bottle, was sprinkling the emperor's neatly arrayed person with eau de cologne, his expression intimating that he was the only one who knew how much cologne to use, and where it should be applied. Napoleon's short hair was wet and pasted down on his forehead. But his face, though puffy and sallow, expressed physical satisfaction. "*Allez ferme .... allez toujours* — brush harder .... put more energy in," he was saying to the valet, as he shrugged his shoulders and grunted.

One of his aides-de-camp, who had been admitted into his sleeping-room to submit a report to the emperor as to the number of prisoners taken during the engagement of the preceding day, having accomplished his errand, was standing by the door, awaiting permission to retire. Napoleon scowled and glared at the aide from under his brows.

"No prisoners," said he, repeating the aide-de-camp's

words. "They compel us to annihilate them. So much the worse for the Russian army. — Go on, more energy!" he exclaimed, hunching up his back, and offering his plump shoulders. "That'll do. Show in M. de Beausset, and Fabvier as well."

"Yes, sire," and the aide-de-camp disappeared through the door of the tent.

The two *valets de chambre* quickly dressed his majesty, and he, in the blue uniform of the Guards, with firm, swift steps, entered the anteroom. Beausset was at that instant engaged in placing the gift which he had brought from the empress on two chairs directly in front of the entrance. But the emperor had dressed and come out with such unexpected promptness that he had not time to get the surprise arranged to his satisfaction.

Napoleon instantly remarked what he was doing, and conjectured that they were not quite ready for him. He did not want to spoil their pleasure in surprising him. He pretended not to see M. Beausset, and addressed himself to Fabvier.

Napoleon, with a deep frown, and without speaking, listened to what Fabvier said about the bravery and devotion of his troops who had been fighting at Salamanca, at the other end of Europe, and who had only one thought — to be worthy of their emperor; and one fear — that of not satisfying him.

The result of the engagement had been disastrous. Napoleon, during Fabvier's report, made ironical observations, giving to understand that the affair could not have resulted differently, he being absent.

"I must regulate this in Moscow," said Napoleon. "*À tantôt* — Good-by for now," he added, and approached De Beausset, who by this time had succeeded in getting his surprise ready — some object covered with a cloth having been placed on the chairs.

De Beausset bowed low with that courtly French bow which only the old servants of the Bourbons could even pretend to execute, and, advancing, he handed Napoleon an envelop.

Napoleon approached him and playfully took him by the ear.

"You have made good time; I am very glad. Well, what have they to say in Paris?" he asked, suddenly changing his former stern expression into one of the most genial character.

"Sire, all Paris regrets your absence," replied De Beausset, as in duty bound.

But though Napoleon knew that De Beausset was bound to say this, or something to the same effect, though in his lucid intervals he knew that this was not true, it was agreeable to him to hear this from De Beausset. He again did him the honor of taking him by the ear.

"I am sorry to have caused you to take such a long journey," said he.

"Sire, I expected nothing less than to find you at the gates of Moscow," said Beausset.

Napoleon smiled, and, heedlessly raising his head, he glanced to the right.

An aide-de-camp with a gliding gait approached with a gold snuff-box, and presented it. Napoleon took it.

"Yes, it has turned out luckily for you," he said, putting the open snuff-box to his nose. "You enjoy traveling; in three days you will see Moscow. You really could not have expected to see the Asiatic capital. You will have had a pleasant journey."

Beausset made a low bow to express his gratitude for this discovery of his proclivity for traveling, till now unknown to him.

"Ah, what is that?" exclaimed Napoleon, noticing that all the courtiers were glancing at the *something* hidden by a covering.

Beausset, with courtier-like dexterity, not turning his back on his sovereign, took two steps around and at the same time snatched off the covering, saying:—

"A gift to your majesty, from the empress."

This was Gérard's brilliantly painted portrait of the little lad born to Napoleon and the Austrian emperor's daughter — the child whom all, for some reason, called the king of Rome.

The perfectly rosy, curly-haired boy, with a face like the face of the child in the Sistine Madonna, was represented playing bilboquet. The ball represented the earth, and the cup in his other hand represented a scepter. Although it was not perfectly clear why the artist wished to represent the so-called king of Rome transfixing the earth-ball with a stick, still this allegory seemed perfectly clear to all who saw the picture in Paris, as well as to Napoleon, and greatly delighted them.

"*Roi de Rome!*" he exclaimed, with a graceful gesture pointing to the portrait. "Admirable." With that facility characteristic of Italians, of changing at will the expression of his countenance, he approached the portrait and assumed a look of thoughtful tenderness.

He was conscious that what he was saying and doing at that moment was history. And it seemed to him that the best thing he could do now was to display the simplest paternal affection, as being most of a contrast to that majesty the consequence of which was that his son played bilboquet with the earth for a ball.

His eyes grew dim; he drew near it, he looked round for a chair — the chair sprang forward and placed itself under him — and he sat down in front of the portrait. He waved his hand, and all retired on their tiptoes, leaving the great man to himself and his feelings.

After sitting there for some time and letting his attention, he knew not why, be attracted by the roughness with which the picture was painted, he got up and again beckoned to Beausset and the aide on duty.

He gave orders to have the portrait carried out in front of his tent, so that his Old Guard, who were stationed around his tent, might not be deprived of the bliss of seeing the king of Rome, the son and heir of their beloved monarch. As he anticipated, while he was eating breakfast with Beausset, on whom he conferred this honor, he heard the enthusiastic shouts of the officers and soldiers of the Old Guard, who came to view the portrait.

" *Vive l'Empereur! Vive le Roi de Rome! Vive l'Empereur*," shouted the enthusiastic voices.

After breakfast, Napoleon, in Beausset's presence, dictated his address to the army.

" *Courte et énergique!* — short and to the point!" exclaimed Napoleon, as he read it aloud, the proclamation which had been written down word for word without a change. The proclamation said : —

" Soldiers! the battle which you have so eagerly desired is at hand. Victory depends on you, but victory is indispensable for us ; it will give you all that you need, comfortable quarters, and a speedy return to your native land. Behave as you behaved at Austerlitz, Friedland, Vitebsk, and Smolensk. Let your remotest posterity recall with pride your exploits on this day. And it will be said of each one of you, 'He was present at the great battle on the Moskova.'"

" *De la Moskowa*," repeated Napoleon, and, taking M. de Beausset with him, who was so fond of traveling, he left the tent and mounted his horse, which was waiting already saddled.

" *Votre majesté a trop de bonté!* — Your majesty is too kind," said Beausset, in reply to the emperor's invitation to accompany him on his ride ; he would have preferred to go to sleep, and he did not like, nay, he even feared, to ride on horseback.

But Napoleon nodded his head to the traveler, and Beausset had to go.

When Napoleon left the tent, the acclamations of his guards in front of his son's portrait were more eager than ever. Napoleon frowned.

" Take it away," said he, pointing to the portrait with a graceful and imperious gesture. "He is too young yet to see a battle."

Beausset, closing his eyes and bending his head, drew a deep sigh, signifying thereby how able he was to appreciate and prize his emperor's words.

CHAPTER XXVII

Napoleon, according to his historians, passed the entire day of September 6 on horseback, inspecting the battle-field, examining the plans suggested by his marshals, and personally giving orders to his generals.

The original position of the Russian army along the Kalotcha had been broken, and the capture of the Shevardino redoubt on the fifth had forced a part of this line, particularly the left flank, to retreat. This part of the line had not been fortified, nor was it protected any longer by the river, and before it extended a more open and level ground.

It was evident to any one, whether soldier or civilian, that this part of the line was where the French would surely make their attack. To reach this conclusion it would seem that there was no need of many combinations, no need of such sedulous and solicitous preparations on the part of the emperor and his marshals, and certainly no need of that high and extraordinary capacity called genius, which men so like to attribute to Napoleon. But the historians who have most recently described these events, and the men who at that time surrounded Napoleon, and Napoleon himself, thought otherwise.

Napoleon rode over the ground, profoundly absorbed in thought, inspected the battle-field, moved his head in silent approval or disapproval ; and, without deigning to reveal to the generals about him the profound ideas that influenced his decisions, he gave them only definite deductions in the form of orders.

Davoust, called the Duke of Eckmühl, having proposed to turn the left flank of the Russians, Napoleon declared that it was unnecessary to do this, but he did not explain why it was unnecessary to do this.

To the proposition of General Campan (who was to attack the fleches) to lead his division through the woods, Napoleon gave his consent ; the so-called Duke of Elchingen (that is, Ney) permitted himself to observe that the march through the woods would be dangerous, and might throw the division into disorder.

Napoleon, having inspected the ground over against the Shevardino redoubt, remained for some time in silent meditation ; then he pointed out the positions where two batteries were to be placed for the bombardment of the Russian fortifications on the next day, and he selected positions on the same line for the field artillery.

Having given these and other orders, he retired to his tent, and at his dictation the plan of battle was committed to writing.

This plan, of which French historians speak with enthusiasm, and which the historians of other nations treat with deep respect, was as follows : —

At daybreak the two new batteries established during the night on the plateau by the Prince of Eckmühl will open fire on the two opposing batteries of the enemy.

At the same moment, General Pernety, commanding the First Corps of artillery, with thirty cannon from Campan's division, and all the howitzers of Dessaix's and Friant's divisions, will advance and begin shelling the enemy's battery, which will thus have opposed to it, —

> 24 pieces of the artillery of the Guard,
> 30 pieces from Campan's division, and
> 8 pieces from Friant's and Dessaix's divisions.

Total: 62 cannon.

General Fouché, commanding the Third Corps of artillery, will place himself with all the howitzers of the Third and Eighth Corps, sixteen in number, on the flanks of the battery attacking the left redoubt, giving this battery an effective of 40 pieces.

General Sorbier will stand ready, at the first word of command, with all the howitzers of the Guard, to bring to bear against one or the other redoubt.

During the cannonade, Prince Poniatowski will move against the village in the woods, and turn the position of the enemy.

General Campan will move along the edge of the woods to carry the first redoubt.

The battle thus begun, orders will be given according to the enemy's movements.

The cannonade on the left flank will begin at the moment when that on the right is heard. A heavy infantry fire will be opened by Morand's division, and by the divisions of the viceroy, as soon as they see that the attack on the right has begun.

The viceroy will take possession of the village,[1] and debouch by its three bridges upon the heights, while Generals Morand and Gérard will deploy under command of the viceroy to seize the enemy's redoubt and form the line of battle with the other troops.

All this must be done with order and method (*le tout se fera avec ordre et méthode*), taking care to hold the troops in reserve as far as possible.

At the imperial camp, near Mozhaïsk, September 6, 1812.

This order — very far from clear in style, and confusing to any one who is so sufficiently lacking in religious awe for the genius of Napoleon as to dare analyze its meaning — contains four points, four commands. Not one of these commands could have been executed; not one of them was executed.

In the order of battle the first command read as follows : —

The batteries established at the points selected by Napoleon, with the cannon of Pernety and Fouché, will place themselves in line, one hundred and two pieces in all, and, opening fire, will storm the Russian outworks and redoubts with shot and shell.

This could not be done, because from the place selected by Napoleon the missiles did not reach the Russian works, and these one hundred and two cannon thundered in vain until the nearest commander ordered them forward, contrary to Napoleon's decree.

The second command was to this effect : —

Poniatowski will move against the village in the woods, and turn the left wing of the Russians.

This could not be done and was not done, because Poniatowski, on moving toward the village in the woods,

---

[1] Borodino.

found Tutchkof there blocking the way, and he could not and did not turn the position of the Russians.

The third command : —

General Campan will move along the edge of the woods to carry the first redoubt.

Campan's division did not carry the first redoubt, but it was repulsed, because, on emerging from the woods, it was obliged to close up under the Russian grape-shot, something which Napoleon had not foreseen.

Fourth : —

The viceroy will take possession of the village [Borodino], and debouch by its three bridges upon the heights, while Generals Morand and Gérard [*who are told neither where nor when to go*] will deploy under command of the viceroy to seize the enemy's redoubt and form the line of battle with the other troops.

As far as it is possible to understand this (not from the vague phraseology employed, but from the viceroy's attempt to carry out the orders he received), it seems he was to move through Borodino from the left against the redoubt, and that Morand and Gérard's divisions were at the same time to advance from the front.

This command, like all the rest, was not carried out, because it was impracticable.

When he had got beyond Borodino, the viceroy was forced back upon the Kalotcha, and found it impossible to advance. Morand and Friant's divisions did not take any redoubts, but were repulsed, and the redoubt was carried by the cavalry at the close of the battle, a contingency which Napoleon apparently had not foreseen.

Thus not one of the commands in this order was performed or could have been.

The order further announced that "during the battle thus begun" instructions would be given in accordance with the enemy's movements, and therefore we might infer that Napoleon, during the battle, made all the suggestions that were necessary. He did, and could have done, nothing of the sort, because throughout the engagement Napoleon happened to be so far away from the field of action that (as it transpired afterwards) the progress of the battle could not even have been known to him, and not one of his orders during the time of the engagement could be carried out.

CHAPTER XXVIII

MANY historians assert that the battle of Borodino was not won by the French because Napoleon had a cold in the head, that if it had not been for this cold, his arrangements before and during the battle would have displayed still more genius, and Russia would have been conquered, and the face of the world would have been changed.

For the historians that believe Russia was formed at the will of one man, Peter the Great, and that France was changed from a republic to an empire and that the French armies invaded Russia at the will of one man, Napoleon, the argument that Russia retained power after the battle of Borodino because Napoleon had a bad cold in his head on September 7 is logically consistent.

If it had depended on Napoleon's will to fight or not to fight the battle of Borodino, on his will to make or not to make such and such dispositions of his forces, then evidently the cold in his head, which had such influence on the manifestation of his will, may have been the cause of the salvation of Russia; and the valet who, on September 5, forgot to provide Napoleon with waterproof boots, was the savior of Russia.

When we have once started on this line of reasoning, this conclusion is inevitable; just as inevitable as that reached by Voltaire when in jest — himself not knowing what he was driving at — he demonstrated that the Massacre of Saint Bartholomew was due to the fact that Charles IX. suffered from a fit of indigestion.

But for men who do not admit that Russia was

formed at the will of one man, Peter I., and that the
French empire arose or that the campaign in Russia
was undertaken at the bidding of a single man, Napoleon, such reasoning will appear to be not only false,
but contrary to all human experience.   To the question,
What is the cause of historical events? a very different
answer presents itself, and one that implies that the
progress of events on earth is preordained; that it
depends on the combined volition of all who participate
in these events, and that the influence of Napoleons on
the progress of these events is superficial and fictitious.

How strange seems at first glance the proposition
that the Massacre of Saint Bartholomew, the order for
which was given by Charles IX., did not come from his
own volition, but that it merely seemed to him that he
had ordered it to be done; or that the battle of Borodino, which cost the lives of eighty thousand men, was
not fought through Napoleon's volition, though he gave
the orders for the beginning and course of the engagement, but that it merely seemed to him that he had
ordered it — how strange seems this proposition ; but
the dignity of humanity, which tells me that each of us,
if he be not more of a man, is at least not less than
every Napoleon, directs me to this solution of the problem, and it is powerfully justified by historical facts.

At the battle of Borodino, Napoleon shot no one and
killed no one.   All that was done by his soldiers.   Of
course he killed no one.

The soldiers of the French army went into the battle
of Borodino to kill Russian soldiers, not in consequence
of Napoleon's orders, but by their own desires.   The
whole army, French, Italians, Germans, Polyaks, fam-
ished and in rags, worn out by the campaign, felt, at
sight of the Russian army barring the road to Moscow,
that the wine was uncorked, and they had only to drink,
— *que le vin est tiré et qu'il faut le boire.*   If at that
moment Napoleon had forbidden them to fight the Russians, they would have killed him and fought with the
Russians ; for this was inevitable for them.

When they heard Napoleon's proclamation, which

offered them, in exchange for mutilation and death, the consoling testimony of posterity that they had been in the battle at Moscow, they cried, " *Vive l'Empereur!*" —just as they cried "*Vive l'Empereur!*" at seeing the picture of the child piercing the terrestrial globe with the bilboquet stick ; and just as they would have shouted " *Vive l'Empereur!*" to any nonsense spoken to them.

There was nothing more for them to do than to cry " *Vive l'Empereur!*" and go into battle in order to reach food and the repose of victors at Moscow. Of course it was not at Napoleon's order that they killed their fellow-men.

And Napoleon did not direct the progress of the battle, for no part of his plan was carried out ; and during the engagement he did not know what was going on before him.

Of course, how these men killed one another had nothing to do with Napoleon, but was independent of his will ; it was determined by the will of the hundreds of thousands of men who took part in the combat. It only seemed to Napoleon that it proceeded by his will.

Thus the question, "Did or did not Napoleon have a cold in his head?" is of no more importance to history than the question whether the most insignificant trainhand had a cold in the head.

The fact that Napoleon was afflicted with a cold in the head on September 7 is still more insignificant because the assertions made by writers that this cold in the head caused Napoleon's dispositions and orders at the time of the battle to be less skilful than those in times past are perfectly false.

The plan here described was not at all inferior — it was even superior — to all the plans by which his previous battles had been won. The imaginary combinations during this battle were not in the least inferior to those of previous battles ; they were just the same as always. But these dispositions and combinations seem less fortunate because the battle of Borodino was the first battle that Napoleon did not win. The best plans and the most sagacious dispositions and combinations in the world seem very poor, and every scientific soldier does not hesitate to criticize them with solemn face, when they do not end in victory! And the feeblest dispositions and combinations seem very excellent, and learned men devote entire volumes to the demonstration of the superiority of wretched plans, when they are crowned with success.

The plan proposed by Weirother for the battle of Austerlitz was a model of its kind, but it was nevertheless condemned for its very perfection, for its superabundance of details.

Napoleon at the battle of Borodino played his part as representative of power as well as in other battles — even better. He did nothing that could hinder the successful course of the battle : he accepted the most reasonable advice, he did not confuse his orders, he did not contradict himself, he did not lose heart, he did not abandon the field of battle, but with all his tact and his great experience in war he played with calmness and dignity the part of a seeming commander.

CHAPTER XXIX

On returning from his second solicitous tour of inspection along the line, Napoleon said : —

"The chessmen are set ; the game will begin to-morrow."

Calling for a glass of punch, and summoning Beausset, he began to talk with him about Paris, and discuss various alterations which he proposed to make in the empress's household — *la maison de l'Impératrice,* — causing wonder at the attention which he gave to the minutest details of court management.

He displayed great interest in trifles, he jested at Beausset's fondness for travel, and with perfect coolness he chatted just as a famous and self-confident surgeon, who knew his business, might do, even while he rolls up his cuffs and puts on his apron and the patient is fastened to the operating table.

"The whole thing is in my hands and in my head, clearly and definitely. When the time comes to act, I will do my work, as no one else could, but now I can jest; and the more I jest and appear calm and collected, the more should you be confident, trustful, and amazed at my genius."

After drinking a second glass of punch, Napoleon went to rest before the serious affair which, as it seemed to him, was waiting for him on the morrow.

He was so much interested in this affair that was before him, that he could not sleep, and, in spite of his cold, which had been increased by the evening dampness, he got up about three o'clock in the morning, and, loudly blowing his nose, passed into the outer division of his tent. He asked if the Russians had not retreated. He was told that the enemy's fires were still burning in the same places. He nodded his head approvingly. The aide-de-camp on duty entered the tent.

"Well, Rapp, do you think we shall have good luck to-day?" he asked.

"Certainly, your majesty," replied Rapp. Napoleon gave him an attentive look. "You remember, your majesty, that you did me the honor of remarking at Smolensk, — 'The wine is uncorked; we have only to drink it.'"

Napoleon frowned, and sat for some time in silence, resting his head on his hands.

"This poor army," he exclaimed suddenly, "has been seriously diminishing since we left Smolensk. Fortune is a fickle jade, Rapp, *une franche courtisane;* I always said so, and I am beginning to experience it. But the Guard, Rapp, the Guard is undiminished?" he said, with a questioning inflection.

"Yes, sire," replied Rapp.

Napoleon took a lozenge, put it in his mouth, and glanced at his watch. He felt no inclination to sleep, though it was still long before morning; but it was impossible to issue any more orders for the sake of killing time, for they had all been made, and were even then being executed.

"Have the biscuits and rice been distributed among the regiments of the Guard?" asked Napoleon, sternly.

"*Oui, sire.*"

"But the rice?"

Rapp replied that he had issued the emperor's orders in regard to the rice, but Napoleon shook his head angrily, as if he had no confidence in his orders having been fulfilled. A servant came in with the punch. Napoleon commanded another glass to be given to Rapp, and silently sipped from his own.

"I have no taste or smell," said he, sniffing at the glass. "This influenza is a nuisance. They talk about medicine. What does medicine amount to when they can't even cure a cold! Corvisart gave me these lozenges, but they don't help me any. What can they cure? What can physic do? Nothing at all! Our body is a living-machine — *une machine à vivre.* It is organized for that purpose, that is its nature; let the life in it be left to itself; let it defend itself; it will do more than if you paralyze it by loading it down with remedies. Our body is like a perfect watch which is meant to go a certain time; the watchmaker cannot open it; he can only regulate it by his sense of feeling and with his eyes shut. Our body is a living-machine, that is all it is."

And Napoleon, having as it were started on the path of definitions, of which he was very fond, suddenly and unexpectedly made still a new one.

"Rapp, do you know what the art of war is?" he asked. "It is the art of being stronger than the enemy at a given moment — that is all."

Rapp made no reply.

"To-morrow we shall have Kutuzof to deal with," said Napoleon. "We shall see. You remember he commanded the armies at Braunau, and not once during three weeks did he mount a horse to inspect the fortifications. We shall see!"

He glanced at his watch. It was only four o'clock. He still had no desire to sleep; the punch was drunk up, and as yet there was nothing to do. He got up, began to pace up and down; then he put on his thick overcoat and hat and went outside the tent. The night was dark and damp; one could almost hear the moisture falling. The bivouac fires, even those near at hand, burned far from brightly, and those in the distance, in the Russian lines, gleamed dimly in the fog. Through the silence clearly could be heard the bustle and trampling of the French troops, already beginning to move to their designated positions.

Napoleon walked out in front of his tent, gazed at the fires, listened to the growing tumult, and, as he passed by a tall grenadier in a wet hat, who was on duty as sentinel by his tent, and who stood stiff and straight like a pillar when the emperor appeared, Napoleon paused.

"How long have you been in the service?" he asked, with his ordinary affectation of hearty and affectionate military bluntness, which he always employed when dealing with his soldiers. The soldier answered him.

"Ah, a veteran! Has your regiment received the rice?"

"We have, your majesty."

Napoleon nodded and left him.

At half-past five, Napoleon mounted and rode to the village of Shevardino.

It was beginning to grow light; the sky was clearing; only a single cloud lay against the east. The deserted bivouac fires were dying out in the pale light of the morning.

At the right thundered a single heavy cannon-shot, prolonged by the echoes, and finally dying away amid the general silence.

There was an interval of several minutes. A second shot, then a third, rolled out, shaking the air; a fourth, a fifth, answered near at hand, and solemnly, somewhere at the right.

The echoes of the first cannon-shots had not died away when still others joined in, then more and more, mingling and blending in one continuous roar.

Napoleon galloped with his suite to the Shevardino redoubt and there dismounted.

The game had begun.

CHAPTER XXX

HAVING returned to Gorki from his visit to Prince Andreï, Pierre gave his orders to his equerry to have his horses ready, and to waken him early in the morning, and then immediately went to sleep behind the screen in the corner which Boris had kindly offered him.

When Pierre was fairly awake the next morning there was not a soul in the cottage. The window-panes in the little windows were rattling. His equerry was standing by him, shaking him.

"Your illustriousness, your illustriousness, your illustriousness!" exclaimed the equerry, stubbornly shaking him by the shoulder, and apparently hopeless of being able to wake him.

"What? Has it begun? Is it time?" demanded Pierre, opening his eyes.

"Be good enough to listen to the firing," said the equerry, who had once been a soldier. "The gentlemen have all gone. His serene highness went long ago."

Pierre hurriedly dressed and went out on the steps. Outside it was bright, cool, dewy, and cheerful. The sun was just making its way out from under the cloud which had obscured it momentarily, and poured its rays through the breaking clouds, across the roofs of the opposite houses, over the dusty road covered with dew, on the walls of the houses, on the windows of the cathedral, and on Pierre's horses standing near the cottage. Out of doors the rolling of the cannon was heard more distinctly. An aide, followed by his Cossack, was galloping down the street.

"It is time, count, time," cried the aide.

Ordering the man to follow him with his horse, Pierre walked along the road to the mound from the top of which, the day before, he had surveyed the field of battle. Here were collected a throng of military men, and he could hear the members of the staff talking French, and he could see Kutuzof's gray head covered with a white hat with red band, and the gray nape of his neck sunk between his shoulders. He was gazing through his field-glass to the front along the highway.

As Pierre mounted the steps that led to the top of the mound, he looked out over the prospect, and was overwhelmed at the beauty of the spectacle.

It was the same panorama he had surveyed the day before from the same elevation ; but now all those localities were covered with troops and the smoke of the cannon ; and the slanting rays of the bright sun, rising behind Pierre at the left, fell upon it through the clear morning atmosphere in floods of light, shot with golden and rosy tones and intermingled with long, dark shadows.

The distant forests which bounded the panorama, just as if they were hewn out of some precious yellow-green gem, could be traced by the curving line of the tree-tops against the horizon, and between them, beyond Valuyevo, the Smolensk highway, now all covered with troops, cut sharply.

Still nearer gleamed the golden fields and groves. Everywhere, in front and behind, at the right hand and at the left, troops were swarming. The whole scene was animated, majestic, and marvelous ; but what surprised Pierre more than all was the spectacle of the battle-field itself, Borodino, and the valley through which the Kalotcha River ran.

Over the Kalotcha at Borodino, and on both sides of the river, more noticeably on the left bank, where, through marshy intervales, the Voïna falls into the Kalotcha, was that mist which so mysteriously veils, spreads, and grows transparent as the bright sun mounts, and magically colors and transforms everything that is seen through it.

The smoke of the cannon was blending with this mist, and over this blended mist and smoke, everywhere, gleamed the lightning flashes of the morning brilliancy, here over the water, there on dewy meadows, there on the bayonets of the infantry swarming along the banks and in the village.

Through this mist could be seen a white church, a

few roofs of Borodino cottages, here and there compact masses of soldiers, here and there green caissons, cannons. And this scene was in motion, or seemed to be in motion, because this mist and smoke was stretched over the whole space. On these lowlands around Borodino, covered with mist, so also above, and especially at the left, over the whole line, over the woods, over the fields, in the hollows, on the summits of the rising ground, constantly born, self-evolved from nothing, rose the puffs of cannon-smoke; now singly, now in groups; now scattered, now clustered; and as they formed, and grew, and coalesced, and melted together, they seemed to cover the whole space.

These puffs of cannon-smoke and, strange to say, the sounds that accompanied them, constituted the chief charm of the spectacle.

Puff! suddenly appeared a round, compact ball of smoke playing in violet, gray, and milk-white colors, and — *bumm!* would follow in a second the report of this smoke-ball.

Puff! puff! arose two balls of smoke jostling and blending, and — *bumm! bumm!* came the coalescing sounds that confirmed what the eye had seen.

Pierre gazed at the first puff of smoke, which he still saw as a round, compact ball, and before he knew it its place was taken by two balls of smoke borne off to one side, and *puff* — with an interval — *puff, puff,* rose three others, then four others, and each was followed at intervals with the *bumm, bumm, bumm* — genuine, beautiful, satisfying sounds. Sometimes it seemed as if these puffs of smoke were flying, sometimes as if they were standing still, while past them flew the forests, the fields, and the glittering bayonets.

On the left, over the meadows and clumps of trees, these great balls of smoke were constantly rising with their solemn voices, and still nearer, over the lowlands and along the forests, burst forth the little puffs of musket smoke which had no time to form into balls, and yet these, in precisely the same way, uttered their little reports. *Trakh-ta-ta-takh!* rattled the musketry.

frequent though irregular and pale in comparison with the cannon-shots.

Pierre had an intense longing to be where those puffs of smoke originated, those glittering bayonets, that movement, those sounds.

He looked at Kutuzof and at his suite, so as to compare his own impressions with those of others. All, exactly the same as he himself, and, as it seemed to him, with the same sentiment, were gazing down on the field of battle. All faces now were lighted up by that latent heat which Pierre had observed the day before, and which he understood perfectly after his conversation with Prince Andreï.

"Go on, my dear,[1] go on ; Christ be with you," Kutuzof was saying to a general standing near him, but he kept his eyes fixed on the battle-field.

On hearing this command, the general went past Pierre on his way to the descent from the mound.

"To the crossing," replied the general, coldly and sternly, to one of the staff, who asked where he was going.

"I too, I too," said Pierre to himself, and he followed in the direction taken by the general.

The general mounted his horse, which his Cossack led forward. Pierre went to his equerry, who had his horses in charge. Asking which was the gentlest, Pierre mounted, grasped his mane, gouged his heels into the horse's flanks, and, feeling that his spectacles were going to tumble off, and that he could not possibly remove his hands from the mane and bridle, he went cantering after the general, arousing the laughter of the staff, who were looking at him from the top of the mound.

[1] *Galubchik.*

CHAPTER XXXI

The general whom Pierre was following rode down the slope the shortest way and then turned to the left, and Pierre, losing him from sight, galloped into a file of infantry marching in front of him. He tried to get past them in front, then at the left, and then at the right; but everywhere there were soldiers, all with anxious, eager faces, all engaged in some invisible but evidently important action. All, with similar involuntarily questioning glances, looked at this portly man in the white hat, who, for some unknown reason, insisted on trampling them down with his horse.

"What makes you ride in front of the battalion?" cried one to him. Another poked his horse with the butt-end of his musket, and Pierre, clinging to the saddle and scarcely able to restrain his plunging horse, galloped in front of the soldiers where there was room.

In front of him there was a bridge, and near the bridge other soldiers were stationed, firing. Pierre rode up to them. Not knowing it, Pierre had unwittingly approached the bridge over the Kalotcha, between Borodino and Gorki, where in the first action of the battle (called Borodino) the French made a charge.

Pierre saw that there was a bridge before him, and that on both ends of the bridge, and on the meadow, among the haycocks which he had noticed the day before, the soldiers were doing something; but, in spite of the incessant firing going on in this place, it never once occurred to him that here was the battle-field. He heard not the sounds of the bullets whizzing on all sides, or the projectiles flying over his head; he saw not the enemy on the other side of the river, and it was long before he saw the killed and wounded, although many were falling not far from him. With a smile which did not leave his lips, he glanced around him.

"What makes that man ride in front of the line?" again cried some one.

"Take the right .... take the left!".... they cried to him.

Pierre took the left, and unexpectedly fell in with one of General Rayevsky's aides whom he knew. This aide looked fiercely at Pierre, evidently with the intention of shouting some command, but then, recognizing him, he shook his head at him.

"How come you here?" he cried, and dashed away.

Pierre, feeling that he was out of place and useless, and fearing lest he should be a hindrance to some one, galloped after the aide.

"What is this here? Can I go with you?" he asked.

"Wait a moment," replied the aide, and, riding up to a stout colonel who was stationed on the meadow, he gave him some order, and immediately turned back to Pierre.

"How do you happen to get here, count?" he asked, with a smile. "Is it out of curiosity?"

"Yes, yes," replied Pierre.

But the aide, wheeling, started to gallop away. "Here it is all right, thank God," said he, "but on the left flank, where Bagration is, there's frightfully hot work going on."

"Really?" exclaimed Pierre. "Where is that?"

"Come with me to the mound; you can see very well from there, and at our battery there it is still safe enough," said the aide.

"Yes, I will go with you," returned Pierre, looking around him and trying to discover his equerry. Then only for the first time Pierre caught sight of the wounded, dragging themselves to the rear on foot or borne on stretchers. On the same plot of meadow-land, with the windrows of fragrant hay, over which he had ridden the evening before, there lay, amidst the ranks, a soldier motionless, with his head awkwardly thrown back and his shako knocked off.

"But why have they not carried him off?" Pierre was going to ask, but, seeing the aide's stern face turned to the same spot, he refrained.

Pierre could not discover his equerry, and so he rode with the aide down across the hollow to Rayevsky's mound. Pierre's horse fell behind the aide's, and shook him at every step.

"You are apparently not used to riding on horseback, count?" suggested the aide.

"No, it's nothing; but somehow he limps badly," said Pierre, in perplexity.

"É—é! but he's wounded," said the aide, "right fore leg, above the knee. Must have been a bullet. I congratulate you, count," said he, "your 'baptism of fire'!"

Making their way through the smoke to the Sixth Corps, behind the artillery, which, unlimbered forward, was blazing away with a stunning thunder of discharges, they reached a small grove. Here in the grove it was cool and still, and smelt like autumn. Pierre and the aide dismounted and went up the hill on foot.

"Is the general here?" asked the aide, as he reached the top.

"He's just gone, he went yonder," was the answer, the men pointing to the right.

The aide glanced at Pierre, as if he did not know what to do with him now.

"Don't disturb yourself," said Pierre. "I will go to the top of the mound, can't I?"

"Yes, do so; you can see everything from there, and it won't be so dangerous. And I will come back after you."

Pierre went to the battery, and the aide went on his way. They did not meet again, and not till long after did Pierre learn that this aide lost an arm on that day.

The *kurgan*, or mound, on which Pierre had come, became afterwards known to the Russians as the Kurgan battery or Rayevsky's battery, and to the French as *la grande redoute, la fatale redoute, la redoute du centre*. It was the place around which tens of thousands of men were slain, and the French considered it the most important point of the whole position.

This redoubt consisted of the kurgan, on three sides of which trenches had been dug. In this place, surrounded by the trenches, were stationed ten active cannon, discharging through the embrasures of the earthworks.

In a line with the kurgan, cannon were stationed, on

either side, also belching forth continuous discharges. A little to the rear of the cannon stood the infantry.

Pierre, on reaching this kurgan, never once dreamed that this small space intrenched with earthworks where he was standing, and where a few cannon were in full blast, was the most important point of the whole battle. On the contrary, it seemed to Pierre that this place, simply because he had come to it, was one of the most unimportant places of the battle-field.

On reaching the kurgan, Pierre sat down at one end of a trench which inclosed the battery, and with a smile of unconscious satisfaction gazed at what was going on around him. Occasionally with the same smile he would get to his feet, and, at the same time trying not to be in the way of the soldiers who were loading and pushing forward the guns or constantly passing him with powder and shot, he would walk through the battery. The cannon in this battery were constantly fired one after another with an overwhelming crash, and the whole place was swathed in gunpowder smoke.

In contradistinction to that sense of gloom which is always felt among the infantry soldiers of a covering force, in a battery where a small band of men are limited and shut off from the rest by a trench, here there is a sort of family feeling, which is shared equally by all.

The appearance of Pierre's unmilitary figure, in his white hat, at first struck these men unpleasantly. The soldiers passing him looked askance at him with a mixture of amazement and timidity. The senior artillery officer, — a tall, long-legged, pock-marked man, — under the pretense of inspecting the behavior of the endmost cannon, came where Pierre was and gazed inquisitively at him.

A young, round-faced little officer, still a mere lad, who had evidently just come out of the "Korpus," and who was very zealously commanding the two guns committed to his charge, looked fiercely at Pierre.

"We must ask you, sir, to go away; you cannot remain here."

The soldiers shook their heads disapprovingly, as they

looked at Pierre. But when all were convinced that this man in the white hat was not only doing no harm as he sat calmly on the talus of the trench or walked up and down the battery, facing the missiles as steadily as if he were on the boulevard, and with his genial smile politely making way for the soldiers, then gradually this feeling of disapproval and perplexity began to give place to an affectionate and jocose sympathy such as soldiers are apt to manifest for dogs, cocks, goats, and other animals that are found in their ranks These soldiers instantly adopted Pierre into their family, and gave him a nickname. "*Nash barin*" — "Our gentleman" — was what they called him, and they good-naturedly laughed about him among themselves.

A round shot tore up the earth within two paces of Pierre. Shaking off the dirt which the missile scattered over him, Pierre glanced around with a smile.

"Did n't that frighten you, barin? truly, did n't it?" asked a broad soldier with a rubicund face, displaying his strong white teeth.

"Why, are you afraid?" retorted Pierre.

"How can one help it?" replied the soldier. "You see, *she* has no mercy. If she strikes, your innards fly! So one can't help being afraid," said he, with a laugh.

Several soldiers with jovial, friendly faces were standing near Pierre. They seemed not to have expected him to speak like other men, and to find that he did surprised them.

"Soldiering 's our business. But this man is a barin, so it 's wonderful! What a barin he is!"

"To your places," commanded the young officer to the soldiers collecting around Pierre. This young officer was evidently for the first or perhaps the second time on duty of this kind, and accordingly he behaved to his men and his superiors with especial preciseness and formality. The rolling thunder of the cannon and of the musketry was intensified all over the field, noticeably at the left, where Bagration's fleches were situated; but Pierre, owing to the smoke of the discharges, could see nothing at all from where he was.

Moreover, Pierre's entire attention was absorbed in watching what was going on in this little family circle, as it were — separated from all the rest. His first unconsciously joyous feeling aroused by the sights and sounds of the battle-field had changed character, now, especially since he had seen that soldier lying by himself on the meadow. As he sat now on the talus of the trench he contemplated the faces around him.

It was only ten o'clock, but a score of men had been already carried from the battery; two of the cannon were dismounted, and the missiles were falling into the battery with greater and greater frequency, and the shot flew over their heads screeching and whizzing. But the men who were serving the battery seemed to pay no heed to this; on all sides were heard only gay talk and jests.

"Old stuffing!"[1] cried a soldier to a shell that flew close over his head with a whizz.

"This is the wrong place. Go to the infantry," added a second, perceiving that the shell flew over and struck in the ranks of the covering forces.

"What is that, an acquaintance of yours?" asked another, with a laugh, as a muzhik bowed under a round shot that went flying over.

A few soldiers collected around the breastwork, trying to make out what was going on at the front.

"Well, they've captured the lines, do you see; they're retreating," said they, pointing across the breastwork.

"Mind your own business," cried an old non-commissioned officer. "If they're retiring, of course it's because they're needed elsewhere."

And the non-commissioned officer, seizing one of the soldiers by the shoulder, gave him a boost with his knee. A roar of laughter was heard.

"Serve No. 5! Forward!" rang out on one side.

"A long pull, and a strong pull, and a pull all together," cheerfully shouted the men who were pushing the cannon forward.

---

[1] *Chinyonka:* any object filled with anything.

"Aï! that one almost took our barin's hat off," cried the rubicund jester, with a laugh which showed his teeth. — "Ekh! you beastly thing," he added reproachfully to the ball, which carried off a gun-wheel and a man's leg.

"Well, you foxes!" cried another, with a laugh, to the militiamen, who, all bent double, came forward to the battery, to remove the wounded. "Is n't this gruel to your taste? Akh! you crows![1] are you frozen stiff?" cried the soldiers to the militiamen, who were dismayed at the sight of the soldier with the leg torn off. "That's only a little one!" said they, imitating the dialect of the peasants. "Don't like to be afraid, do you?"

Pierre observed how after the fall of each new missile, after each new loss, the general excitement became more and more intensified.

Just as when a heavy thunder-shower is approaching, more and more frequently, more and more dazzlingly, flashed forth on the faces of all these men the lightnings of that latent but now developing heat. It was apparently called forth by resistance.

Pierre did not look out on the battle-field, and he was not interested in knowing what was going on there; he was entirely absorbed in the contemplation of this ever more and more developing fire, which now in exactly the same way — he was conscious — was also kindling in his own soul.

At ten o'clock, the infantry, who had been in front of the battery, in the thickets, and along the Kamenka, or Stony Brook, retreated. From the battery they could be seen running back past it, carrying their wounded on their muskets.

A general with his suite dashed up the kurgan, and, after exchanging a few words with the colonel and giving Pierre a fierce look, rode back down again, ordering the covering infantry who were stationed behind the battery to lie down, so as not to expose themselves to the missiles. Immediately after this, in the ranks of the infantry, at the right of the battery, were heard the

---

[1] *Voronui :* crows; means also simpletons.

rolling of a drum and shouts of command, and they in the battery could see how the ranks of infantry moved forward.

Pierre looked over the breastworks. One face especially struck his eye. This was a pale-faced young officer, who was marching with them backwards, holding his sword-point down and looking anxiously around.

The ranks of infantry disappeared in the smoke, their prolonged cheer was heard and the continuous rattle of their musketry fire. After a few minutes a throng of wounded men walking and on stretchers came straggling back.

The missiles kept falling with greater and greater frequency on the battery. A number of soldiers lay unattended. The men around the cannon were working with renewed vigor and zeal. No one any longer paid attention to Pierre. Twice he was angrily told that he was in the way. The senior officer, with a frowning face, strode with long, swift steps from gun to gun. The young officer, with his face more flushed than ever, gave his commands to his men with ever increasing vehemence. The soldiers came and went with the projectiles, and loaded and did their duty with ever more zealously burning activity and dash. They jumped about as if they were moved by springs.

The thunder-cloud had come close at hand, and brightly on all faces burned that fire the kindling of which Pierre had been watching. He was standing near the senior officer. The young officer came hastening to the elder and saluted him, finger at vizor.

"I have the honor of reporting, Mr. Colonel, that there are only eight shot left. Do you order us to go on?"

"Grape!" cried the old officer, gazing over the rampart, and not giving any definite answer.

Suddenly something happened: the little officer shrieked, and fell upon the ground all of a heap, like a bird shot on the wing. Everything became strange, dark, and gloomy in Pierre's eyes.

One following another the projectiles came screaming, and buried themselves in the breastwork, among the soldiers, among the cannon. Pierre, who before had not heard these sounds, now heard nothing except these sounds. At one side, at the right of the battery, with their cheers — hurrah! hurrah! — the soldiers were running, not forward as it seemed to Pierre, but back to the rear.

A shot struck on the very edge of the rampart where Pierre was standing, scattered the earth, and a black ball flashed in front of his eyes and at the same instant fell with a dull thud into something. The militia, who had been coming up to the battery, were in full retreat.

"All grape!" cried the officer.

The non-commissioned officer hastened up to his senior, and in a frightened whisper — just as at dinner the butler reports to his master that the wine called for is all out — reported that all the ammunition was used up.

"The villains! what are they doing?" cried the officer, turning round to Pierre. The old officer's face was flushed and sweaty, his eyes were gleaming fiercely. "Run back to the reserves, have the caissons brought," he cried, crossly avoiding Pierre's glance and addressing his command to his orderly.

"I will go," cried Pierre. The officer, without answering him, went with long strides to the other side.

"Don't fire!.... Wait!" he shouted.

The soldier who had been commanded to go after ammunition ran into Pierre.

"Ekh! barin, this is no place for you here," said he, and started on the run down the slope.

Pierre ran after the soldier, avoiding the place where the young officer lay.

One shot, a second, a third, flew over his head; they struck in front of him, on both sides of him, and behind him. Pierre ran down the slope.

The question, "Where am I going?" suddenly occurred to him, even while he was hastening up to the green caissons. He stopped irresolutely, undecided whether to go forward or back. Suddenly a terrible shock threw him back on the ground. At the same instant a sheet of a mighty fire flashed into his eyes, and at the same instant a noise like a thunder-clap, stunning and terrific, a crash and a whizz, overwhelmed him.

Pierre, having recovered his senses, sat up, supporting himself on his hands. The caisson near which he had been standing had disappeared; only on the scorched grass were scattered a few pieces of the green painted wood of the carriage, and smoking rags; and one horse, shaking off the fragments of the shafts, was galloping off, while another — like Pierre himself — was lying on the ground, and uttering a long penetrating scream of agony.

CHAPTER XXXII

PIERRE, in his terror, not knowing what he was doing, sprang to his feet and ran back to the battery, as if it were the only refuge from the horrors surrounding him.

When he reached the intrenchment, he observed that there was no sound of firing any longer from the battery, but that men were engaged in doing something there. Pierre had no time to make out who these men were. He saw the old colonel leaning over the breastwork, with his back to him, as if he were watching something below, and he saw one of the artillerists, whom he had already observed, struggling to get away from some men who had him by the arm, and crying "Brothers! Brothers!" and he also saw something else that was strange.

But he had no time to realize that the colonel was killed, and that the man was crying for help, and that under his very eyes a second soldier was stabbed in the back by a bayonet thrust. He had hardly set foot in the intrenchment before a lean, sallow, sweaty-faced man, in a blue uniform, with a sword in his hand, leaped upon him, shouting something. Pierre instinctively avoided the shock, as men do who are about to run into each other, and, putting out his hand, he seized this man—

he was a French officer — by the shoulder with one hand and grasped his throat with the other. The officer, dropping his sword, seized Pierre by the collar.

For some seconds they each gazed with startled eyes into the other's face, and both were uncertain as to what they had done and what they were going to do. "Has he taken me prisoner, or have I taken him prisoner?" each of them was wondering. But apparently the French officer was rather inclined to believe that he was taken prisoner, for the reason that Pierre's powerful hand, involuntarily clenching under the influence of fear, was squeezing his throat ever tighter and tighter. The Frenchman was just trying to say something, when suddenly over their very heads, narrowly missing them and terribly screeching, flew a projectile, and it seemed to Pierre that the French officer's head was torn off, so quickly he ducked it.

Pierre also ducked his head, and released his hand. No longer puzzling over the question which had taken the other prisoner, the Frenchman ran back to the battery, while Pierre ran down the hill, stumbling over the dead and wounded, who, it seemed to him, grasped after his feet. But he had not more than reached the bottom before he came full upon a dense mass of Russian soldiers, who, stumbling and falling and cheering, full of dash and spirit, were on the double-quick toward the battery.

This was the charge for which Yermolof took the credit, declaring that only by his gallantry and good fortune was it possible to have achieved this success — the charge during which one might say he scattered over the mound the St. George crosses that had been in his pockets.

The French who had taken the battery fled. Our troops, with cheers, drove the French so far beyond the battery that it was hard to bring them to a halt.

The prisoners were led away from the battery, in their number a wounded French general, around whom the officers crowded.

A throng of wounded, Russians and French, some

of them known and many unknown to Pierre, their faces distorted with agony, crawled or limped, or were carried away from the battery on stretchers.

Pierre went up on the mound again, where he had spent more than an hour already, and of that little "family circle" which had, as it were, adopted him, he found not one. There were many dead lying there, but they were strangers. Some he recognized. The young officer was lying, all in a heap, as before, in a pool of blood at the edge of the parapet. The rubicund soldier was twitching a little, but they did not carry him away.

Pierre went down again.

"No, now they must surely put an end to this ; now they must begin to feel remorse for what they have been doing," thought Pierre, aimlessly taking the same direction as the line of litters moving from the battle-field.

But the sun, obscured by smoke, was still high in the heavens, and at the front, and especially at the left at Semenovskoye, there was a great commotion in the smoke, and the thunder of guns and cannon not only did not slacken, but rather increased, even to desperation, like a man who, perishing, collects his forces to utter one last cry.

CHAPTER XXXIII

THE principal action in the battle of Borodino took place on a space of a thousand sazhens,[1] between Borodino and Bagration's earthworks.

Outside of this space there had occurred, about noon, on one side, a demonstration on the part of Uvarof's Russian cavalry ; on the other, beyond Utitsa, the skirmish between Poniatowski and Tutchkof had taken place ; but these were two distinct engagements, and insignificant in comparison with what went on in the middle of the battle-field.

On this field, between Borodino and the fleches, near

[1] A sazhen is seven feet; five hundred sazhens make a verst.

the forest, on an open tract visible from both sides, the principal action of the battle was fought in the simplest, most artless manner imaginable.

The action began with a cannonade on both sides, from several hundred cannon.

. Then, when the smoke had settled down on the whole field, forward through it, on the side of the French, at the right, moved the two divisions of Dessaix and Campan against the earthworks, and at the left moved the viceroy's regiments against Borodino.

From the Shevardino redoubt, where Napoleon had taken up his position, the distance to Bagration's fleches was about a verst, while Borodino was upwards of two versts distant in a straight line, and, consequently, Napoleon could not see what was going on there, — all the more from the fact that the smoke, mingling with the mist, covered the whole locality.

The soldiers of Dessaix's division, as they moved against the fleches, were visible only until they began to descend the ravine which separated them from the earthworks. As soon as they descended into the ravine, the smoke of the cannon and musketry from the earthworks was so dense that it wholly curtained off everything on the farther side of the ravine.

Through the smoke, here and there, gleamed some black object, apparently a body of men, and from time to time the glittering of bayonets. But whether they were moving or standing still, whether they were French or Russians, it was impossible to distinguish from the Shevardino redoubt.

The sun came out bright, and shone with its slanting rays full into Napoleon's face, as he looked from under the shade of his hand toward the fleches.

The smoke hung like a curtain in front of them, and sometimes it seemed that the smoke was in motion, sometimes that the troops were in motion. Occasionally, above the noise of the musketry, the shouts of men could be heard ; but it was impossible to know what they were doing.

Napoleon, standing on the knoll, gazed through his

field-glass, and in the small circlet of the instrument he could see smoke and men, sometimes his own, sometimes Russians; but when he came to use his naked eye, he could not find even where he had been looking but the moment before.

He went down from the redoubt, and began to pace back and forth in front of it.

Occasionally he paused and listened to the firing, or strained his sight to see the battle-field.

Not only from that lower ground where he was standing, not only from the mound on which some of his generals were left, but likewise from the fleches themselves, where, now together and now alternately, Russians and French were in the fore, crowded with soldiers, dead and wounded, panic-stricken or frenzied, was it impossible to make out what was going on in that place.

For several hours, amid the incessant firing of musketry and cannon, now the Russians appeared in the ascendant, and now the French; now the infantry, and now the cavalry; they showed themselves, they fell, they fired, they struggled hand to hand; not knowing what they were doing to one another, they shouted and they retreated.

Napoleon's aides and his marshals' orderlies kept galloping up from the battle-field with reports as to the progress of affairs; but all these reports were false for the reason that, in the heat of the engagement, it was impossible to say what was taking place at a given moment; and for the reason that many of the aides did not reach the actual place of conflict, but reported what they had heard from others; and again for the reason that, while any aide was traversing the two or three versts which separated his starting-point from Napoleon, the circumstances must have changed, and the tidings have become false.

Thus the viceroy sent an aide post-haste with the tidings that Borodino had been captured and the bridge over the Kalotcha was in the hands of the French. The aide asked Napoleon whether he would command the troops to make a flank movement.

Napoleon commanded them to be drawn up into line on the other side of the river and to wait, but at the time when Napoleon issued this command — nay more, even before the aide had fairly left Borodino — the bridge was recaptured and burned by the Russians, in fact, during that very skirmish in which Pierre had participated at the beginning of the battle.

Another aide, galloping up from the fleches with frightened face, reported to Napoleon that the charge had been repulsed, and that Campan was wounded and Davoust killed; but, in reality, the fleches had been recaptured by another division of the troops at the very moment that the aide was told that the French were defeated, and Davoust was alive, and suffering only from a slight contusion.

Drawing his own conclusions from such unavoidably false reports, Napoleon made his dispositions, which either were already fulfilled before he had made them, or else could not be, and never were, fulfilled.

The marshals and generals, who were at closer touch with the battle-field, but who, nevertheless, just like Napoleon, did not actually take part in the battle itself, and only rarely came actually under fire, did not ask Napoleon, but made their dispositions, and gave their orders as to where and whence to fire, and when to have the cavalry charge and the infantry take to the double-quick.

But even their dispositions, exactly like Napoleon's, were only in small measure and rarely carried out. For the most part, exactly the opposite of what they ordered was carried into effect. Soldiers commanded to advance would be exposed to a fire of grape, and retreat; soldiers commanded to hold their ground, suddenly seeing an unexpected body of Russians coming against them, would sometimes rush on to meet them, and the cavalry without orders would gallop off to cut down the fleeing Russians.

Thus two regiments of cavalry dashed down through the ravine of Semenovskoye, and as soon as they reached the hilltop they faced about and galloped back at breakneck speed.

In the same way, the infantry soldiers oftentimes moved about, sometimes going on the double-quick in directions entirely different from what they were ordered to go.

All dispositions as to where and when cannon were to be unlimbered, when the infantry were to be sent forward, when to fire, when the cavalry were to hammer down the Russian infantry, — all these dispositions were made on their own responsibility by the subordinate heads who were close at hand, in the ranks, and they did not stop to consult either with Ney or Davoust or Murat, and certainly not with Napoleon. They had no fear of blame for their commands not being carried out, or for arbitrary orders issued, because in a battle the issue at stake is man's most precious possession — his own life, and it often seems that his safety lies in retreating, often in advancing at the double-quick; and so those men who were in the smoke of the battle acted in conformity with the needs of the moment.

In reality, all these movements back and forth did not relieve and did not change the positions of the troops. All their collisions and charges, one against the other, produced very little injury, but the injuries, the deaths, and the mutilations were brought by the projectiles and shots which were flying in all directions over that space where these men were pelting one another. As soon as these men left that space where the shot and shell were flying, then immediately their nachalniks, stationed in the rear, would bring them into order again, subject them to discipline, and, under the influence of this discipline, lead them back to the domain of the projectiles, where again under the influence of the fear of death they would lose their discipline and become subject to whatever disposition was paramount in the throng.

CHAPTER XXXIV

NAPOLEON's generals, — Davoust, Ney, and Murat, — finding themselves near to this domain of fire, and sometimes even riding up into it, more than once led into this domain of fire enormous and well-ordered masses of troops. But, contrary to what had invariably happened in all their former engagements, instead of the expected report that the enemy were fleeing, these well-ordered masses of troops returned *thence* in disorderly, panic-stricken throngs.

Then again they would collect them, but each time in diminished numbers. In the afternoon, Murat sent his aide to Napoleon for reinforcements.

Napoleon was sitting at the foot of the mound, drinking punch, when Murat's aide-de-camp came galloping up with the report that the Russians would be defeated if his majesty would send one more division.

"Reinforcements?" exclaimed Napoleon, in grim amazement, as if not realizing the meaning of his words, and looking at the handsome young aide, who wore his dark hair in long curls just as Murat wore his. "Reinforcements!" muttered Napoleon. "How can they ask for reinforcements when they already have in their hands half of the army to throw against the weak, unfortified Russian flank! — Tell the king of Naples," said Napoleon, sternly, "tell the king of Naples that it is not noon, and that I do not yet see clearly on my chess-board. .... Go!" ....

The handsome young aide-de-camp with the long hair, not removing his hand from his hat, drew a heavy sigh, and galloped back again to the place where they were slaughtering men.

Napoleon got up, and, calling Caulaincourt and Berthier, began to discuss with them concerning matters that had nothing to do with the battle.

In the midst of this conversation, which began to engross Napoleon, Berthier's eyes were attracted to a general with his suite who came galloping up to the mound on a sweaty horse.

This was Belliard. Throwing himself from his horse, he approached the emperor with swift strides, and boldly, in a loud voice, began to show forth the imperative necessity of reinforcements.

He swore on his honor that the Russians were beaten if the emperor would only give them one division more.

Napoleon shrugged his shoulders, and, without making any reply, kept on walking back and forth. Belliard began to talk loud and earnestly with the generals of the suite gathered round him.

"You are very hot-headed, Belliard," exclaimed Napoleon, again approaching the general who had brought the message. "It is easy to make a mistake in the thick of battle. Go back and look again, and then return to me."

Hardly had Belliard time to disappear from sight when, from the other side, a new messenger came hastening up from the battle-field.

"Well, what is it ? " demanded Napoleon, in the tone of a man annoyed by importunate difficulties.

"Sire, the prince ...." began the aide-de-camp.

"Wants reinforcements?" said Napoleon, with a furious gesture, taking the words out of his mouth. The aide-de-camp bowed his head affirmatively, and began to make his report ; but the emperor turned away, took a couple of steps, paused, turned back, and addressed Berthier.

"We must give them the reserves," said he, slightly throwing open his hands. "Which shall we send, think you?" he asked, addressing Berthier, "that gosling which I made into an eagle — *oison que j'ai fait aigle*," as he was of late in the habit of calling him.

"Sire, send Claparède's division," suggested Berthier, who knew by heart every division, regiment, and battalion.

Napoleon nodded approval.

The aide-de-camp dashed off to Claparède's division, and, within a few minutes, the Young Guard, who were drawn up back of the mound, were on the way. Napoleon looked on in silence at this movement.

"No," he cried, suddenly turning to Berthier, "I cannot send Claparède. Send Friant's division," said he.

Although there was no advantage in sending Friant's division rather than Claparède's, and the delay caused by recalling Claparède and sending Friant was unfortunate, still this order was carried out to the letter. Napoleon did not see that in thus treating his forces he was playing the part of a doctor who, by his very remedies, hinders recovery — a part which he thoroughly appreciated and criticized.

Friant's division, like the others, also vanished in the smoke that hung over the battle-field. From all sides aides kept galloping up with reports, and all, as if by previous agreement, had one and the same story to tell. All asked for reinforcements, all declared that the Russians were holding desperately to their positions and that they were returning an infernal fire — *un feu d'enfer* — under which the French troops were melting away.

Napoleon, in deep thought, sat down on a camp-chair.

M. de Beausset, who was so fond of traveling, and had been fasting since early morning, came up to the emperor, and permitted himself the boldness of respectfully proposing to his majesty to eat some breakfast.

"I hope that I am not premature in congratulating your majesty on a victory," said he.

Napoleon silently shook his head. M. de Beausset, taking it for granted that this negation was a disclaimer of victory and did not refer to breakfast, permitted himself in a playfully respectful manner to remark that there was no reason on earth why they should not have some breakfast when they could have some

"*Allez vous* ...." suddenly cried Napoleon, gruffly, and turned his back on him. A beatific smile of pity, regret, and enthusiasm irradiated M. Beausset's face, and with a swaggering gait he rejoined the other generals.

Napoleon was under the sway of a gloomy feeling like that experienced by a universally fortunate gamester,

who has senselessly staked his money because he was
always sure of winning, and suddenly, just at the time
when he has calculated all the chances of the game, is
brought to the knowledge that the more he puzzles over
its course, the more surely he is losing.

The troops were the same, the generals were the
same, the preparations were the same, the same dispositions, the same *proclamation courte et énergique;* he
himself was the same, — he knew it; he knew that he
was vastly better in experience and skill than he had
ever been before; even the enemy were the same as at
Austerlitz and Friedland; — but the terrible crushing
blow of the hand fell powerless as if magic interfered.

All those former measures which had been invariably
crowned with success, — the concentration of all the
batteries on one spot, and the attack of the reserves for
crushing the lines, and the charge of the cavalry — his
men of iron, — all these measures had already been employed, and not only there was no victory, but from all
sides the same stories about generals killed and wounded,
about the necessity of reinforcements, about the impossibility of defeating the Russians, and about the
demoralization of the troops.

Hitherto, after two or three moves, two or three
hasty orders, marshals and aides-de-camp would come
galloping up with congratulations and joyous faces,
announcing whole corps of prisoners as trophies, *des
faisceaux de drapeaux et d'aigles ennemis* — sheaves of
standards and eagles taken from the foe — and cannon,
and provision trains; and Murat would only ask for permission to let the cavalry set forth to gather in the booty.
This was the case at Lodi, Marengo, Arcole, Jena, Austerlitz, Wagram, and so on, and so on. But now, something strange had happened to his warriors!

Notwithstanding the report that the fleches had been
captured, Napoleon saw that this success was different,
entirely different, from what had been the case in all his
other battles. He saw that the feeling which he experienced was also experienced by all the men around him
who were familiar with military affairs. All faces were

gloomy, all eyes were averted. Beausset alone failed to understand the significance of what was happening.

Napoleon, after his long experience of war, well knew what it meant that, after eight hours' steady fighting, after the expenditure of such efforts, victory had not crowned the attacking columns. He knew that it was almost a defeat, and that the slightest mischance might now, at this critical point on which the battle was balancing, ruin him and his army.

When he passed in review all this strange Russian campaign, in which not one victory had been won, — in which, for two months, not a standard, not a cannon, not a squad of men had been captured ; when he looked at the openly dejected faces of those around him, and heard the reports that the Russians still stood their ground, — a terrible feeling, like that experienced in nightmares, seized him, and all the unfortunate circumstances that might ruin him came into his mind.

The Russians might fall on his left wing, might break through his center, a random projectile might even kill him! All this was possible. In his previous battles, he had reckoned only with the chances of success ; now, an infinite number of possible mischances confronted him, and he expected them all. Yes, this was just as in a dream, when a man imagines that a murderer is attacking him, and the man, in his dream, brandishes his arms, and strikes his assailant with a tremendous force which he knows must annihilate him, and then feels that his arm falls weak and limp as a rag, and the horror of inevitable destruction, because he is helpless, seizes him.

The report that the Russians were really charging the left flank of the French army awoke in Napoleon this horror. He sat in silence at the foot of the mound, on his camp-chair, with his head bent, and his elbows on his knees. Berthier came to him, and proposed to him to ride around the line, so as to assure himself how affairs really stood.

"What? What did you say?" asked Napoleon. "Yes, have my horse brought."

He mounted, and rode toward Semenovskoye.

In the slowly dissipating gunpowder smoke that spread all over this space where Napoleon was riding, in the pools of blood, lay horses and men, singly and in heaps. Such a horror, such a collection of slaughtered men, neither Napoleon nor any of his generals had ever seen on so small a space. The thunder of the cannon, which had not ceased rolling for ten hours, and had become a torment to the ear, gave a peculiar significance to this spectacle (like music to *tableaux-vivants*).

Napoleon rode to the height over Semenovskoye, and through the smoke he could see ranks of men in uniforms the colors of which were unfamiliar to his eyes. They were the Russians.

The Russians, in dense rows, were posted behind Semenovskoye and the mound, and their cannon, all along the line, were incessantly roaring, and filling the air with smoke. This was not a battle. It was wholesale butchery, incapable of bringing any advantage to either the Russians or the French.

Napoleon reined in his horse, and again fell into that brown study from which Berthier had aroused him. He could not put an end to this affair which was going on in front of him and around him, and which seemed to have been regulated by him and to have been contingent upon his fiat; and this affair, in consequence of this his first failure, for the first time made him realize all its uselessness and horror.

One of the generals who came galloping up to Napoleon permitted himself to propose that the Old Guard should be sent into the battle. Ney and Berthier, who were standing near Napoleon, exchanged glances, and smiled scornfully at this general's senseless proposal.

Napoleon let his head sink on his breast, and was long silent.

"We are eight hundred leagues from France, and I will not have my Guard destroyed!" said he; and, turning his horse, he rode back to Shevardino.

CHAPTER XXXV

KUTUZOF, with his gray head sunk down, and his heavy body sprawled out on a rug-covered bench, was sitting in the same place where Pierre had seen him that morning. He gave no definite orders, but merely approved or disapproved of what was reported to him.

"Yes, yes, do so," he would answer to the various suggestions. "Yes, yes, go, my dear, go and see!" he would say to this one or that of those near him; or, "No, it is not necessary, we had better wait," he would say.

He listened to the reports brought to him, gave his commands when this was considered necessary by his subordinates; but even while he was listening to what was said to him, he was apparently not interested in the sense of the words so much as in the expression of the faces, in the tone of voice, of those who brought the reports. Long experience in war had taught him, and his years of discretion had made him realize, that it is impossible for one man to direct a hundred thousand men engaged in a death struggle, and he knew that the issue of a battle is determined, not by the plans of the commander-in-chief, not by the place where the troops are stationed, not by the number of the cannon or the multitude of the slain, but by that imponderable force called the spirit of the army; and he made use of this force, and directed it, as far as it was in his power.

The general expression of Kutuzof's face was one of calm concentrated attention and energy, scarcely able to overcome the weariness of his old and feeble frame.

At eleven o'clock in the morning, he was informed that the fleches captured by the French had been retaken, but that Prince Bagration was wounded. Kutuzof groaned, and shook his head.

"Go to Prince Piotr Ivanovitch, and learn the particulars what and how," said he to one of his aides; and immediately after he turned to the Prince of Würtemberg, who was standing just back of him: —

"Would not your highness like to take command of the first division?"

Soon after the prince's departure, so soon, in fact, that he could not have reached Semenovskoye, the prince's aide came back, and informed his serene highness that the prince wished more troops.

Kutuzof frowned, and sent word to Dokhturof to take command of the first division, and begged the prince to return to him, as, so he said, he could not do without him at this important crisis.

When the report was brought that Murat was taken prisoner, and the staff hastened to congratulate Kutuzof, he smiled.

"Wait, gentlemen," said he. "There is nothing extraordinary in the victory being won, and Murat being a prisoner. But it is best to postpone our elation."

Nevertheless, he sent one of his aides to ride along the lines, and announce this news to the troops.

When Shcherbinin came spurring up from the left flank to report that the French had captured the fleches and Semenovskoye, Kutuzof, judging from the sounds on the battle-field and by Shcherbinin's face that he was bringing bad news, got up, as if to stretch his legs, and, taking Shcherbinin by the arm, he led him to one side.

"Go, my dear,"[1] said he to Yermolof, "go and see if it is impossible to do anything."

Kutuzof was at Gorki, the center of the position of the Russian troops. The assaults on our left flank, directed by Napoleon, had been several times repulsed. At the center the French had not pushed beyond Borodino. On the right Uvarof's cavalry had put the French to flight.

At three o'clock the French attack began to slacken in violence. On the faces of all who came from the battle-field and of all who stood around him, Kutuzof read an expression of the most intense excitement. Kutuzof was satisfied with the success of the day, which surpassed his expectations. But the old man's

[1] *Galubchik.*

physical strength began to desert him. Several times his head sank forward, as if out of his control, and he dozed. They brought him something to eat.

Flügel-adjutant Woltzogen, the one who, as he rode past Prince Andreï, had declared that the war must spread into the country, — *im Raum verlegen*, — and whom Bagration so detested, came riding up while Kutuzof was eating his dinner. Woltzogen came from Barclay with a report as to the course of affairs on the left wing. The prudent Barclay de Tolly, seeing the throngs of wounded hastening to the rear, and the ragged ranks of the army, and taking all circumstances into consideration, decided that the battle was lost, and sent his favorite with this news to the general-in-chief.

Kutuzof laboriously mumbled a piece of roasted chicken and gazed at Woltzogen with squinting, jocose eyes.

Woltzogen, stretching his legs negligently, with a half-scornful smile on his lips, came to Kutuzof, barely lifting his hand to his vizor. He behaved to his serene highness with a certain affectation of indifference, which was intended to show that he, as a highly cultured military man, permitted the Russians tò make an idol of this good-for-nothing old man, but that *he* knew with whom he was dealing. " *Der alte Herr* — the old gentleman," as Kutuzof was called by the Germans in his circle — " *macht sich ganz bequem* — is taking things very easy," said Woltzogen to himself ; and, casting a stern glance at the platter placed in front of Kutuzof, he proceeded to report to the old gentleman the position of affairs on the left flank, as Barclay had told him to do, and as he himself had seen and understood them.

"All the points of our position are in the enemy's hands, and we cannot regain them, because we have no troops ; they are in full retreat, and there is no possibility of stopping them," was his report.

Kutuzof, ceasing to chew, stared at Woltzogen in amazement, as if he did not comprehend what was said to him.

Woltzogen, observing the *alter Herr's* excitement, said,

with a smile, — "I did not feel that it was right to conceal from your serene highness what I have been witnessing. The troops are wholly demoralized."....

"You have seen it? You have seen it?".... screamed Kutuzof, scowling, and leaping to his feet, and swiftly approaching Woltzogen. "How.... how dare you?".... and he made a threatening gesture with his palsied hands, and, choking, he cried: "How dare you, dear sir, say this *to me?* You know nothing about it. Tell General Barclay from me that his observations are false, and that the actual course of the battle is better known to me, the commander-in-chief, than it is to him!"

Woltzogen was about to make some remark, but Kutuzof cut him short: —

"The enemy are beaten on the left and crushed on the right. If you saw things wrong, my dear sir, still you should not permit yourself to say what you know nothing about. Be good enough to go to General Barclay and tell him that it is my absolute intention to attack the enemy to-morrow," said Kutuzof, sternly.

All was silent, and all that could be heard was the heavy breathing of the excited old general.

"They are beaten all along the line, thank God and the gallantry of the Russian army for that! The enemy are crushed, and to-morrow we will drive them from the sacred soil of Russia," said Kutuzof, crossing himself, and suddenly the tears sprang to his eyes and he sobbed.

Woltzogen, shrugging his shoulders, and pursing his lips, silently went to one side, expressing his amazement at the old gentleman's conceited stubbornness — *über diese Eingenommenheit des alten Herrn.*

"Ah, here comes my hero," exclaimed Kutuzof, to a stalwart, handsome, dark-haired general, who at this moment approached the mound.

This was Rayevsky, who had been all that day at the critical point of the field of Borodino.

Rayevsky reported that the troops were unmoved in their positions, and that the French did not dare to attack them any more.

On hearing this, Kutuzof said in French, — "Then you do not think, *as some others do*, that we are forced to withdraw?"

"On the contrary, your highness, in drawn battles it is always the stubbornest who can be called victorious," replied Rayevsky, — "and my opinion...."

"Kaïsarof!" cried Kutuzof, summoning his adjutant. "Sit down and write an order for to-morrow. And you," he said, addressing another, "hasten down the lines and have them understand that we attack to-morrow."

While Kutuzof was talking with Rayevsky and dictating his order of the day, Woltzogen came back from Barclay and announced that General Barclay de Tolly would like a written confirmation of the order which the field-marshal had delivered to him.

Kutuzof, not looking at Woltzogen, commanded his aides to write out the order, which the former commander-in-chief desired to have in order completely to relieve him of personal responsibility.

And by that intangible, mysterious connection which preserves throughout a whole army one and the same disposition, the so-called *esprit du corps*, and constitutes the chief sinew of an army, Kutuzof's words and his order for renewing the battle on the following day were known simultaneously from one end of the force to the other.

The exact words or the absolute form of the order were not indeed carried to the utmost limits of this organization; in the stories which were repeated in the widely separated ends of the lines there was very likely nothing like what Kutuzof really said; but the gist of his words was conveyed everywhere, for the reason that what Kutuzof said sprang not from logical reasoning, but was the genuine outcome of the sentiment that was in the heart of the commander-in-chief, finding a response in the heart of every Russian.

And when they knew that on the next day they were going to attack the enemy, and heard from the upper circles of the army the confirmation of what they wished to believe, these men, tortured by doubt, were comforted and encouraged.

CHAPTER XXXVI

PRINCE ANDREÏ's regiment was among the reserves, which had been stationed until two o'clock behind Semenovskoye, doing nothing under the severe fire of the artillery. At two o'clock, the regiment, which had already lost more than two hundred men, was moved forward upon the trampled field of oats, on that space between Semenovskoye and the "Kurgan" battery, whereon thousands of men were killed that day, and toward which was now concentrated a tremendous fire, from several hundreds of the enemy's guns.

Without stirring from that spot, and not themselves replying with a single shot, the regiment lost here two-thirds of its effective. In front and especially at the right-hand side, amid the perpetual smoke, the cannons were booming,[1] and from that mysterious domain of smoke which shrouded all the space in front constantly flew the hissing and swiftly screaming projectiles, and the more deliberately sputtering shells. Sometimes, as if to give a respite, a quarter-hour would pass during which all the shot and shells would fly overhead, but then, again, several men would be struck down in the course of a moment, and they were constantly engaged in dragging the dead to one side, and carrying the wounded to the rear.

With each new casualty the chances of life were diminished for those who were as yet unscathed. The regiment was posted in battalion columns at intervals of three hundred paces, but, nevertheless, all the men were under the influence of one and the same mood. All the men of the regiment were without exception silent and melancholy. Once in a while a few words were spoken in the ranks, but this conversation was always abruptly cut short each time when the thud of the falling missile was heard, and the cry of "Stretchers!"

The larger part of the time, the men of the regiment,

[1] *Bubukhali.*

by their chief's orders, lay low on the ground. One man, having taken off his shako, was assiduously untying and again tying up the strings; another, with dry clay fashioned into a ball in his palms, was polishing up his bayonet; another had taken off the strap and was buckling his bandoleer; still another was carefully untwisting his leg-wrappers and tying them on again, and changing his shoes.

Some dug shelters out of the plowed land, or plaited wattles out of the stubble straw. All seemed entirely absorbed in their occupations. When any of them were killed or wounded, when the litters were brought into requisition, when our men were forced back, when great masses of the enemy were seen in the smoke, no one paid any attention to these circumstances.

But when the artillery or the cavalry were moved forward, or our infantry could be seen executing some manœuver, approving remarks were heard on all sides. But the most attention was excited by incidents entirely extraneous, which had absolutely no relation to the battle. These morally tormented men seemed to be relieved by having their attention turned to the ordinary affairs of every-day life.

A battery of artillery passed in front of the regiment. The off horse attached to one of the caissons got entangled in the traces.

"Hey! look out for your off horse!".... "Take care! He'll be down!".... "Ekh! Haven't they any eyes?" Such were the remarks shouted all along the line.

Another time, general attention was attracted by a small cinnamon-colored puppy which, with its tail stiffly erect, came from God knows where, and went flying at a desperate pace in front of the ranks, and, frightened by the sudden plunge of a round shot which fell near it, set up a yelp, and sprang to one side with its tail between its legs. A roar of laughter and shouts ran along the line.

But diversions of this sort lasted only for a few minutes, while the men had been standing there for more

than eight hours, without food, and inactive, under that
ceaseless horror of death, and their pallid and anxious
faces grew ever more pallid and more anxious.

Prince Andreï, like all the other men in his regiment
anxious and pallid, paced back and forth along the
meadow, next the oat-field, from one end to the other,
with his arms behind his back, and with bent head.
There was nothing for him to do or to order. Everything went like clockwork. The dead were dragged to
one side, away from the front; the wounded were carried to the rear; the ranks were closed up. If the soldiers stood aside, they instantly hastened back to their
places again.

At first Prince Andreï, considering it incumbent upon
him to encourage his men and to set them an example
of gallantry, kept walking up and down along the ranks;
but afterwards he became convinced that they had
nothing to learn from him. With all the energy of his soul,
— and this was true also of every one of the soldiers, —
he unconsciously tried to blind himself to the horrors of
their situation.

He marched along the meadow, dragging his feet,
trampling down the grass and contemplating the dust
that covered his boots; then again with long strides he
would try to step from ridge to ridge left by the mowers'
scythes along the meadow; or, counting his steps, he
would calculate how many times he must go from one
boundary to the other in order to make a verst. He
would pluck up the wormwood growing on the edge of
the field, and rub the flowers between his palms, and
sniff the powerful, penetrating bitter of their odor.

Nothing remained of the fabric of thought which he
had so painfully elaborated the evening before. He
thought of nothing at all. He listened with weary ears
to that perpetual repetition of sounds, distinguishing the
whistling of the missiles above the roar of the musketry.
He gazed at the indifferent faces of the men in the first
battalion, and waited.

"Here she comes!.... That's one for us," he would
say to himself as he caught the approaching screech of

something from that hidden realm of smoke. " One, a second! There's another! It struck!"

He paused, and looked along the ranks. " No, it went over. Ah! but that one struck!"

And once more he would take up his promenade, trying to measure long steps, so as to reach the boundary in sixteen strides.

A screech, and a thud! Within half a dozen steps from him a projectile flung up the dry soil and buried itself. An involuntary chill ran down his back. Once more he looked along the ranks: evidently many had been struck down; a great crowd had come together in the second battalion.

" Mr. Adjutant," he cried, "tell those men not to stand so close together."

The aide, having fulfilled the command, returned to Prince Andreï. From the other side the battalion commander rode up on horseback.

" Look out!" cried a soldier in a terrified voice; and, like a bird whistling in its swift flight and settling earthward, a shell came plunging down, not noisily, within two paces of Prince Andreï, and near the battalion commander's horse.

The horse, not pausing to consider whether it were well or ill to manifest fear, snorted, shied, and, almost unseating the major, darted off. The horse's panic was shared by the men.

" Lie down!" cried the aide, throwing himself on the ground.

Prince Andreï stood undecided. The shell, with its fuse smoking, was spinning like a top between him and the aide, on the very edge between the plowed land and the meadow, near the clump of wormwood.

" Can this be death?" wondered Prince Andreï, casting a fleeting glance full of a newly born envy at the grass, the wormwood, and the thread of smoke that escaped from the whirling black ball. " I cannot, I will not die; I love life, I love this grass, the earth, the air.... "

All this flashed through his mind, and at the same time

he remembered that they were looking at him. "For shame, Mr. Officer!" he started to say to the aide. "Any...."

He did not finish. There came simultaneously a crash, a whizzing of fragments, as of broken glass, a powerful odor of gunpowder smoke, and Prince Andreï was struck in the side, and, throwing his arms up, he fell on his face.

Several officers hastened to him. From the right side of his abdomen a great gush of blood stained the grass.

The infantry who acted as bearers came up with their stretchers, and stood behind the officers. Prince Andreï lay with his face buried in the grass, gasping painfully.

"Now, then, why loiter? come on!"

The muzhiks came close and lifted him by the shoulders and legs; but he groaned piteously, and the men, exchanging glances, laid him down again.

"Bear a hand there! Up with him! it's all the same!" cried some one's voice. Once more they took him by the shoulders, and laid him on the stretcher.

"Ah! my God! my God! What?".... "In the belly? That finishes him!".... "Akh! Bozhe moï!" exclaimed various officers.

"Na! a fragment whizzed past my ear," said the aide. The muzhiks, lifting the stretcher to their shoulders, hastily directed their steps along the path that they had already worn toward the "bandaging-point."

"Fall into step!.... Oh! you men!" cried an officer, halting the muzhiks, who were walking out of step and jolting the stretcher. "In step there, can't you, Khveodor, ... now, then Khveodor!" exclaimed the front muzhik.

"Now that's the way!" cheerfully replied the rear one, falling into step.

"Your illustriousness.... prince!" said Timokhin in a trembling voice, as he came up and looked at the stretcher.

Prince Andreï opened his eyes, and looked out from

the stretcher in which his head was sunken, and when he saw who spoke, he again shut them.

The militiamen carried Prince Andreï to the forest, where the wagons were sheltered, and where the field lazaret had been established. This field lazaret, or bandaging-place, consisted of three tents with upturned flaps, pitched on the edge of the birch grove. Within the grove stood the wagons and horses. The horses were munching oats in haversacks, and the sparrows were pouncing down and carrying off the scattered grains; crows, scenting blood, and impatiently cawing, were flying about over the tree-tops.

Around the tents, occupying more than five acres [1] of ground, lay, and sat, and stood blood-stained men in various attire.

Around the wounded stood a throng of stretcher-bearers, soldiers, with sad but interested faces, whom the officers, attempting to carry out orders, found it impossible to keep away. Not heeding the officers, the soldiers stood leaning on the stretchers and gazed steadily, as if trying to grasp the meaning of the terrible spectacle before their eyes.

From the tents could be heard now loud, fierce sobs, then pitiful groans. Occasionally, assistants would come hurrying out after water, and signify the next ones who should be brought in. The wounded by the tents, waiting their turn, hoarsely cried, groaned, wept, screamed, cursed, clamored for vodka. Some were delirious.

Prince Andreï, as regimental commander, was carried through this throng of unbandaged sufferers, close to one of the tents, and there his bearers waited for further orders. He opened his eyes, and it was some time before he could comprehend what was going on around him. The meadow, the wormwood, the plowed field, the black whirling ball, and that passionate throb of love for life occurred to his recollection.

Two paces from him, talking loudly and attracting general attention, stood a tall, handsome, black-haired,

[1] Two desyatins; a desyatin is 2.7 acres.

non-commissioned officer with a bandaged head, and leaning against a dead tree. He had been wounded in the head and leg with bullets. Around him, attracted by his talk, were gathered a throng of wounded and of stretcher-bearers.

"We gave it to him so hot that they dropped everything; they even left the king," cried the soldier, snapping his fiery black eyes and glancing around. "If only the reserves had been sent up just at that time, I tell you, brother, there would not have been left a show of him, because I am sure...."

Prince Andreï, like all the circle gathered around the speaker, gazed at him with gleaming eyes, and felt a sense of consolation. "But why is it that it is not a matter of indifference to me now?" he asked himself. "What is going to happen, and what does it mean? Why do I have such regret in leaving life? There was in this life something which I have not understood, and which I still fail to understand."

CHAPTER XXXVII

ONE of the surgeons, with blood-soaked apron, and with his small hands covered with gore, holding a cigar between thumb and little finger, so as not to besmear it, came out of the tent. This doctor lifted his head and proceeded to look on all sides, but beyond the wounded. He was evidently anxious to get a little rest. Having for some time looked toward the right and then toward the left, he drew a long sigh and dropped his eyes.

"In a moment now," said he, in reply to his feldscher, who called his attention to Prince Andreï, and he gave orders for him to be carried into the tent.

The throng of wounded who had been waiting was disposed to grumble. "In this world it seems only ' gentlemen ' are permitted to live !" exclaimed one.

Prince Andreï was taken in and deposited on a table which had only just been vacated. The feldscher was that instant engaged in rinsing something from it.

Prince Andreï could not distinctly make out what there was in the tent. The pitiful groans on all sides, the excruciating agony in his ribs, his belly, and his back, distracted him. All that he saw around him was confused for him, in one general impression of naked, blood-stained human flesh, filling all the lower part of the tent, just as several weeks previously, on that hot August day, the same flesh had filled the filthy pond along the Smolensk highway. Yes, this was the same flesh, the same cannon-meat which even then the sight of, as if prophetic of what he now experienced, had filled him with horror.

There were three tables in this tent. Two were occupied. Prince Andreï was laid on the third. He was left to himself for some little time, and he could not help seeing what was doing at the other two tables. On the one nearest lay a Tatar, — a Cossack to judge by his uniform, which was thrown down beside him. Four soldiers held him down. A surgeon in spectacles was cutting into his cinnamon-colored, muscular back.

"Ukh! Ukh! Ukh!" — the Tatar grunted like a pig, and, suddenly turning up his swarthy face with its wide cheek-bones and squat nose, and unsheathing his white teeth, he began to tug and to struggle, and set up a long, shrill, penetrating screech.

On the other table, around which were gathered a number of people, a large, stout man lay on his back, with his head thrown back. His streaming hair, its color, and the shape of the head seemed strangely familiar to Prince Andreï.

Several of the assistants were leaning on this man's chest, and holding him down. His large, stout, white leg was subject to an incessant and rapid trembling, as if it had the ague. This man was convulsively sobbing and choking. Two surgeons — one was pale and trembling — were silently doing something to this man's other handsome leg.

Having finished with the Tatar, over whom they threw his cloak, the spectacled surgeon, wiping his hands, came to Prince Andreï. He looked into Prince Andreï's face, and hastily turned away.

"Undress him. What are you dawdling for?" he cried severely to his feldschers.

Prince Andreï's very first and most distant childhood occurred to him, as the feldscher, with hasty hands, began to unbutton his clothes and remove them. The surgeon bent down low over the wound, probed it, and drew a heavy sigh. Then he made a sign to some one.

The exquisite agony which Prince Andreï felt within his abdomen caused him to lose consciousness.

When he came to himself, the broken splinters of ribs were removed, the torn clots of flesh cut away, and the wound was dressed.

They were dashing water into his face. As soon as Prince Andreï opened his eyes, the surgeon bent silently down to him, kissed him in the lips, and hastened away.

After the agony which he had endured, Prince Andreï was conscious of a well-being such as he had not experienced for a long time.

All the best and happiest moments of his life, especially his earliest childhood, when they used to undress him and put him to bed, when his old nurse used to lull him to sleep with her songs, when, as he buried his head in the pillows, he had felt himself happy in the mere consciousness of being alive : all recurred to his imagination, no longer as something long past, but as actuality.

Around that wounded man, whose features seemed familiar to Prince Andreï, the doctors were still busy, lifting him and trying to calm him.

"Show it to me..... Oóooo! O! Ooooo!" he groaned, his voice broken by frightened sobs, subdued by suffering.

Prince Andreï, hearing these groans, felt like weeping himself : either because he was dying without fame, or because he regretted being torn from life, or because of these recollections of a childhood never to return, or because he sympathized in the sufferings of others, and this man was groaning so piteously before him ; but, at any rate, he felt like weeping good, childlike, almost happy tears.

The wounded man was shown the amputated leg, still in its boot, which was full of blood.

"O! Ooooo!" and he sobbed like a woman. The surgeon, who had been standing in front of the patient, and prevented his face from being seen, stepped to one side.

"My God! what does this mean? Why is *he* here?" Prince Andreï wondered.

In this wretched, sobbing, exhausted man, whose leg had only just been taken off, he recognized Anatol Kuragin. They lifted Anatol's head, and gave him water in a glass; but his trembling, swollen lips could not close over the edge of the glass. Anatol was still sobbing bitterly.

"Yes, it is he! yes, this man who has been somehow so closely, so painfully, connected with my life!" said Prince Andreï to himself, not as yet realizing clearly all the circumstances. "What has been the link that connects this man with my childhood, with my life?" he asked himself, and could not find the answer to his question. And suddenly a new and unexpected remembrance from that world of the childlike, pure, and lovely past arose before Prince Andreï. He recalled Natasha just as he had seen her for the first time at the ball, in 1810, with her slender neck and arms, with her timid, happy face so easily wakened to enthusiasm, and his love and tenderness for her arose more keenly and powerfully in his soul than ever before. He remembered now the bond which existed between him and this man, who, through the tears that suffused his swollen eyes, was gazing at him with such an expression of agony. Prince Andreï remembered everything, and a solemn pity and love for this man welled up in his happy heart.

Prince Andreï could no longer restrain himself, and he wept tears of compassionate love and tenderness over other men and over himself, over their errors and his own.

"Sympathy, love for one's brothers, for those who love us, love for those who hate us, love for our enemies, yes, the love which God preached on earth, which the Princess Mariya taught me, and which I have not understood, — that is what made me feel regret for life; that is what would have remained for me if my life had been spared. But now it is too late. I know it."

CHAPTER XXXVIII

THE terrible spectacle of the battle-field, covered with corpses and wounded men, together with the heaviness of his head and the news that a score of famous generals had been killed and wounded, and together with the consciousness that his formerly powerful hands were powerless, had produced an unusual impression upon Napoleon, who, as a general thing, was fond of contemplating the killed and wounded, this being (as he thought) a proof of his mental force.

On this day the horrible spectacle of the battle-field overcame this moral force whereby he had always manifested his worth and greatness. He hastened away from the battle-field and returned to the hill of Shevardino. Sallow, bloated, apathetic, with bloodshot eyes, red nose, and hoarse voice, he sat down in his campchair, involuntarily listening to the sounds of the firing and not raising his eyes.

With sickening distress he awaited the end of this action, of which he regarded himself the principal participant, but which he was powerless to stay. A personal feeling of humanity for a brief moment became paramount over that artificial phantom of life which he had followed so long. He bore the weight of all the suffering and death which he had witnessed on the battle-field. The dull feeling in his head and chest reminded him of the possibility that he also might have to suffer and to die. At that instant he desired neither Moscow nor victory nor glory (and yet what glory he still required!). The one thing that he now desired was rest, repose, and liberty.

But as soon as he reached the Semenovskoye heights, an artillery general proposed to him to station a few batteries there for the sake of increasing the fire on the Russian troops massing in front of Kniazkovo. Napoleon acquiesced, and ordered a report to be made to him as to the effect produced by these batteries.

An aide-de-camp came to say that, in accordance with the emperor's orders, two hundred cannon had been directed against the Russians, but that the Russians still held their ground.

"Our fire mows them down in rows, but still they stand," said the aide.

"*Ils en veulent encore!* — They want some more of the same!" said Napoleon, in his husky voice.

"Sire?" inquired the aide, not quite understanding what the emperor said.

"*Ils en veulent encore!*" repeated Napoleon, in his hoarse voice, with a frown. "*Donnez leurs-en* — Give it them."

Even without his orders what he did not wish was accomplished, and he repeated the form of the injunction, simply because he imagined that the injunction was expected of him. And again he returned into that former artificial world of illusions as to his majesty, and once more — like a horse which walks on the sliding plane of the treadmill and all the time imagines that he is doing something for himself — again he began stubbornly to fulfil that cruel, painful, and trying and inhuman *rôle* which was imposed upon him.

Not on this day and this hour only the intellect and conscience of this man, on whom weighed more heavily than on all the other participants of this action the responsibility for what was taking place, were darkened; but never, even to the end of his life, was he able to realize the goodness, or the beauty, or the truth, or the real significance of his actions, since they were too much opposed to goodness and right, too far removed from all that was human, for him to be able to realize their significance. He could not renounce his actions, since they were approved by half of the world, and conse-

quently he was compelled to renounce truth and goodness and all that was humane.

Not on this day only when, having ridden round the
field of battle strewn with dead and mutilated men, —
through his volition as he fondly supposed, — as he contemplated these men, he tried to calculate how many
Russians one single Frenchman stood for, and, deceiving himself, found good reason for rejoicing that one
Frenchman was equal to five Russians! Not on this
day only he wrote in his letter to Paris that *le champ de
bataille a été superbe* — that the battle-field was magnificent — because there were fifty thousand corpses
on it; but on the Island of Saint Helena as well, in the
silence of his solitude, where he declared that he was
going to devote his leisure moments to an exposition
of the mighty deeds which he had accomplished, he
wrote : —

The Russian war should have been the most popular war of
modern times : it was one of sound common sense and genuine
advantage, calculated to bring peace and security to all ; it was
purely pacific and conservative.

Its great purpose was to put an end to contingencies and to
establish security. A new horizon, new labors, would have
opened up and brought well-being and prosperity to all. The
European system was established ; all that was left to do was to
organize it.

Satisfied on these great questions, and at peace with all the
world, I also should have had my CONGRESS and my HOLY AL-
LIANCE. Those ideas were stolen from me. In this great council of monarchs we should have discussed our interests as in a
family, and ruled the nations with a high sense of our responsibilities.

Thus Europe would soon have become in reality but a single
people, and every man, wherever he might travel, would always
find himself in the common fatherland. I would have insisted
on all navigable rivers being free to all, on all having equal
rights to all seas, and on all the great standing armies being
henceforth reduced to a guard for the sovereigns.

On my return to France, being established in the heart of a
country rendered great, magnificent, tranquil, glorious, I should
have proclaimed her boundaries unchangeable : all future war

purely *defensive;* all new aggrandizement *anti-national.* I
should have made my son my partner on the throne ; my *dictatorship* would have ended and his constitutional reign would
have begun —

Paris would have become the capital of the world and the
French the envy of the nations.

Then my leisure and my old days would have been devoted,
during my son's royal apprenticeship, to making tours in company with the empress — with our own horses and taking our
time, like a worthy country couple — through all the nooks and
corners of the empire, receiving petitions, redressing wrongs,
establishing wherever we went and everywhere monuments and
benefactions.[1]

This man, foreordained by Providence to play the painful, predestined part of executioner of the nations, persuaded himself that the end and aim of his actions was
the good of the nations, and that he could have ruled
the destinies of millions, and loaded them with benefits,
if he had been given the power !

[1] *La guerre de Russie a dû être la plus populaire des temps modernes :
c'était celle du bon sens et des vrais intérêts, celle du repos et de la securité
de tous ; elle était purement pacifique et conservatrice. C'était pour la
grande cause, la fin des hasards et le commencement de la securité. Un
nouvel horizon, de nouveaux travaux allaient se dérouler, tout plein du
bien-être et de la prosperité de tous. Le système Européen se trouvait fondé :
il n'était plus question que de l'organiser. Satisfait sur ces grands points
et tranquille partout, j'aurais eu aussi mon congrès et ma* sainte-alliance.
*Ce sont des idées qu'on m'a volées. Dans cette réunion de grands souve-
rains, nous eussions traités de nos intérêts en famille et compté de clerc à
maître avec les peuples. L'Europe n'eut bientôt fait de la sorte véritable-
ment qu'un même peuple, et chacun, en voyageant partout, se fut trouvé
toujours dans la patrie commune. J'eus demandé toutes les rivières navi-
gables pour tous, la communauté des mers et que les grandes armées perma-
nentes fussent réduites désormais à la seule garde des souverains. De
rétour en France au sein de la patrie, grande, forte, magnifique, tranquille, glorieuse, j'eusse proclamé ses limites immuables ; toute guerre
future, purement* defensive; *tout agrandissement nouveau* anti-national.
J'eusse associé mon fils à l'empire ; ma dictature *eut fini, et son régne con-
stitutionnel eut commencé. Paris eut été la capitale du monde, et les français l'envie des nations. Mes loisirs ensuite et mes vieux jours eussent été
consacrés, en compagnie de l'impératrice et durant l'apprentissage royal de
mon fils, à visiter lentement et en vrai couple campagnard, avec nos propres
chevaux, tous les recoins de l'empire, recevant les plaintes, redressant les
torts, semant de toutes parts et partout les monuments et les bienfaits, etc.*

He wrote further concerning the Russian war as follows : —

Out of the four hundred thousand men who crossed the Vistula, half were Austrians, Prussians, Saxons, Poles, Bavarians, Würtembergers, Mecklenbergers, Spaniards, Italians, and Neapolitans. The imperial army, properly speaking, was one-fourth composed of Dutch and Belgians, the inhabitants of the banks of the Rhine, Piedmontese, Swiss, Genevese, Tuscans, Romans, the inhabitants of the thirty-second military district, — Bremen, Hamburg, etc.; it counted scarcely one hundred and forty thousand men who spoke French. The Russian expedition cost France less than fifty thousand men; the Russian army, during the retreat from Vilna to Moscow, in the various battles, lost four times as many as the French army; the burning of Moscow cost the life of one hundred thousand Russians, who perished of cold and starvation in the forests, and moreover, in its march from Moscow to the Oder, the Russian army suffered from the inclemency of the season. On its arrival at Vilna it counted only fifty thousand men, and at Kalish less than eighteen thousand.

He imagined that the war with Russia came about by his own will, and the horror of what took place did not stir his soul within him. He audaciously assumed the entire responsibility of the event, and his darkened intellect found justification in the fact that, among the hundreds of thousands of men destroyed, there were fewer French than Hessians and Bavarians!

CHAPTER XXXIX

SEVERAL score thousands of men lay dead in various positions and uniforms on the fields and meadows belonging to Mr. Davuidof and certain crown serfs, on those fields and meadows where for centuries the peasants of Borodino, Gorki, Shevardino, and Semenovskoye had with one accord harvested their crops and pastured their cattle.

Around the field lazarets, for several acres, the grass

and ground were soaked with blood. Throngs of men, wounded and not wounded, belonging to various commands, from the one side fell back to Mozhaïsk, from the other to Valuyevo. Other throngs, weary and hungry, led by their chiefs, moved onward to the front. Still others stood in their places and went on firing.

Over the entire field where, in the morning, the sun had shone on glittering bayonets and wreaths of smoke, now lowered a wrack of damp and smoke, and the air was foul with a strange reek of nitrous fumes and blood.

Clouds had gathered, and the raindrops began to fall on the dead, on the wounded, on the panic-stricken, and the weary, and the despairing. It seemed to say to them : —

'Enough!.... enough! ye men! Cease!.... Remember! What are ye doing?'

The men on either side, utterly weary, without nourishment and without rest, began alike to question whether it were any advantage for them longer to exterminate one another, and hesitation could be seen in every face, and in every mind the question arose : —

"Why, wherefore are ye killing and being killed? Kill whomever ye please, do whatever ye please, but as for me I will no more of it!"

This thought, toward late afternoon, burned with equal force in the heart of each. At any moment all these men might suddenly manifest their horror at what they had been doing, give it all up, and fly anywhere it might happen.

But although, toward the end of the struggle, the men began to feel all the horror of their actions, although they would have been glad to cease, some strange, incomprehensible, mysterious power still continued to direct them, and the surviving gunners, — one out of every three, — covered with sweat, grimed with powder, and stained with blood, staggering and panting with weariness, still lugged the projectiles, charged the guns, sighted them, applied the slow-matches, and the shot flew just as swiftly and viciously from the one side and the other, and crushed human forms, and still that strange affair went on which was accomplished, not by the will of men, but by the will of Him who rules men and worlds.

Any one who had looked at the vanishing remnants of the Russian army would have said that all the French needed to do would be to put forth one small last effort and the Russian army would vanish; and any one who had looked at the remnants of the French would have said that all that the Russians had to do was to make one small last effort and the French would be destroyed. But neither the French nor the Russians put forth this last effort, and the flame of the conflict slowly flickered out.

The Russians did not make this effort because they did not charge the French. At the beginning of the battle they merely stood on the road to Moscow, disputing it, and in exactly the same way they continued to stand at the end of the battle as they had stood at the beginning. But if the aim of the Russians had been to defeat the French, they could not put forth this last effort because all the Russian troops had been defeated, there was not a single division of their army that had not suffered in the engagement, and, though the Russians still held their own, they had lost a HALF of their troops.

The French, with the recollections of all their fifteen years of past victories, with their confidence in Napoleon's invincibility, with the consciousness that they had got possession of a portion of the battle-field, that their loss was only a quarter of their contingent, and that they had still twenty thousand in reserve, not counting the Guard, might easily have put forth this effort. The French, who were attacking the Russian army, with the intention of defeating it, ought to have made this effort, because, as long as the Russians disputed the road to Moscow, as they did before the battle began, the aim of the French was not attained, and all their efforts and losses were thrown away.

But the French did not put forth this effort.

Certain historians assert that Napoleon had only to send forward his Old Guard, who were still fresh, and the battle would have been won. To say what would have happened if Napoleon had sent forward the Guard is just the same as to say what would happen if autumn turned into spring.

It was an impossibility.

Napoleon did not send forward his Guard, not because he did not want to do it, but because it was impossible for him to do it. All the generals, all the officers and soldiers of the French army knew that it was impossible to do this, because the dejected spirit of the army would not allow it.

Napoleon was not the only one to experience that nightmare feeling that the terrible blow of the arm was falling in vain, but all his generals, all the soldiers of the French army who took part or who did not take part, after all their experiences in former battles, when, after exerting a tenth as much force as now, the enemy would be vanquished, now experienced alike a feeling of awe at that enemy which, having lost a HALF of its troops, still stood just as threateningly at the end as it had stood at the beginning of the engagement.

The moral force of the French attacking army was exhausted.

Victory is not that which is signalized by the fastening of certain strips of cloth called flags to poles, nor by the space on which troops have stood or are standing; but victory is moral, when the one side has been persuaded as to the moral superiority of the other and of its own weakness; and such a victory was won by the Russians over the French at Borodino.

The invading army, like an exasperated beast of prey, having received, as it ran, a mortal wound, became conscious that it was doomed; but it could not halt any more than the Russian army, which was not half so strong, could help giving way. After the shock which had been given, the French army was still able to crawl to Moscow; but there, without any new efforts on the part of the Russian troops, it was doomed to perish, bleeding to death from the mortal wound received at Borodino.

The direct consequence of the battle of Borodino was Napoleon's causeless flight from Moscow, the return along the old Smolensk highway, the ruin of the five hundred thousand men of the invading army, and the destruction of Napoleonic France, on which at Borodino was for the first time laid the hand of an opponent stronger by force of spirit!

END OF VOL. IV.

J